Sacrifice

ALSO BY CLYDE PHILLIPS

Blindsided

Fall from Grace

SACRIFICE

Clyde Phillips

WILLIAM MORROW
An Imprint of HarperCollins*Publishers*

SACRIFICE. Copyright © 2003 by Clyde Phillips. All rights reserved.
Printed in the United States of America. No part of this book may be used
or reproduced in any manner whatsoever without written permission except
in the case of brief quotations embodied in critical articles and reviews. For
information address HarperCollins Publishers Inc., 10 East 53rd Street,
New York, NY 10022.

HarperCollins books may be purchased for educational, business,
or sales promotional use. For information please write:
Special Markets Department, HarperCollins Publishers Inc.,
10 East 53rd Street, New York, NY 10022.

FIRST EDITION

Designed by Debbie Glasserman

Printed on acid-free paper

Library of Congress Cataloging-in-Publication Data
Phillips, Clyde.
Sacrifice / Clyde Phillips.—1st ed.
p. cm.
ISBN 0-06-621237-5
1. Candiotti, Jane (Fictitious character)—Fiction.
2. Police—California—San Francisco—Fiction. 3. San Francisco
(Calif.)—Fiction. 4. Policewomen—Fiction. I. Title.
PR6063.I3175 S33 2003
813'.54—dc21   2002035750

03 04 05 06 07 JTC/QW 10 9 8 7 6 5 4 3 2 1

For Michael Tronick and Ken Marks . . . best men.

And for Jane and Claire, my wife and daughter . . .
my compass and my sail.

. . . sirens in the darkness tell sad stories in the night.
—DAVE ALVIN, "(I Won't Be) Leaving"

CHAPTER 1

———■———

IT WAS PHILIP Iverson's big night.

He stood at the podium of the Golden Gate Grand's Crystal Ballroom and basked in the applause of San Francisco's elite. As the audience rose to its feet, he took a step back and held up his hands, gesturing for everyone to sit down. In his midfifties, his trim runner's body—draped tonight in an elegant tuxedo—and his close-cropped salt-and-pepper hair made him seem ten years younger. His pale blue eyes glistened as the emotion of the evening caught up with him, and he nodded to the people at the front tables. Some of them sat, then others, until, gradually, everyone in the ballroom took their seats.

The huge room hummed in anticipation as Philip Iverson, the city's best-loved citizen, finally stepped forward and adjusted the microphone.

"Thank you, my friends." He picked up the award he'd just received. "Thank you for this honor. Thank you for this incredible evening . . . and thank you for the many opportunities this great city has given me." He returned the plaque to the lectern. "It is because of those opportunities that I feel especially fortunate to announce tonight my pledge of an additional fifty million dollars for a new cancer wing at Children's Memorial Hospital."

The audience erupted in cheers. Philip Iverson held his hands out toward the crowd. "Thank you. Thank you so much. I just want to add that, with this gift, I and my Make It So Foundation have now passed *one billion dollars* in donations. And, my friends, we're not stopping there." He raised a champagne glass. "Here's to you. Here's to our beautiful city. And here's to the *next* billion dollars . . . with love . . . from me to you!"

Everyone in the ballroom lifted their glasses to join him in the toast.

Beyond the faces beaming up at him, beyond the shimmering chandeliers, beyond the smoked glass of the towering floor-to-ceiling windows, the man who would kill Philip Iverson waited in the coming fog.

■

FOG.

Like the cold breath of God, it descended on San Francisco. The heavy clouded air moved through the parking structure of the Golden Gate Grand. The dark shapes of the luxury cars on Level Seven grew more and more indistinct. And then they were invisible—afterimages of themselves in the mist.

The green light of the exit sign above the stairwell door glowed dimly. A tiny beacon.

The door burst open, throwing a sudden wedge of light onto the slick concrete surface. Philip Iverson, his hair now damp with sweat, raced through the door. His breath coming in desperate searing gasps, he jabbed in his coat pocket, frantically searching for his keys. He ripped them out and thumbed the remote as he ran.

The door locks on a black Mercedes S600 popped up like sentries, and Iverson, thinking the haven of his car would save him, ran even faster. He chanced a look back.

The light in the doorway was filled by the hulking body of his pursuer. He spotted Iverson, and without hesitation, he pushed forward, parting the fog before him like a ghost.

Philip Iverson was almost to his car when he slipped on a wet patch of grease. He scrambled to regain his footing and hurled himself toward the Mercedes.

But it was too late. His pursuer was upon him.

A sob of resignation catching in his throat, Iverson grabbed at the door of his car.

A flash of light. An echoing pop.

Philip Iverson gasped and stumbled forward, the bullet in his brain extinguishing his life even before he crumpled facedown on the cold concrete floor.

Kneeling beside him, his pursuer barely had time to tear Iverson's wallet out of his trousers when the squeal of tires—above or below he couldn't tell—sent him racing back toward the stairwell.

As he pulled the door shut, there was music, a fanfare coming from the ballroom, and applause. The fanfare reached its crescendo and the applause died away.

The fog covered Philip Iverson like a shroud.

∎

JANE CANDIOTTI STOOD at her bedroom window watching the fog roll into San Leandro. It moved onto Oak Street, she thought, like some great enveloping cloud in a science-fiction movie.

The grandfather clock at the bottom of the stairs chimed. Announcing midnight. Jane turned at the sound. Kenny Marks, her partner in the SFPD Homicide Division, snored softly in their bed. She crossed the room, brushed a kiss across his lips, and went out the door.

Jane and Kenny had been married for four months.

The floorboards of the upstairs hallway creaked as she walked. Passing the room that had been hers as a child, Jane entered the bathroom. This one bathroom, small and simple, had been the only one in a household of four when she was growing up.

Jane flicked on the bathroom light and went to the mirror. She studied her face. Her eyes, black and shining, stared back at her as she touched her high cheekbones, her pale, almost translucent skin.

She knew she was pretty—some thought her beautiful—but lately the gray hairs and the fine etching of tiny wrinkles around her eyes had begun to make her feel her age.

Poppy used to say that her hair was the color of a blackbird's wing. She grasped a gray hair between her thumb and forefinger and yanked it out.

She would turn forty this month.

"Hey, knock it off," Kenny said as he came into the bathroom. He wrapped his arms around her. "I like those guys." He flashed his easy smile and Jane kissed the scar on his chest. The size of a small coin, the bullet scar was a constant reminder that they were in a very dangerous business.

She looked up to his eyes, youthful and spirited. It's what she loved most about him: his spirit. "You're the one who wanted to marry an older woman."

"Not any older woman." Kenny squeezed her to him. "*This* older woman."

The phone rang. Kenny snapped up the portable from next to the small white television on the counter. "Hello?" He listened for a moment, then handed the phone to Jane. "It's the chief. He wants to talk to *Lieutenant* Candiotti. He kinda sounds intense."

"The chief?" Jane took the phone. "Hello?" Jane listened. "Oh, my God."

Kenny touched her shoulder and mouthed the word "Who?"

Jane held her hand over the mouthpiece. "Philip Iverson."

"Dead?"

Jane nodded. "We're there in twenty, sir." She clicked off the phone.

"Philip Iverson." Kenny shook his head. "Motherfuck."

"Well put." Jane nudged him toward the door. "Get my stuff ready, will ya?"

"You got it, Lieutenant."

When he had gone, Jane reached under the sink and came up with an EPT kit. Even though she knew she was supposed to wait until morning, she sat on the toilet, peed into the plastic cup, and dipped the stick.

Negative.

Again.

Kenny stuck his head in the door. "Where's my . . ."

Jane flushed the toilet, trying to conceal what she'd been doing. Kenny went to her, took the kit, and looked at the stick. Then he saw the worry in her face. He put his palm to her cheek. "We can do this."

"You sure you want to?"

Kenny tapped his wedding ring against hers. "More than anything." He kissed her forehead. "Let's go," he said as he hurried out. "We've got a dead billionaire out there . . . and one very pissed-off chief of police."

CHAPTER 2

■

"STINKS IN HERE," Jane said as she and Kenny climbed the stairs of the Golden Gate Grand's parking structure.

"The heady but unpretentious bouquet of fine urine." Kenny stepped aside as two young uniformed cops rushed down the stairs.

"You see him?" one said to the other.

"Yeah. Philip fuckin' Iverson. Wait'll I tell my wife."

"Highlight of their lives." Kenny tugged open the door at Level Seven. "Whoa." He and Jane passed from the dingy stairwell into a full-blown, big-ticket crime scene.

SFPD light trucks illuminated the entire parking level, rows of fifty-thousand-watt lamps cutting wide swaths in the swirling fog. The forensics van had pulled up next to the medical examiner's wagon, and a squadron of other police vehicles was parked at all angles around the crime scene's center. Police officers and detectives from a dozen different departments went about their work quietly and efficiently. But there was an unmistakable tension in the air.

This one was different.

Jane and Kenny passed under the green exit sign and moved around an unmarked police sedan sitting in the handicapped spot. "Uh-oh," Kenny said. "Some jerk-off parked too close."

As they cleared the sedan, they saw the center of all this activity.

Philip Iverson lay as he had fallen next to his Mercedes, his body now covered by a yellow plastic sheet. The patent-leather shoe on his left foot gleamed in the artificial light as a breeze lifted a corner of the tarp.

Lieutenant Aaron Clark-Weber, in charge of the forensics detail, came up to them. "Welcome to *Celebrity Death Match*."

"What do we have?" Jane asked as she and Kenny knelt next to the body.

Aaron, wincing from his arthritic knee, squatted beside them and lifted the sheet. "Small-caliber entry . . . here." He pointed his penlight at an oozing starburst circle at the base of Philip Iverson's skull. "No exit. Best guess is a twenty-two."

Jane started to ask a question.

"No shell casing," Aaron said. "Some shoe stuff between here and the stairwell. We're doing prints, hair and fibers, as we speak."

Jane looked at the wound and let her eyes travel, absorbing the scene. The deep maroon trickle of blood running down Iverson's meticulously groomed hair, staining the collar of his tuxedo shirt. The manicured nails of his right hand. His left arm still under his torso. His right eye, the only one she could see, still open; a pinpoint of light reflecting from the power trucks. Like a doll's eye.

Jane rose and turned to Aaron. "Anything else?"

"The victim's wallet was missing. Patrol woman"—he indicated a female officer standing next to a steam vent, drawing on its warmth—"found it in the alley next to a storage shed. Money's gone. Credit cards and photos still inside."

"Think it's a mugging gone sour?" Jane asked.

Kenny shook his head. "Doesn't feel like it, y'know?"

"I know." Jane nodded for Aaron to lower the sheet.

The sudden glare of a news camera's key light caught her attention. Chief of Police Walker McDonald was moving to the yellow police tape perimeter, about to address the media. He had pulled open his bow tie and his tuxedo jacket was rumpled under his arm. Other lights came on as the news crews jostled for position.

Jane and Kenny started toward the makeshift press conference when Linda French caught up to them. "Philip Iverson, huh? Man, this is big." Linda French was in her midthirties and a little taller than Jane. There was a formality about her that some found off-putting. Her blond hair was always perfect, her suits always fresh and pressed. But Jane had been impressed by the recommendations of Linda's previous supervisors and had decided to bring her aboard as a homicide inspector when she herself had moved up to the lieutenant's office.

"Big enough," Jane said as they closed in on the chief. Everything about Walker McDonald seemed thick tonight, Jane thought. His chest, his hair, his mood.

"Can you tell us the name of the deceased?" one reporter called out. Many of them were dressed in tuxedos as well, having covered Philip Iverson's banquet for their local stations.

Chief McDonald took a step forward. "Guys, this is gonna be brief. We have a Caucasian male gunshot victim. He was found by—"

"Any ID yet, sir?"

"We have an idea who he is," the chief went on, "but we need to notify his family before we release his identity. I sure as hell do not want his loved ones learning about this tragedy on television. Please respect that, fellas. Soon as I can, I'll turn you over to Sergeant Alvarez in Press Relations and he'll bring you up to speed. Thank you."

He turned away and motioned for Jane to join him as he walked toward his limousine. His driver, Devon Haskell, opened the back door for him.

Jane moved forward, Kenny half a step behind.

"I'm coming with," he whispered.

"You better," Jane whispered back.

The chief shook her hand. Jane nodded to Kenny. "You remember my husband, Inspector Marks?"

"Of course. You all healed?"

"Good as new, sir."

Jane brought Linda in close. "And this is Linda French of my department. Moved up to homicide inspector a month ago."

Linda took a quick step forward. "Pleasure, sir."

"Here's what we know," McDonald began. "The guy over there . . ." He pointed to a silver Lexus, where a man in a very expensive tuxedo was talking on a cell phone. A woman sat inside the car, a fur over her shoulders. Her head was back against the seat and her left arm was over her eyes.

"Isn't that Barry Stein?" Kenny asked, recognizing one of San Francisco's most prominent restaurateurs.

"Yeah. He's the one found the body. Called Security." McDonald tilted his chin toward an Asian man in his early twenties. Dressed in a dark blue windbreaker with the Golden Gate Grand's security logo on both shoulders, he shifted from foot to foot, trying to stay warm.

A forensics tech knelt next to Iverson's body and slipped plastic bags over each of the dead man's hands. Then he wound tape around the wrists. A police photographer hunched down and fired off half a dozen frames in as many seconds.

The chief blew a long sigh. "Tonight, after he accepted his award, Iverson announced a huge donation to Children's Memorial. He didn't even want his own name on the building, but the name of some kid who died last year. The place went crazy. All these people standing and cheering and whistling . . . and then this." Disgusted, he threw his jacket into the limousine. "Jane, I want you to personally inform Alice Iverson about what happened here tonight. No phone calls, no kid cops . . . you."

"Consider it done, sir." Jane pulled her phone from her bag. "I'll have Central pull their address."

"She's not at their San Francisco place," the chief said. "She's up in their Dos Rios cabin. Hour and a half north of here. It's why Iverson left his own banquet early. The long drive."

Linda French turned to him. "How do we know that, sir?"

The chief got into his car. "Because I sat next to him on the fucking dais. Posed for pictures with him. And that's what the papers are gonna run tomorrow. San Francisco's most beloved citizen murdered while the city's police chief is two hundred feet away." He yanked the door closed and lowered the window. "Find me this shooter."

Kenny nudged in. "We will, sir."

Chief McDonald didn't look at him. "Candiotti," he said to Jane, "do *not* let me down."

Before Jane could respond, he raised his window, bringing her reflection with it.

Devon Haskell approached Kenny. " 'Scuse me, Mr. *Candiotti*," he whispered out of the side of his mouth. He brushed past Kenny and hurried around the car. A young cop cleared a path and the limousine pulled away, its tires squealing on the concrete. Haskell caught Kenny's eye in the rearview mirror and smirked before the limo disappeared down the incline.

"Here's a question," Jane began, drawing Kenny's attention from the retreating limousine. "Why wasn't the famous wife here? Shouldn't the spouse of our city's favorite son be at his side on such an important night?"

"Good point," Kenny said. "Not like her to miss a photo op."

Jane started toward the security guard. "Let's do a few prelims before the big drive up north."

The security guard looked up as they approached. "I go home now? I work two job. I need go sleep."

Jane gestured for Linda to take notes. "Soon, sir. But first tell me what you saw this evening."

"I already tell two peoples. Please I go home now?"

"I promise if you just tell me one more time, you'll be able to go home."

The guard sighed. "That man . . ." He pointed to Barry Stein. "He come my office. Say man dead up here. I come back with him. See that man on ground. Call 911. Then I wait and everyones show up." He chewed his lower lip, looking as if he were going to cry. "Nothing bad ever happen here before. Car stolen once; but not when I work. Sometime a bum bother peoples. But never this."

Linda leaned in. "You said sometimes a bum bothers people. Was there anyone hanging around here who was a threat to the patrons of the hotel?"

"Lady, this San Francisco. Always bums. Sleep in stairs, beg money. But not this." He stole a glance at Iverson's body.

"Besides," Kenny added, "this is hardly the MO of a panhandler. There's something too clean about it."

"I agree," Jane said. "Sir, does this facility have security cameras?"

"At cash booths."

"Hey, Aaron," Kenny called. "Your guys pull the videos from the security cameras yet?"

Aaron Clark-Weber looked up from the back of his van. "Coupla minutes ago."

Jane's radio crackled. "3H58."

Jane pressed the mic. "3H58. Go."

"This is Dispatch. We have an eight-oh-two at Pier Twenty. First on-scene reports a black male. Homeless type. Late forties. Apparent stabbing."

"Two in one night," Kenny said. "Christ."

"Thank you, Dispatch. 3H58 out." Jane turned to Linda. "Time to get your feet a little wetter. I want you to go out there and run that scene. If it's a clean one, write it up yourself. If not, call for a supervisor."

Linda started to say something. Jane could tell she didn't want to leave this high-profile case for the dreary prospect of a no-profile murder of a homeless man. She put her hand on Linda's shoulder. "Go on now," she said gently. "I need your help on this."

Linda nodded and made her way toward the unmarked sedan that had been parked in the handicapped space. Jane looked to Kenny and shook her head. Then she caught up to Linda. "Next time, park your car as far away from the body as possible. Last thing we need is for one of our own to compromise a crime scene."

Linda opened her car door. "I screwed up. Sorry." She got in, started the engine, and pulled away.

Jane watched her go as Kenny came up. "She's young and full of mistakes," he said. "Just like us way back when."

"This is the big-time, Ken. I can't have mistakes on my watch." She turned back to the crime scene. "Let's finish up here. We gotta go tell Alice Iverson her husband is dead."

CHAPTER 3

—■—

JANE PUT HER feet up on the dashboard as Kenny drove his black Explorer north toward the Golden Gate Bridge. Lost in thought, she'd been silent since they left the Philip Iverson murder scene.

Informing a family member about the death of a loved one was the single worst aspect of her job. There was always that time when she knew of a murder; and the husband or wife or father or mother was still unaware, safe in his or her ordinary day. And then the news she carried would shatter the ordinary, and everything from then on would be remembered by the family as before or after that day.

Jane thought of Alice Iverson asleep in her bed in Dos Rios. Asleep in her ordinary night. Not knowing that her husband lay dead, a bullet in his head, surrounded by two dozen strangers, on the cold floor of the parking structure of a downtown hotel. She played the crime scene back in her head—from when she first got there up to reprimanding Linda French for parking so carelessly.

Kenny touched her cheek with the back of his hand. "Hey, where are you?"

"Lost in the land of second thoughts."

"Career, marriage, kids?"

Jane slipped her hand under his right thigh. "Nothing so global. At first I was thinking about Alice Iverson. Then I sort of drifted to Linda French."

"Alice I get. What about Linda?"

"It's just that she looked so good on paper. Her performance reports were off the charts and she gave a great interview. But something's eating at me about her. I'm getting this knot that I get when I know something's not right."

"Homicide is a huge learning curve. If you want, I'll keep an eye on her. Try to help till she catches up."

"Thanks." Jane pressed her forehead to the coolness of the window. "Ken?"

"Hmm."

"Back there, the chief's driver . . ."

"What about him?"

Jane glanced over to him. "He seemed a little—I don't know—edgy. You know the guy?"

"Used to." Kenny kept his eyes on the road.

Jane let it drop, knowing that if and when Kenny wanted to talk about it, he would. As the Explorer rounded the last turn before San Francisco Bay, she noticed the strobe of a paramedic unit near the water. Peering into the fog, she barely made out the shapes of other vehicles, their headlights on, parked in a circle. Occasionally, someone would pass through the beams of one car to another. "That Pier Twenty?" Jane asked.

"Yep." Kenny slowed the car. "Wanna take a quick look-see?"

"Accent on *quick*." Jane sat up. "Two minutes. Make sure Linda's doing the right thing. Then we're back on the road."

▪

JANE JOINED KENNY in front of the Explorer and saw that Linda French had parked her car a good distance from the crime scene.

"Climbing that old learning curve already," Kenny said as they approached the circle of lights.

"Philip Iverson gets every light truck in Northern California," Jane observed. "Some bum dies and our guys have to use their high beams."

Linda French looked up from her notebook and spotted Jane and Kenny. She flipped back a few pages as she crossed to them. "No ID yet. Deep stab wound to the chest seems to be the cause of death." She slid something out of her notebook. "Uniform found this in the vic's coat pocket. Meal coupon from a shelter called Santuario in the Mission District. We put in a call. The director is on his way. Maybe help with the ID."

Jane threw a look to Kenny. "Good work," she said to Linda. The supervising sergeant handed Jane a flashlight and she trained it on the body.

A small black man in tattered clothes lay on his back in a vast pool of blood. His hands were clutched at the front of his blood-soaked shirt, as if in a vain attempt to keep his life from draining away.

"Jesus," Kenny said.

"EMT says his aorta's cut," Linda explained. "He pumped himself out."

Jane played the flashlight along the body. There was a small hole on the right side, just below the rib cage. "M.E.?"

"Yeah," Linda said. "TOD around midnight."

The hole had been made by the medical examiner when he had inserted a thermometer into the victim's liver. Time of death was then determined from the organ's residual temperature.

Jane moved the beam past the ravaged chest to the victim's face. There was blood around his mouth and chin, evidence that one or both of his lungs had been penetrated.

Then she noticed something. "Ken, look at his eyes."

Kenny knelt beside her. "I see it."

Jane looked across the body to Linda. "Anyone touch him other than the EMT or the M.E.?"

"First on-scene felt for a carotid. Why?"

"See the blood streaks on his eyelids?" Jane waggled the light from eye to eye. "Someone closed his eyes for him."

Linda leaned in for a closer look. "What's that tell us?"

"Don't know yet," Jane said as she stood up. "But it's something."

"Uh, 'scuse me, Inspector . . ." A Latina patrol officer beckoned to Jane from just outside the perimeter.

Jane and Kenny crossed to the tape. "It's lieutenant," Kenny said. Jane almost elbowed him, but held back.

"Sorry," the young cop said. "But I got something weird over here."

They followed the patrol woman, her utility belt creaking as she walked, to a pile of loading pallets. She aimed her flashlight on a pallet that was leaning against the stack. The light caught an S-shaped pattern of dark red, about six inches long, on the top cross-board. "Kinda looks like blood."

"Looks like it," Kenny said, " 'cause it is."

Jane turned to Linda. "Have Forensics quick-type this and the blood on the victim's eyelids."

Linda made a note. "You got it."

Jane ran her flashlight over the patrol officer's name tag. "Canseco, huh? Any relation?"

"I wish."

Jane smiled. "Secure this area for me, will ya?"

"Yes, ma'am."

Kenny took Jane's flashlight and shined it directly on the bloody S-shape. "Is it a symbol? An initial? A gang thing?"

"Don't know," Jane said, "but somebody's talking to us."

A white late-model Crown Victoria pulled up at the perimeter and a tall black man in a navy-blue Adidas sweatsuit climbed out. He spoke to the supervising sergeant and was escorted under the tape and to the body.

"That would be Reggie Mayhew," Linda said to Jane. "From that place we called about the meal coupon."

"I know this guy," Jane said.

"You left out 'can't stand this guy,' " Kenny said.

Reggie Mayhew not only ran Santuario, he was an outspoken and volatile activist for the homeless who thrived on his well-publicized confrontations with the police. A star athlete at San Francisco State around the time of O. J. Simpson, he had a brief stint with the Raiders before injuries sent him back to the real world. After a few scrapes with the law in the late seventies—including some prison time—he had found his calling working with San Francisco's huge homeless population.

"Short and quick," Kenny reminded Jane. "We're not even supposed to be here."

Before Jane could say anything, Mayhew was in her face. "So, Lieutenant, what are you going to do about this tragedy?"

Kenny wedged himself between Mayhew and Jane. "What we do about every murder." He tried not to let his intense dislike for this man rise to the surface. And he failed. "Solve it."

"A homeless black man?" Mayhew laughed. "What you been smokin'?"

Jane spoke in a voice carefully modulated to offer respect while still showing she was in charge. "Mr. Mayhew, we appreciate your concern and all the good work you do for the community. But right now this man—"

"Willie Temple."

"Pardon me?"

"Man's name is Willie Temple."

Linda French jotted the name in her notebook.

"Thank you," Jane said. "Right now Willie Temple isn't a symbol of anything other than the violence and cruelty of whoever killed him. And we will do everything we can to bring that person to justice."

Kenny tugged at her elbow. "We've got to go."

"Excuse us, sir," Jane said to Mayhew. She turned to Linda and walked her away. "This crime scene just got complicated. Don't provoke Mayhew. But don't take any shit from him either. I want theories on the eyelid blood and the S-thing by the time we get back from Alice Iverson's."

"I'll do my best."

"I know you will."

Jane took one last glance at Willie Temple's body as she and Kenny started toward the Explorer. That's when she noticed he was wearing mismatched sneakers. A black Nike high-top on his right foot. A black Nike low-cut on the left. "Check out his shoes."

Kenny turned back. "Hey, he's lucky he had two of them." He pulled her under his arm. "Gonna be a long night."

"Already is."

CHAPTER 4

◼

THE CORRUGATED ROADWAY of the Golden Gate Bridge thrummed under the Explorer's tires as Jane and Kenny sped north toward the Marin side. The wipers slapped intermittent arcs at the mist on the windshield. "Not even ten minutes," Kenny said.

"Not even ten minutes, what?"

"We were at Pier Twenty less than ten minutes. We'll be okay." He nudged the speedometer past eighty.

Jane turned to look back at the bridge. The top of the South Tower, virtually lost in the fog, was where Kenny had taken that bullet in the chest one terrifying night before they were married. He had saved her life, and she had finally understood that he was the man she should be with.

A few heavy trucks whooshed by in the opposite lanes, heading for a city they couldn't see.

Jane twisted the cap off a water bottle and sloshed back a handful of vitamins. "I really hate this night shit."

Kenny reached for the water. "Tell me about it. We average what— one homicide a week? And now it's two in one night. What's that about?"

The Explorer swept under the North Tower and began to ascend the foothills of Marin County. Kenny pressed the accelerator and pushed the car even faster.

"Ken?"

"I'll slow down."

"No, it's not that. I keep thinking of Alice Iverson lying in bed not knowing that her husband is dead."

"Charmed life, huh?"

"Until now." Jane thought about Alice Iverson, California's golden girl. They were roughly the same age and Jane could remember reading about her when she was growing up. Formerly Alice Trumbull of the pioneering television family, she had been as close to California royalty as anyone in the early eighties.

A long-legged beauty with honey-blond hair, she had led Stanford to the NCAA championship in swimming. Still in college, she was the sentimental and odds-on favorite to win four gold medals in the Los Angeles Olympics.

They were hers to lose.

And she did.

Alice Trumbull was leading the hundred-meter butterfly, her best event, when a twelve-year-old Chinese girl came from out of nowhere and touched the wall two one-hundredths of a second before her. Alice never recovered from the shock of coming in second. She went on to compete in her three remaining events, taking one bronze and finishing out of the medals in the others.

After the Olympics, she disappeared from the public eye for almost two years. Occasionally a photo of her would wind up in *People* showing her dancing with some soccer star in a London club or sitting in the stands watching her latest tennis-phenom boyfriend at the French Open.

Eventually, she had returned to California to work as an on-air reporter for one of her father's stations. It was while covering a story in the Silicon Valley that she met Philip Iverson.

Already a millionaire many times over at twenty-five, Iverson had come of age during the computer revolution. While others were perfecting operating systems and interface design, Philip Iverson devoted himself to making the components smaller, then smaller still. It was largely through his foresight and ingenuity that the computer industry was able to make their product accessible to the private consumer.

His fortune grew a hundredfold, then a thousandfold; and soon he and Alice found themselves to be the reigning sovereigns of Northern California society.

Philip eventually moved his factory to Costa Rica, and built an elegant administrative and research complex called RiverPark on its site in the mountains just north of San Francisco.

"Can I say the unsayable?" Kenny asked, pulling Jane out of her contemplation.

Jane smiled. "I'd expect nothing less."

"The Iversons don't have any kids, right?"

"Right . . ." Jane knew where this was going. She had thought the same thing.

"Then the widow Alice is about to become the unbelievably rich widow Alice." He changed lanes to blow past a slow-moving delivery van. "Here's the unsayable part . . ."

"I know." Jane sighed. "The surviving spouse is always a suspect."

"All I'm saying is, as long as we have to do this shitty thing and inform her about her husband, let's at least monitor how she reacts."

"Some job we have, huh, when it comes to this?"

"Hey, we *chose* Homicide."

"What were we thinking?"

Kenny's radio came to life. "3H61."

Kenny flicked on the two-way. "Moby, that you?"

"Yes, Inspector. Late-shift lieutenant called me in to help out with all that's going on tonight. Not that I'm sleeping all that much anyways."

"How's the new baby doing, Mike?" Jane asked.

"He's got one mission in life: eating."

Jane held a finger up to Kenny, imploring him not to make a joke.

Patrolman Mike Finney was vastly overweight. Jane's predecessor, Lieutenant Spielman, had put him on temporary desk duty years ago. Temporary somehow became permanent and now Mike Finney was part of the homicide support team at Precinct Nineteen. The other cops, except for Jane, all called him Moby.

"Like father, like son," Kenny whispered.

"Anyways," Finney continued, "we got the surveillance tape from the Golden Gate Grand parking structure. I stowed it in the evidence locker." There was a pause. "Lieutenant, can I ask you something?"

"Sure, Mike."

"Was it really Philip Iverson got killed tonight?"

"Yes, it was."

"Hard to believe." The rustling sound of cellophane came over the speaker and Jane and Kenny knew that Finney was enjoying his first meal of the new day, or his last meal of the night before. "Also," Finney went on, his mouth full, "also, I called the sheriff up in Dos Rios. Local guy named A. J. Guthrie. Former SFPD. I told him you were coming up, but I didn't tell him why."

"Good thinking," Jane said.

"Thanks. Sheriff Guthrie said to meet him at the station and he'd escort you to the Iversons' cabin. It's way out in the backcountry and kinda hard to find. Plus there's all sorts of security and stuff."

Kenny turned off the 101 at the exit for Route 12. Within seconds, they were traveling along a deeply wooded two-lane country road. "Hey, Moby," Kenny called. "You got an address for the sheriff's station?"

"One Main Street."

"I think we can find that."

■

RIVERPARK, PHILIP IVERSON'S corporate headquarters, sat nestled in the crook of a mountain pass. A series of low buildings faced with mirrored glass, they reflected the forest in which they had been built.

The Halaby River coursed through the property, providing an eye-soothing contrast to the high-voltage intensity of this huge multinational company. Despite its low-key image, RiverPark was a fierce competitor in the cutthroat world of computers.

After about a half mile, the Halaby dropped off precipitously at the eastern end of the property, the plunge creating a waterfall that was part of the company's logo. The cascading river formed a small lake at the base of the waterfall before descending into the Arleta Valley and joining up with the larger Paloma River. The town of Dos Rios was situated at the merge of the Halaby and the Paloma.

"Main Street looks like the only street," Kenny said as he drove the Explorer past the dark, sleepy storefronts. A hardware store, a Laundromat, a grocery store, a diner—all sat in silent repose.

"I'd kill for a Starbucks right now," Jane said.

"I don't think cappuccinos have made their way to Mayberry just yet."

"There." Jane pointed to a bare flagpole at the end of the street. "A light's on next to the post office."

"Gotta be our guy." Kenny pulled in next to a battered Jeep Wagoneer. "I smell coffee."

"Thank the baby Jesus."

The door opened and a big soft bear of a man stepped onto the short porch. He paused to tuck his blue cotton work shirt into his rumpled brown corduroys.

Jane climbed down from the Explorer. "Sheriff? I'm Lieutenant Candiotti and this is Inspector Marks from SFPD. Sorry to bother you so late."

"No trouble, Lieutenant." A. J. Guthrie held the screen door for them. "I got coffee on. Hope you don't want decaf."

Jane entered the station. "I think I love you."

"Then it's my lucky night."

An old rolltop desk was the center point of the room, a typewriter and an ancient computer on a side table. An electric space heater, its coils glowing red orange, sat next to a threadbare couch. Fishing poles and tackle were stacked in a corner next to a gun cabinet that held a double-barreled shotgun and a deer rifle.

A. J. Guthrie filled two mugs and handed them to Jane and Kenny. "I'm not famous for nothing," he said, "but when I die, some folks're gonna miss my coffee." He slid an unlit cigar between his teeth. "Don't worry, ma'am. I ain't gonna light it with a woman around."

Jane sipped the coffee and smiled. "Now I know I love you."

A.J. sat at his desk and rested his left foot on an open drawer. "Not that I don't appreciate the company, but aside from the coffee, there anything else I can do for ya? Your Officer Finney was rather circumspect on the phone."

"Sheriff . . ." Jane began.

"A.J., please, ma'am."

"Okay, A.J., Inspector Marks and I need to see Alice Iverson."

"And it can't wait till morning?"

"No, sir. It can't."

"Because?"

"Because Philip Iverson has been killed. Murdered tonight in San Francisco."

A. J. Guthrie took the cigar from his mouth and snicked a piece of tobacco from the tip of his tongue. "Well, shit." He shook his head. "Poor Philip. How?"

"Gunshot," Kenny answered. "Single bullet to the head."

"You catch the guy?"

Jane held the coffee in both hands, grateful for its warmth. "Not yet." She sat on the couch.

"Got any suspects?"

Kenny sat on the arm of the couch, at the opposite end. "No, sir. But we may want to come back and pick your brain."

"Anything I can do." He let out a long slow breath and Jane saw his eyes moisten. "Then I guess you're here to formally inform the wife. Nice of you to drive all this way. Coulda called, you know. I'da done it for ya."

Jane put the mug on the desk. "Mr. Iverson was a friend of our chief. He wanted us to do it this way. Besides, it's the right thing to do."

"You never regret doin' the right thing." A.J. emptied the coffeepot into a thermos. "Don't expect Alice'll have coffee goin' at this hour." He draped his holster over his shoulder, a .357 Magnum hanging heavily against his broad chest.

Kenny opened the door and descended the two steps to the Explorer. A.J. held the screen open for Jane. "You don't mind me askin', but how long you two been married?"

Jane stopped. "How'd you know?"

"Two of you were careful not to sit too close to each other. Regular partners usually don't care about that stuff." He let the screen door slap shut. "That and you got the same wedding rings."

Jane regarded him. "You don't miss a thing, do you, Sheriff?"

"I 'spect you don't, either, Lieutenant."

CHAPTER 5

■

KENNY AND JANE followed A. J. Guthrie's Wagoneer up a narrow back road. The blacktop soon gave way to dirt, the surface furrowed like a washboard.

Jane watched the thin white exhaust puffing from the sheriff's car. One taillight blinked at infrequent intervals. The Wagoneer slowed as it approached a pair of tall iron gates.

Video cameras atop the gate posts swiveled for a better look as A.J. leaned out to speak into the intercom. After a moment, the electric gates parted to reveal a rambling three-story log structure with expansive picture windows and wraparound porches on every level. "This is a cabin?" Jane asked.

"More like a ski lodge." Kenny parked the Explorer next to the sheriff on the far side of the entry-court fountain.

A light came on in an upstairs room, then another. A. J. Guthrie emerged from his Jeep and reached back in for the thermos. Jane put her hand on Kenny's arm. "Let's remember the reason we're here."

"Both reasons," Kenny said. "To inform Mrs. Iverson of the tragedy . . . and to watch her reaction."

■

THE HUGE RIVERSTONE fireplace was large enough to stand in. Every available surface of the sitting room was arrayed with framed photographs. Alice Iverson with Ronald Reagan, both as governor and president. With Frank Sinatra. With George Bush. With George W. Bush.

A massive oak door on the far wall was pulled open by a Korean housemaid. She stepped aside and Alice Iverson entered the room.

Even at this hour she looked like a Thoroughbred, Jane thought. Her blond hair was pulled back into a loose ponytail, and she wore an ivory silk robe that clung to her body like water. She strode over to A. J. Guthrie in old unlaced Converse tennis shoes and rose up on her toes to give him a kiss on the cheek. As she did, her robe parted slightly, offering a glimpse of her legs. Lithe and athletic, they had a firmness, a perfection almost, that was breathtaking. Jane glanced over to see if Kenny was watching.

He was.

"I'm so sorry to keep you waiting, A.J.," Alice said. "But I'm fighting this cold and it took me an extra minute to throw myself together."

Jane felt Kenny's eyes, but she wouldn't return his look. Alice Iverson had fresh makeup on. The doorbell had rung at three in the morning and she'd taken the time to fix her face before coming downstairs.

"Alice," A.J. began, "this is Lieutenant Candiotti and her . . . partner . . . Inspector Marks from San Francisco. We're real sorry to be comin' up so late, but it's important."

Alice's fingers trembled slightly, like twigs in a breeze. She sat in a leather reading chair. "It's Philip. Something's happened to him."

"Mrs. Iverson . . ." Jane said softly. "Your husband was killed tonight. He was shot as he left the banquet. We don't know who did it, but we will. I promise."

There came a cry from the doorway as the housemaid fled down the hall. Everyone turned at the sound.

Then Alice Iverson pulled a tissue from the sleeve of her robe. Her lip quivered involuntarily. She waited for it to stop. When it didn't, she spoke slowly, fighting to control her emotions. "Can I see him?"

Kenny studied her carefully. "Yes, of course. We'll help make that happen."

Alice turned to Jane. "Did he suffer?"

"No, Mrs. Iverson. He was shot once. It . . . death . . . was instantaneous. And painless."

A sudden sob escaped Alice Iverson's lips, her upper body heaving. "When he didn't come home, I kept calling his car and our apartment in the city. I left three messages, but he didn't call back. Of *course* he didn't call back. Oh God . . ." She fell back in the chair and wiped her eyes. "Oh God . . ."

Jane gave her a minute to collect herself. "We're very sorry for your loss, Mrs. Iverson. Chief McDonald is distraught over this. He sends his warmest personal regards."

"Thank you."

"May I ask you a few questions while everything is still fresh in your mind?"

"Anything."

An older Korean man appeared in the doorway. His eyes brimmed with tears as he carried a tray of coffee, tea, and ice water to the end table.

"Thank you, Mr. Kim," Alice Iverson said.

"You're welcome, miss." Mr. Kim nodded tightly and left.

"Is there anyone you can think of who might be responsible for this?" Jane asked. "Someone from business or—"

"No one." Alice shook her head. "Philip didn't have an enemy in the world." She drew several quick breaths. "Oh God."

Kenny poured her a glass of ice water. "Mrs. Iverson, we'd like to speak with someone from your husband's company. Who's the best person for us to talk to?"

Alice stared at the water glass in her hands. "Bob Lewis. He's RiverPark's CFO and Philip's closest business confidant."

Kenny made a note. "Can we get a number from you?"

Alice Iverson looked up. "He's in Costa Rica, at the manufacturing site. But I'm sure as soon as he hears about . . . this . . . he'll take the jet back here."

"Why is it, Mrs. Iverson," Jane asked, "that you stayed up here rather than accompany your husband to the city?"

"I wanted to go." Alice sipped the water. "But I have this damn cold. Philip insisted I stay here and get better." She looked away. "Maybe if I'd gone, this never would have happened."

A. J. Guthrie leaned back against the stone hearth and watched as Jane and Kenny felt their way along this difficult path.

"Did your husband go to the banquet from here or from your place in San Francisco?" Jane asked.

"From here. I helped him get ready. He looked wonderful." Alice stopped, fighting for composure. "So proud of what he was going to do tonight. He looked forward to the banquet as another opportunity to give, not just as an evening about honoring him."

"Did he call you from the hotel?" Kenny asked. "Was he concerned about anything?"

"No, he didn't call. I went to bed after *Charlie Rose*. But the phone didn't ring. I'm sure of it." She crouched forward and reached for the china coffeepot.

A.J. stepped in. "Brought some of my own." He unscrewed the top of the thermos and filled her cup.

Alice added a spot of milk and sat back. "Thank you, A.J."

Jane nodded to Kenny and they rose together. "Mrs. Iverson, we're going to head back to the city." She slid a business card from her pocket and set it down on the tray. "But if anything . . . or anybody . . . comes to mind that you think we should know about, I want you to give us a call."

Kenny buttoned his jacket. "Someone from our office will contact you about . . . seeing your husband."

Alice Iverson looked at the card and put it in her pocket. She started to say something, but it was lost in a sigh.

"I'll show you out," A.J. offered.

As they started across the room, Jane turned back. Alice Iverson had closed her eyes, her head gently rocking from side to side. Jane glanced at Kenny. He nodded with his eyes. Agreeing that she had to do this.

"Mrs. Iverson," Jane said.

"Hmm?"

"Who was on *Charlie Rose* tonight?"

"Alan Dershowitz and some mystery author I'd never—" She stopped. Opening her eyes, she found Jane and glared at her. "How dare you!"

Jane held her gaze. Whatever sorrow she felt for her, and it was considerable, was tainted by a visceral dislike for Alice Iverson. "Sorry to be indelicate," she said finally. "Just doing my job."

Alice stood up quickly. "Why don't you do your fucking job and find whoever murdered my husband!" She gathered up her robe and stormed out of the room.

There was a long silent beat, then they could hear someone running up the stairs.

"That went well," Kenny said, guiding Jane into the foyer.

A. J. Guthrie held the front door open. "I'm gonna stay awhile. Do the country-sheriff thing. I learn anything, I'll give you a call."

"Thanks for everything, A.J. Nice meeting you."

A.J. smiled. "Wish it coulda been under better circumstances." He started to close the door. "Oh, one other thing?"

Jane and Kenny looked up.

"How'd she do?"

Kenny pulled the car keys from his pocket. "What do you mean?"

The sheriff shrugged. "The notification test. The old spouse-as-suspect theory. How'd Alice do?"

"Ooh." Jane smiled. "You're good."

"Used t' be." A.J. nodded and pushed the door closed.

CHAPTER 6

■

"YOU WERE GREAT," Kenny said as they climbed Route 12 out of the Arleta Valley. Behind them, the eastern sky bloomed with promise, the sun just now brimming the horizon.

Jane watched as a flight of swallows swooped across the lake at the base of the RiverPark waterfall. "Thanks, but it still feels shitty to throw a curve like that at a woman who's just lost her husband."

"Not just any husband."

"Not just any woman."

"3H61." The mountains interfered with the clarity of the signal, causing the call to fade in and out.

"This is 3H61," Kenny said. "Go, Moby."

"Uh, hi, Inspector. Just calling to tell you that Reggie Mayhew's ID of the eight-oh-two from Pier Twenty is confirmed. Army records positively identify the victim as William Thomas Temple, fifty-one, of Daly City."

"Thanks, Mike," Jane said. "Hang on a second till we get over this hill. You're breaking up."

The Explorer slid over the last rise and, passing RiverPark on the right, began the descent toward Highway 101.

"All those people who work there," Kenny said, "don't know their boss is dead."

Jane nodded as she spoke into the radio. "Okay, Mike. Should be better now."

"Loud and clear on this end, Lieutenant." He slurped some sort of drink.

"Great. Have someone check the answering machine at Philip Iverson's San Francisco apartment. Also, see if the voice mail on his cell phone has any messages. Then pull the phone records of the Dos Rios address and—"

Kenny put his hand on her arm. "We going straight to the office?"

Jane nodded. "Got to."

Kenny turned to the radio and spoke. "Put it all on my desk." He looked to Jane. "I know how much you hate that stuff."

Jane smiled her thanks. "And, Mike? I need someone to find Bob Lewis, the CFO of RiverPark. He's down at their plant in Costa Rica. I want to talk with him as soon as possible."

"Will do, Lieutenant. Oh . . . Becka Flynn's here. Really wants to speak with you."

Becka Flynn was a reporter for KGO-TV. She and Jane had met while Jane was working the difficult case of an ex-con who was killing cops, including Lieutenant Spielman's son. Becka was a beautiful redhead who was ten years younger than Jane. Over the past several months, they'd gotten together for drinks a couple of times, dinner once.

Becka was bright and ambitious . . . and lonely.

She reminded Jane of herself at that age.

"Patch her through, Mike."

There was a moment of low static. "Lieutenant, that you?"

"Hi, Becka. You're up early."

"We both are. Looks like we've got a big story brewing and I'm not waiting for the other guys to get it first." She paused. "Jane, the chief's put the muzzle on the whole department and everyone here is stonewalling me. We know Philip Iverson was killed last night, but I can't get anyone to confirm it. And I can't go with the story until I do."

Jane started to speak, but Becka Flynn pushed on.

"Here's what I've got so far. There's a photo of the crime scene going around. In it is a body and three vehicles. We ran the plates of all three cars. Called the owners. Got two of them. The one we couldn't get was Philip Iverson."

Jane smiled. Becka Flynn was resourceful and relentless. "If you let me get a word in edgewise, Becka, I will confirm for you that we've informed the widow and that the victim was indeed Philip Iverson."

"Suspects, motives, leads?" Becka was breathless. "This is huge. I need something."

"You got something," Jane said. "You got the story first. Maybe those guys at CNN will finally notice what a fine reporter you are."

"That's it?"

"That's it. We'll make an official statement later."

"C'mon, Jane."

"Becka." Jane's voice was tinged with annoyance. "We got zero sleep last night and we still have to drive down to the city. Don't push it."

"Okay . . . you're right. I'll talk to you later."

"No doubt," Jane said. "Oh hey, how'd the blind date go?"

"The usual." Becka sighed. "Another lawyer type wanting to get close to the news chick he watches on TV every night."

"It'll happen, Becka. It'll happen."

"From your mouth. Talk to you later."

Jane switched off the radio. "Poor kid."

"So now you're talking blind dates and stuff. I'm glad you guys are bonding."

"Why, 'cause she's such a babe?"

"No," Kenny said, "because you've said a thousand times that it's important for us to have friends outside the department. Makes us pass for almost normal."

Jane nodded. It was something she'd been thinking about more and more lately.

Kenny cranked the Explorer onto the on-ramp for Highway 101 and, new sunlight streaming through the mountain pass on their left, headed south to San Francisco.

"Floating a balloon here," Jane said as they settled in for the long drive. "Is it possible that Alice Iverson's reaction was too perfect? Prepared, rehearsed . . . and maybe just a little flawless?"

"Possible. I mean, the woman's virtually flawless already."

Jane shot him a look.

"What?" Kenny asked. He eased off the accelerator as the flow of inbound traffic thickened, like slow-moving water.

"You see her legs?"

"Not really." Kenny kept his eyes on the road.

"Bullshit."

"Okay, maybe a little. But she's like what, thirty-two or something?"

"She's my age."

"Oh." Kenny pulled the sun visor around to shield the driver's-side window. Then he slid his hand under Jane's left thigh. "You're everything I want."

Jane took his hand and kissed his fingers. "Thanks. You, too."

They drove on, caught in the stream of traffic.

After a while, Jane let go of Kenny's hand. "I'm gonna start jogging again."

CHAPTER 7

■

KENNY AND JANE entered the homicide bullpen.

Everyone looked up, a still life of anticipation. The murder of Philip Iverson was a big case, easily as big as the cop killer case, and this time Jane was in charge.

She crossed to the dispatch desk. Cheryl Lomax, an overweight black woman with elaborately painted fingernails, sat at the console. Silver was the nail color of the day. Silver with flecks of glitter.

Cheryl, monitoring a call on her headset, handed Jane a thick stack of messages and raised an eyebrow. This is a big one, the eyebrow said. Jane responded with two raised eyebrows. Tell me about it.

Jane sifted through the messages. "Every reporter in town, plus a couple of network guys in New York."

"What're you gonna do?" Kenny asked as they passed Linda on the phone at her desk.

"Send 'em to Press Relations. Let Alvarez handle them. I've got" —she stopped at Linda French's desk—"two new murders to solve."

"I know this is difficult, Mrs. Temple, but I already told you all we know about your son at this time." Linda looked up at Jane. She seemed put out. Not quite agitated, but unsettled. "I'm sorry, ma'am," she continued into the phone. "But we keep going over the same things. Is there anyone you can call? Anyone who could maybe

take you down here? No, ma'am, like I said, we don't provide trans-
portation."

Jane looked across Linda to Kenny. He had noticed it, too. Linda
French, while not being impolite, was not being particularly compas-
sionate. Willie Temple's mother had just had her world blown apart
and there was no room in Jane's universe for anything less than complete surrender in the face of that kind of grief.

Jane touched Linda's shoulder. "Send a car."

Linda put her hand over the mouthpiece. "But I thought—"

"Send a car," Jane said firmly, and went into her office.

Mike Finney's head gophered up over the top of his cubicle. He
saw Kenny across the room and, a breakfast burrito in one hand and
a sheaf of papers in the other, crossed to him.

"Got those phone records for you, Inspector Marks." He dropped
the papers on Kenny's desk, oblivious to the grease stain on the top
sheet.

"Thanks, Mobe. It's gonna get pretty busy around here. Up for
it?"

"You bet."

Jane sat at her desk in Lieutenant Spielman's old office. She dusted
off a picture of herself and Kenny taken on the Sausalito Ferry just
after they were married. Through the glass window that separated
her from the rest of the squad room, she watched as the detectives
and patrol officers in her charge went about the business of solving
San Francisco's most elite crime. Homicide.

Usually the work was pure drudgery. Wading through avalanches
of files, pursuing dead-end lead after dead-end lead, shivering
through endless stakeouts. But when it worked, when the bad guy
who had dared to, or had been cruel enough to, deprive someone else
of his or her life had been caught, there was no feeling on earth that
compared with that rush.

It was a drug.

And, like the high off a drug, it was fleeting. They needed to move
to the next fix, the next murder.

There was always a next murder.

Lately, Jane had been wondering if the high was worth it anymore. If the risk and the toll were still offset by the reward.

And lately, the answer was no.

She had been feeling weary and confused. Not sure if accepting this command had been the right thing to do. She wanted more out of life, to work on her marriage.

To have a baby.

Roz Shapiro tapped on her door. Jane motioned for her to come in. A widow in her early seventies, Roz had been working as a volunteer at Precinct Nineteen for almost five years. She put a cappuccino and two Equals on Jane's blotter. "A little wake-me-up for ya. Chief's on two."

"Thanks, Roz."

Roz Shapiro stood there for a moment. "Philip Iverson, huh?"

Jane poured the Equals into the coffee. "Yeah."

"Well, God rest his soul. Good man like that." She left, pulling the door closed, extinguishing the sounds of the bullpen.

Jane saw Kenny cross to the dispatch desk, the phone records in his hand. She punched line two. "This is Lieutenant Candiotti."

"Hold for Chief McDonald."

A few seconds. Then: "Lieutenant, the incident report shows you at the Pier Twenty murder scene. I specifically told you to get up to Dos Rios to inform Alice Iverson without delay."

Jane tilted back in her chair, surprised at the chief's tone and lack of civility. "Chief, all homicide cases in the city go through my office. There happened to be two of them last night. Pier Twenty is directly on the way to Dos Rios from the Golden Gate Grand. We . . . I was there less than ten minutes."

"And what if, in those ten minutes, some busybody reporter had called Alice Iverson and that was how she learned of her husband's death?"

Jane's instinct was to apologize, to smooth the chief's feathers. But she fought it. If she gave in to him now, on her first major case since assuming command, he'd make her life miserable. "The point's moot, sir. Because it didn't happen."

"Speaking of Alice Iverson, I just got a call from her. Seems you were a little . . . provocative . . . with her."

So that's what this is about, Jane thought. She pushed her cappuccino away, the taste for it lost in the bile rising in her throat. "Sir, I was professional and respectful. I informed Mrs. Iverson of her husband's death with reserve and compassion . . . as you'll see in my report."

There was a long pause. Jane could hear the muffled voice of the chief talking to someone in his office. He returned to Jane. "Look, Lieutenant, this is an extremely sensitive case, and as soon as this city wakes up and hears about it, all hell's gonna break loose."

"I know that, sir. And if you let me do my job without second-guessing me, I'll solve it for you."

Another pause. "You do that, Lieutenant." The line went dead.

Unnerved by the call, Jane reached across her blotter and retrieved her cappuccino. Sipping it, she noticed Kenny leaning over the dispatch desk, talking to Cheryl Lomax, and reminded herself that she was a lucky woman.

Her husband had a great ass.

CHAPTER 8

———◼———

"WATCH THIS," KENNY said, his eyes bright with excitement. He stood before a television set in Interrogation Room One and pressed "play" on the VCR. The image of a parking-garage cashier's booth flickered on. "The arm's up because it's midnight and everyone paid on the way in."

Jane stepped deeper into the room.

"Okay, here we go," Kenny said. "Nothing. Nothing. Nothing . . . *Boom!*" He pointed at the screen as a late-model sedan screamed past the booth. It fishtailed into a hard right turn and disappeared.

"Again," Jane said.

Kenny twisted the jog wheel to the left. The car raced backward toward the camera. He pressed "play" again. "Nothing. Nothing . . . There!" He froze the picture.

Jane crossed to the table and peered into the screen. "BMW, seven series. Partial license . . . four, H, B, something something, three, something. The rest is obscured by the glare coming off the floodlights."

"Look at the time code," Kenny said. "Eleven fifty-seven P.M. Only exactly when Philip Iverson was killed."

"First thing we gotta do is check the accuracy of the time code," Jane said. "If someone didn't reset it for daylight savings, or if it's fast or slow, then it's useless to us."

Mike Finney sat at the back of the room next to an older detective. "I'll do it, Lieutenant."

"Thanks, Mike. Also, do a rundown on identical vehicles with plates similar to the partial we have here."

Kenny popped the tape from the VCR. "This needs to get to Forensics for full-spectrum enhancement right away."

"I'll hand-carry it over," Linda French said from the doorway.

"Thanks, Linda," Jane said. "But I need you on the Willie Temple killing. Incident reports, forensics, autopsy follow-up. We'll take care of this." She thought she saw a hint of irritation cross Linda's face as she retreated back to her desk. "Ken, we should look into the whole philanthropy thing. Lots of people applied to Iverson's Make It So Foundation. That means lots of people were turned down. Maybe someone was more than just a little disappointed."

"I'm all over it," Kenny said. "Moby, any news on that RiverPark exec who was in Costa Rica?"

Mike Finney turned back a page in his notebook. "Bob Lewis will be taking the corporate jet to SFO in about an hour." He looked up and shrugged. "Customs and stuff."

Jane turned to the detective next to Finney. Lou Tronick always wore one of his two suits to work, gray or blue. He was already an old-timer when Jane had moved up to Homicide. Patient and persistent, he was the perfect candidate to pursue some of the less glamorous aspects of a murder case. "Lou, do me a favor and check on Alice and Philip Iverson's financials. While you're at it, see if there were any reports of domestic problems between them. Check with the police and neighbors at both their homes."

"I'll also call in for the banquet guest list."

"That'd be great. There were a slew of reporters there. Local TV, maybe some network. Get copies of all the video they shot last night and—"

"Go through it," Lou said.

Jane nodded. "All of it. And talk to the hotel staff. See if anything turns up. Okay, guys, it's ten o'clock. Let's recap at noon."

As Lou Tronick and Mike Finney started out, Roz Shapiro stuck her head in. "Jane, chief's on two. Your aunt Lucy on one."

Jane reached for the phone and pressed line one. "Hi, Aunt Lucy." She signaled that she'd call the chief back. Roz Shapiro retreated into the bullpen just as Linda French pulled on her coat and headed for the stairwell door.

"So, Auntie, how ya doin'?" Aunt Lucy was Poppy's only surviving sibling. It was Lucy, widowed for almost thirty years, who had looked after Jane and Timmy when their mother died; and it was Lucy who had taken care of Poppy—cooking for him, taking him to his doctor appointments—in the last years of his life. Now her five brothers were gone, and Lucy was alone. "Yeah, this is a big one. Sure I'll be careful. You wanna maybe come over for dinner this week? Great. Yeah, I'll tell him."

Jane hung up and turned to Kenny. "She said to say hello to that handsome husband of mine."

■

"ONE BLACK GIORGIO Armani tuxedo. Black label. One pair black patent-leather dress shoes. One pair of black socks. One Hugo Boss bow tie."

Jane checked the items on the coroner's manifest as Kenny reached back into the box. Each of Philip Iverson's belongings was neatly packed in a clear plastic bag.

"One Giorgio Armani formal dress shirt." Kenny held it up, the bloodstain on the collar now almost black. "Two silver monogrammed cuff links. One black leather wallet." He flipped it open. "No cash. Everything else seems normal." He turned it to Jane to reveal a photo of Alice Iverson.

"Whatever you're going to say," Jane warned, "don't."

"Moving on." Kenny tossed the wallet onto the table. "Comb. Keys. One Chap Stick, cherry . . ." He dug into a corner of the box and came up with the last plastic bag. "One platinum Rolex watch." Kenny held the bag between his thumb and forefinger and let it dangle between them. They were both thinking the same thing.

"If we're going to even begin to think of this as a robbery gone bad," Jane said, putting down the checklist, "then what's a twenty-thousand-dollar watch still doing on the victim's wrist?"

"Good question, Lieutenant. But . . ." Kenny opened a folder and riffled through a stack of eight-by-ten color crime-scene photos. "Iverson fell facedown. His left arm was under his body, obscuring the Rolex. This was a hit-and-run shooting and the bad guy didn't stick around."

"I don't buy it," Jane countered. "If this guy took the trouble to kill Philip Iverson and take his wallet, he would have searched for other goodies."

"Only one explanation, then."

"Someone scared him away."

■

LINDA FRENCH GOT off the elevator at Parking Level Seven.

She felt tense, slightly nervous. Jane had specifically told her to stay on the Willie Temple case. But as soon as she rounded the corner, the excitement and drama of the previous night all came rushing back.

The wind had blown the detritus of the Philip Iverson crime scene—coffee cups, snippets of yellow police tape, film canisters—against the wall where his Mercedes had been parked. There was a small white patch amid all the other grease stains, and Linda knew that someone had scrubbed Iverson's blood away.

She crouched next to the spot where he had fallen and looked around. A white Chevy Suburban with a wheelchair rig on the rear bumper was in the handicapped spot where she had mistakenly parked her car last night. Jane had been right, she thought, to reprimand her. But she didn't have to come on so strong.

Beyond the nearest row of cars, she noticed a plume of steam billowing out of a heating vent. She thought she saw the outline of a man's body standing on the other side of the steam, barely visible in the mist. She looked away and looked back again.

It was a man, a large man in an overcoat. And he was watching her.

Linda French rose and called out to him. "Sir, can I talk to you?"

He turned to go, his greatcoat whirling in the steam.

Linda called out again, filling her voice with authority. "Sir! I need you to come over here and talk to me!"

The man stopped and stared at her through the rolling vapor. Then he reached into his coat.

Linda French fell to one knee behind the Suburban and ripped her service revolver from her waistband. "Don't!"

A gunshot echoed through the concrete parking structure. The passenger window of the Suburban shattered, sending a tuft of fabric exploding from the headrest. Linda French trained her weapon on the man in the mist and tensed her finger against the trigger.

But he just stood there, looking off to his left. Confused.

She realized that he hadn't fired. Turning to where he was looking, she saw that the stairwell door was slightly ajar. A muzzle flash, another echoing shot. A slug ricocheted off a nearby pillar and the man she had first drawn on went down.

Before she could return fire, the shooter slammed the door closed and fled. Her pistol clutched in both hands, Linda French scooted to the door and tried the knob. It was locked. She heard the fading sound of footsteps as someone pounded down the steel stairs.

"Help me . . ." The man by the steam vent raised a trembling hand. "I've been shot!"

CHAPTER 9

■

"HERE'S WHAT WE have so far."

Kenny stood at the bulletin board and indicated the crime-scene photos and a blowup of the BMW. "TOD is somewhere around midnight. This Beamer was videotaped speeding from the scene of the crime. Time code—which is correct—has it at eleven fifty-seven. Ipso facto: It's connected."

Jane picked up for him. "Our thinking is: Either the driver was scared off by the killer and perhaps frightened the bad guy into leaving before he could grab Iverson's Rolex or—"

"Or the driver *is* the shooter," Kenny said, "and something else scared him off." He turned to Lou Tronick. "What can you add?"

"Well, I'm still working on all the domestics and financials, but . . ." He opened the coroner's report. "Initial M.E.'s findings concur with Forensics. Single twenty-two slug. Entry at the base of the skull. No exit. Nothing under the victim's nails." He turned to another page. "Speaking of Forensics, Aaron's team did a power-suck of Iverson's clothing. Since he had spent the previous three hours at a banquet in his honor and had probably been hugged by a couple of hundred people, there should be a smorgasbord in there. They'll get back to us on that. There were some scuff marks on the floor of the parking structure that match the victim's shoes. Best guess is he slipped while running away from his assailant."

Roz Shapiro came in and handed Mike Finney a note. He read it and looked up.

" 'Scuse me, Inspector. There's a limo downstairs. Come for Mr. Iverson's effects."

Kenny turned to Jane. She took a pen from the table and signed the release. "Okay, Mike, you can take it down."

Finney carefully repacked the plastic box, pressed the cover to seal it, and carried it out.

"That fancy box for the lim-o-zine?" A woman's angry voice boomed from the squad room. Jane and Kenny hurried to the doorway.

A black woman in her early seventies stood in front of Finney, blocking his way. She wore a faded green housedress beneath a tattered woolen overcoat. The backs of her tennis shoes were flattened beneath her heels.

Loretta Temple.

Willie Temple's mother.

"I got to beg for a ride down here 'cause some lady cop calls me up and says I gotta pick up my boy's things *in person*. I ask her for help and she tells me no exceptions!" She poked a finger into Finney's chest. "I can see there's maybe *one* exception . . . and his name's Philip goddamn Iverson!"

Jane quickly crossed the room. She took Mrs. Temple by the elbow and motioned for Finney to go on. Loretta Temple pulled her arm away. "You the lady cop called to tell me about my boy?"

"No, ma'am."

Dismissing Jane, Loretta Temple turned to Kenny as he came into the bullpen. "You the Lieutenant Candiotti they told me about downstairs?"

Kenny's ears flushed red.

"I'm Lieutenant Candiotti," Jane said.

Loretta narrowed her eyes. She wore a black wig, thin tendrils of gray hair peeking out the back. "You a lieutenant? For real?"

"For real." Jane held out her hands. "Can I get you anything?"

"My boy's stuff so's I can get out of your motherfuckin' po-lice station, that's what you can get me. I been downstairs for an hour messing with paperwork and that rich bitch sends a lim-o-zine? Why ain't she come *in person?*"

"She's sick and . . ." Jane regretted it as soon as she said it.

"I'm sick, too," Loretta shouted. "Sick my baby's dead."

Her face was the very face of grief and Jane knew she had no choice but to yield to it. Besides, Mrs. Temple had been treated poorly through a whole confluence of missteps by people in her department.

Jane called over to Cheryl. "Where's Linda?"

"Said she had some fieldwork. Be back in an hour."

Roslyn Shapiro emerged from the holding room with a plain brown paper bag. Willie Temple's belongings. Kenny motioned for her to bring it into Interrogation One.

Loretta followed Roz with her eyes, understanding what she was carrying.

"Come," Jane said softly. "Come, Mrs. Temple, and you can examine your son's things. Then I'll have someone take you home."

Loretta Temple's jaw clenched and Jane braced for the next outburst. But the older woman just turned and shambled into Interrogation Room One. "Let's do this quick. I got family waitin' back to the house."

Kenny used his pocketknife to pop the security tape and opened the paper bag. Then he stepped aside and motioned for Loretta Temple to come closer. She hesitated for a moment, then went to the table. Roz Shapiro handed Kenny the manifest. "Everything your son had with him last night," Kenny said, "is in this bag. We can go through it if you like."

Mrs. Temple started to reach for the bag, her hand quavering. She pulled it back. "I want to."

Jane moved forward and laid the bag on its side. "May I?"

Loretta Temple pulled a wad of Kleenex from her coat pocket. She dabbed at her eyes and nodded. The reality of what was in the bag pressed down on her, cooling her anger.

Jane took the first items from the bag. "Pack of Kent cigarettes.

Meal coupon from Santuario. Cigarette lighter with military insignia. Eleven dollars and forty cents."

"Wait. My boy wasn't killed for his money?"

"Apparently not."

"Then why was he killed?"

"We don't know."

Mrs. Temple sat heavily in a folding chair. "He heard voices. Every since he was a little boy, he heard voices. They was always telling him to do things. Good things. Give his things away. I couldn't keep him in clothes, he was always giving them to somebody who didn't have none. His clothes, his food. Social Services said he wasn't sick enough for them to help. I wanted him with me. But the voices wanted him to be out there." She drew a long breath and nodded for Kenny to continue.

"Two BART tokens."

"The train was warm. He would ride the whole day."

"A hand mirror, keys—"

"They wasn't keys to nothin'. He just liked them in his pocket. Made him proud."

"Snickers candy bar. San Francisco Opera schedule."

Roz Shapiro leaned in from the doorway, trying to make contact. "Did your son enjoy the opera, Mrs. Temple?"

Loretta Temple shook her head in a tiny repetitive motion. Lost.

"Lots of homeless people around here keep schedules to the opera," Jane said, "or the theater, or the symphony. It's where the affluent people go." She glanced at Mrs. Temple. "And sometimes they can be generous."

"One pair of tennis shoes."

"Gimme them."

Kenny handed the shoes to her.

Loretta Temple turned them over in her hands, drifting on a memory. "He loved these sneakers," she said. "Thought they made him look like all them kids at the park. Made him look like . . . normal." She clutched the shoes to her chest, lowered her head, and kissed them—a low sob catching in her throat.

As Kenny started to repack the bag, Jane again noticed that the shoes were mismatched. Not uncommon for a homeless man. "Whenever you're ready, Mrs. Temple."

Loretta passed her son's shoes to Kenny and rose. As she did, she saw Mike Finney returning to the bullpen. Her mood darkened and her temper returned. She grabbed the bag from Kenny and stormed back into the squad room.

Jane hurried after her. "There's a car waiting for you down—"

Loretta Temple spun around, her wet eyes blazing. "My son wasn't just some street bum panhandlin' on rich folks. He was a hero. Two times with the army in Vietnam. He got a Purple Heart *and* a Bronze Star. What about Philip goddamn Iverson? You think he put his ass on the line when there was niggers to go instead?"

She jammed the bag under her arm and yanked open the stairwell door. "Anyone in here wanna bet which killer gets found first? Iverson's or my boy's?" She passed through the door and slammed it closed.

Everyone sat still for a moment, shaken by her intensity and her pain. Then the phones rang again. And the printers whirred again. And the elevator doors opened again.

The bullpen caught its collective breath and went back to work.

Jane noticed Finney staring out the window and went to him. "Lookit, Lieutenant," he said.

On the street below, a herd of photographers ran alongside the limousine that Alice Iverson had sent, scrambling for a shot.

A few seconds later, the patrol car carrying Loretta Temple back to Daly City slipped out of the garage, turned left, and drove, unnoticed, up the street.

"Jane!" Cheryl called out from the dispatch console. "Linda French was just in a shots-fired situation. We've got backup and paramedics rolling."

CHAPTER 10

—■—

YELLOW POLICE TAPE ran from the stairwell door of Parking Level
Seven, around the white Suburban in the handicapped space, and
along the row of parked cars.

Linda French spotted Jane and Kenny approaching and hurried
from behind the ambulance to intercept them. "Two shots fired," she
said breathlessly. "I never had a chance to return."

"You hurt?" Kenny asked.

"No." Linda looked toward the stairwell where a forensics tech
was dusting the door. "But the shooter got away."

"Long as you're okay." Jane gestured toward the ambulance.
"What's EMT doing here?"

"There was this guy standing off to the side watching me," Linda
explained. "I called to him and he refused to respond. I called to him
again. He reached into his coat and . . . I drew down on him. Then
the shots came from over there and he was hit."

Jane started around the ambulance. "Was he going for a weapon?"

Linda caught up with her. "No . . . a badge."

A. J. Guthrie sat in the open doorway of the ambulance. His left
pant leg had been cut up to the knee by a paramedic and his calf was
wrapped in a bandage. "Hello, Lieutenant. Sorry for all the trouble."

"Sheriff Guthrie, Jesus," Jane said. "How bad?"

"Through and through," the EMT said as she pulled off her rubber gloves. "Lucky as you can get. We're gonna transport him to Mercy to irrigate the wound. Should be released in like an hour." She started repacking her medical kit.

"You see who shot you?" Jane asked.

A.J. shook his head. "No, ma'am. Tell the truth, I kinda flinched when I heard the first shot. Next thing I know I'm on the ground."

"Lemme guess," Kenny said, "you being at the exact spot where Philip Iverson was killed is not entirely a coincidence."

A.J. stuck a cigar in his mouth, but didn't light it. "Truth is, Mrs. Iverson asked me to help her out with her husband's case."

"And do what?" Jane asked.

"The word she used, and I'd never heard it before, was 'liaise.'"

"Means act as a liaison," Linda French offered.

"So I surmised, ma'am." A.J. looked to Jane. "Mrs. Iverson wants me to be her private investigator because . . ." He paused, not sure if he should go on.

"Because?" Jane said.

"Because . . . well, because she doesn't like you, Lieutenant."

"What a load of shit," Kenny said. "If she had half a brain, she'd—"

"Y'know what?" Jane interrupted. "I gotta agree with my partner that she's full of it. But she and I are never going to be best friends. So if it helps us catch the bad guy, I'm all for it. Now here's the deal, Sheriff. This is my city, my jurisdiction, and my case. Anything you come up with, you give it to us the same time you give it to Alice Iverson. Anything we come up with—"

A.J. held his hand up. "—you are under no obligation to give to me or Mrs. Iverson. I worked with plenty of PIs when I was on the force." He reflexively reached for his lighter, then caught himself. "I'm gonna behave the way I wanted them to behave back then. Only better."

"And the good people of Dos Rios," Kenny asked, "are cool with you doing this?"

"I got some vacation time saved up." A.J. shrugged. "Postman's holiday."

The EMT slid her case into the ambulance. "Okay if I take him now, Lieutenant?"

"Sure, thanks." Jane stepped back as A.J. gingerly climbed aboard. "You take care of yourself, Sheriff."

"I'll try to, ma'am."

The EMT closed the doors and hustled around to the driver's side. A uniformed cop cleared a path and the ambulance pulled away, winding its way down the spiraling ramp of the parking structure.

The sergeant-in-charge came up to Jane. " 'Scuse me, Lieutenant."

"Hey, Max," Jane said, "what've you got?"

"Bad guy got away clean." Max Batzer was a veteran cop. Solid and reliable, he had a line in his face for every case he'd worked on. "Fellow down in the cash booth says nobody sped away or otherwise acted strange around the time of the incident. We pulled the surveillance tapes just in case, but I think he was on foot. Could have gone into the hotel or—"

Kenny picked it up. "—or down one of the alleys to a parked car."

Max nodded. "Right, Inspector. One thing, though, Forensics pulled a slug from the headrest of that Suburban. It's in pretty good condition."

"I want the ballistics report as soon as possible," Jane said.

"I'll push it through myself."

"Thanks, Max. Good work." Jane turned to Kenny and Linda. "Let's start with the obvious: This shooting and Philip Iverson's murder are related."

"Killer returns to the scene of the crime," Kenny said, "sees a cop"—he nodded to Linda French—"with her weapon out and starts shooting to cover his escape."

"Possible," Jane said. "But why was he even here? I mean, why come back?"

Kenny watched as the forensics team fanned out and began a systematic grid sweep of the area. "Because he wanted to retrieve something . . ."

"Something . . ." Linda French added, "he left behind when he killed Philip Iverson. But what?"

"Don't know," Jane said, ". . . yet." She turned to Linda. "What the hell were you doing here after I told you I needed you on the Willie Temple killing?"

"I was on my way to Pier Twenty, trying to get some traction on the Temple case," Linda explained, "and I decided to stop off here. I just figured it couldn't hurt to experience as many crime scenes as possible." She averted her eyes. "But you're right, you did tell me to stick with Willie Temple's murder, and I had no business being here."

"Okay," Jane said. "Let's move on. You got anything on your case?"

Linda tossed open her notebook. "The guy who found Willie Temple's body is a transient from Nevada. No address, not even any hard ID. It's the old homeless-equals-hopeless syndrome."

"Willie Temple's mother came by for his stuff," Jane said, allowing just the slightest whiff of admonition to slip through.

"There were eleven or twelve bucks in his pockets," Kenny added. "So it wasn't one of those 'life is cheap, I'm gonna kill you for a quarter' deals."

"If robbery wasn't the motive," Jane said, "what was?"

Linda turned the pages of her notepad as if the answer were hidden in there. "I . . . I don't know."

"Try this," Jane offered. "Revenge. Maybe Willie Temple stole somebody's blanket, or girlfriend, or needle."

Kenny picked up on it. "Or maybe there's a psycho out there targeting bums. Check with Santuario. Go talk to Reggie Mayhew. Sure he's belligerent, but he knew Willie and the people in his world."

"Got it." Linda finally found what she was looking for. "What about the S-thing?"

"Any theories?" Jane asked.

"Not yet."

"Something to pursue. Could be a gang thing. Also, Temple was found at the docks. Was that a place he frequented?"

"I don't know."

"Then find out."

Linda looked away, embarrassed.

"Look," Jane explained, "if all you have are questions, then that's still something. The thing is to never stop thinking of new ones to ask." She started toward the elevators. "If the docks were someplace Willie liked to go, then maybe somebody there—another homeless person, a dockworker, anybody—has some information about his life, his friends . . ."

". . . his enemies," Kenny said.

"If not," Jane went on, "then what was he doing down there? The last twenty-four hours of a victim's life can tell you everything you'd ever want to know, if you just ask the right questions." She pressed the "down" button. "What about the body itself? What have we learned? What has it told you?"

"Nothing yet. Still waiting for the M.E.'s report."

"Don't wait. Do." The doors slid apart. Jane motioned to Linda. "C'mon."

Linda looked from Kenny to Jane. "Where we going?"

"The morgue," Jane said. "Let's see if Mr. Temple will talk to us."

CHAPTER 11

■

KENNY BROUGHT THE Explorer to a stop in a no-parking zone in front of the Hall of Justice and started to turn off the ignition.

Jane grabbed her purse and undid her seat belt. "Ken, can you go back to the parking structure and oversee the forensics sweep? I need my best man covering this. And that would be you."

Kenny's eyes darted to the rearview mirror. Linda French was just climbing down to the sidewalk. He turned to Jane. "Uh, sure. Why should those forensics guys have all the fun?"

Vast, leaden clouds, heavy with rain, were pushing their way in from the bay. Seagulls swirled in the parking lot across the street. "Storm coming," Jane said as she opened the door. "Drive carefully."

"Always," Kenny called. He watched them climb the steps and enter the Hall of Justice. Jane and Linda showed their badges and crossed the lobby toward the low white building in back that housed the city morgue.

Then he turned to watch the seagulls dip and dart in frenzied circles. He blew a huge sigh, caught in his own cycle of frustration. Every once in a while, his subordination to Jane got to him. He understood it was the nature of the beast. She was a lieutenant, *his* lieutenant . . . and she was his wife. They had discussed it all before they were married, and for the most part, he had made his peace with it.

But sometimes, and he could never see it coming, it all caught up to him.

He snatched the mike from the dash. "3H61 to Dispatch."

"This is Dispatch. Go, Ken."

"Cheryl, I got a Code J-4-0-B-D and need assistance right away."

"Inspector, what in the world is a J-4-0-B-D?"

"Jane's fortieth birthday. What the hell am I gonna get her?"

■

LINDA FRENCH STARED up at the number panel as she and Jane rode the elevator down to the morgue.

"I know I've been screwing up lately," she began without looking over, "but I'll get it together."

"You have to," Jane said evenly.

Linda glanced at her, surprised at her tone.

"Look," Jane went on, "I want to let you off the hook. But this is Homicide. Like it or not, we're working the cases with the highest stakes. I just have a limit as to how much I can tolerate."

They rode in silence for a few seconds.

"Wanna know why I wanted to transfer to Homicide so badly?" Linda asked.

"Why?"

"Because of you." She turned to Jane. "You probably have no idea, but you're kind of a role model among the women on the force."

Jane shook her head. "You're right. I had no idea."

"You have this great way about you," Linda continued, "that makes even this rough job look easy." The elevator reached the bottom floor. "But now that I'm actually doing it, on the front lines and all, I see how hard it really is."

"As hard as it gets," Jane said as the doors slid open. She started out, then turned back to Linda. "You'll be fine."

■

THE COLD ROOM.

Jane and Linda drew their coats around them as they were ushered in by Dr. Anthony Tedesco, San Francisco's chief medical examiner.

A dozen gurneys, nearly all of them occupied, were lined against the walls on both sides of the large space. It looked to Jane like a hospital ward in an old movie, except that all the patients were in body bags.

"Freezing in here," Linda French said, her breath steaming in front of her.

"Actually, two to four degrees above," the M.E. said as he stepped deeper into the room. "We got the natural causes back there," he explained for Linda's benefit. "We'll get to them later today. Over here"—he gestured to the first gurney—"is Philip Iverson. I brought my team in early for him. Under the circumstances, I think it's OT well spent."

Jane crossed to gurney number one and looked to Dr. Tedesco. He pulled the zipper down.

The face of Philip Iverson, a face known to everyone in San Francisco, stared back at her. Gray, almost blue now, his skin had the pallid appearance of candle wax. His body was a patchwork of bloodless incisions from the autopsy. They were closed with coarse black stitches, cosmetic considerations lost on the dead.

Jane looked into his pale blue eyes. She wondered if Philip Iverson had seen his killer, had known him.

"Damn shame is what it is," Dr. Tedesco said. "You wanted to see Mr. Temple, too?"

He led Jane and Linda to a gurney on the opposite wall and matter-of-factly opened the body bag.

Willie Temple was as much a contrast to Philip Iverson in death as he was in life. He was small, almost boyish in size. The dark skin of his chest was ravaged by several deep stab wounds.

His hands were covered in the grime of someone who made doorways and Dumpsters his home. There were smooth, hairless strips above his wrists where the tape had been ripped off when Forensics removed the bags from his hands.

"What's that?" Linda pointed to a weblike scar on his upper right thigh.

Dr. Tedesco turned the leg for a better look. "Old bullet wound."

"Probably a gang-banger," Linda said. "Might be some connection between this and the S-thing we found on-scene."

"That's large-caliber," Jane observed. "Not usually the weapon of choice with our gangs. Besides, his mother said he won the Purple Heart in Vietnam."

"Looks like a rifle entry," Dr. Tedesco agreed. "I'll check it against his records. Army just sent them over."

Jane looked back to Philip Iverson. His body was pale and clean, almost pristine. He died of a single small bullet to the head, a dime-size hole at the base of his skull the only blemish to his meticulous appearance.

Willie Temple's death, on the other hand, had been messy and violent.

Each man had died as he had lived.

Jane pulled her attention back to Willie Temple's body. Leaning in, she noticed a round discolored bump on the side of his head. "What's that?"

The cooling system kicked in and Dr. Tedesco had to raise his voice to be heard. "Contusion," he said. "Not fatal."

Linda scribbled in her notepad.

"You got a magnifying glass?" Jane asked.

"You bet." The M.E. handed her a stainless-steel magnifier.

Jane trained it on the swollen contusion.

"Might have happened when he hit the ground," Linda said.

"Or it could have been a blow to the head," Dr. Tedesco added.

Jane looked at Willie Temple's hands again. "No defense wounds. Unusual in a stabbing as brutal as this."

"What's that mean?" Linda asked.

"Either he was overpowered by a much larger man," Dr. Tedesco said. "Not unlikely given how small Mr. Temple is. Or . . ."

"Or," Jane said, "he was unconscious when he was knifed and never had a chance to defend himself. If he'd been knocked out first, then the question is where. Could be the docks. Could be anywhere in the city."

Dr. Tedesco made a note on Willie Temple's chart. "I'll run a particle analysis. See if there's anything in the head wound that rules in or rules out where the body was found."

"Thanks, Tony." Jane focused the magnifying glass on Willie's eyes and examined the thin dark streaks of blood on each eyelid.

Dr. Tedesco watched her closely. "Forensics determined those smears to be the victim's blood."

"And the S-thing," Jane asked. "Whose blood is that?"

"Victim's also."

Jane moved the glass past Willie's nose to his mouth. "Whoever did this is taking the time to tell us something."

"But what?" Linda asked.

"Don't know yet. But—" She stopped. Something in the glass had caught her eye. Something small and white was barely visible between Willie Temple's lips. "Tony, look at this," Jane said, her voice hushed with excitement.

The M.E. seized Willie's jaw and squeezed until it fell open. Then he took a pair of hemostat clamps from his lab coat and extracted a three-inch piece of flesh from Willie's mouth. "Jesus," he whispered.

"What the hell is that?" Jane asked.

"Piece of someone." Dr. Tedesco dropped the specimen into a tray and held it up for a closer look. "Human. Definitely white. From the hairs, I'd say a male."

Jane's beeper vibrated on her hip. She glanced at it.

Call me. 3H61.

Kenny.

"Linda, I want you to stay for the autopsy. Then I want you to check the hospitals and clinics for reports of bite victims and tetanus shots. Get together with Aaron Clark-Weber and go over the on-scene forensics. Come back to me for recap first thing tomorrow." She turned to Dr. Tedesco. "Do me a favor, Tony, and handle this one yourself?"

"You got it, Lieutenant."

"Thanks. And please make sure this"—she indicated the chunk of flesh—"is measured, weighed, typed, and DNA'd."

Jane crossed the cold room and leaned into the door with her shoulder. Then she turned back to Linda French. "Looks like Mr. Temple had something to say after all."

■

A LIGHTNING FLASH.

Then another. Washing the pewter sky in a startling burst of white. The deep rumble of far-off thunder reverberated through the lobby of the Hall of Justice.

"You hear that?" Jane said into her cell phone.

"Sounds like the end of the world," Kenny said. He sat on the hood of the Explorer watching the forensics team wrapping up their investigation in the parking structure. "How'd it go down there?"

"Wonders never cease."

"Iverson or Temple?"

Jane saw people running up the steps, taking them two at a time, and she knew that the rain had started. "Temple. I'll tell you later." She stopped at the windows and looked for her driver. "You beeped?"

"Yeah, Moby called. The phone records from Alice Iverson's Dos Rios house corroborate her statement. Also, the answering machine at their San Francisco place has two messages from the widow-to-be looking for her husband."

"Anything new on the video or the banquet guest list?"

"Still enhancing and compiling."

An SFPD patrol car pulled up behind a parking enforcement vehicle. Jane recognized a uniformed cop from her precinct. "My ride's here." She let a couple of people hurry in through the double doors. "We need to speak with Alice Iverson again. Will you call her in for tomorrow?"

"We could always take that romantic drive to the mountains."

"We could," Jane agreed. "But I don't want to show any more preference over Loretta Temple than we already have."

"Good point. I'll make the call."

"See you back home." Jane pushed her way outside, the rain falling in flat bouncing drops. "Oh, and Inspector Marks?"

"Yes, Lieutenant Candiotti?"

"Will you take a bath with me?"

■

"I INVITED AUNT Lucy to dinner this week," Jane said as Kenny washed her back with the long-handled wooden brush.

It was one of her favorite things to do, bathing. Especially tonight because she was sharing her tub with Kenny, and the brush he was using had been made for her mother by Poppy. Two vanilla candles flickered in the mirror. The small television on the counter played ESPN with the sound off. The rain whipped against the windows, the trees in the yard bending in the wind.

So this is marriage, Jane thought. I'll take it.

"The way Aunt Lucy cooks, she can come live with us full-time."

"I love that you love my family."

A close-in clap of thunder rattled the windows. Kenny laid the brush on the edge of the tub and drew Jane to him. Half-floating and half-sliding, she pressed back into his chest.

"I ever tell you about my first thunderstorm?"

"Tell me again."

"It was just like this one. Loud and powerful and bright. Poppy was putting me to bed when the storm came up. I was maybe three or four and ready to be frightened by the sheer force of it all. But he jumped out of bed and yanked open all the blinds, bringing the storm in to us. Taking the fright away; but not the wonder.

"And he told me about mountaintops where clouds crash together. And oceans that capture beams of sunlight and turn them into lightning. And the thunder roared and the lightning flashed, filling the room with this beautiful light. 'Like daytime at midnight,' Poppy said. And I looked up and saw his face, just simply loving me. And in that moment I was . . . safe." She sat quietly, allowing another layer of the memory to reveal itself. "Know what I just realized?"

"What's that?"

"That night, that talk during the storm all those years ago, happened in this house. Ten feet from where we are now. And the noise and the light and Poppy and I were as present in our lives then, as you and I are now."

Kenny nuzzled his nose into her hair. "I miss him, too."

"Yeah." Jane sighed. She looked to the TV. "What time is it?"

" 'Bout eleven."

"Can I change this?"

"Sure."

Jane zapped the remote, changing the station to the local news. Becka Flynn's image came on, behind her a picture of Philip Iverson.

"That's the third report on Iverson tonight," Jane said. "And nothing about Willie Temple at all. Can you imagine his mother sitting at home, watching television?"

"Truth be told," Kenny began, choosing his words carefully, "you never said anything about Willie Temple to Becka Flynn either."

Jane shut the TV off, its screen turning gray-white then black. It struck her that she was part of the greater problem: She'd gone so far out of her way to notify Alice Iverson in person, while Loretta Temple was told of her son's murder over the phone.

She let the remote fall to the floor. "You're right."

CHAPTER 12

■

ALICE IVERSON WAS coming to Precinct Nineteen.

Jane hated herself for it, but she wished her good suit hadn't been at the cleaners. As it was, she had put just a little too much time into thinking about what she was going to wear today.

Sipping her cappuccino, Jane leafed through the stack of newspapers on her desk. The *Chronicle,* the *New York Times,* the *Los Angeles Times, USA Today.* All led with the murder of Philip Iverson. Most ran the photo of his body lying next to the Mercedes. Others ran a picture provided by the RiverPark publicity department; the same one that had been on the KGO newscast last night.

The *Chronicle* ran both. Below them was a shot from the banquet showing Iverson sitting next to Chief McDonald on the dais. Next to that was a small departmental photo of "Lt. Jane Candiotti, SFPD Homicide, lead detective on the Philip Iverson case."

Jane rose, dropped the papers on the couch, and looked out her window. The rain pounded the streets, rising at one flooded sewer onto the sidewalk. The news vans, their satellite disks rising into the rainfall like flowers, idled at the curb. Jane thought one of the women huddled beneath the overhang was Becka Flynn.

"So who's it gonna be?" Kenny asked from the doorway.

"What are you talking about?"

"We're taking bets which high-powered attorney the widow Iverson shows up with." He picked up the newspapers, put them on Jane's desk, and flopped on the couch. "You look great today, by the way."

"Oh, I didn't—"

"Jane, it's a compliment. Accept it, say 'thank you,' and shut up."

"Thank you." Jane glanced into the bullpen. Lou Tronick was pushing a cart loaded with videotapes from the local stations that had covered the Iverson banquet. Linda French had a computer printout on her desk. She had been on the phone all morning. "What's Linda doing out there?"

"Tetanus and bite-wound follow-ups. Calling every hospital within a hundred miles of here. After that, she and Aaron are going over to Berkeley to see some sociology professor about that S-thing. Aaron figured there's some sort of symbology thread they should follow."

"Anyone check to see how Sheriff Guthrie's doing?"

"I did. He said, and I quote, 'No piddly-shit flesh wound is gonna keep me off the job.' "

A long black limousine snaked its way through the gauntlet of news trucks, cameramen scurrying in its wake.

"She's here."

■

ALICE IVERSON STRODE toward Roz Shapiro's reception desk. All work in the bullpen stopped for a second.

She was dressed in a dark gray Chanel suit with a light gray silk blouse and a simple strand of pearls. She had a navy-blue cashmere overcoat draped across her shoulders. And sunglasses—inside, in the middle of winter, during a rainstorm, Jane thought as she crossed the squad room to greet her. Lighten up and stay objective, she reminded herself. The woman's husband was just murdered, for God's sake.

"Mrs. Iverson, welcome," Jane greeted her. "Thank you for coming on such a dreary day."

"Anything to help." Alice Iverson's voice, her manner, were cool, almost remote; their last encounter in Dos Rios clearly still very much on her mind. "Is there any news?" They moved toward Jane's office. Finney watched her pass, his second of three Egg McMuffins poised halfway to his mouth. Linda French glanced up, then was drawn back to her phone call.

"Nothing concrete yet," Jane answered. She let Alice pass into her office and pulled the door closed. "You remember Inspector Marks."

"Of course. Good morning, Inspector."

"Good morning, Mrs. Iverson. Please have a seat."

Alice Iverson sat on the couch and crossed her legs, allowing just the briefest glimpse of thigh before she smoothed down her skirt.

Kenny made a point of not looking. "Coffee?"

"Nothing, thanks. Can we begin? I have a busy day."

"Oh, uh, sure," Kenny said. "We thought you might want to wait for your attorney is all."

"Attorney?" Alice Iverson shrugged out of her coat. "Why? Do I need one?"

"No, it's just that . . ." Kenny was angry that he'd allowed himself to be put on the defensive so quickly.

"Inspector Marks, I haven't done anything except lose my husband. I think I can handle this interview myself."

Kenny glanced over to Jane and tilted his head. Your turn.

"Mrs. Iverson," Jane said, "now that you've had some time to think about this . . . tragedy . . . does anyone come to mind? Someone in business, or someone from your husband's past perhaps."

"I called Bob Lewis on the company jet and asked him that same question."

Jane sat on the edge of her desk. "What'd he say?"

"Bob said that he couldn't think of a single person in Philip's life who would even contemplate doing such a thing."

"That speaks for the professional side of his life," Kenny said. "What about the private side? Did your husband, even in what may have seemed like an inconsequential aside, a throwaway, ever mention anything that would—"

"My husband, Inspector, quite simply did not have an enemy in this world . . . at least not that he knew of." She paused, as if to put her thoughts in order. "Let me make this easier for you. Philip and I had a warm, loving marriage. No domestic disturbances, reported or otherwise." She threw a look to Jane. "Philip was a kind and generous man, both in our marriage and in the business community." Her fingers trembled slightly and she clasped her hands together, holding them tightly in her lap. "He was lucky enough to have made an enormous fortune, almost unfathomable wealth, and he had pledged to devote the rest of his life to using that money to make the world a better place . . . especially for children."

"And he did," Jane said.

Alice looked up, surprised. "Thank you." She lifted her sunglasses to the top of her head and dabbed at her eyes.

"Forgive the bluntness of this, Mrs. Iverson," Jane said. "But you stand to inherit this . . . unfathomable amount of money, as you call it."

"Yes, I do," Alice Iverson said frankly. "We had a prenuptial. But Philip tore it up on our tenth wedding anniversary." She allowed herself a faint smile. "It was a very loving and very trusting thing to do and, I think, speaks to the strength of the bond between us." She looked directly at Jane. "His money, other than RiverPark operating funds, some trusts, and the Make It So Foundation, goes to me."

Kenny leaned against the bookcase, his arms folded across his chest, and watched intently.

"Did Mr. Iverson have any siblings?" Jane asked.

"There was one. A sister who died."

Kenny pushed away from the bookcase. "When?"

"Forty years ago, in a car accident. She was four." Alice Iverson looked from Kenny to Jane. A look that said, Are we finished?

Jane held her gaze. "Mrs. Iverson, I have something delicate to ask you and I don't want you to take it the wrong way. Would you consent to taking a lie-detector test?"

Alice Iverson lifted her chin. "Toward what end?"

"Toward the end we're all searching for: the truth."

Alice's cheeks flushed a quick angry crimson. "If you're even beginning to suggest that I either know something I'm not telling or that I may have had something to do with my husband's death, you're sorely mistaken, Lieutenant."

"I'm not suggesting anything, Mrs. Iverson. It's my job to ask questions. And that includes difficult ones."

"What if I decline?"

"That's within your rights."

"Then my answer to your difficult question, Lieutenant, is no." Alice rose to her feet and smoothed her skirt. "If that's all you—"

"One other thing, Mrs. Iverson," Kenny said. "Have you spoken to Sheriff Guthrie since yesterday?"

Alice Iverson turned to him. "Yes, and he told me about what happened at the parking structure. That shooting. Thank God he's all right."

"He was very lucky," Kenny said. "Y'know, he mentioned to us that he was there working for you. Is that right?"

"Yes, I hired him. He came to me and offered his services; said he'd been on your police force and understood the intricacies, the policies. A.J. basically promised to cut through the red tape and get me some answers." She looked to Jane. "And that's what I want, Lieutenant. I want answers."

"We all do, Mrs. Iverson," Jane said. "Let me get this straight: A. J. Guthrie came to you and asked you to hire him? Not the other way around?"

"Yes, that's how it happened."

Jane caught Kenny's eye. Yesterday A.J. Guthrie had told them that Alice Iverson had asked *him* to come aboard.

CHAPTER 13

—■—

THE INTERCOM BUZZED. Jane reached back across her desk and pressed the speakerphone. "Yes?"

"Sorry to bother, Lieutenant," Cheryl said, "but Miss Flynn's on the line. Says she's calling on behalf of all the drowning rats outside. She wants to know if, since Mrs. Iverson is already here and the reporters are already here, if Mrs. Iverson would consent to a brief news conference."

Jane smiled. Becka Flynn had a way. She turned to Alice Iverson. "Your call."

"Could it help?"

"Maybe."

"Okay," Alice said. She pushed forward on the couch and stood up, her skirt riding up slightly. Kenny stared at the sunglasses on top of her head.

"Cheryl," Jane said into the intercom. "Tell Miss Flynn, five minutes in the lobby."

"Will do, Lieutenant."

Alice Iverson went to the window. She found her reflection and tucked a few strands of wayward hair behind her ears. Looking down, she could see a redheaded woman addressing the other reporters gathered beneath the overhang. Within seconds, newsmen were hefting their cameras and hurrying inside.

Alice turned to Jane. "I'm ready."

Kenny grabbed his coat. "I'm gonna go call about that ballistics report."

Jane nodded. "Could you check on Linda, too? See how she's doing with Willie Temple?"

Kenny moved to the door. "I'll meet you down there."

Alice Iverson started to cross the office when she noticed the picture of Jane and Kenny on the Sausalito Ferry. She found another snapshot of the two of them at a Giants game. She looked to Jane. "How nice for you," she said, and walked out.

Jane watched her go, her every instinct telling her, screaming out to her, that this woman was involved in her husband's murder. She pressed the intercom and buzzed Kenny. He looked up from his desk as he picked up the phone. "What's up?"

"Ken, I want to pin a tail on Alice Iverson."

Kenny swiveled in his chair as Alice crossed the bullpen toward the elevators. "You sure?"

"Completely," Jane said. "I want level-one surveillance. Twenty-four/seven."

"But the chief—"

"I'll handle the chief," Jane said impatiently. "Just make it happen, okay?"

"You got it . . . Lieutenant."

▪

ALICE IVERSON RESPONDED to the glare of the TV cameras like a sunflower. Turning to the brightest light. Thriving.

The questions came in rapid succession, often overlapping, and she made sure to answer each one, favoring whichever camera belonged to her questioner.

"This isn't a news conference," Kenny remarked as he came up behind Jane. "It's a performance."

"You just got here. She's been like this for a while."

"We were watching upstairs."

"This is going out live?"

Kenny held up his watch. "Ten-oh-five. All the local stations broke in."

"Did you make that call?"

Kenny started to say something, then drew it back. "Twenty-four/seven, it is."

"Mrs. Iverson," Becka Flynn began from the front of the clutch of reporters, "how are *you* holding up, ma'am?"

Alice Iverson found the KGO camera and spoke directly into it. "As many of you know, I have had a life blessed with privilege . . . But I would trade all of my days up to now for one more day with my husband." She paused, composing herself and the rest of her statement. "I came down here today . . ."

"She came down here today," Jane said to Kenny, her voice rising in anger, "because we called her in."

"I came down here today . . . to offer a one-hundred-thousand-dollar reward for information that will lead to the arrest and conviction of whomever murdered my husband."

"Motherfuck," Kenny said under his breath.

"Well put."

The still cameras whirred and strobed. The reporters pressed forward as they hurled question after question at Alice. "Have you discussed this with the police?" "Wasn't your husband friendly with Chief McDonald?" "Why one hundred thousand dollars?" "How long will this reward be in effect?"

Alice Iverson seized on the last one. "For as long as it takes."

■

THE CABLE CAR churned up Russian Hill.

Nearly empty on this cold wet morning, it clanged a quick greeting as it ground past the once-elegant apartment building on Hyde Street.

In a frozen-in-time two-bedroom flat on the street side of 740 Hyde, Ellen Schubert watched Alice Iverson on television. In her early sixties and once quite beautiful, Ellen felt a knot of nausea at the base of her throat as a sudden wave of unwanted memories washed over her. She thought of a time, years ago, when all was right in her world.

And then it had happened. A loss so wrenching and complete that her soul and spirit would never recover.

And since that day, so long ago now, Ellen's life had been in steady and irreversible decline. Her will and her beauty slipping away like sand.

Luna, her calico cat, old beyond all expectation, jumped heavily off the couch and waddled to the heater. She stretched the ache from her feeble hind legs and coiled herself into a ball, falling asleep with a deep sigh.

Today, Ellen thought to herself as she watched Alice Iverson—the grieving widow still somehow radiant—today is the day I finally do something.

■

"MY HUSBAND BELIEVED in the dignity of all human beings." Alice Iverson spoke steadily, fueled by the persistent questioning of the reporters.

"And when he saw suffering, he tried to do something about it. Especially children. It was his dream to ease the pain of children everywhere. 'To smooth the stones on the path of life,' he used to say." She paused, feeding on the anticipation of the faces before her. "And it is to the children of San Francisco and across this country that I promise the Make It So Foundation will continue to support causes that nurture you, care for you, educate you, and cure you. We will do everything we can to make your lives healthy, productive, and safe."

Kenny leaned into Jane. "This is impromptu?"

"Let's just say the occasion presented itself and she rose to it."

"Lieutenant Candiotti!" Becka Flynn hailed from across the lobby. "Anything to report? Any leads on the case?"

Alice Iverson gestured for Jane to come up to the microphones.

"Well," Jane said as she approached, "I can't really comment on an ongoing investigation. But I will say this: San Francisco loved Philip Iverson. We will find his killer and we will bring him to justice."

Alice Iverson lowered her head slightly, bringing her lips to Jane's right ear, and hissed a whisper. "When?"

■

Ellen Schubert thought the two women looked uncomfortable next to each other as they addressed the media. Watching from her desk now, she read the name at the bottom of the screen: Lt. Jane Candiotti, SFPD Homicide.

The radiator rattled with steam, the cat stretching in her sleep. Ellen knew she couldn't stay silent any longer. No matter what they did to her.

She began to compose a letter on her computer. "Dear Lieutenant Candiotti, Things are not as they seem . . ."

■

"What do you have?" Becka Flynn asked Jane as the press conference broke up. They watched together as Alice Iverson's limousine pulled away from the plaza in front of Precinct Nineteen.

"Not much," Jane said. "But some."

"C'mon, Jane, gimme a crumb. I have to go on the air with something tonight."

Kenny pointed to his watch, indicating they had to go upstairs.

Jane knew better than to favor one reporter over another, even if they were friends. But she also knew that Becka was ingenious and extremely well connected. It couldn't hurt to have someone like that on her team.

"Try this," Jane said. "There were two murders that night. Philip Iverson and a homeless man. I'm a little concerned that we're only concentrating on the death of a wealthy man."

Becka pondered this while her soundman unclipped her lapel mike.

"I'll do an *Upstairs/Downstairs* angle. Any man's death diminishes all of us. That sort of thing."

Jane started for the elevator. "Do I see a Pulitzer with your name on it?"

Becka smiled. "The Pulitzer can wait. I want that CNN gig first."

"What, and leave San Francisco?"

"Like I'm ever going to meet a straight man in this city?"

"I did."

"I think you got the last one." Becka looked through the lobby windows. Her crew was waiting. "I'm still going to dig into the life of Philip Iverson, y'know. We've both been at this long enough to know that nobody could be that much of a saint."

"And you'll give me anything you get?"

Becka Flynn smiled cryptically. Both already knowing that neither would give anything up for free.

Jane stepped into the elevator.

"Hey," Becka called. "What are you doing for your birthday?"

"You remembered?"

"Off the record, let's just say a certain straight husband of yours might have called for a gift suggestion. So, what are you doing?"

"Dreading it."

The elevator doors slid closed between them.

■

"THAT TRANSIENT FROM Nevada is gone," Linda French said as she began her briefing in Interrogation Room One. "I've got uniforms searching for him, but it doesn't look promising. Nothing's turning up on the tetanus and bite-wound front either, but I'll keep making calls."

"I'll help you with that," Mike Finney offered.

"Thanks. Lieutenant Clark-Weber and I . . ." She nodded to Aaron, leaning against the back wall, his weight on one hip to ease the pain in his arthritic knee. "We're going over to Berkeley later today to talk with a professor friend of his about the S-thing."

"What about the gang angle on that?" Kenny asked.

"Billy Ling of the Asian Gang Task Force looked at the photos. He doesn't think it's any of the gangs he's tracking. But he's passing them on to the other gang smash units in the city and the East Bay. Should hear back tonight."

Linda turned a page in her notebook. "Reggie Mayhew—*Reverend* Reggie Mayhew as he likes to be called—said that Willie Temple had only recently been showing up for meals at Santuario. It's not an unusual pattern. A lot of missions shut down after Christmas when the donations dry up. So the homeless are always looking for new places to crash just when it's the coldest. Willie Temple, says Reggie Mayhew, pretty much kept to himself. Didn't really have any friends. But I'll go down there and follow up."

"I read the M.E.'s report," Jane said. "What do you make of it?"

"The thing that jumps out at me right away is that there were no fingerprints connected to the S-thing."

"What's that tell you?"

Linda French put her notebook on the table. "Whoever left that mark on that loading pallet was wearing gloves."

"It was wicked cold that night," Lou Tronick commented. "Maybe that's not so strange."

"We thought so, too, but . . ." Linda French looked to Aaron Clark-Weber.

Aaron shifted his weight. "There were traces of something odd in the blood. We performed a second-tier microscan and came up with a molecular structure consistent with latex."

"Latex?" Kenny asked. "As in rubber gloves?"

"Yup."

Lou Tronick shrugged. "So much for my brilliant cold-weather theory."

"A bum killer who wears latex gloves," Kenny mused. "This spices up the soup."

"Good work, Linda," Jane said. "Stay on top of all these threads and keep coming up with new questions." She turned to Finney. "Mike, what about the BMW from the Golden Gate Grand surveillance video?"

"We've got it narrowed down to fourteen possibles that match the partial license plate."

"Any reported stolen?"

"No. Inspector Tronick and I are in the process of making calls and talking with the owners of the vehicles."

"In all my spare time," Lou Tronick said. "When I'm not working my way through the news-station videos of the banquet." He indicated the stacks of videotapes next to the VCR and monitor.

Roz Shapiro entered and handed Kenny two sheets of paper.

"Ballistics?" Jane asked.

"And Forensics." Kenny scanned the top sheet. "Forensics found the usual junk that you'd find at any parking structure. Bottle caps, cigarette butts, coins, stuff like that. Everything's bagged and tagged." He passed the page along to Jane and looked at the next one. "Holy shit."

"What?" Jane asked.

Kenny crossed to her. "Ballistics has the slug from the headrest of the Suburban and the bullet that killed Philip Iverson as a match."

"Then, if our theory holds," Jane said, "Iverson's killer returned to the scene to retrieve something."

"But why?" Linda French asked. "Why would he shoot at Sheriff Guthrie and me over something that wasn't there?"

"It wasn't there when *we* looked for it," Jane said.

Kenny handed the report to Jane. "Could be he had already found what he was looking for and got spooked when he saw a cop with a drawn weapon."

"Ken," Jane said, "it's a long shot, but check with City Patrol. See if anyone issued a parking ticket in the area of the Golden Gate Grand at the time of the shooting. Both shootings."

"You got it."

"Streets and alleys," Jane added.

"Streets and alleys, driveways and loading zones," Kenny said, a slight trace of irritation rising in his voice. He looked around at the other cops in the room. They were all busy with their assignments.

Roz Shapiro came back in with a phone message for Jane. Jane unfolded the pink slip of paper and read it. Then she slipped it in her pocket. "Okay, everyone, a good Day One. Keep the heat turned up on both these killings. Keep careful notes. And keep me posted." She took her coat from the back of a chair and motioned for Kenny to follow her.

"Where we going?"

"Bob Lewis called. He's back at RiverPark. He'll be there all day if we want to talk to him."

"How 'bout he comes down here?"

"Sheriff Guthrie's also up in Dos Rios. His story about how he got involved in all this doesn't jibe with Alice Iverson's. Now we have two reasons to take a drive." She held the door open for him. "But first, I want to make a stop."

"To do what?"

"To set things straight."

■

ELLEN SCHUBERT REREAD the letter and pressed "Control P" on her keyboard. Her printer hummed to life, and in a few seconds, a sheet of paper rolled into view. She started to pick it up, then thought better of it. Her heart pounding, she hurried to the kitchen and reached under the sink.

As she returned to her desk, she pulled on a pair of yellow Playtex rubber gloves.

She took the letter from the printer tray, folded it neatly, and slipped it into a self-stick envelope. Then she peeled a stamp from an adhesive sheet and placed it in the corner. Finally, she applied the address label she had printed out earlier:

LIEUTENANT JANE CANDIOTTI

SFPD HOMICIDE

PRECINCT NINETEEN, THIRD FLOOR

10 PRINCE STREET

SAN FRANCISCO, CA 45010

Ellen Schubert dropped the envelope into her purse, fetched her scarf and umbrella, and unlocked the door. The cat stirred at the clicking of the lock and opened one eye.

As she let herself out, Ellen Schubert knew that her dear cat would die before the summer; and that she would be alone.

Again.

CHAPTER 14

—■—

THE RAIN HAD let up by the time Jane and Kenny got to Daly City. They sat in the Explorer, the windshield coated with a fine mist, in a tumbledown neighborhood of tiny single-family houses.

Jane had noticed that Kenny had been unusually subdued during the drive. "Something bugging you?"

"Nah, just busy."

"You sure?"

Kenny laughed. "Want me to take a lie-detector test?"

"I don't think that'll be necessary." Jane smiled. She started to open the door.

Kenny put his hand on her arm. "Want me to come with?"

She almost said no, she'd do this herself. But she recognized that as a reflex response to all the years she'd spent on her own. "Yes, come with me."

"I don't want to."

"Asshole."

They climbed out of the Explorer and unlatched the gate of the chain-link fence. Bending into the wet air, they hurried up the broken walkway to a wretched pale yellow house. Kenny rang the doorbell. Nothing. He rapped on the screen door. It bounced on rusty hinges.

The front door opened and a black man in his late twenties said, "You cops?"

"Yes, we are," Jane answered. "I'm Lieutenant Candiotti and this is Inspector Marks—"

"Been too many cops already. Leave us alone." He started to close the door.

"Please," Jane said. "We're not here on official business. I just want to talk with—"

"Ma'am, *I* just don't give a shit."

"Andrew! Who at the door?" a woman's voice called from inside.

Andrew shouted back over his shoulder. "More po-lice. A lady lieutenant and some—"

"You show them in, hear?"

"Yes, Mama." Andrew, his bravado evaporating, moved aside. Kenny creaked the screen door open and he and Jane stepped up into the darkened living room. It wasn't until they walked past Andrew that Jane realized what a small man he was. Five-five tops.

Like his brother.

"So, lady lieutenant, you find who killed my baby?" Loretta Temple sat on a brown Naugahyde lounger next to the fireplace. The fireplace had a plastic basket of pink artificial flowers where the logs should go. The shades were drawn and the flickering gray of the television screen was the only source of light in the room.

"No, Mrs. Temple," Jane said. "But we will."

"You told my Andrew you ain't here on business." Loretta Temple poked a thread of gray hair back under her wig. "Then why you here?"

"To pay my respects . . . and to apologize."

"What for?"

Jane looked to Kenny. He had moved toward the television, keeping one eye on Mrs. Temple and the other on Andrew. Something in Jane warmed as she remembered what a good cop her husband was. "Well," she went on, "mistakes were made and—"

"By who?"

"By me. And I'm sorry. I and the people who work for me should have been more sensitive."

"Little late," Andrew snorted. "Damage is done. Insult to injury."

"Yes, you're right; and that's why I'm here." Jane inched closer to Loretta Temple. "My father died last summer . . . and I know how you must feel."

Mrs. Temple lowered the footrest of her lounger and leaned forward. "You got kids?"

"No, ma'am. I don't."

"Then no way you know how I feel." She fell back in the chair, retreating to her shadows.

Andrew started toward Jane. Kenny felt he was moving a little too aggressively and stepped in front of him. Andrew stopped. "Maybe you should go, miss."

"Yes," Jane said. She nodded to Loretta Temple. "Maybe I should."

As she and Kenny got closer to the front door, she noticed a picture on a side table. An army portrait of Willie Temple. Taken thirty years ago, he stood in dress uniform in front of a rippling American flag. So young, Jane thought, and hopeful and whole.

There was a small glass-topped box next to the picture. In it were two service medals.

A Bronze Star and a Purple Heart.

■

"3H58."

Jane and Kenny ran the last few yards to the Explorer and climbed in.

"3H58. Go, Cheryl."

"I got the chief holding for you. He's kind of agitated."

"Shit," Jane groaned, "I forgot to call him back. Patch him through."

There was a spit of static. Then: "Hold for Chief McDonald."

"Where the *hell* are you?" the chief demanded.

"Daly City, sir. At the home of Willie Temple's mother."

"Willie Temple!" Chief McDonald roared. "Goddammit Lieutenant, you've got a whole department to deal with Willie Temple. I want you to stay on the Iverson case and stay on it hard!"

Jane took a deep breath, trying not to match her boss's anger. "Inspector Marks and I are on our way to Dos Rios right now. Is that good enough for you?"

"Lieutenant Candiotti, I can live without your attitude."

"And I, sir, can live without you yelling at me."

"Yikes," Kenny whispered. "Nice knowin' ya."

There was a long pause. Then the chief came back on, his tone more moderate. "Jane, you took this job, this promotion, and I want you to do it. Find me Philip Iverson's killer and then we can talk about attitude and temper. Do you understand me?"

Jane was seething. Old wounds burning beneath her skin, her face flushed with resentment at being talked to this way. She had always been troubled by the old-boy network in the SFPD, and the chief's bombastic mind-set just pushed those buttons all over again. "Yes . . . sir," she finally said through clenched teeth.

"Fine, then," Chief McDonald said, and hung up.

"Well," Kenny began as they pulled away from the curb, "that was . . . endearing."

"Fuck him," Jane snapped. "And fuck this job."

CHAPTER 15

■

JANE SPENT THE entire ride on the phone. Pushing her team harder, then harder still.

"Lou?" The Explorer crested the last hill and RiverPark lay before them. "You're breaking up. If you can hear me, I'll call you back in half an hour. Lou?" Frustrated, she ended the call and dropped the phone into her bag.

Kenny slowed at the security gate and flashed his shield. The guard waved them through. He drove the Explorer across the gravel parking lot and pulled into a visitor's spot near the front entrance. Jane started to get out, but Kenny put his hand on her arm. "Look, the command structure of this department is bordering on Neanderthal. I just want you to know that I understand how hard this is for you."

Jane smiled. Kenny's words were like a salve for her torn feelings. "Thank you," she whispered, and climbed out of the car.

Kenny jumped down from the Explorer and followed her toward the main building. "You're the best homicide cop on the force," he said. "And I'm lucky because I get to go home with you every night."

Jane started to respond, but then stopped. Looking down, she saw that she was standing in Philip Iverson's empty parking space.

Someone had put a pinecone laced with daisies next to his name on the log bumper.

■

JANE EXPLORED THE RiverPark lobby while Kenny signed in at the security desk.

Huge black-and-white photographs covered three walls. All of them pictures of Philip Iverson with children. Kids in the hospitals he funded. Kids in caps and gowns on their way to college on Make It So scholarships. Black kids. Chinese kids. White kids. Latin kids.

A well-known photo of Iverson kissing the bald head of a beaming seven-year-old girl undergoing chemotherapy was displayed between the two elevators. Beneath it was a small bronze sign: MR. IVERSON →. Jane guessed the photograph had been placed there so that all who passed, virtually everyone in the building, would get used to seeing a seriously ill child. Would see that there was no threat or cause for revulsion in the image of someone this young going through such an ordeal. Only enduring innocence.

■

BOB LEWIS'S EYES were red-rimmed and glassy. "I have never been so sad . . . or weary . . . in my life."

Everything about him said Ivy League. His clothes, his faint New England accent, his close-cropped sandy-blond hair.

When Jane and Kenny had come into his large, conservatively appointed office, Bob Lewis had come around from his desk and ushered them to a corner sitting area. Jane had chosen a deep brown leather club chair, as had Bob, and Kenny sat on the arm of an oxblood leather sofa.

"Thank you for agreeing to see us so quickly," Jane said. "I know how awful this must be for you."

"For all of us." Bob nodded to the far glass wall. Through it they could see the employees of RiverPark quietly going about their jobs. It was as if, Jane thought, they were moving through water, slowed by their own grief. "Philip was an extremely kind and generous boss. He was my friend . . . my teacher."

"Is there anyone, sir," Kenny asked, "anyone who may have felt slighted in a business transaction, or who was turned down by the Make It So Foundation, or—"

"—or someone in his personal life," Jane interjected, "who comes to mind?"

Bob Lewis sat back in his chair and raised his foot to the coffee table. The sole of his tassled loafer balanced on the edge and his leg vibrated slightly. "I thought about that all during my flight. I even called some of my colleagues from the plane and asked them. But they came up empty. And so did I. Until . . ."

Jane leaned forward. "Until . . . ?"

"Until I thought of this one guy. Not a businessman, not an applicant to Make It So, and definitely not part of Philip's personal world."

"Then who was he?" Kenny asked.

"A stockholder. He only owns a few shares. But the company took a pretty big dip this year, as did just about everyone in the tech industry, and our last meeting was pretty . . . lively." Bob Lewis rose and crossed to a mahogany armoire. "This guy, Randall Thomas, got kind of worked up at the meeting and had to be escorted from the hall." He opened the doors to expose an audio-video setup. "After that, we started getting some rather provocative, you might even call them threatening, e-mails from him. All large companies have cranks who come out of the woodwork when the market's in a down period. But, under the circumstances . . ."

He pressed "play" on the VCR and the screen jumped to life. "This was two months ago."

The face of Philip Iverson filled the screen.

The camera pulled back to reveal that he was standing on a stage in front of a huge monitor. Striding confidently, holding a microphone casually in his hand, he paused to look up at the image of himself on the monitor. Then he addressed the audience. "It may look like there's two of me up here, but one is all you get."

The crowd laughed.

He was about to go on when a voice called out: "*One* of you is too goddamn many!"

The people stirred, looking around anxiously.

Philip Iverson shielded his eyes from the glare of the lights, almost as if he were saluting. The camera panned off him and found a short stocky man with tousled hair hurrying up the aisle. His clothes were mismatched and wrinkled.

Bob Lewis pointed to the screen. "Meet Randall Thomas."

On the tape, Iverson squatted down. "Can I help you, sir?"

"Yeah, you can help me!" Thomas yelled. "You can help all of us by getting out of this fucking company before you run it into the ground!"

Iverson rose back up. "For a moment there, I thought we might be able to have some sort of constructive discourse. But that kind of language simply crosses the line of what I'll tolerate." He nodded to two burly security guards. "Gentlemen, please escort our friend out of this hall."

The guards moved in and grabbed Thomas firmly on each upper arm. He struggled briefly, but quickly realized he was overmatched. As he was hustled back up the aisle, he turned and shouted, "You'll be hearing from me, asshole!"

Philip Iverson gave a little wave. "I'd expect nothing less, my friend."

Bob Lewis pressed "pause," freezing the close-up image of Philip Iverson's face. Kenny reached over and touched Jane's shoulder. She turned to follow his gaze.

About a dozen office workers stood on the other side of the window wall. Watching. When they saw Jane and Kenny looking at them, they quietly dispersed.

Jane stood up. "What can you tell us about this Mr. Thomas?"

"Your classic corporate pain-in-the-ass. We've had people like him before in stockholder meetings. There's a subculture of anti-big-business whackos out there. Angry, paranoid."

Kenny rose as well. "Did you ever hear from him again?"

"For a couple of weeks. Then his e-mails just stopped."

"E-mails?" Kenny asked. "Can we see them?"

"Of course." Lewis handed him a manila folder.

Kenny flipped through the pages. "Do you have an address? A phone number?"

"Just the P.O. box where his statements go." Bob Lewis went behind his desk and tapped at his keyboard. A piece of paper scrolled out of his printer. "Appears to be San Francisco Central Post Office. But maybe you guys can track him down."

"We can, sir." Jane took the page from him. "And we will."

CHAPTER 16

■

The way u run your compny is no good!
I have los to much mony!!!
Sinserely, Randall Thomas

U r a evel man!
Where is my mony???
Sinserely, Randall Thomas

Jane held the e-mails up so Kenny could see them as he drove.
"This last one is dated the day after the stockholders' meeting, a little over seven weeks before Philip Iverson was killed."

I will sue your ass 4 embaras me!!!
U will here from my loyers!!!
Sinserely, Randall Thomas

"Nothing like a good public-school education." Kenny guided the
Explorer down the last hill and into Dos Rios. "That's it?"
"That's it." Jane checked the folder. "No further contact." She di-
aled her cell phone as Kenny turned onto Main Street.

"Homicide, Finney."

Jane shifted in the seat to get a better signal. "Mike, I need you to find somebody for me."

"Will do, Lieutenant."

"His name's Randall Thomas. Caucasian. Late thirties. Maybe five-seven or -eight. Long black hair. I've got an e-mail address and a P.O. box in the city. E-mail is 'rt622 at mediabox dot com. P.O. box is sixteen eighty dash nine zero."

"Got it, Lieutenant. I'm all over it."

Jane rang off just as Kenny pulled up to A. J. Guthrie's office.

■

SHERIFF GUTHRIE SAT at his desk, his left leg propped on an open drawer.

"How's the leg today?" Jane asked as she poured herself a cup of coffee.

"I've had pleasanter experiences," A.J. said. "But I'll be fine."

Kenny sat on a wooden chair and leaned back against the wall. "Can we ask you a couple of questions, Sheriff?"

"You bet."

"Ever hear of someone named Randall Thomas?"

"No, sir. Can't say that I have. He involved in Mr. Iverson's case?"

Jane sat on the couch. "Might be. We're checking him out."

"Then I'll keep my ears open. I hear anything, you'll be the first to know."

"Or second"—Jane smiled—"after Alice Iverson. By the way, is she still getting her money's worth out of you?"

"Well, I been slowed down a bit." A.J. indicated his leg. "But I can still do my job." He took a long reflective beat, letting the silence float between them. "But you all didn't drive up here to check on whether Mrs. Iverson is getting what she paid for."

"No, A.J., we didn't," Jane said. "When we were talking with you at the parking structure, you told us that Alice Iverson asked you to help her out. To 'liaise' for her."

"Right, I did. There a problem?"

"Only that when we met with her, she told us *you* approached *her* and asked for the job." Jane drew his eyes to hers. "Where I come from that's called an—"

A.J. broke eye contact. "—an inconsistency. I know." He lowered his injured leg and let his chair rock forward. "I'm gonna be sixty-five this year," he said without looking at them. "Town of Dos Rios has mandatory retirement for all civic employees . . . including sheriff. That's two careers that finished with me before I finished with them. All the more reason to use up my vacation time helping Mrs. Iverson."

He watched the steam rise from his coffee. "I was born here," A.J. continued. "Fished with my father and my granddad over where the rivers meet. Went to the only school hereabouts back when it was behind the fire station. Played baseball and football here." His face creased into a soft smile. "Kissed my first girl after the homecoming game. Six months later, I joined the marines. After bein' an MP a coupla years over in Germany, I came home and married that girl. Guess that kiss kind of stayed with me."

Reaching across the desk, he turned a picture frame around. In it was a photograph of himself as a much younger man with his arm around a small boy. They both had a fishing pole and a string of river trout in their hands. "We had a little boy. Sweetest kid you could ever dream of. Couple years later we got divorced." A.J. paused to look at the picture, then he picked up his story. "After my divorce, I moved to San Francisco. Back in those days, with my MP training, it was pretty easy to hook up with the force. I put in almost ten years down there. Other than a little blip of excitement chasing down piddly-shit leads on Zodiac, it was entirely uneventful.

"Then . . ." A.J. paused, his jaw clenching and unclenching.

"Then what, A.J.?" Jane asked softly.

"Well, ma'am . . . then my boy died."

Jane pulled in a quick breath, catching the gasp in the back of her throat. She looked to Kenny, then back to A.J. "How? What happened?"

Sheriff Guthrie closed his eyes and sat quietly for a long moment. "Car accident." His voice was barely audible. He opened his eyes and stared off to the middle distance. "I was taking him home to his mom. It was late. Some salesman who'd been on the road nonstop for three days fell asleep at the wheel and crossed the center line. It was just a country road, no dividers or nothing."

A.J. tilted his head back, holding the tears in place. "Took the fire department half an hour to tear open the car. But my little boy was already gone." He sucked in his upper lip, his head rocking back and forth. "All my life, all I wanted to do was keep my child alive. Not just feed him and clothe him and educate him . . ." He tugged his pant leg down over his boot. "I mean, a father has one responsibility and that's to protect his child . . . and I didn't."

He raised the corner of his mouth in a rueful grin. Then he arched his back and stood up. Weary from the memory. Weary from the telling. "My wife married the guy she'd been living with and moved down to the valley. So I came back up here to Dos Rios and now I live in the same house we all used to live in. It's too big and filled with ghosts. But I stay."

"Why?" Jane asked.

"Habit . . . fear. Don't know exactly." A.J. reached down for his mug. "After my son died," he continued, "people didn't know how to talk to me. Couldn't look me in the eye. But Mr. Iverson, he always made a point to ask how was I doing. He remembered me every Christmas; and always remembered me on the anniversary of my . . . loss. That all means something to me."

A. J. Guthrie dipped his head in apology. "So all that's my long way of telling you that maybe I embellished how I came to be on this case. Maybe my need for approval, for trying to do something for Mr. Iverson . . . for one last sense of purpose, maybe they all caught up to me, and next thing you know, I'm making myself sound a little more important than I really am. I'm sorry, Jane. It won't happen again."

He went to the coffeemaker and topped off his mug. "My son would have been thirty-one come April. A grown man. Maybe with a wife, a kid or two. Can't even begin to imagine that because, to me, he'll be a little boy forever." He turned back to Jane and Kenny. "Now, when I die, there'll be no ripple in the pond."

"Oh, A.J.," Jane said. "I'm so sorry."

"Thank you." A.J. took a sip of his coffee and wiped his mouth with the back of his hand. Then he did it again and Jane could see that he was really swiping at a tear that was coursing down his cheek. "So now you can see why I want to help. Even if they try to kill me again, I ain't gonna stop."

Kenny stood up and touched Jane's elbow. "C'mon," he said. "We've got a long drive."

CHAPTER 17

∎

JANE PUSHED ON into the third mile of her jog, the cool evening air wrapping around her.

She ran past where Famiglietti's Italian bakery had been; where she used to pick up sweet rolls with her mother on Saturdays. Now it was a Blockbuster. Past the pharmacy, now a coffee bar. At the corner, in front of her father's old grocery store, she touched the lamppost and started back home. She ran past her father's grocery again without looking.

Now it was a travel agency. People still wanted to get out of San Leandro, if even for a little while.

Jane jogged past the church where she'd gone to Catholic school. Davey Tasca, one of the few kids whose family hadn't moved away, was shooting baskets in the playground. He was just finishing his second year at Oakland Community College and still lived at home to save money. Jane used to baby-sit for him. Now he was a handsome young man, just over six feet tall. He spent his weekends working on his car in the driveway. Like he used to do with his father.

"Hey, Janie!" he called. "You chasing the bad guys or running away from them?"

"Chasing them down like dogs!" Jane laughed. "Say hi to your mom for me!" She rounded the corner at the end of the wrought-iron fence and turned onto Oak Street. Her street. The trees sagged, their leaves heavy from the rains.

Jane quickened her pace, her feet hitting a steady one-two on the sidewalk. With each footfall, she blew a breath from her mouth. Clearing her mind for just a moment before allowing the details and worries of her job to flood back in. Loretta Temple in her darkened living room. The photograph of A. J. Guthrie's son. And Alice Iverson; perfect, angry Alice Iverson.

Up ahead, she saw Kenny raking the soggy leaves that had fallen in the last storm. He wore an inside-out sweatshirt and a Giants cap turned backward on his head. Two yellow wires snaked down from under the cap and Jane knew he was listening to the blues on his Walkman.

He looked, she thought, like a college kid.

Jane turned onto the lawn and ran across to him. As she got closer, she could hear the music leaking from his headphones. Stevie Ray Vaughan. He'd been teaching her about the blues gods, and she had been teaching him how to cook without using the microwave.

"Y'know," Jane said as she approached, "we could always get a gardener."

But Kenny couldn't hear her. He kept tugging at the broad leaf rake, scraping it across the grass.

"Yo, Kenneth!" Jane shouted.

Kenny turned and pulled off his earphones. "Hey you. How was the run?"

"If anything's gonna remind me that I'm getting old, jogging has to be high on the list."

Kenny leaned the rake against the tire swing hanging from an old oak tree. "Aunt Lucy came by. Loaded up the refrigerator with a bunch of Italian stuff I can't even begin to pronounce."

Jane shook her head. "It's how she used to spend her days. Taking care of her brothers. Now they're all gone and she's a little lost."

Kenny took her hand. "C'mere, I want to show you something." He pulled her along to another, smaller tree. "Found it when I was taking down the hammock."

Jane stood on her toes and saw that someone had carved something into the tree trunk.

Maria aed Paolo. Sempre.

Beneath it was a more recent entry, still more yellow than gray. Jane recognized it as her mother's date of birth and the date of her death. Poppy had come back to this tree after losing his wife and done this.

Maria and Paolo. Always.

▪

KENNY STIRRED AT the soft chiming of the grandfather clock. TWO A.M.

Stretching, he realized he was alone in bed. He swung his legs around, got up, and went down the hall. Jane wasn't in the bathroom. He stood at the top of the stairs and listened. Nothing but the hum of the refrigerator. Then her voice, speaking almost in a whisper, drew him around.

Jane was lying on the twin bed in her old room, a blanket of yellow light from the streetlamp falling across her. She was talking on the telephone. "Mike, I know I don't have to stress again how important this is, and how much I appreciate all that you're doing." She listened for a moment. "That's a good idea. Go for it. Okay, let's both try to get some sleep. See you in the morning." She hung up.

Kenny stepped into the doorway, the floorboards creaking. "Mike? As in Moby?"

"Yeah, this Randall Thomas thing is eating me up."

"And you called Finney?"

"Paged him on the chance he'd be awake. He called back in about five seconds. The baby already had him up."

"And?"

"And . . . nothing yet. For now, Randall Thomas is a ghost."

"There's no such thing as ghosts," Kenny said. "We'll find him."

"What makes you so sure?"

"Because we know how to do this stuff. We'll get your Mr. Thomas."

Jane slid toward the wall, wanting him to join her.

Kenny lay next to his wife on the narrow bed.

She rested her head on his shoulder. "Lot on my mind."

"I know. Me, too."

"Anything you can tell me?"

Kenny started to speak, but then pulled it back. "Maybe another time."

Jane glanced up at him. "Then I'll do the talking . . . When I saw those dates on that tree, it all caught up to me. Poppy and Ma planted that tree when I was born. They were ten years younger than I am now. Time just doesn't wait." She traced the scar on his chest with her fingertip. "That streetlight out there was my night-light for years."

"I'm not going to talk you out of feeling blue." Kenny kissed the top of her head and pulled her close. "And you can't talk me out of telling you about one of the things I'm getting you for your birthday."

Jane tilted her head up to him. "What is it?"

"Got us a room at the Shanghai Dragon Palace for Chinese New Year's. Fortieth floor. One for each of your years." His eyes sparkled. "We'll be at eye level for the fireworks. Our own private pyrotechnic show."

"What if it's a foggy night?"

"Oh, man." Kenny laughed. "You *are* in a bad mood. If it's a foggy night, which ain't gonna happen, we'll do this." He kissed her deeply, pulling her on top of him.

Jane responded hungrily. Needing to be touched.

Kenny peeled off her T-shirt and brushed his lips across her breasts.

"Oh, hon," Jane moaned. She wrapped her arms around his head, clutching him to her.

Kenny rolled over until he was on top of her. "Let's make our baby," he whispered.

"Oh God, I love you." Jane sighed, a single tear falling back from the corner of her eye.

And there, on her childhood bed, too small and too rickety, they made love.

CHAPTER 18

■

JANE SAT ON the porch swing watching her neighborhood wake up.

A minivan cruised by. Driven by a woman Jane didn't recognize, it was carpooling several kids she'd never seen before. A young boy was trying to throw a pair of tennis shoes over a telephone wire. They kept coming up short, landing with a dull thump on the street.

The throaty rumble of an old Firebird caught Jane's attention. Davey Tasca backed out of his driveway and, showing off a little, sped away. He'd had a crush on Jane since he was five. Across the street an elderly woman, Blanche Sands, sat in a rocker on her front porch. Jane started to raise her hand in a wave, but then realized Mrs. Sands was dozing.

The screen door squeaked open and Kenny came out with a mug of tea. He handed it to Jane and went down the walkway to retrieve the *Chronicle*. Flipping it open, he held it up.

WIDOW OFFERS $100,000 REWARD

There was a photograph of Alice Iverson, beautiful and refined, at the makeshift press conference. Jane was one of a mosaic of faces in the background. "Other than Philip Iverson getting killed, it's the only real news in the case."

"Good news and bad news," Kenny said.

Jane nodded. Rewards often led to the solving of a difficult case. But they also opened the floodgates to the crackpots who had imaginary leads that wasted everyone's time.

Kenny sat next to her and, pushing against the railing with his foot, set the swing to gently swaying.

Jane leaned into him. "Ken, I think I know what's bugging you. But I need you to say the words. So just know that, when you do, it'll be okay. *We'll* be okay."

Kenny took a sip of her tea and handed it back. "I've just got some guy stuff I'm trying to work out." He quickly skimmed the rest of the paper. "Still nothing on Willie Temple."

"Becka was right. This really is *Upstairs/Downstairs*."

A junkman's wagon puttered down the street, looking for something to pilfer from the recycle bins.

Kenny put his arm around Jane until she folded into him. "What do you miss most about your house in the Marina?"

"Hmm. Not the house so much as the stuff we lost in the fire. Your guitars . . . my photographs. That picture of Poppy and me at the barbecue right here in this yard."

Kenny waited a moment for the memory to settle. "How about the view?"

The young boy down the street finally got the tennis shoes to catch on the phone wire. He pulled on his backpack and ran to the end of the block. Then he turned right and disappeared.

"You kidding?" Jane said. "What could be better than this view?"

The phone rang.

Kenny untangled himself from Jane. "I got it." He went inside.

Jane sipped her tea and wondered if that little boy went to the same church school she had gone to.

"We gotta go," Kenny said through the screen door. Jane turned at the gravity of his voice. "That was Linda French. A homeless man was found murdered in the Pleasant Avenue underpass."

Jane felt a well of dread at the base of her throat. "Similarities?"

"Many."

■

"TOW TRUCK DRIVER called it in." Linda French pointed to a white tow truck on the fringe of the highway below. "He stopped to pick up an abandoned vehicle—that junker over there—came up here to relieve himself, and found our John Doe here."

Jane and Kenny squatted next to her in the crotch of the underpass bridge.

The victim, a white man with scraggly blond hair, lay faceup on a ragged scrap of mattress, soaked through with his blood. There was debris from a cooking fire and a black Hefty bag filled with aluminum cans. The sour smell of urine pervaded the air. "Be it ever so humble," Kenny said.

"The victim's eyes were closed," Linda French continued, her excitement growing, "in the same way as Willie Temple." She trained her flashlight on his face. "There's blood on them." With a twist of her wrist, she brought the beam down to a single stab wound in the left side of his chest. Dark blood pooled in its depth and spilled across the man's torso until it was absorbed by the sodden mattress.

"Single wound," Jane said. "The killer's getting better."

"This guy's a big one," Kenny said, "and still no defense wounds."

Jane nodded to an empty half-gallon vodka bottle. "May not have known what hit him." She turned to Linda French. "What else?"

"This." She aimed her flashlight at the grimy cement wall. "See under that old graffiti, next to the drainpipe, there's a—"

"I see it," Jane said.

Another S-shaped figure.

This one was larger and better defined than the one before. There were two dots to the left of the top of the symbol.

"Blood?" Jane asked.

"Blood," Aaron Clark-Weber confirmed as he approached from his van. He shook a vial in his hand and held it up to Jane. "Same blood type as the victim's, which also matches the smears on the eyes."

"Any traces of latex?" Kenny asked.

"Wouldn't be surprised 'cause there's no fingerprints other than John Doe's here." Aaron dropped the vial into his pocket. "We're not set up for that in the field. But I'll grease this sample through the lab and get you some results as soon as possible."

Jane bent over the victim's head. "His mouth. Check his mouth."

Aaron knelt on one knee and pried open the dead man's mouth. He looked back to Jane. "Nothing."

Jane turned to Linda French. "Soon as you finish up here, I want to set up the war room back at the precinct."

Linda moved closer to Jane. "Do you think we have a serial killer?" Her eyes bounced with anticipation. She could feel her no-profile murder investigation into the death of a homeless man getting a lot sexier.

"Everything says it's the same killer," Jane said. "But we don't know if it's a serial sequence. So let's just do our work and keep quiet about any theories until I've reviewed all the facts." She motioned for Kenny to join her. They headed for the Explorer.

"I hate this shit."

CHAPTER 19

■

JANE COULD FEEL it.

An elevation in the energy level, the tension in the air. She stood in the back of Interrogation Room One as her Homicide Team went through their show-and-tell.

"Let's start with the big stuff." Aaron Clark-Weber stood in front of a large blackboard. Willie Temple's name headed a column on the left. Then John Doe and next to it, ominously, a blank space.

"Latex trace microscan came back positive," Aaron said. "Plus— and here's the news of the day—this red cloth fiber"—he passed around a color Xerox—"was found on both victims. Caught in the belt buckle of John Doe and . . . in the mouth of Willie Temple."

Kenny looked at the picture. "Something exotic I hope."

"No such luck," Aaron said. "Standard-issue plaid-work-shirt kind of thing. Available at The Gap or Sears or a dozen catalog companies." He handed out a second color Xerox. "Side-by-side comparison photos of the fatal stab wounds are identical . . ."

Linda French picked up the story. "Which tells us it was probably the same weapon. Both victims were stabbed in the upper torso and the knife was then twisted and dragged until it penetrated the heart. Severing the aorta. Each of them had smudges of their own blood on their eyelids. Neither had defense wounds. In the case of Willie Temple, he was a small man and may have been overpowered. Or, as the contusion on his head suggests, knocked unconscious and then stabbed."

Jane started to ask a question, but Linda French anticipated it. "Particle analysis of the contusion is inconclusive. Willie Temple may or may not have been struck on the head at the Pier Twenty murder scene."

Aaron Clark-Weber walked through the room, limping slightly, and handed out a third color Xerox. "The S-thing. Professor Akiyama at Berkeley is one of the world's foremost authorities on religious, tribal, and cult symbology. So far he's stumped. But he'll keep on it." He worked his way back to the blackboard. "As you can see, the photos from the two scenes are interesting in their similarities as well as their dissimilarities. For instance: Both are S-shaped. Both were made with the victim's blood. But one, Willie Temple's, was left in plain view; and the John Doe's was left on a graffiti-covered wall. If we hadn't already been looking for it, we might not have seen it."

"The second one," Linda French added, "is much bigger than the first, almost twice as big. Plus there are those dots at the top of the second one that the first one didn't have. So it's growing and becoming more intricate."

"I've sent hard-copy photos over to Dr. Akiyama," Aaron said. "Maybe this new stuff will help him help us."

Lou Tronick looked up from the photo. "What about the contents of the John Doe's pockets?"

"It's interesting," Linda French said. "There were almost eighty dollars in cash, plus an American Express and a Visa. So, once again, robbery wasn't the motive." She glanced at her notebook. "The credit cards belonged to a Rosabeth Miller, who had reported her purse stolen earlier last night."

"Anyone check her out?" Lou asked.

"Patrol went to interview her," Linda said. "She's seventy-eight; and, when I said her purse was stolen? It was stolen from the back of her wheelchair."

"Seventy-eight, huh?" Lou Tronick made a note. "She single?"

Laughter rippled through the room.

Jane pushed away from the back wall and walked to the black-board. "Great job, everyone." She nodded to Linda French. "We've got a lot of good information going here. We need to concentrate not only on what we know, but what we don't know." She directed this to Linda French. "Motive. Why were these men killed? Find the why and find the who."

Jane saw Mike Finney motioning to her from his cubicle in the bullpen. He pointed to his computer, then to Jane. "Okay, guys," Jane said. "We all know these two murders were committed by the same man. Let's keep a lid on serial killer talk until I go over this stuff with the chief." She started from the room.

"When?" Linda asked.

Jane stopped and turned to her. "When what?"

"When will you talk to the chief?"

Given her lesser rank and relative inexperience, it was an impertinent question and everyone in the room knew it. Especially Linda French.

Jane looked around to the faces of her Homicide Team. Only Kenny didn't look away. Then she took a small step back into the room and locked eyes with Linda.

"When I think it's appropriate." She left the room, closing the door hard. The sound of its slam ricocheted through Interrogation Room One.

■

"THE P.O. BOX you gave me for Randall Thomas is no longer active," Mike Finney said to Jane. "Postal service being what it is, could take days to dig up his records."

Kenny joined them at Finney's cubicle. "What about the e-mail address?"

"He was using Safeweb. It's what they call an 'anonymizer,'" Finney explained. "Basically it's a computer program that covers your footprints and makes your correspondence impossible to trace."

"What if we call the Safeweb people," Kenny began, "and—"

"Can I interrupt?" Finney said.

"Sure, Moby."

"Well, I was hitting all these dead ends and got to thinking. Randall Thomas threatened Philip Iverson in public. Screamed at him even. Not exactly a rational man. So what if Mr. Thomas had done this before . . . to someone else?"

Kenny put his hand on Finney's arm. "Moby, cut to the chase, please."

"And I was right. Except his real name isn't Randall Thomas; it's Thomas Randall. That's why we couldn't find him."

"But now you have?" Jane asked.

Finney tapped a few keys on his keyboard and a color mug shot appeared on his screen.

Jane stood up. "That's him! That's the guy from the stockholders' meeting."

Finney nodded. "He's got two TROs against him. One from Nu-Logic Technology, the other from Cornerstone Computers."

Jane kept her eyes on the screen. "What are the restraining orders for?"

"Threats against management. Every time he loses money, he goes nuts."

"This mug shot," Kenny said, "what was he arrested for?"

"Blowing up the mailbox of the CEO of a dot-com company that went belly-up last year."

Jane studied the face on the monitor. The wild angry eyes, the defiant tight-lipped grin. "Mike, you got an address?"

"I got an address."

CHAPTER 20

■

PALM COURT MANOR
LUXURY APARTMENTS
POOL / CABLE / HBO
VACANCY
SEE MGR. APT. 101

PALM COURT MANOR was a long-neglected apartment building in North Beach. It had a two-tiered open balcony surrounding a grimy, partially drained swimming pool. The music and aromas from a half-dozen cultures seeped through the cracked louvered windows of the one-bedroom and studio units.

"Luxury apartments?" Kenny said as he and Jane climbed the stairs to number 214. "Looks like a horse died in that pool."

They reached the top of the stairway. Jane put her hand into her purse and gripped her pistol, flicking off the safety with her thumb. "Focus," she cautioned.

"Focusing," Kenny said. He reached inside his coat and gave his Glock a slight tug to loosen it in its shoulder holster for quicker release. Chambered and ready, it didn't have a safety.

Walking slowly, their eyes registering every visible doorway and window, their minds calculating every possible escape route—both for the suspect and themselves—they passed Apartment 210. The flimsy beige drapes were closed, but the throbbing pulse of hip-hop music caused the window to vibrate. They glanced into the next window, 212. Two men, one in his twenties, the other in his forties, sat at the dinette table rolling joints. Another man, not much more than a teenager, sat on the floor, puffing on a bong. The sweet smell of marijuana smoke drifted under the door.

"Bad boys," Kenny said as they passed.

Jane nodded tightly.

Two-fourteen.

They pressed against the wall and peeked in through a part in the drapes. Thomas Randall was in the tiny kitchen, kneeling in front of the open oven. He was wearing a white T-shirt and jeans, an apron, and oven mitts.

Kenny looked to Jane. "Report has him blowing up that CEO's mailbox. Think he's cooking up another batch of explosives?"

Jane slipped her gun out of her purse. "Anything's possible." She glanced inside again. "Ken, look."

On the far wall, above a threadbare sleeper couch, was a collage of photos and newspaper articles. Prominent among them was an eight-by-ten picture of Philip Iverson.

"Jesus." Kenny snapped his Glock out of its holster. "Probable cause?"

"Probable cause," Jane agreed. "Wanna call it in and wait for backup?"

"And take the chance of him blasting the luxury apartments of Palm Court Manor into next Tuesday?" Kenny held his pistol close to his chest. "Let's make a house call."

Jane assessed the situation. The apartment building was teeming with people. A large-scale police action could deteriorate into chaos. Right now they held the element of surprise. Thomas Randall was on his knees in his kitchen. Vulnerable. It was time to go in. "Let's do it," she said. "On my three." She took a deep head-clearing breath. "One . . . two . . . *three!*"

Moving in unison, they kicked down the front door of Apartment 214 and charged inside.

"SFPD, freeze!" Kenny shouted.

Thomas Randall, still on his knees, immediately raised his hands, two navy-blue oven mitts thrusting over his head.

Jane, her weapon trained on the suspect, closed in on him while Kenny checked the bathroom.

"Clear!" he shouted as he came back into the living room. Now that they were inside, they could see the other walls of the apartment. Photographs of other corporate CEOs and newspaper articles covered almost the entire area, floor to ceiling, like wallpaper.

"On your stomach," Jane ordered. "Hands behind your head."

Thomas Randall flattened himself on the kitchen floor.

Kenny yanked off the oven mitts and slapped on a pair of handcuffs. Then he hoisted the suspect to his feet and pushed him into a chair.

Randall tossed his head to one side, trying to get his long greasy hair out of his eyes.

Kenny gestured to the open oven door. "What d'you got going in there?"

"Baking."

"Baking what, asshole?"

Randall lifted his shoulder against his face, still trying to get the hair out of his eyes. Then he looked up at Kenny. "A pie. I was baking a pie. That one in there's mince. But I got pumpkin and custard in the fridge. I like custard the best."

Jane returned her pistol to her purse. "Mr. Randall, we're placing you under arrest as a suspect in the murder of Philip Iverson. Inspector Marks will read you your rights and then we'll—"

"Philip Iverson?" Thomas Randall started to rise. Kenny shoved him back down. "I didn't kill that money-squandering son of a bitch. Wish I had, but I didn't."

Kenny tilted his chin toward the walls. "This place is like a museum exhibit of a confession. Why should we even be listening to you?"

" 'Cause the night Iverson was killed? I got an alibi from the day before to the day after."

Kenny sneered. "Which would be?"

Thomas Randall stuck out his lower lip and blew upward, temporarily sending the hair out of his eyes. "I was in jail."

The first thing Jane thought was why hadn't it shown up in Finney's research? Then she realized that if Randall were telling the truth, the arrest must have been in a different jurisdiction. "Where?" she asked.

"San Jose," Thomas Randall said. "I sort of attacked the senior financial officer of Hewlett-Packard."

" 'Sort of attacked'?" Kenny said. "What the hell does that mean?"

"He was giving a speech at San Jose State and I charged him. Before they could stop me, I . . ." Thomas Randall sat back smugly, savoring the memory.

"You what?" Kenny asked.

"Threw a pie at him. Custard. Like I said, I like custard the best. It has a certain heft, y'know?"

"No I don't know," Kenny said. "I never went to clown school." He turned to Jane. "You believe this guy?"

But Jane had been scanning the collage of papers around Philip Iverson's picture on the wall over the couch. "Ken, c'mere. Look at this."

Just below the photograph, in the middle of various articles about Philip Iverson and RiverPark, was an e-mail.

Subj: A response.
From: RAL@RP.com
To: rt622@mediabox.com

Dear Sir:

I am in receipt of your several e-mail correspondences over the last six months.

In them you remark that RiverPark is like all of the other large technology companies with whom you either invest or have some other financial relationship. You accuse us of being monolithic, inhuman, and faceless.

I am sorry for that perception.

Granted, we are a large multinational corporation. And granted, too, when an individual investor tries to personally contact senior management, it might be frustrating in that we, with our busy work and travel obligations, might not always be accessible to people like yourself. For that, too, I apologize and am trying to rectify the impression you have of us with this note.

RiverPark is anything but a faceless or inhuman company. Indeed Philip Iverson, our founder and chairman, has striven to run our company along forward-looking and humane principles. And Mr. Iverson's public generosity through the Make It So Foundation is well known and well publicized.

A company like RiverPark may seem like a huge dark wall. If so, then there's a window shining brightly at the heart of that wall. And that's Philip Iverson.

He is the conscience and soul of our company. He carries RiverPark on his broad shoulders, and without him, it would surely collapse.

All of us who work for him are eternally grateful to be able to follow his profound leadership.

Yours sincerely,
Robert "Bob" Lewis
CFO, RiverPark Enterprises

Thomas Randall snorted from the kitchen. "Bunch of patronizing horseshit."

Jane guided Kenny out of earshot of Thomas Randall. "On the surface, that e-mail is an articulate defense of a huge company's seeming indifference to the complaints of an average citizen. But—"

"I'm way ahead of you," Kenny interrupted. "A letter like this could easily be construed by someone with as active an imagination as our friend here as placing the blame for whatever outrages, real or imagined—"

Jane finished the thought for him. "Squarely on Philip Iverson. Painting a bulls'-eye on his forehead."

"Long as we're being so paranoid," Kenny went on, "we should consider who else stands to gain from the death of RiverPark's number one executive."

"RiverPark's number two executive," Jane said as she reached for her cell phone.

CHAPTER 21

———■———

FD-498 (Rev. 6-24-87)

POLYGRAPH REPORT

DATE OF REPORT: 8 February 2003
DATE OF EXAMINATION: 8 February 2003
BUREAU FILE NUMBER: 0901-SF-7818645
FIELD FILE NUMBER: 0901-SF-7818645
FIELD OFFICE: San Francisco, California
EXAMINEE NAME: Lewis, Robert Alexander

CASE SYNOPSIS: Examinee's employer, Philip Marc Iverson, was murdered on approximately 4 February/5 February 2003. It is at the request of Lieutenant Jane Candiotti (SFPD, Homicide) that this polygraph test be administered.

On 8 February 2003, Examinee arrived at the Nineteenth Precinct Station House of the SFPD. Purpose of the examination is to determine if Examinee was or was not involved in the murder of the above-named deceased.

QUESTIONS

1. Q: What is your full name?
    A: Robert Alexander Lewis

2. Q: Are you sometimes known as Bob?
    A: Yes.

3. Q: Do you have a wife and three children?
    A: No.

4. Q: Do you have a wife and one child?
    A: Yes.

5. Q: Did you freely consent to this polygraph interview?
    A: Yes.

6. Q: Regarding the murder of Philip Marc Iverson, do you
    intend to be completely truthful with me about that?
    A: Yes.

7. Q: Are you convinced that I won't ask you any surprise
    questions on this test?
    A: Yes.

8. Q: Are you the chief financial officer of a company known
    as RiverPark?
    A: Yes.

9. Q: Is there a "keyman clause" in your contract with River-
    Park?
    A: Yes.

10. Q: Now that Philip Marc Iverson has been murdered, will
    your percentage of ownership of RiverPark increase?
    A: Yes.

11. Q: Will the aforementioned increase be substantial?
    A: Yes.

12. Q: Did you murder Philip Marc Iverson?
    A: No.

13. Q: Have you ever broken the law?
    A: Yes.

14. Q: Is your child's name Alexander?
    A: Yes.

15. Q: Did you hire anyone to murder Philip Marc Iverson?
    A: No.

16. Q: Do you have a valid California driver's license?
    A: Yes.

CONCLUSION

It is the conclusion of this examiner that the recorded responses are indicative of truthfulness on the part of Examinee.

Signed: Alejandro Rivera, Examiner

■

BOB LEWIS EMERGED from the tiny examination room with his attorney, Jordan Shepherd.

Jane and Kenny, the polygraph report in hand, approached them. "Mr. Lewis," Jane said, "thank you for your cooperation today. I know it's a difficult time for you. But, under the circumstances, I'm sure you'll agree it was for the best."

"Under the circumstances, Lieutenant," Jordan Shepherd said, "I think it best that from now on, all further contact between you and my client go through me."

Shepherd was young, not even thirty. He wore his Yale Law School ring on the fourth finger of his left hand as if it were a wedding ring. His self-confidence, bordering on arrogance, represented, Jane thought, all that was good and bad about the new generation of Ivy League pit-bull lawyers.

"Mr. Shepherd," Kenny said evenly, "this is a murder case. Following leads and pursuing new information is extremely time-sensitive.

We are not going to waste our time chasing you down whenever we want to talk to your client."

Shepherd stood his ground. "I can get a court order requiring you to—"

Jane stepped forward. "Sir, Mr. Lewis did very well in there today, why would you possibly want to antagonize the situation?"

Jordan Shepherd's ears burned red, a combination of indignation and embarrassment. He had overplayed his hand and was searching for a graceful way out. Jane gave it to him.

"Tell you what," she said, "anytime we contact Mr. Lewis, we'll inform your office simultaneously."

Shepherd nodded curtly. "Fine, Lieutenant." He took Bob Lewis by the elbow and guided him toward the elevators.

Kenny turned to Jane. "Very diplomatic."

"I do my best."

"But next time, could you just—"

Mike Finney stepped up. " 'Scuse me, Lieutenant, Inspector. We got this letter? I think you need to see it."

CHAPTER 22

■

Lieutenant,

Things are not as they seem.
The devil's grave is a place to dance.

For he has brought suffering.
Endless, black suffering.

And now he is gone.
And the silence is lifted.

The dead will speak.
And the dead will be heard.

I know this is true,
For I am dead, too.

Keep your money.
There has been enough blood.

01436937471

THERE WAS A second, smaller envelope with the letter. Kenny used the tip of his pocket knife to unseal it.

A newspaper clipping of Philip Iverson floated like a feather to the table in Interrogation Room One.

Lou Tronick came over from the monitor where he was watching news camera outtakes from Philip Iverson's banquet.

Kenny stripped off his rubber gloves. "What the fuck is this?"

Aaron Clark-Weber stood next to Lou. Mike Finney sat at the end of the table, jotting notes in his casebook.

"Look at this language," Jane said. " 'Things are not as they seem. The devil . . . suffering . . . The dead will speak. I am dead, too.' At face value this is telling us that at least one more person out there isn't exactly mourning the death of Philip Iverson. If this is real, it could be the key to taking the word *random* out of our vocabulary."

"That's a big *if,* Jane," Lou Tronick said. "What's telling us that, given Mrs. Iverson's reward, this isn't just another crank?"

"For one, it's anonymous," Kenny said. "Most of the others we've gotten were traced either to people incarcerated in prison or to someone with a history of writing these things."

Jane regarded the letter. "I agree." She turned to Aaron. "Do your magic and make this thing fly through your lab."

Aaron nodded.

Using the eraser tip of a pencil, Jane turned the letter. "Also, Aaron, please send a copy of this over to Ruth Holmes at FBI—"

Mike Finney looked up from his casebook. " 'Scuse me, Lieutenant, how do you spell that?"

Kenny couldn't resist. "F . . . B—"

Jane cut him off. "Holmes, as in Sherlock. She's the best document examiner out there."

"But," Finney said, "this letter is typed."

"I know, Mike. There are key words and phrases, choice of typeface, page positioning, that sort of stuff, that the experts can use to profile the letter writer."

"What about the numbers?" Kenny asked.

Jane read them out loud and looked up. "Anything, guys?"

"Could be a phone number," Lou Tronick offered. "With a country code or something."

"Or a bank account," Kenny said. "Or maybe some bizarre numerology."

Aaron Clark-Weber took a pair of tweezers from the breast pocket of his sport coat. He slipped the letter and newspaper clipping into an evidence packet. "We ran this with the field kit when you first opened it, and came up empty. We'll go deeper." He started for the door. "I'll get a copy of this to Ruth Holmes right away."

"While you're at it," Jane said, "make us a blowup for the interrogation room. The more we look at it, the more likely something will hit us about it." She looked to Mike Finney as Aaron left. "Mike, what else do you have?"

Finney held up the surveillance tape from the Golden Gate Grand. "I called all the owners of the BMWs whose license plates matched our partial."

"And . . ." Kenny prodded.

"And . . . they all have alibis."

Jane reached for the tape. "I don't buy it. I'm taking this home."

"Ooh," Kenny said, "an evening of watching a parking garage's security video. I love being married." He turned to Jane to share in the joke. But she was watching something through the window.

Kenny followed her gaze.

Chief Walker McDonald was crossing the bullpen. Heading their way.

■

"YOU NEED TO take the word *anonymous* out of the equation," Chief McDonald said after he reread a copy of the letter. "This thing"—he held the letter up—"is dripping with innuendo. We find who wrote it, we start getting some answers."

"*If* it's real, sir," Jane said. They were in her office, the chief's broad body filling every inch of the guest chair. Jane sat at her desk. The tension from yesterday's argument hovering like a shadow on the periphery. "Lieutenant Clark-Weber took the original to his lab, and we sent a copy over to Ruth Holmes at FBI."

"She's the one," the chief acknowledged. "I'm authorizing funds for manpower, OT, science . . . anything you need on this case." He waited for some expression of gratitude from Jane. There was none forthcoming. "Problem, Lieutenant?"

"We had another homeless man killed last night."

"I saw the incident report. What's that have to do with what we're talking about?"

"Everything. Sir . . . with respect . . . I just can't treat the death of Philip Iverson differently than any other homicide on my watch. So either the funds are for all my pending cases . . . or I don't want them."

The chief closed his eyes and drew a long frustrated breath. When he opened them again, they were burning with anger. "Jane . . . I've reviewed the Willie Temple and John Doe paperwork, and I agree with your assessment that it's the same killer—"

"Then let me go out with a Serial Killer Alert—or at least voice our concern—and warn the street community. Even if we're wrong, we still get everybody acting with caution. Where's the harm in that?"

The chief shook his head. "Right now this city's about at its lowest point since Moscone and Milk . . . and you want to go out with an SKA? For all we know, the bum killer had only two enemies in the world, and now he has none. The sequence could be over just when we're gearing up to scare the shit out of everybody." He offered a little half smile. "So let's move off this, okay?"

"No."

The chief shot to his feet. " 'No'? What do you mean 'no'?"

"Sir, you come in here throwing money at the Philip Iverson case. You refuse to issue an SKA on the homeless murders. I don't agree."

"Last I checked, I was the chief of police in this city!" Chief Mc-Donald was shouting now. "And you, Candiotti, are a lieutenant. A *new* lieutenant."

Jane refused to engage in the histrionics. It wasn't that she was afraid. It was simply that given the circumstances, she knew she couldn't win.

But she held her ground.

"What if it had been two *philanthropists* who had been killed instead of two derelicts? What would the chief of police's position be then?"

Chief McDonald narrowed his eyes. "I recommended you for this job."

Jane held his gaze. "And you knew exactly what you were getting."

"You may think you're being idealistic, Lieutenant. But I prefer to call it naive." He buttoned his coat. "Someone like Philip Iverson is *not* the same as a homeless person. It may not be politically correct, but let's face facts. How many kids did Willie Temple send to college? How many kids' lives did your John Doe save with his generous donations to Children's Memorial?" He went to the door. "There's a real world out there, Jane. You might try living in it." He tore the door open and left, striding across the squad room to the stairwell door.

Jane watched him go, trying to make sense of it all. The beeper vibrated on her hip. She snatched it from her belt. *You okay? 3H61.* She looked into the bullpen. Kenny smiled back at her. "Yeah," she said through the window. "I'm okay." She rose and crossed to the doorway. "Do we have a whereabouts on Mrs. Iverson?"

"Last I heard she was in her San Francisco apartment."

"Good. Who's assigned to watch her today?"

Kenny checked the duty manifest on his bulletin board. "Madeiros."

"Give him a call and see if Alice is home."

"Because?"

"Because I want to pop by to talk about this letter and I don't want her refreshed . . . or rehearsed."

CHAPTER 23

———■———

THE LATE-DAY SUN was a perfect circle of white behind the thin layer of clouds.

A hole in the sky.

Kenny coaxed the Explorer into the gentle left curve past the Safeway. The traffic on Marina Boulevard was surprisingly light for this time of day. A few sailboats, just small white triangles at this distance, leaned into the wind on the restless gray waters of San Francisco Bay. A group of college kids played soccer on the Green, their shouts lost in the offshore breeze. A homeless man, his world in a shopping cart, rummaged through a trash can.

Jane knew that Kenny would slow down at the next block. There was a narrow vacant lot on the left. The low sun found the two freshly painted houses on either side, accentuating the dark empty space between them.

All that was left of Jane's house after it was burned down by the cop killer who had come after her last year was a chain-link fence and a field of weeds. Who would have thought, Jane mused, that as she was building a life for herself, moving away from her parents, advancing her career . . . getting married and trying to have a baby, that she would end up living in the same house where she grew up?

"You okay with this?" Kenny asked. "We could go another way."

". . . I'm okay."

And they both knew she was lying.

Kenny cranked hard on the wheel and stepped on the gas. The Explorer jumped forward, passing a taxi out trolling for a fare.

■

"I WAS JUST leaving," A. J. Guthrie said.

He stood with Jane and Kenny in the massive foyer of the Iversons' San Francisco apartment.

"This a social call," Kenny asked, "or work?"

"Work. I heard from a woman I know—actually I went to high school with her and now she's a secretary at RiverPark . . . anyway, she called me about Bob Lewis being brought in for a polygraph. So I came by to tell Mrs. Iverson what I knew."

"What else do you know?" Jane asked.

" 'Nother friend of mine from back when I was on the force told me about Thomas Randall and how that didn't pan out. Too bad, it sounded like a good lead."

"We thought so, too," Kenny said.

The door to the library opened and Mr. Kim announced, "Mrs. Iverson is available to you now."

Jane touched A.J.'s arm. "The leg okay?"

"Just fine, Lieutenant." Sheriff Guthrie, with just the slightest show of discomfort, crossed the foyer to the private elevator. He turned and smiled. "I learn anything you don't already know, I'll call ya."

"You do that," Jane said. "Be careful out there."

A. J. Guthrie tilted his head in a grin. "I'll do that, too."

■

"I THINK IT'S all finally catching up to me." Alice Iverson sat in the corner of a plush green velvet sofa, a dressing gown pulled loosely around her. She was wearing the same unlaced white Converse sneakers, Jane noticed, as the night they met. Her eyes were soft and puffy from crying. "I have just been overwhelmed. All the details, the phone calls . . . the arrangements. I finally had to stop and try to find a moment to sleep." She sat quietly for a second, staring up into a corner of the cathedral ceiling.

"This place"—she gestured to the richly appointed two-story library—"was more Philip's than mine. There's such a masculine feeling to these rooms."

Jane looked around. Alice was right. The Iversons' San Francisco apartment had the darkly elegant character of a university club.

"So what do I do with it now?" Alice went on. "Sell it? Or worse, preserve it as some sort of grieving widow's shrine to her slain husband?"

"Time will tell," Jane said. "Surely there's no rush."

Alice shook her head slowly. "Surely there isn't."

"We're sorry to disturb you," Kenny said. He was standing with his back against the expansive mahogany wet bar. "We know that Sheriff Guthrie told you about Bob Lewis coming in for a polygraph test today."

Alice nodded. "I can't even begin to imagine that Bob had anything to do with my husband's death. He loved Philip."

Jane knew that in her statement was an implied question: How did Bob Lewis do? She thought about not answering it, but decided to disclose what she knew in the interest of making Alice more talkative. "I think you're right. He did love your husband. Mr. Lewis has essentially been eliminated as a suspect."

Kenny approached Alice Iverson. "Was there anything in that letter that jumped out at you? The language, the numbers maybe?"

Alice Iverson reread the piece of paper in her lap. "I wish there were." She sighed. "One thing about the language, though . . ."

"Yes?" Jane said, ready to seize on the slimmest of leads.

"If they're talking about Philip," Alice said, "then these are very ugly words. I mean calling him the 'devil' and his 'grave is a place to dance'?" She regarded the letter. "And 'he has brought suffering.' What did my husband ever do to anyone?"

"Your husband," Jane said, "amassed his fortune by being brilliant and aggressive. I hate to keep coming back to this, but was there someone along the way—even before you were married—whom Mr. Iverson may have slighted? Someone back in the start-up days who may have been cut out of the company, who's been harboring a grudge all these years and finally decided to act on it?"

Alice Iverson shifted her weight to face Jane. As she did, her left shoe slipped off. "And I hate to keep telling you the same thing, Lieutenant. But the answer is no." She held up the letter. "May I keep this?"

"Of course you can," Jane said as she rose. "It's a copy." She dropped a business card on the coffee table. "I know you'll call if you think of anything."

Alice reached across and Jane thought she was going to pick up the card. But she bent farther and retrieved her tennis shoe. As she did there was the expected, and seemingly inadvertent, show of thigh. It became the brief focal point in the room.

For Kenny.

Jane was looking at Alice Iverson's bare foot.

The sleepless grieving widow, overwhelmed by details and arrangements, had a new pedicure.

CHAPTER 24

■

JANE AND KENNY were four blocks away from Alice Iverson's apartment when the call came in.

"3H58."

Jane grabbed the mike. "This is Candiotti."

"Lieutenant, Rudy Madeiros here. Mrs. Iverson just left her place. She was kinda in a rush. She's in a new Range Rover, dark gray, heading south on Gough."

"*We're* heading south on Gough."

"Roger that. I watched you leave. I could tail her and report in or—"

Kenny looked in the rearview mirror. "Check it out."

The Range Rover sped by them, the silhouette of Alice Iverson barely visible through the tinted windows.

"We'll pick it up from here, Rudy," Jane said. "You stay behind us."

Kenny pressed the accelerator, nudging the Explorer through the rush-hour traffic. Up ahead, Alice Iverson wove from lane to lane without signaling. "Somebody's in a hurry."

Alice Iverson turned right onto Van Ness just as the light turned yellow. Kenny floored it and squealed into the turn a split second after the light went red.

The Range Rover slipped past a city bus and turned left into a Denny's parking lot. Kenny pulled over to the right and cruised to a stop. He and Jane waited until Alice got out of her car, hurried across the lot, and entered the nearly empty restaurant. Then he eased the Explorer back onto Van Ness and worked his way across the traffic. He bumped up into the lot and parked, partially hidden by a sour-dough bread delivery van.

Jane scanned the broad windows. "There."

They watched as Alice Iverson, slipping on a pair of sunglasses, quickly walked down the row of booths until she came to the second-to-last one. A man, handsome and tan, with short black hair, rose to greet her. Alice pulled him into a deep hug, then kissed him hungrily on the lips.

■

"3H58."

"This is Candiotti."

"Lieutenant, this is Rudy Madeiros. I got a shift change coming. Backup's here in less than five. But I'll hang if you need me."

Jane peered across the parking lot. Alice Iverson had been huddled with the man for almost half an hour. "You can take off, Rudy. Thanks."

Across Van Ness, the unmarked police sedan pulled away from the curb in front of a convenience store. Madeiros merged with the traffic and, in a few seconds, disappeared behind a broad curve.

"Perfect timing," Kenny said. "She's on the move."

Inside the restaurant, Alice Iverson rose from the booth and dropped some money on the table. Laughing, she kissed the man one last time, then headed for the front door. The man drained the last of his soft drink, then he, too, got up and started to leave.

"Two of them," Kenny said. "One of us. Your call."

Jane had already thought of this. "If Alice turns back toward her place, we let her go and follow the boyfriend."

The man emerged from the Denny's and gave a little wave to Alice

Iverson as she went out the driveway and turned right. Toward her apartment.

"Uh-oh," Kenny said.

Jane turned to see what he was talking about.

The man was running right at them. As he got closer, he reached into his pocket. In an instant, Kenny had his Glock out of the shoulder holster and in his lap. Jane had her bag up off the floor, her in hand inside, squeezing the grip of her pistol. But the man pulled out a ring of keys and pointed the remote at a new white Lexus LS430 just behind the Explorer.

Oblivious to Jane and Kenny, he climbed in, started it, and peeled away. Blasting over the sidewalk, he swung a sweeping left across Van Ness and tore away.

"Hang on," Kenny said as he whipped the Explorer into a tilting U-turn and shot left through the traffic on Van Ness. "You get a plate?"

Jane narrowed her eyes, trying to focus on the speeding car ahead. "I don't think there is one."

"Car's brand-new. Makes sense."

The Lexus powered into the Makepeace Tunnel.

Kenny pushed past a red plumbing truck and entered the dark tunnel. The Lexus slowed with the traffic. Kenny saw an opening and jammed the Explorer over to the right. The moment he did, the Lexus accelerated into a screeching U-turn and joined the flow going in the opposite direction.

Jane and Kenny were trapped on the far right side of the tunnel. Jane pivoted in her seat. The Lexus broke back into the sunlight, turned left, and was gone.

"Shit!" Kenny slammed the steering wheel with the heel of his hand.

Jane snapped up the microphone. "3H58 to Dispatch."

Cheryl Lomax came on immediately. "Go, Lieutenant."

"Cheryl, I need Finney."

"Hang on."

When the traffic finally started going again, Kenny maneuvered into the left lane and, other cars honking, threw the Explorer into a U-turn. Just as they pushed their way out of the tunnel, Finney's voice crackled over the radio.

"3P66 to 3H58. Go ahead."

"Mike, listen carefully. White Lexus. Model LS430. Brand-new. No plates. Canvas all dealers in the area . . . San Francisco, Oakland, North Bay. I want to know all purchases recent enough that the plates haven't come in yet."

"Will do, Lieutenant," Finney said. "Any luck with the surveillance tape of that BMW from the parking structure?"

"We've been a little busy, Mike. But that'll be tonight's homework. 3H58 out."

Kenny turned left and accelerated, instinctively following the route the Lexus had taken.

"This guy is long gone, Ken." Jane touched his arm.

Kenny reflexively tensed, his eyes still straining for the white Lexus.

"Kenny," Jane said softly, "let's go home."

Easing off the gas pedal, Kenny sighed and let the Explorer slow down. Other cars passed him, their drivers looking back and shaking their heads.

CHAPTER 25

■

"WHAT'RE YOU WATCHING?" Jane asked. She set a tray of home-made pizza and two Sierra Nevadas on the coffee table.

"Nineteen eighty-eight World Series. Oakland–L.A. Bottom of the ninth. Kirk Gibson's up." Kenny twisted the tops off the beers. "Watch this. *Boom!* Look at Lasorda. He must have jumped an entire inch off the ground."

Jane sat next to him on the couch. "Help me here. You're watching a baseball game—"

"World Series game."

"—from way back in the, I don't know, *twentieth century.* You already know what's going to happen, and then when it does, you still get this excited?"

"It's a classic."

"And, because there just aren't enough sports on television, someone comes up with a station that shows all these old games; and people like you stay up all night watching *repeats* of these games over and over again?"

Kenny slid a slice of pizza onto his plate and sat back. "Ain't life grand?"

An arc of headlights swept across the curtains as a car, its tires shishing on the rain-dampened street, passed slowly by. Jane turned to the sound and watched the car, a maroon Buick sedan, drive up to the corner, its receding taillights like rubies shrinking in the night.

Aunt Lucy.

"C'mon." Kenny held up the VCR remote. "Let's watch some cop porn."

"Hmm," Jane said, her mind still on Aunt Lucy driving past her brother's house at night. Prowling the streets in her melancholy.

"Okay." Kenny pressed "play." "This is regular size and regular speed." They watched as the BMW tore past the cashier's booth at the Golden Gate Grand parking garage. "Now super-enhanced slow-mo." The car, repositioned in the frame, stuttered past the booth in slow motion.

"Again," Jane said. She reached for her beer.

Kenny looked at the readout on the video box. "This one's slower and enlarged another fifty percent."

The BMW, broken into a mosaic of pixilated images, crept into the entry plaza. Jane started to put her beer to her lips when she spotted something. "There!" She leaped from the couch and pointed to the TV set. "Back it up and freeze it just before this."

Kenny rewound the tape, then pressed "frame advance."

"Stop!" Jane said. She was on her knees in front of the television, peering into the crackling gray light. Kenny came around and knelt beside her.

"See it?" Jane asked.

"Yeah."

The BMW's license plate was still partially blown out by the glare of the security floodlights. But just below it and to the right, on the black rubber part of the rear bumper, was a two-inch-square field of white.

A parking decal.

Kenny pressed the "eject" button. "I'll call for a patrol messenger to take this downtown. If that decal is for a school or business or condo complex—"

"—and we cross it with the names on Finney's list, we're gonna find this fucker."

"Well put." Kenny pulled Jane to her feet. "Good work, Lieutenant." He turned and went into the kitchen.

Jane leaned against the doorjamb, her eyes following Kenny as he took the wall phone from its cradle in the breakfast nook and dialed their precinct. While waiting for the connection, he bent over and touched his toes. Stretching the long day out of his back. Jane smiled. There was her husband, not knowing he was being observed, presenting his wonderful butt to the world.

Jane promised herself that tomorrow morning, on her fortieth birthday, she would think back to tonight and remember this moment.

CHAPTER 26

■

JANE HAD BEEN determined for weeks that she wouldn't be blue on her birthday. Now, as she and Kenny drove along the Oakland side of the bay, she felt a weight, a tugging, on her soul.

Turning forty was part of it.

Where they were going was the rest of it.

She looked over to Kenny. He felt her watching him and touched her cheek. "We can do this later, y'know."

"Thanks," Jane said. "But I want to do it now."

A city bus, filled with a standing crowd of people going to work and school, chuffed black smoke in front of them. Kenny pulled hard on the wheel and passed it in one practiced motion.

"When I was jogging this morning . . . ?" Jane began.

"Yum?"

"Three different people called out to me and wished me happy birthday." She gave a little halfhearted laugh. "Davey Tasca yelled down from his bedroom window. 'Yo, the big four-oh!' "

"Three people at six-thirty in the morning? Pretty good."

"Used to be a dozen."

Kenny turned left through an arched stone gateway. Jane fell quiet as the Explorer climbed a gentle tree-lined slope. Just over the crest, Kenny pulled to the side and stopped.

Jane grasped the door handle. "I'll just be a minute."

Beads of water caught the morning sunlight and glistened like diamond dust in the grass. Jane came to a broad oak tree, her beacon in this meadow of tombstones, and stood before her parents' grave.

They lay side by side beneath the tree, the plot overlooking the Oakland Navy Yard, where Poppy and two of his brothers had worked during World War II. This and the house in San Leandro, Poppy used to say, were all the real estate he'd ever need in this life and the next.

Now all five brothers were buried in this cemetery.

On a low hill across the way, an elderly woman knelt next to a small tombstone and pinched a few weeds from its base.

Jane noticed that there was still a vague outline in the grass on Poppy's side of the grave, his burial having been only a few months ago.

She squatted on her heels and put the palm of her right hand on the moist grass at her father's feet. As she prayed silently, meditatively, her whispered words gathered their own rhythm until they were almost a chant.

Then she looked up. "Forty years ago this day," she said, "you were building a family. You were happy and proud as you brought your first child into this world. You worked hard and you loved me. And you taught me how to love." Jane looked back to Kenny. He stood in the open door of the Explorer, talking on the radio. "Thank you for teaching me how to love."

Her eyes pooled with tears as she rose. She walked up to the tombstone, put both hands on it, and lowered her head. "Thank you," she whispered again. Then she bent at the waist and kissed the stone, cold and rough against her lips. Wiping her eyes, she turned to start back and saw Kenny approaching.

"I'm sorry to do this," he said, "but . . ."

"What is it?"

"Linda French just called."

Jane crossed to him. "Another one?"

Kenny nodded. "Another one."

"Jesus." Jane started running toward the Explorer. "Let's go."

Kenny opened the passenger door, then hustled around and climbed in the driver's side. He waited for Jane to get in, started the car, and threw it into gear.

As they picked up speed, Jane turned back for one last glimpse of her parents' grave. But a rise in the land blocked her view. She kept looking back until the oak tree disappeared.

■

THE CARPET WAS so saturated with blood that the Homicide Team had trouble avoiding it as they did their work.

The victim, a white man in his early twenties, lay in the middle of a tiny flophouse room. Heroin works and a box of Milky Ways were strewn near his feet.

His arm was still tied off.

"Everything's the same," Linda French reported to Jane and Kenny. She was coiled, kinetic, ready to lunge at the slightest slackening of her leash. "Will you go back to the chief?"

Jane took in the scene. The deep dark well of the chest wound, the closed eyes smudged with blood, the victim himself. "Yes, I will." She turned a slow three-sixty, pulling it all in. "Where's the S-thing?"

"Haven't found one," Aaron Clark-Weber said.

"Yet," Linda added.

Kenny rose from examining the body. "Try the closet, under the furniture . . ."

"When you can move it," Jane said, "look under the body."

Aaron leaned in. "Happy birthday, Jane."

Jane gestured to the activity around her. "You shouldn't have."

A scrawny teenage girl sat in the only chair. Jane sidled over to listen to the last of her statement, a patrolwoman busily scribbling. ". . . sometimes in the park. Sometimes here. His mother sent him some money? And we took this room? Bought some food and . . . well, some stuff we shouldn'ta?" She looked over to the victim. Her eyes were lifeless, any hint of youth already gone. "What's gonna happen to that stuff?"

"It'll go back with us," the patrolwoman answered. "Any of it yours?"

"Yeah," the girl said. "The"—she looked longingly at the drugs— ". . . the candy bars." She let her head fall back. "What the fuck am I gonna do?"

The patrolwoman looked up to Jane. "Says her name's Talia. The vic's name is Alan Ray."

"Alan Ray something?" Jane asked. "Or just Alan Ray?"

"Asked her that myself, Lieutenant. Said she didn't know."

"Hey, Lieutenant," Aaron said. "Look at this."

One of the EMTs had rolled the victim onto his side and lifted his shirt. There was a narrow wound near his spine.

"Stabbed in the back?" Jane asked.

"Looked like it at first," Kenny said. "But it's an exit wound."

"Exit wound?" Linda French leaned in for a closer look. "How do you get a knife exit . . . oh, my God."

"Right," Aaron said. He motioned for the EMT to return the body to the floor. "The blade went all the way through the torso."

As the medic lay the body back down, a red dot suddenly appeared on Alan Ray's forehead. Then another. Then a third, splattering onto his chin. Jane and Kenny were just starting to raise their heads to find the source of the falling drops when Talia screamed. Her shrill girlish cry shattered the hushed atmosphere in the cramped room.

She shot to her feet, sending the chair crashing into the wall, and pointed to the ceiling. "What the fuck is *that*?"

Everyone looked up, following her waggling finger toward the overhead light.

A two-foot-long S-figure was smeared onto the water-stained ceiling. In blood. There were three elongated dots on the right side of the uppermost section. It was dripping blood, returning it to its source.

Kenny turned to Jane. "This guy's talking to us."

"No," Jane said. "He's screaming at us."

CHAPTER 27

—■—

"... AND WE'VE DETERMINED it to be a serial sequence." Chief Walker McDonald addressed the media in the memorial plaza in front of Precinct Nineteen. His black Suburban was parked to the side, out of the camera shot. Devon Haskell stood by the rear door, listening to his boss.

"Therefore, I have instructed my Homicide Team to issue a Serial Killer Alert. All homeless shelters, soup kitchens, missions, clinics, and known indigent camps will be notified and monitored by officers of the San Francisco Police Department, all under the auspices of Homicide Lieutenant Jane Candiotti." He glanced over to where Jane, Kenny, and Linda French were standing.

Jane nodded slightly. Kenny looked across the plaza to the Suburban. Haskell lifted the corners of his mouth in a smirking grin.

"Some call the homeless population of our city the forgotten people." The chief found the lens of the KGO camera. "Well, I'm here to promise you they will not be forgotten by us."

Sergeant Alvarez from Press Relations stepped up to the microphone cluster. "That's it, folks. The chief has to get to City Hall to brief Mayor Biggs. Any further questions will be handled by my office."

Chief McDonald started toward his Suburban, four chase motorcycles idling next to it. Someone yelled, "We appreciate how you feel about the homeless, sir! But what about Philip Iverson?"

Becka Flynn.

The chief stopped, a flush of irritation blooming in his cheeks. "No one on my force will rest until the person responsible for Mr. Iverson's death is behind bars. And . . ." He leveled his eyes at Becka. "I assure you that is going to happen." Devon Haskell opened the rear door of the Suburban. Chief McDonald turned his back on the press and climbed in, pulling the door and its opaque window closed behind him. Without looking back, Haskell ran to the driver's side and got in.

A traffic control officer cleared a lane and the Suburban, flanked by its escort, raced away.

Jane turned to Linda. "Set up in I-One and get Aaron down here for a full report in twenty minutes."

Linda pulled open the stairwell door. "Lieutenant," she began, the words coming as if she'd been waiting for hours to say them, "I'll do a good job for you." Excited and filled with purpose, she hurried up the stairs.

"Happy birthday, Jane."

Jane turned.

Becka Flynn was crossing the plaza. Her cameraman was already at the van, motioning impatiently for her to join him.

"Thanks. Where you going now?"

"Reggie Mayhew is holding a news conference any minute. We gotta fight the traffic and beat the other guys there. I've got some kid intern duking it out with the other kid interns, saving me a spot up front."

"Nice going on the Philip Iverson question."

"Do you have anything?"

"We have what you have."

"What's that?" Becka asked.

"Questions."

■

"WILL THE OUTRAGE never end?"

Reverend Reggie Mayhew stood on the sidewalk in front of Santuario. Several other homeless activists fanned out behind him as he went about his unique method of making a statement to the press.

He asked questions.

"How many more unfortunate souls have to be murdered, cut down in the streets, before this city does something about it? Why weren't my colleagues or I notified after the second slaying?"

His colleagues, their hands folded in front of them, muttered their approval.

Jane, watching the TV in her office, noticed that Becka Flynn had gotten her place in front for the Reggie Mayhew Show.

"How can it *be*," the reverend continued, warming to it now, "that *three* of our lost children have to die before the police department of San Francisco says to itself, 'Oops, we have a problem'?" He shook his head gravely. "Do you find it as sad, as *infuriating*, as I do?"

Roz Shapiro entered with a phone message. Aunt Lucy. She glanced at the TV and left. Jane used the remote to turn off the television and picked up the phone.

"Happy birthday, sweetie," Aunt Lucy said.

"Thank you, Auntie." Jane turned her attention to her paperwork. Dr. Tedesco's report on Alan Ray, evidence release slips, victim possession manifests, a performance review form for Linda French. She initialed the pages and dropped them into her out-box for Finney to deal with.

Her pager pulsed. She snapped it from her belt. *Happy birthday, sexy. I love you. 3H61.* Smiling, she looked into the bullpen. Kenny smiled back and indicated that they were ready in Interrogation Room One.

Jane let her swivel chair fall forward. "I gotta go, Auntie. See you tonight." She rang off and started for the door. But something pulled her back.

Reaching across her desk, she retrieved Linda French's performance review form and slipped it into her bottom drawer.

■

THE BLOWUP OF the anonymous letter rested on an easel in the corner of Interrogation Room One.

But all eyes were on the blackboard.

Alan Ray's name now headed the third column, alongside Willie Temple and the John Doe. Beneath each name was a list, written in white chalk, of the evidence and facts known so far. Cause of death, the closed eyelids, the S-imagery, the absence of robbery as a motive, homeless victims.

Next to each of those was another list, written in yellow, of differences and unknowns. Willie Temple was black. John Doe and Alan Ray were white. Willie Temple had been in the army. Military service for the other two was still to be determined. Alan Ray was a drug user. Toxicology on the other two was pending. The flesh found in Willie Temple's mouth.

"Coupla new things to add," Linda French said. "Fingerprints on the third victim came back. Name's Alan Ray *Cross*." She wrote his last name on the board. "From Oakland. Multiple drug-related arrests. No military service. Also, I think Aaron has something for us."

Aaron Clark-Weber moved toward the blackboard. "The red cotton fiber turned up again. Not on the body of Mr. Cross, but in the rough wood on the bottom of the coffee table. Best guess is the perp brushed against it while he was on the floor doing the deed."

"Latex?" Kenny asked.

"In several places."

Jane studied the board. "What about the S-thing?"

"I faxed a copy of the latest one to Professor Akiyama. Also sent photos of all three to the FBI Behavioral Sciences Section. They both said the same thing: They were troubled by the progressive increase in size and detail of the images."

Lou Tronick sipped coffee from a World's Greatest Granddad mug. "What'd they think it meant?"

"The word they both used was *escalation*."

Jane let the portent of what Aaron had just said hang in the room. Then she looked to him and Linda French. "Any theories on the three dots?"

Aaron and Linda started to speak at the same time. Aaron demurred. Linda pointed to a photo of the latest S-message taken in the fleabag hotel. "What if each one represents a victim? Of course, we can't be sure until . . ."

"We catch the guy?" Kenny asked.

"Or," Linda added, "there's another killing."

"We're not going to wait around to prove or disprove that theory," Jane said. "I want you to triangulate the locations of the murder scenes. See if there's a geographical paradigm we should be paying attention to. I'm dedicating whatever we need of the funds the Chief authorized to double the manpower exposure. I want uniforms all over this city talking to everyone who ever laid eyes on these guys. Then . . ." She nodded to Finney. "Mike will input all of that data and give Inspectors Marks and French any cross-hits he comes up with. If they went to the same clinic. Crashed at the same mission. Did time in the same jail. Whatever. These guys have to have something in common besides being dead."

Finney wrote frantically on his clipboard, trying to keep up. "You got it, Lieutenant."

"Lou," Jane went on, "it's a long shot, but please go through all the old unsolved murder books. See if we're not dealing with somebody coming out of retirement. Also, how you doing with the videos of Iverson's banquet?"

"Almost done."

"Good." Jane gestured back to the blackboard. "And Linda . . ."

Cheryl Lomax ran in, out of breath. "Jane . . . uh, Lieutenant. The chief's on the phone. Says it's urgent!"

Jane started for the door.

Kenny rose from his chair. "I'll come with."

For a brief disconnected moment, Jane felt the others in the room following her into the bullpen. Before it could register fully, she had walked into her own surprise party.

The dispatch console was decorated with a handmade banner: 40 IS GOOD . . . 19 IS BETTER! HAPPY BIRTHDAY FROM YOUR FRIENDS AT PRECINCT 19!

A table had been set with champagne, presents, and a cake.

"That cake better be chocolate!" Jane said, thoroughly surprised and thoroughly delighted.

"I cannot tell a lie." Mike Finney turned the cake around to reveal a deep divot. "It's definitely chocolate!"

Everyone laughed. Kenny and Lou popped the champagne bottles and passed around foaming plastic cups. Roz Shapiro gathered up the presents and put them on Kenny's desk. As they all sang "Happy Birthday," their faces beaming, Jane couldn't help but think that it had been far too long since there had been any real joy in this squad room.

Kenny waded through the crowd and handed Jane the first present. "Happy birthday . . . partner."

Jane tore the wrapping from the gift and flipped the top off the box. "Oh, my God!"

"Let's see!" Aaron called from the back.

"I don't know, guys . . . I'm not sure if it's—"

"Lieutenant," Roz Shapiro said, "we're all either married or widowed. We can handle it!"

"Okay, you asked for it." She reached into the box and lifted out a sheer silk camisole.

Kenny pulled Jane into a hug and nodded to Cheryl. "I had help picking it out."

"And, girl?" Cheryl teased. "You is a *tiny* little thing!"

The bullpen erupted into laughter again.

Jane looked at their faces, loose and relaxed, and realized she was happy for them. Happy for herself.

She was about to pick up the next present when she noticed Aaron Clark-Weber. He was staring off to his right. One by one, the others sensed the change, their laughter subsiding. An uneasy silence rushed in to fill the vacuum.

There, standing by Roz Shapiro's empty reception desk, was Alice Iverson. A. J. Guthrie a few feet behind her.

She was livid.

"This is how you conduct a murder investigation?" Alice's teeth were clenched, her words coming in angry spurts. "My husband lies dead in his coffin, and his murderer is still somewhere out there with nothing to worry about because Homicide is having a party . . . with champagne and lingerie!" She whipped off her sunglasses and glared at Jane. "How dare you?"

Spinning on her heel, her pleated skirt catching the air, she stormed back into the elevator. A. J. Guthrie nodded slightly, then joined her.

Alice Iverson held Jane's eyes with her rage as the doors slid closed.

A long awkward beat passed. Then Kenny started to say something.

Jane held up her hand, stopping him. "Guys, thank you for this party. For the thought and the planning and the affection. But, when all is said and done . . . Mrs. Iverson is right."

"It was an innocent little diversion," Linda French said. "Can't we have lives, too?"

Jane dropped the camisole into the box. She picked up the top and fitted it onto the package. Pressing on it, closing it tighter than she needed to. Then she looked up and said, "No."

CHAPTER 28

∎

"Knock knock?"

Jane looked up from scouring the follow-up reports on the Iverson and homeless murders as Kenny came into her office.

"Just heard from Ruth Holmes. She's on a plane to some handwriting analysis meeting in Brussels, but she sent us an in-flight fax on that anonymous letter." He dropped it on her desk. "Basically, she's interested in the fact that the letter writer isn't asking for any reward money. The language is oblique, and she thinks that means the writer is frightened."

"Of what?"

"Or of whom. We don't know yet. But she'll keep working on it."

"Something to go on. How about the BMW tape? Any news on that decal?"

"Nothing yet. I think maybe I should go down there and rattle their cages."

"I think maybe you should."

Kenny crossed to the door. But he didn't leave. He stood in the doorway watching Jane read the fax. She lifted her eyes from the page. "What?"

"Just watching my wife." He turned to go. "I'll be at Com Lab rattling the aforementioned cages."

"You do that, tough guy."

Kenny grabbed his coat and keys from his desk and made his way toward the stairwell door. Roz Shapiro was taking down the birthday decorations. Mike Finney was on the phone with his list of Lexus dealers.

Beyond them, Lou Tronick was still working his way through the news footage of the Iverson banquet.

Jane felt separated from them all. Separated by the pane of glass that was always between them. By her rank.

" 'Scuse me, Jane." Linda French was at the door.

"What's up?"

Linda was charged, unable to stand still. "Got an ID on our John Doe." She came partway into the office. "Johnny O'Meara. Went to St. Francis here in the city. Dropped out of junior college . . ." She glanced at her notes. "Been in and out of alcohol treatment centers since he was fourteen. Mostly in."

"Military?"

"No." Linda closed her notebook. "Something interesting, though."

"What's that?"

"His father was SFPD. Uniform sergeant. Did his thirty and took his check."

Jane leaned forward. "We should go talk to him."

"He died in a nursing home three years ago. Also an alcoholic."

"Then dig into his file. See if anything calls your name." Jane stood up, drawing on Linda French's intensity. "Also, if Johnny O'Meara was in all those treatment centers, he may have crossed paths with Alan Ray Cross."

"You're right. I'll look into it." Linda took her car keys from her pocket.

"Where you going?" Jane asked.

"To inform the families"—Linda looked to Jane—". . . in person." She hurried away.

Jane pressed the intercom.

"What's up, Lieutenant?"

"Cheryl, I'm going out for about an hour. I'll have my cell phone and pager."

"Roger that." There was a moment of static. Neither of them wanting to disconnect. ". . . Hey, Jane?"

"Yeah?"

"You okay?"

Somewhere outside a siren wailed, dopplering past the precinct.

"I will be," Jane said. She took her coat from the door hook and left her office, drawn to go visit someone she hadn't seen for far too long.

■

A CHOCOLATE LAB, its tail wagging like a metronome, barked its greeting as Jane boarded Lieutenant Spielman's sailboat in the Tiburon Marina.

"Hershey, down, girl!" Ben Spielman shouted as he emerged from the cabin. He had aged years in the months since Jane had seen him. His thinning brown hair had yielded to gray and his once lively blue eyes were now dull, as if without moisture.

He had lost so much weight, his clothes seemed to belong to someone else.

Everything about him said loss.

Ben came across the afterdeck and embraced Jane. "I was so happy to hear from you. How's Ken?"

"He sends his love."

An oversized power cruiser was just leaving its slip, turning the water out as it churned along. Its wake rolled to either side, causing all the other boats at mooring to rise, then fall. Jane grabbed a halyard and rode it out.

"C'mon," Ben said, "let's go below. Get out of this chill." He lifted the hatch. "Watch your head. Hershey, come."

The dog bounded down the steps. Jane held both rails and followed her.

The cabin was cramped and very much lived in. Newspapers and magazines were strewn along the bunks. Fast-food wrappers and empty soup cans were piled in the sink. The coffeemaker was stained black, a chicory smell mingling with the salt air.

Jane pushed aside some old periodicals and sat down. "Mary around?"

Ben Spielman leaned back against the galley. "Nah, she was never much for boats. She's been volunteering, though, down at the crisis center and I . . ." He made a small sweeping gesture. "Well, I pass my days being a little self-indulgent." He poured himself a mug of coffee and sat heavily in a captain's chair. "So, the cases getting you down?"

"They're kicking the shit out of me, Ben." Jane was instantly grateful to talk to someone who had been there. "Sure, we've got stuff, but we can't pin down a motive in either one. We've been literally chasing our tails on Philip Iverson. And the homeless men? Not your usual serial sequence. It's like the stakes are being raised with each homicide."

"No motive there either?"

"We don't have fuck-all."

Hershey padded over to a well-worn L.L. Bean dog bed and flopped down with a breathy grunt.

"Jane, you've got a phenomenal solve rate. And you know that the physical aspects of a murder case—the victim, the witnesses, the evidence, all the science—combined with hard work and the occasional fresh idea almost always lead to a good catch."

"It's the *almost* that I'm worried about, Ben. That and the fact I'm getting grief from everywhere."

"The chief?"

"Especially the chief."

Ben tilted his chair back on its hind legs. "That's really the problem, isn't it? The whole issue of command is so complicated. You strive for it your whole career. Then, when you finally attain it, you start to feel . . ."

Jane seized the thought. ". . . removed from the process."

Ben Spielman's lips curled into a faint smile. But his eyes remained flat and distant. "Exactly."

"Any pearls?"

"Just one: Fuck the chief. You want to talk removed? He's so busy grooming himself for a mayoral run, he's completely out of the crime-solving loop. He should be thanking his lucky stars he has someone like you to take point on these cases."

"I can't ignore the guy, Ben. He's my boss and I knew what I was signing on for when I said yes to this promotion."

"I'm not telling you to ignore him. I'm telling you to do your job, follow your instincts, and crack these cases open. The irony is Walker McDonald can't live without *you*, not the other way around . . . and neither of you realizes it."

"So . . . ?"

"So . . . you've got a gift for this game. Just be the talented cop that you are and don't ever worry about what anybody thinks about you. Take your chances, make your mistakes, recover, and bust the bad guys."

The phone rang, its high-pitched trill feeling out of place in the timeless space of an old wooden sailboat. Hershey's ears turned like antennae at the sound. Ben dropped his chair back to the deck and got up to grab the portable handset off the chart shelf. "Hello . . . Hi, hon . . . Doesn't matter, whatever you like . . ." He bent down and passed into the forward cabin.

Jane noticed a row of framed photographs screwed to the wall behind where Ben Spielman had been sitting. She slid off the bunk and leaned in for a closer look. Benjy was in each of them. As a young boy on a carousel. With his mother and father in Tijuana. At his high-school graduation. His official Police Academy portrait.

Below these was a wide-angle group photo taken in the squad room of Precinct Nineteen. Jane and Kenny were on either side of Lieutenant Spielman. The rest of the cops were spread out in order of rank. Benjy stood at the far right, reaching up to put his arm around Mike Finney's shoulder.

The picture had been taken less than a week before he was killed.

"Mary says to tell you happy birthday."

Jane turned as Ben put the phone back in its cradle. She felt like she'd been caught peeking into someone's photo album. "Ben, I . . ."

The boat rocked over the swell of another craft's wake. Ben looked at the gallery of pictures. "They say time heals, Jane." He turned his head and Jane saw his eyes suddenly fill. And now she knew why they had seemed so dry before. He was always crying. Always wiping the tears away. "But that's bullshit. Time is a thief. A thief because it takes me further and further away from Benjy. Time is stealing my son from me."

Hershey whimpered and uncircled herself from her bed. She crossed the cabin, her nails clicking on the teak deck, and leaned against Ben's legs.

Like a child.

Ben Spielman dropped his hand and scratched the dog behind her ear.

Jane tried for a smile. "She's a good pup."

"She was Benjy's."

■

A SEAGULL HOVERED on an updraft above the harbormaster's office. It tilted its wings, letting the pocket of air slip by, and floated down to the roof. Squinting in the wind, it squatted next to the bare flagpole. Its head turned as if on a swivel as it watched Jane come up from the dock to the parking lot.

Crossing toward the Explorer, Jane thought about Lieutenant Spielman, her mentor and friend, and the gaping wound in his soul that would never heal. She looked across the bay to San Francisco's skyline, a panorama rendered colorless by the cloaking late-day haze.

And her thoughts went to Loretta Temple and A. J. Guthrie, and even to Alice Iverson.

And she knew why she had become a homicide cop.

And she understood that it was her job to bring relief, a brief sense of closure, to those who were left behind.

"3H58."

Jane reached into the car and picked up the microphone. "3H58. Go."

"Lieutenant, it's Mike Finney. Cheryl told me you were taking some personal time, but I think I have something."

"What's that?"

"Well, I talked to all the Lexus dealers like you said. Got the names of everyone who made a recent purchase of an LS430. Then I remembered, when Vicki and I bought that van a couple of years ago? The dealer wouldn't let me take it for a test drive without first Xeroxing my license . . ."

Jane got in the Explorer and twisted the key in the ignition. "Mike, tell me you got the licenses, the photo IDs, of everyone who test-drove a new Lexus."

"Sure did."

"Call Kenny and have him come back to the precinct." Jane stomped on the accelerator. She tore across the marina parking lot, startling the seagull off the roof. "I'll be right there."

CHAPTER 29

———■———

"HIS NAME'S EDDIE Lukic." Kenny slid a photocopy of a driver's license across the table. "Finney's running a background bio as we speak." Jane studied the face in the picture. Then she read the license itself:

CALIFORNIA
DRIVER LICENSE
D9333710
EDWARD PETER LUKIC
1401 SIERRA MADRE
SAN FRANCISCO, CA 94551
SEX: M   HAIR: BLK   EYES: BRN
HT: 5'11"   WT: 175
DOB: 8-19-74

"Born in seventy-four," she said. "Makes him what—twenty-eight, twenty-nine?"

"Naughty Alice is seeing a younger man."

Finney came into Interrogation Room One. "Got the vitals on Mr. Lukic."

Kenny started to reach for them, but Finney, not noticing, handed them to Jane. She quickly scanned the page. "Native of the Czech Republic. Former military. Tae Kwan Do instructor. Permit to carry concealed weapons, issued three years ago. Owns two registered handguns. A Walther nine-millimeter and"—she looked to Kenny—". . . a twenty-two." Jane turned to the second page. "One arrest. March 2000. Aggravated assault. Later dismissed when the witness refused to press."

"A Tae Kwan Do instructor," Kenny said, "driving a fifty-five-thousand-dollar car?"

"Sixty-two thousand," Finney said. "With extras."

"You're proving my point, Moby."

"Money?" Finney asked.

"And lots of it."

Lou Tronick crossed from the coffee setup toward the video monitor. "Got something?"

"A solid lead on a suspect," Jane said.

"Homeless or Iverson?"

Kenny handed him the photocopy. "Iverson."

Lou blew on his coffee and took a sip as he checked out the picture. Then he put his mug on the table so abruptly, a half inch of liquid sloshed out. "Jesus, guys, c'mere!"

He hurried to his monitor and VCR; Jane, Kenny, and Finney following. Lou ejected a tape and inserted another. Then he pressed "FF" and the image chattered quickly ahead. "This one's from KBBI. What they call B-roll. Background footage of whatever story they're covering so they have something to cut away to." He pressed "stop," then "rewind," "stop" again, then "play." After a few seconds, he pushed "pause."

Kenny leaned forward. "Holy shit."

There, in a shimmering still image, standing in the crowd at the rear of the Crystal Ballroom of the Golden Gate Grand, was Eddie Lukic. He was wearing a tuxedo and his eyes were riveted on a man who was just entering the banquet hall.

Philip Iverson.

■

THE STRIP MALL on Octavio Street, just across from Lafayette Park, was like a hundred others in the city. A florist, a Vietnamese nail salon, a defunct bookstore, a liquor store, and a shoe repair shop.

Between the nail salon and the closed bookstore—sheets of white paper covering its windows—was a Tae Kwan Do studio.

Eddie Lukic led a small class of teenagers, middle-aged men, and housewives through the final stages of a rigorous workout. When they finished, the students bowed deeply at the waist, paying respect to their master. Eddie pressed his palms together at his chest and returned the ancient Korean gesture.

"He is one limber son of a bitch," Kenny said.

He and Jane sat in an unmarked car at the far end of the parking lot, Eddie's new white Lexus between them and the studio. After the previous day's chase, they didn't want to chance Lukic recognizing the Explorer.

"Remember," Jane cautioned, watching Eddie through the studio window as he zipped up his gym bag. "He could be packing. Let's play this cool. If he runs on us, let backup take over."

Kenny checked the rearview. Two plainclothes cops sat in an idling muscle car at the near curb. Two more were in another car across the street, pointed in the other direction. Just in case.

Jane touched his arm. "Here he comes."

Eddie Lukic slung his gym bag over his shoulder, waved to a few lingering students, and stepped out of his studio. He pointed his keys at the Lexus and pressed the remote. The headlights and taillights pulsed for an instant as the automatic door locks popped up.

Jane and Kenny climbed out of their car and approached Lukic, ready to intercept him before he could get to his car.

"Mr. Lukic?" Kenny said.

"Maybe." Lukic, immediately wary, let his gym bag slip to the ground. "Who are you?"

Kenny started to reach into his coat for his shield. As he did, Eddie Lukic suddenly spun on the ball of his right foot and whipped his left leg around. Kenny instinctively ducked, the heel of Lukic's foot glancing off the top of his head. But the blow was still strong enough to send Kenny down to one knee.

Flattening his hands into weapons as lethal as ax handles, Lukic drew back for the kill.

Jane threw down her purse to reveal her pistol pointed at Lukic's face. She thumbed back the hammer and strode forward. "You so much as flinch and you're dead where you stand!"

Lukic let his whole body relax, a thin smile playing across his lips.

Kenny regained his feet, turned Lukic around, and slapped a pair of cuffs on him.

"You're cops?" Lukic said over his shoulder in a thick Eastern European accent. "Why didn't you say so?"

The backup officers were just running into the lot as Kenny shoved Lukic across the hood of his Lexus and patted him down. "You never gave us the chance."

"I don't give chances . . . or take them."

"He's clean." Kenny stepped back and motioned to one of the other cops. "Take him to Nineteen. Check his gym bag and the studio. We'll send someone to his house."

As Eddie Lukic was led away, Jane came up and put her hand on Kenny's back. "He hurt you?"

Kenny pushed his hair back off his forehead. "Nah, I'm okay." He bent down to pick up Jane's purse. "Thought you said we were gonna play it cool."

"No way he gets away from us again." Jane eased the hammer forward on her gun and dropped it into her bag. "Besides, the guy kicked my husband."

CHAPTER 30

■

EDDIE LUKIC WAS incredulous. "You think I *what?*"

He sat on a metal chair in Interrogation Two, his cuffed hands on the small table before him. Jane sat across from him, a tape recorder between them. Kenny stood with his back against the doorjamb.

"I will repeat for the record, Mr. Lukic," Jane said, "that you are being detained because you are a suspect in the murder of Philip Iverson."

"On what grounds?"

Kenny pushed away from the wall. "It's the proverbial laundry list. You own a twenty-two-caliber handgun. Philip Iverson was shot with a twenty-two-caliber handgun. You have a history of physical violence. You were videotaped at the Crystal Ballroom the night of the crime. You make something like twenty-seven thousand dollars a year and you drive a sixty-thousand-dollar car. You made a deposit in your personal account of one hundred thousand dollars a week before the murder . . ."

Jane picked it up. "And, Mr. Lukic, you have an intimate relationship with Alice Iverson, the decedent's widow."

Eddie Lukic started to say something, his lips parting slightly. Then he drew it back. His shoulders slumping, he looked away and shook his head.

Jane shot a quick glance to Kenny, then turned back to Lukic. "Do you have anything to say, sir?"

"Yes. Yes, I do." Eddie looked directly at Jane, then pressed closer to the tape recorder. "I want a lawyer."

■

"YES, EDDIE AND I are lovers."

Alice Iverson's manner was matter-of-fact, as if she were talking about what she'd had for lunch. She took a bottle of Evian from the refrigerator behind the bar. Without offering anything to Jane or Kenny, she unscrewed the top and took a sip.

"Did your husband know?" Kenny asked. He was standing across the room near the massive bookcases.

"Yes." Alice came around the bar and sat on the arm of the couch.

Jane sat in the club chair and crossed her legs. "How'd he find out?"

"I told him."

Kenny moved into a splash of light coming in the west-facing window. "What was his reaction?"

"The same as with all the others," Alice said, already annoyed with the triviality of these questions. "He understood that it was part of our arrangement. A significant part."

"Had this . . . arrangement . . ." Jane asked, "been a part of your marriage since the beginning?"

"No. It was six or seven years ago that Philip started becoming distant, withdrawn. He wouldn't talk about it, but it had to be some sort of midlife crisis. He just lost interest in his work, in his friends . . . in his wife. Everything except the foundation. He was obsessed with leaving something behind, with making a difference in this life."

Jane regarded Alice Iverson, struck by her utter lack of emotion as she revealed the darkest secrets of her marriage. "Did you feel abandoned by your husband?"

"Not really. Truth is, our sex life was never all that . . . satisfying. It's one of the reasons we never had children."

"Did you want to have kids?" Jane asked.

"Very much so at first." Alice put the Evian bottle on the end table and toyed with the cap. "But as I got older, the prospect of having children became more and more improbable . . . and less and less important. I had to make my own peace with that."

Jane hesitated, her own feelings about motherhood and the possibility of missing that opportunity pushing their way forward. She willed herself to stay focused. "Didn't you feel abandoned, betrayed, by your husband?"

"More like compromised."

"And did this feeling of being compromised," Kenny asked, "make you angry?"

"Not angry so much as disappointed. But, like I said, I made my peace with it. I got a privileged lifestyle from Philip. And I got physical comfort and sex from other men."

"That's all it was with Mr. Lukic," Jane asked, "physical?"

"That's all."

Kenny approached the couch where Alice was sitting. "What about the hundred thousand dollars Mr. Lukic recently put into his bank account. Do you know anything about that?"

"I gave it to him."

"Why?"

Alice sighed. "Because he's boring, in bed and out of bed. And I'm going to break off with him. Giving money to these men reminds me and them that the relationship is just a convenience. Something I'm willing to pay for. It's how I avoid becoming attached to them."

"But don't they become attached to you?" Jane asked.

"Sometimes."

"In love with you?"

"Sometimes."

Jane rose from the club chair. "Did Eddie Lukic fall in love with you?"

"I suppose he did."

"In love with you enough to want to kill your husband? To have you all to himself?"

Alice stood up as well. She inched forward, closer and closer, to Jane. "Y'know, Lieutenant, that thought simply never occurred to me. But then I don't have to think in such suspicious and ugly terms, do I?" She abruptly turned away, tossing the bottle cap onto the coffee table. It bounced once and rolled off. Alice Iverson ignored it. She had people who would pick it up. "If you think Eddie was involved in Philip's murder," she said as she headed for the door, "why don't you ask him?"

Just as she reached the door, it was pushed open by Mr. Kim and Alice walked out. Mr. Kim stepped into the room, picked up the bottle cap, and addressed Jane and Kenny. "Come, I call elevator for you."

CHAPTER 31

━━━━━■━━━━━

"ALICE SAID THAT?" Eddie Lukic asked. "You're sure?"

He was back in Interrogation Two. A young female lawyer now at his side.

Jane adjusted the microphone attached to the tape recorder. "Yes, Mr. Lukic. I'm sure."

Eddie sagged. "Then I mean nothing to her."

"Mr. Lukic," Kenny said from the doorway. "How did you meet Mrs. Iverson?"

Eddie Lukic looked to his attorney. She nodded.

"You were right. I don't make much money teaching tae kwon do. So I take jobs working security, as a bodyguard. One night I was at this function providing security for someone else and I meet Alice in the lobby. We got to talking and she said she was interested in learning self-defense. I offered to teach her. 'In private,' she says." He shrugged. "Anyway, two things led to another and we started . . . seeing each other."

"What were you doing at that banquet the night Mr. Iverson was murdered?" Jane asked.

"Providing security for Judge Blevins."

The young lawyer cleared her throat. "Superior Court, Alameda County."

Jane nodded. "Thank you."

"But we left early, the judge and me," Eddie added.

"How early?"

"Ten-thirty maybe."

"Where does the judge live?"

"Greenbrae."

"That's in Marin," the lawyer offered, justifying her presence.

"Philip Iverson was killed roughly around midnight," Kenny said. "That would leave you plenty of time to get up to Greenbrae . . . Marin . . . and get back again."

The lawyer pushed back in her chair and started to rise. "My client has responded truthfully to your questions. It's my responsibility to advise him to—"

"Counselor," Jane said sternly, "your client had motive, opportunity, and method to commit this crime. Everything we're saying in this room is being recorded. If anything is out of line, let the court decide."

Caught between standing and sitting, the young lawyer hesitated. Then she sat back down.

Eddie Lukic cleared his throat. "Please. I want to talk. I didn't kill Philip Iverson."

Kenny put both his hands on the table. "Can you prove it?"

"No," Eddie said, ". . . but Judge Blevins can."

■

THE PHOTOGRAPHS IN Judge Blevins's study spanned the life of a marriage. The eager young man in a tuxedo and the beautiful young woman in her wedding dress. The couple with their two small children. Graduations, vacations, holiday meals, Christmas mornings.

The door opened and a woman in her early sixties hurried in. She was the woman in the pictures. Somewhere along the way she had passed from beautiful to handsome. She thrust out her hand to Kenny. "Lieutenant Candiotti, I'm Judge Monica Blevins. So sorry to keep you waiting. But I've got company for dinner."

Kenny took her hand. "I'm Inspector Marks." He nodded to Jane. "This is Lieutenant Candiotti."

Monica Blevins shook Jane's hand and laughed. "Well, aren't I the sexist pig? My apologies to both of you."

"We'll be brief, Judge," Jane said. "Then you and your husband can get back to your evening."

The judge moved to a photo on the fireplace mantel. She and her husband were on a cruise ship, dining at the captain's table. "My husband passed four years ago, Lieutenant."

"Now I'm the one who's sorry."

"That's quite all right. What can I do for you?"

"This is about Philip Iverson's murder."

"Damn shame that was. I was at his banquet the night he was killed," the judge began. Then she stopped and smiled. "But you already know that. That's why you're here."

"Judge," Kenny said, "we want to ask you about Eddie Lukic."

There was the slightest, almost imperceptible change in Judge Blevins's posture. "What about him?"

"Was he working security for you that night?" Kenny asked.

"I had been presiding over a pretty serious drug case and my department thought it best that I had an escort."

"We understand," Jane said. "Did you leave the dinner early?"

"Sometime after ten. Tell the truth, I'm not big on those things, and I was rather tired from some long hours at work. So I made my appearance, ate my chicken, and left."

Kenny made a note in his pad. "And got back here to Greenbrae around when?"

"Somewhere between ten-thirty and eleven."

"So conceivably," Jane said, "Mr. Lukic could have had time to get back to the Golden Gate Grand and commit—"

Judge Blevins held up her hand. "No, he couldn't have."

"Couldn't have what," Kenny asked, "committed the crime?"

"Eddie Lukic, Inspector, couldn't have had the time . . . because he was here, in my house, until after two in the morning."

The door opened slightly. An older woman in an apron stepped partway into the room. "Dinner, Judge."

"I'll be there in a minute. Thank you, Olga." Judge Blevins turned to Jane and Kenny. "Draw your own conclusions if you must . . . and you'll be right. If called, I'd even testify in court as to his whereabouts." She went to the door. "But I'd hate to."

■

JANE AND KENNY headed south over the Golden Gate Bridge, against the early-evening traffic.

"You're quiet," Kenny said as they passed beneath the North Tower, the city's striking skyline to their left.

"This case is making me crazy." Jane turned to him, the setting sun behind her. "And I hate being wrong."

"They were all solid leads, and now they're out of the way." Kenny's eyes wrinkled into a smile. "Besides, it's not so much being wrong as it is not being right yet. It's the process."

"But you always say process is just the kind of girl talk that drives you up a wall."

The traffic slowed. Kenny tapped the brake. "I'm older now. And wiser."

"And married."

"That, too."

They drove along in silence. Jane watched her husband as the muscle in his jaw worked up and down. "Ken?"

"Yum?"

"It happened again tonight. Someone automatically assuming that you're in charge because you're the man in the room."

"Does that bother you?"

Jane let out a little laugh of surprise. "Not at all. I've been up against that kind of sexist shit since I joined the force." She slid her hand under Kenny's right thigh. "I was really concerned about how it affected you."

Kenny drew a deep breath through his nose, his chest filling. Then he let the air slip out between his lips. "Full disclosure? I hate it." The traffic loosened up and he accelerated. "I'm trying to deal. But sometimes it's hard. Now, when we meet someone for the first time, I want to jump in and say, 'She's the lieutenant, I'm the inspector' before it gets too awkward." He glanced over to Jane. "But it's not natural. We're cops. I want to walk into a room and just listen, not start yakking and making excuses."

They cruised under the South Tower, picking up speed. "But the fish we have to fry right now are so much bigger, we'll deal with my stuff later." Kenny took Jane's hand. "Besides, it's someone's birthday."

"I can't believe it," Jane said. "I completely forgot."

"It's kind of been a busy day."

■

OKAY, ONE MORE . . . hold it, hold it . . . nice."

Jane and Aunt Lucy leaned across the corner of the dining-room table, cheek to cheek. Timmy made one last focus adjustment on his Nikon and took the picture.

"That's all, Timmy," Jane said to her brother. "I want to have my cake and eat it, too."

"Your slightest wish." Kenny handed Jane a kitchen knife and slipped the cake onto her place mat.

Jane turned the knife around and offered it to Aunt Lucy. "You do the honors."

As Lucy took the knife, Kenny leaned over to refill Jane's wineglass. "You all right?"

"Yeah, fine. Just . . . forty."

"Presents!" Timmy scooped the gifts off the sideboard and laid them on the table. Although they were different sizes, they were all vaguely the same shape.

Jane smiled as she realized what they were. The only things she wanted.

She peeled the wrapping off the first one. A framed photograph of Poppy and his brothers taken in the early fifties. Five handsome men caught in a moment in time in some dark forgotten room with heavy brocade drapery. Poppy, the youngest, was in the center, his eyes gleaming like new coins.

The next gift was Aunt Lucy's wedding portrait. She wore an

ivory-colored gown; Uncle Rocco, home from the navy, wore his uniform. Then a picture of Jane's mother walking down a street wheeling a baby carriage. She smiled shyly for the camera, her left hand clutching the hand of a little girl. Jane's hand.

Finally, a photo of Jane and Poppy taken at a backyard barbecue a few days before he died. Jane had her head on his shoulder, and his eyes, still gleaming fifty years later, were looking directly into the lens.

Father and daughter.

Jane's eyes brimmed as she raised her eyes and looked at her family. "Thank you all so much. There's nothing in this world I would rather have."

CHAPTER 32

———■———

IT SEEMED TO Jane that the cops on her Homicide Team were coming in earlier and earlier every day. She and Kenny had barely set foot in the squad room when Mike Finney hustled up to them.

"Got it," he announced, unable to suppress a grin.

Kenny pulled off his jacket while Jane checked the stack of messages on Cheryl's dispatch console.

"Got what?" Kenny asked, looking over Jane's shoulder at the pink phone slips.

"The BMW."

Jane and Kenny looked up at the same time.

"Lab called five minutes ago. Because Inspector Marks went down there and stressed how important this is, someone pulled an all-nighter."

"So," Jane said, "what was on that bumper? Was it a decal?"

"Yes. For a company called JefTek. Some big-deal start-up. Owner's name is Jeff Levy."

"Owner of the car," Kenny asked, "or owner of the company?"

"Owner of both."

Kenny cocked his head. "Was it someone on the banquet list?"

"Nope," Finney said. "And he wasn't a guest at the hotel that night either. I checked." His smile grew wider.

"What?" Jane asked.

"So . . . I called Mr. Levy and asked him was the car his. And he said yes, but it was totaled a month ago. And . . ." Finney paused, almost too proud to go on.

Kenny made a show of reaching for his pistol. "Are you going to tell us why you're smiling, or do I have to shoot you?"

Finney glanced at Kenny's Glock 17. "So I have Cheryl find me a patrol unit in the area and they cruise JefTek's parking lot. And the Beamer is . . ."

"There?" Jane asked.

"You bet, there," Finney said. "Untotaled."

"Great work, Mike," Jane said. She and Kenny started toward the door.

"Hey, Moby," Kenny called back. "Find whoever's in charge of security for JefTek and patch him through to my car." He turned to Jane. "Ready?"

"Come on!" She raced down the stairs, drawn at last by the hope that one clue had finally led to another.

■

KENNY HATED EVERYTHING about Jeff Levy.

The long black hair, the rectangular yellow-tinted eyeglasses, the black suit with too many buttons, the black phone on his black leather belt.

His rich daddy.

Jane and Kenny stood across from Jeff Levy in his enormous office in the Cannery, overlooking Fisherman's Wharf; and overlooking the parking lot where his anthracite-gray BMW 740il sat in his parking place. Pictures of Levy with his family were lined up in perfect rows along the black enamel divan.

Everything about this place and this person exuded confidence, control.

"Yeah, I lied about the car being totaled," Jeff Levy said dismissively. "I make it a policy never to get involved in police business."

"Too late," Kenny said. "You're involved. We've got you, or at least your car, at the exact same place at the exact same time as the murder of Philip Iverson." He thrust his face into Jeff Levy's. "I'll only ask you once, Jeff. Where were you that night?"

Levy sat back, pulling away from Kenny. "I was home. My family was asleep . . . and I was watching television."

"Bullshit!" Kenny slammed his fist on Levy's desk. "Do *not* waste our time, Jeff."

"Mr. Levy," Jane said softly.

Jeff Levy leaned toward her, seeking the calm in her voice.

"Mr. Levy, on our way over here," Jane continued, "we called your wife. She said you were working that night. Working way past midnight."

"That kind of discrepancy," Kenny said, "makes us curious. And a little bit suspicious."

Levy's shoulders fell, his bravado evaporating. He started to say something, then held it back.

Jane and Kenny could feel it. This guy was a goner.

"Being we're so suspicious, we checked with your chief of security on our way over here," Kenny went on. "He pulled the in-out records for that night. Guess what? You were out."

"But, Mr. Levy," Jane said, "in that it's your policy never to get involved in police business, maybe we should call your wife, bring her down to the station, and ask *her* about the discrepancy."

Kenny inched forward, wanting Levy to feel them closing in. "We could show her the surveillance video from the Golden Gate Grand. Jeff racing away in his Beamer. After that we could run the enhanced surveillance video that clearly shows—"

"Okay." Jeff Levy sagged. "I was there."

"We already know that," Kenny said. "The question is: What were you doing there?"

Levy's eyes drifted to the photos of his family. "I was . . . with someone. In my car."

"Doing?" Kenny asked.

"Not exactly doing . . . more like receiving." He looked to Jane, then quickly looked away.

"Don't be shy on my account, Mr. Levy," Jane said. "I'm a cop. There's no way you're going to offend or surprise me."

"So," Kenny prodded, "you're in your BMW . . . receiving. And . . . ?"

"And I heard a shot. From above us. And I split. End of story."

"What was her name?" Jane asked.

"Whose name?"

"The hooker's."

Jeff Levy swiveled in his black Aeron chair until he faced the photos of his family. "*His* name," he said. "I was with a guy." He dropped his head back. "He was so . . ."

"Young?" Kenny urged. "Talented?"

"Beautiful."

Jane glanced at Kenny, then returned to Levy. "Did he tell you his name? Even a street name?"

"No."

"Where'd you meet him?" Kenny asked.

"I picked him up in the Castro. By the bookstore. He was wearing this necklace. Pukka shells, y'know? We talked about it for a minute. Then he got in the car." Levy turned back to them, his eyes red and teary behind his yellow-tinted glasses. "Look, I've got a wife and kids. I don't want my life to be ruined by the police."

"Seems to us," Kenny said, "you're doing a pretty good job of that yourself." He put both hands flat on the desk and pressed closer. "And if you're lying to us, if you waste another second of our time . . ."

Jeff Levy started to rise. Kenny gave the slightest shake of his head and he settled back down. "Please . . ."

"I believe you," Jane said.

Relief swept across Levy's face.

They owned him.

"Here's what we need you to do," Jane continued. "Come to the station and sit with a police artist. Go through some mug books of known male prostitutes, stuff like that. Everything checks out, we'll stay out of your life." She dropped a card on his desk. "I'm assuming that when we look into it, there will be no connection between you and Philip Iverson."

"No, none."

"Good. It's best you don't leave town for a while."

"But I've got—"

"Cancel it, Jeff," Kenny said. He and Jane moved to the door. "By the way, what sort of business is JefTek?"

"We make . . . surveillance equipment."

▪

"ELEVATOR OR STAIRS?" Jane asked.

"Stairs." Kenny pulled the stairwell door open. "I know how much you love your exercise." They started down. At the first landing, Jane turned back to him.

"This is a good lead. Something feels right about it."

Kenny caught up to her. "I agree. But that thing about Levy's wife saying he was working late? You never made that call, did you?"

"Nah." Jane grinned. "I was fishing."

"Well, he sure bit," Kenny said as they worked their way down the next flight. "Big-time."

▪

JANE RODE IN silence as Kenny moved the Explorer up Stockton Street.

Once clear of the construction sites near the Wharf, he accelerated up the hill and passed a cable car. "I'll talk to the vice guys about Mr. Levy's hooker," he offered, feeling his way around Jane's mood. "Might even have to do some field research."

He glanced over to Jane. She was staring out the window. Kenny reached across and put his hand on her leg. "What?"

"I don't know if you want to go there right now."

"From the way you sound," Kenny said, "I *know* I don't want to go there right now . . . but we probably should. What is it?"

"You were a little rough on Jeff Levy back there."

"Levy?" Kenny said, surprised. "He's an asshole."

"Maybe so. But you jumped down his throat without provocation. In fact, *you* were provoking him. Antagonizing him for no good reason."

"There's a good reason," Kenny protested. "He's a spoiled rich kid who's had everything in life handed to him. Not unlike, by the way, how you feel about Alice Iverson."

"Ken?" Jane said gently.

"Yeah?"

"I'm gonna step onto some thin ice here."

"Okay," Kenny said warily. "Go."

"You're deflecting. What happened between you and Jeff Levy has nothing to do with how I feel about Alice Iverson."

"Deflecting? From what?"

Jane paused, searching for the right words. "From what we talked about last night. The fact that I'm in command."

Kenny started to protest, but Jane pressed on.

"Look, every time I bring it up, you tell me it's not a good time." She put her hand on his shoulder. "But there's this current of anger in you just beneath the surface. When someone like Levy is added to the mix . . . you blow."

Kenny turned onto Prince Street and entered the precinct's parking garage. He worked his jaw, his cheek flexing. Finally, he turned to Jane. "I don't agree."

"Fine. Then tell me what's going on between you and Chief McDonald's driver. What big button of yours is he pushing?"

Kenny pulled into Jane's spot, the one closest to the stairs. "I'm gonna go talk to the vice guys."

"So this is us, once again, saying it's not a good time to talk about it?"

"This is us." Kenny shifted into reverse and waited for Jane to open her door.

Frustrated, Jane climbed down from the Explorer and there was Linda French. "Sorry to bother."

"No bother," Jane said. She turned to watch Kenny leave. He drove the Explorer through the exit without stopping, causing a motorcycle officer to come up short.

"He all right?" Linda asked.

"Yeah, sure. Just in a hurry, like always," Jane said. "So . . . what do you have?"

Linda held the stairwell door open. "Every angle I try on Johnny O'Meara's ex-SFPD father comes up as dead as he is. Except for one thing."

"What's that?"

"I got to talking with all these veteran cops about O'Meara's dad and about how Johnny O'Meara turned homeless and got himself killed and—"

Jane stopped at the first step. By now she recognized the current of excitement in Linda's voice. "I'm all ears."

Linda French took her notebook from her purse. "Anyway, a couple of them told me about some ex-con way back when. This tough street guy who killed a homeless man for a half bottle of T-Bird. With a knife."

"And the fuzzy recollections of a bunch of old-timers is relevant to us because . . . ?"

"Because I checked it out and the ex-con is Reggie Mayhew."

Jane started toward Linda's car. "The good Reverend Mayhew is about to be visited by two cops on a mission."

CHAPTER 33

■

THE LINE OUTSIDE Santuario snaked around the block.

Homeless men, women, and children huddled into one another. Wanting out of the cold, out of the fear. Santuario was about to serve lunch, and the ones who were lucky enough to get in were not going to leave until morning.

The aroma of something savory floated to Jane and Linda as they entered the dining hall. Half a dozen cooks stood, like spirits in the steam, over huge kettles. They stirred their pots with what looked like canoe paddles. A middle-aged black woman moved quickly from station to station. Tasting, spicing, cajoling.

"That's Esther Peacock." Reggie Mayhew had come up behind them. "She was a cook in the army. Desert Storm, the whole thing. Esther can feed a hundred people on a chicken, an onion, and a bag of rice. And leave them smilin' their thank-yous all day long."

He took Jane and Linda by the arms and guided them to a corner. "This joint's gonna be jumpin' in five minutes and I'm gonna be kinda busy. So we should maybe have our little meeting right here, if you ladies don't mind."

Reggie Mayhew's grip on Jane's arm was firm and potent in a way that turned suggestions into commands. This was a man, she thought, a former athlete, who still very much lived in the physical world.

They sat at a picnic table, a tray of plastic utensils and saltshakers in the center.

"I'm hoping," Reggie said, "that you're coming all the way down here with some good news. Like you caught the man's been doing these awful things."

"I wish I could tell you that too, sir," Jane said. "It's what we all want."

"But we have a lot of good evidence," Linda French added.

"Evidence?" Reggie Mayhew snorted. "Should I tell my flock it's safe to sleep on the steam vents and in the alleys and in the parks because you have 'a lot of good evidence'?"

"Well, no . . ." Linda reflexively reached for her notebook, then stopped. "Perhaps if—"

"Reverend Mayhew," Jane said, "can we just ask you a few questions?"

"Of course, Lieutenant." He smiled, his gold teeth catching the false light of the fluorescents.

A kitchen worker started for the front doors. Jane could see the faces, dark silhouettes in the steamy windows, pressing forward as he got closer, keys in hand.

"Tell me about you serving time," Jane said abruptly.

Reggie Mayhew's smile dropped as if it had been cut. "I had a debt to society, Lieutenant, and I paid it. In full." He stood up so quickly, he seemed to do it without moving. First he was sitting; then he was standing, towering over Jane and Linda. "I hit bottom. The hard undignified bottom of despair. Of shame! And I climbed out, scraping and scratching and bleeding, to a place where I, with the help and grace of God, am blessed to be able to help others!"

He was yelling now. The kitchen staff stopped to watch. Esther Peacock scurried among them, barking at them to finish preparing the food.

"And that's what I do every day, *every* day, of the year. I work in service to those people out there. And *every* day I thank God for the privilege to do His work in His name!"

Jane rose, trying to stay calm in the storm of Mayhew's anger. "Put yourself in my place, Reverend. Homeless people are being murdered. The director of one of the city's biggest shelters has a manslaughter conviction for killing a homeless man . . . What would *you* do?"

"My fucking homework," Reggie seethed. "When Willie Temple was killed, I was addressing the Homeless Advocacy Council at the Church of the Good Shepherd in Oakland. Do some homework and you'll see I had over five hundred witnesses that night. When John O'Meara was killed, I was in San Diego visiting my mother. Do some homework and you'll see I was seven hundred miles away . . . *overnight.* And when Alan Ray Cross was killed, I was conducting a prayer vigil for one of my colleagues at the AIDS Hospice." He stopped to catch his breath, his eyes flashing with anger. "Now get out of here, Lieutenant."

The doors opened and a cascade of people poured in; cold, hungry, anxious.

Reverend Mayhew turned to them, his arms outstretched like a player in his own biblical movie. "Come, children. Oh yes. Eat. Chase away the chill. Thank you all for coming here. God loves you so."

CHAPTER 34

—■—

"GUESS WHO'S GAY."

Kenny strode into Jane's office. Any vestige of their earlier confrontation now gone.

Jane accepted this . . . for now. It was how they survived. "Guess who's an asshole," she said as she hung up the phone.

Mike Finney was sitting on the couch. He had been taking notes while Jane was on the phone with Ruth Holmes, the handwriting analyst. Uncertain as to where this conversation was going, he started to get up. The couch was soft and deep, and given Finney's prodigious size, extricating himself was not an easy task.

"You first," Kenny said.

"The Reverend Reggie Mayhew is an asshole."

"There's a surprise." Kenny came around and sat on the edge of her desk. "What'd he do now?"

"Linda French came to me. One of O'Meara's old cronies from the force told her about Mayhew having done a manslaughter turn. He killed a homeless man back in 1977. Killed him with a knife."

"No shit?"

"Absolutely none."

Just as Finney finally got out of the couch, Jane signaled for him to stay. "So we go down to Santuario to talk to him and he goes all . . ."

"Indignant?"

Jane nodded. "The man eats, sleeps, and breathes indignation. He also has three airtight alibis." She closed the folder on her desk and handed it across to Finney. "So who's gay?"

"I've been out with the vice guys tracking JefTek's male hooker." Kenny unfolded a copy of the police artist's sketch.

Jane smoothed it out on her blotter. "Mr. Levy was right. This kid is gorgeous."

"Down, girl," Kenny said.

Finney craned for a better look.

"Anyway," Kenny continued, "there's this whole subculture of high-end hookerdom. We've heard about it before. Politicians, businessmen, actors. And the name of a very prominent professional baseball player was mentioned."

"Local?"

"Yup."

"Giants or A's?"

Kenny smiled. "You really want to know?"

"You know what?" Jane said. "As the last bastion of decency in this division, I don't."

"I'll tell you later."

"Any progress finding Pretty Boy, or were you too busy looking into closets?"

Kenny stood up and stretched. "We did a full distribution of the sketch. It'll be in every patrol car and briefing room by tonight. Vice will take care of the Castro for us. If he's still in town, we'll find him."

"Great, thanks for doing that," Jane said. "I just got off the phone with Ruth Holmes from—"

"The FBI," Finney interjected.

"—from *Brussels*. Something turned up in that letter." Jane pulled a copy of the anonymous letter from one of the "active" folders. "She's sending it on to the Bureau's Behavior and Psyche Sections. What she did come up with was the fact that the letter writer is a woman. Something about the indentation, the punctuation, the whole presentation."

"She sure?" Kenny asked.

Jane nodded. "Pretty positive."

"Interesting. Spurned lover?"

"Anything's possible."

"I'll do some follow-up with Ruth," Kenny offered. "She have anything to say about the numbers on the bottom?"

"Not yet. We've got Com Lab sequencing and resequencing them. Running them backward and forward, out of order, et cetera. We'll cross every combination with their mainframe. Plus FBI, plus NCIC. Plus, plus, *plus!*" Jane slammed the letter down on the desk, a wave of frustration washing over her. "Plus I've got two killers still out there and we don't know who or where the fuck they are!"

Finney cleared his throat. "Uh, Lieutenant?"

Jane looked over to him.

Chief McDonald was standing in the doorway.

"Lieutenant," he began, "I just got a call from Reverend Mayhew. He was quite . . ."

"Indignant?" Jane asked.

▪

KENNY SAT AT his desk, watching Jane's door.

Her office had been closed, the blinds drawn, for almost half an hour. He gathered up his notes and crossed to Reception. "This needs to be messengered over to Lieutenant Clark-Weber as soon as possible," he said to Roz Shapiro.

Roz looked up from the phone log she was typing. "I'll take care of it, Inspector."

"Thanks." Just as Kenny turned to go back into the homicide bullpen, the elevator doors opened and Devon Haskell stepped out. Kenny was stuck. He couldn't ignore Haskell and just walk away. It felt weak, inadequate somehow. And there was no way to stay where he was and have a civil conversation with this man. He nodded tightly. "Seeing a lot of you lately, Dev."

"Only because my boss has to keep such close tabs on *your* boss."

Roz Shapiro swiveled her chair around and went back to work; typing even faster.

Kenny closed in on Haskell. "What is this stick you have up your ass?"

Haskell sniffed a contemptuous laugh. "Like you don't know."

"If you're talking about what I think you are, all that's so far in the past I forgot it even happened." Kenny shrugged. "So let's just move on, okay?"

Devon Haskell peered into Kenny's eyes, holding his gaze without blinking. "No."

There was a sudden change in the bullpen as people reacted to Jane's door opening. Chief McDonald paused in the doorway to shake Jane's hand. Then he crossed the squad room, nodding hello to Lou Tronick as he went.

Jane looked across and saw Kenny standing jaw to jaw with Devon Haskell. With a slight tilt of her head, she motioned for Kenny to join her. "The whip cracks," Haskell whispered as the chief approached. Kenny let it slide and headed for Jane's office.

"Please tell me," Kenny said as he came in, "we don't have to go make nice to the reverend."

"Oh God, no. The chief hates Reggie Mayhew. Calls him that Sharpton-Lite prick. And you please tell me you and Devon Haskell were just making nice out there."

"Two old friends catching up."

"Bullshit, Ken."

Kenny reached over and pushed the door closed. "Are you so concerned because you're my wife, or because you're my lieutenant?"

"C'mon, Ken. That's unfair."

"Actually, it's pertinent." Kenny looked out to the squad room. "It's true there's some tension between me and Haskell." He came around to face Jane again. "But I feel that because he works for Chief McDonald, you're *ordering* me to tell you about it."

Jane let her desk chair fall back until her head was resting against the wall. "Okay, maybe you're right. It's just that everything we do, every minute of our days and nights, are so intertwined . . . so over-lapped . . . it's hard to know where the line is."

"Tell me about it."

"How 'bout this? Talk to me about Haskell, and I promise to listen as a civilian . . . as the good wife."

"Think you can?"

"Probably not." Jane smiled. "But I can fake it."

Kenny smiled back at her. "It's about a girl."

"I'm liking this already."

"Haskell and I were in the Academy together. He had this girl-friend from when he was in junior college. On the surface, it all looked great. But he was always saying how she didn't mean all that much to him and he was going to dump her as soon as he met some-one else."

"How noble."

"Anyway," Kenny continued, "I bumped into her one night at the Navigator. We had a couple of drinks and—"

"You didn't!"

Kenny shrugged. "I did."

"And of course Haskell finds out."

"Julie told him the next day. She dumped him before he could dump her. Next thing you know, she and I are a couple and Devon's pissed off at me."

"You can't tell me," Jane said, "that Haskell's been carrying this grudge since the Academy."

"That's only the half of it." Finney came to the door with some pa-pers. Kenny shook his head and Finney retreated. "Julie and I stayed together maybe a year—she's the one in my Academy graduation photos—and then I broke it off with her."

"Why?"

"She wanted to get married. I wasn't even close to ready. Simple as that. Anyway, a couple of years pass. Haskell and I go our separate ways in the department. Then I hear he's back with Julie again, and next thing I know, they're married. But . . ."

"But . . . ?" Jane urged.

"But, not long after that, I get a call from her . . . from Julie. Can we meet? So I have coffee with her and she tells me she's still in love with me and would I want to get back together?"

"And you say?"

"I say no." Kenny pushed away from the door and sat on the couch. "So she goes back and tells Devon that she's still in love with me and that she's leaving him."

"Wait a minute. I thought you told her no."

"I did. But she needed some excuse to get out of a shitty marriage . . . and I was it. Needless to say, Devon didn't take it well. It didn't really affect us all that much until he started driving for the chief. Now we're always in each other's faces and he's got this big hard-on for me."

"Nicely phrased," Jane said. "One last question, I promise."

"Shoot."

"Why did you turn Julie down that second time?"

"I'd already met you."

Jane let her chair fall forward. "Thank you for telling me that story. And thank you for telling Julie no."

Kenny nodded. "Now, can we move on?"

"Moving on."

"So, what were you and the chief talking about?"

"At first it was Alice Iverson," Jane said. "She called to complain about me again."

"Surprise, surprise. What else did he want to talk about?"

"A. J. Guthrie."

"A.J.?" Kenny stretched his legs across to the guest chair.

"They were cops together in the old days. Chief says A.J. was one of the good ones. Tough, committed, and honest."

"And then his son died."

"Right." Jane looked at Kenny. "And so did A.J. in a way. He lost the light. Moved back home."

"Understandable. I would have gotten the hell out of here, too."

"Exactly what I said. But the chief says it wasn't quite like A.J. tells it. He didn't quit the force, he was asked to leave."

"Drinking?"

"Big-time. Which led to fucking up. Which led to discipline . . . which led to more discipline."

Kenny sat forward, dropping his feet to the floor. "So that's what he meant when he told us that the mandatory retirement up in Dos Rios was the *second* job that was finished with him before he was finished with it."

Jane nodded solemnly. "It's why he's always trying so hard to prove himself."

A flurry of motion caught her eye. Cheryl Lomax was saying something to Linda French at the dispatch console. She was gesturing with her hands, her long nails cutting arcs in the air. Linda tore through the bullpen toward Jane's office.

Jane pushed her chair back and rose. "Uh-oh."

"Uh-oh what?" Kenny asked, turning toward the doorway.

Linda threw Jane's door open.

She caught her breath and said, "Another."

CHAPTER 35

■

"NAME'S MARIO TONELLI," Aaron Clark-Weber said as he stood up and brushed off his pant leg. "First on-scene found this in his pocket." He held up a small glassine bag.

Jane took it from him. "Marijuana?"

Aaron nodded. "Decent grade. Personal-use stuff."

They were on the roof of a recently gentrified three-story building in Potrero Hill. The top two floors were made up of small overpriced apartments. The ground floor housed a coffee bar, an ale house, and a used-CD store.

The victim's body lay splayed out in the center of the roof. There were faint smears of blood across his closed eyelids. Blood from the wound in his chest had seeped out, forming a flat shiny pool beneath him. So much blood, Jane noticed, that she could see the clouds reflected overhead.

"Nothing in his mouth," Aaron said.

Kenny nodded. "That chunk of flesh seems to be a onetime thing."

Jane looked around.

More than twenty-five police personnel swarmed over the black tar-paper rooftop. They worked quietly, steadily. Dusting, photographing, measuring, videotaping. Searching. "What about the—"

Linda French anticipated the question. "No sign of the S-thing yet."

"It's here," Jane said soberly. "Broad daylight. I don't like this."

"Think it's a sign," Linda asked, "doing this in the daytime?"

Jane dropped her eyes to the body. "Everything this fucker does is a sign."

The powerful strobing *thrup* of a police helicopter filled the air. The chopper circled far above, getting its bearings, before lowering altitude to observe and assist.

"Jane!" Lou Tronick called.

He was standing near the rear of the access door housing, a small shedlike structure that jutted up from the rooftop. Jane and the others crossed to Lou.

"Found it," he said. He led them to the far side of the housing, to a remote corner of the building. "There."

Linda gasped. "Oh, my God."

The S-figure was over six feet long. The lower half was on the roof; the upper half was climbing the dull gray stucco of the housing wall.

It was now clearly a snake.

There were four teardrop-shaped dots to the right of its head.

"Look at the size of that damn thing," Aaron said. "Took a lot of time."

Jane studied it, her eyes tracing its incredible length. "And a lot of blood."

They were rendered still for a brief moment, absorbing the enormity, the sheer enterprise and portent of it all.

A forensics photographer quick-snapped a roll of film.

Kenny hurried up with the victim's wallet. "There's maybe a hundred in cash here. Business card says Mr. Tonelli's an associate producer for programming at KKSF Radio. You know what this means, right?"

"This guy's no bum," Aaron Clark-Weber said.

Jane looked from the snake to the body. "Our killer's expanding his horizons."

■

THE CROWD OF onlookers pressed against the yellow tape of the crime-scene perimeter.

Kenny was huddled with Aaron Clark-Weber in the maw of the forensics van. Doing field tests and cataloging evidence.

The first news truck arrived.

Becka Flynn.

She had her arms outstretched, her soundman hooking her up, as Jane approached. Becka dropped her arms and adjusted her lapel mike. Her cameraman nodded. Ready. "Any chance I can get a statement?" she asked Jane.

"Sorry, Becka. Alvarez will be on-scene any minute. I gotta run things through him."

"How 'bout some off-the-record background? Not for attribution."

The helicopter peeled away, taking the jangling persistence of its rotor noise with it. A mile away in just a few seconds, it banked right and raced for the horizon. Jane nodded to Becka Flynn. "Try me."

Becka took out her reporter's notebook. "Same killer?"

"Appears to be."

"Same sort of victim?"

"All I can say is, there are similarities."

Becka Flynn pressed on. "What about differences?"

Jane started away. "I gotta get back in there."

"Before you go, I've got a little heads-up for you."

Jane stopped.

Becka leaned over the perimeter tape. "Watch CNN tonight. Ten P.M."

"Wally Powers?"

"And a very special guest."

Jane searched Becka's eyes. "Don't tell me."

"They just firmed it up. Our own golden girl will leave no show unturned in the desperate hunt for her husband's killer."

"Christ almighty," Jane groaned.

CHAPTER 36

■

"YOUR OFFICER FINNEY called," Sheriff Guthrie said.

He had just come out of the elevators and bumped into Jane at Roz Shapiro's reception desk. "Said I could pick up the sketch of that male prostitute."

"Down the hall," Jane said, "first right after the water fountain."

A.J. looked across to Interrogation Room One. It was crowded with the Homicide Team and their support staff, waiting for Jane to begin breaking down the latest killing. "Heard you had another one."

"We're doing everything we can," Jane said, "to make sure it's the last one."

"My money's on you." A.J. turned and walked away.

Jane watched him go, then put her hand on Roz Shapiro's shoulder. "Roz, do me a favor and let me know when it's ten o'clock."

■

MIKE FINNEY HAD FOUND a second blackboard.

It stood next to the first one in Interrogation Room One, Mario Tonelli's name heading the first column. The next two were blank.

It was going to be a long night.

"As far as I'm concerned," Jane said, addressing her Homicide

Team, "escalation just became explosion." She indicated the police photographs from that afternoon. "Virtually everything about the crime scene in Potrero Hill matches the previous three. The cause of death, the closed eyes, the red fibers." She sat on the table and took a sip of Diet Coke. "But there are notable, and disturbing, exceptions.

"First the obvious. This victim was gainfully employed, not a homeless man like the others. He was killed in broad daylight. And the S-image, the snake, has grown exponentially over all the others before it."

She turned to Aaron Clark-Weber. "Did you find Professor Akiyama?"

"I got him at home," Aaron said. "I e-mailed him a digital of the snake. The thing that was most interesting about what he said was how *un*interesting the symbol was."

"Meaning?"

"Meaning it wasn't particular to any known religion or sect or tribe. It wasn't necessarily primitive or sophisticated. It was just . . . ordinary."

"I sent it over to the Gang Task Force," Lou Tronick said. "They're stumped, too." He picked at the deli tray one of the uniforms had picked up.

"Then if it's coming up zeroes," Jane said, "we have to move on. Linda, add the Potrero Hill murder scene to the triangulation grid you're working on. Show me a geographical overlay. Might be something there." Jane jumped down from the table. "Also, guys, this is all over the news and, needless to say, very sensitive—both as a murder investigation and as a political hot potato. I don't want anyone talking to the press. If the *Chronicle* calls trying to sell you a subscription, hang up on them. No exceptions."

"And I have to stress," Kenny added, "that we're keeping this thing with the killer closing the eyes as our holdback. Everyone involved with this case—from EMT to the chief—has been sworn to secrecy about that. Some loony comes in to confess, or if there's a copycat, he better know about the eyes or it's bogus. Last thing we need in a serial killer case is to blow the all-clear too early."

"What about witnesses?" Jane asked. "This murder happened in the daytime, in a relatively well-traveled area."

"No one's come up with anything yet." Lou Tronick poured another cup of coffee. "But I'll keep banging away on it."

"Looks like," Aaron said, "Mr. Tonelli, who lived in the building, by the way, went up to his roof for a little toke and was in a very wrong place at a very wrong time."

"I know it's doubtful," Jane said, "but check the victim's drug history. Might be something there that can hook him into some of the others."

Stacey Moran, a female forensics specialist from Aaron's team, slipped in and handed Aaron a fax. He read it and turned to Jane.

"Workup came back on that letter." He indicated the blowup in the corner.

"Anything?" Jane asked.

Aaron shook his head. "Not much. No prints. Postmark is Central Office. The envelope and stamp are both self-stick. And the stationery is standard-issue computer stock. Three bucks a ream at any Staples."

"Then someone went to a lot of trouble to make it untraceable," Kenny said.

"I agree." Jane crossed to the easel. "And, like we've been saying, if the 'keep your money' phrase means the writer doesn't want the reward, then that makes me even more hopeful it's not some crank jerking us around."

Roz Shapiro came to the doorway. She caught Jane's attention and pointed to her watch. Jane glanced at the wall clock. Ten P.M.

Time for *Wally Powers*.

"Roz," Jane said gently, "why don't you go home?"

"To what?" The old woman smiled ruefully. "Should I turn on the TV?"

"I got it," Kenny said. He took up the remote and hit "power." A hockey game came up. "Hey, Lou, the Sharks are in overtime."

"Ken," Jane chided.

"Okay," Kenny said. "But we're clicking back during commercials."

The familiar logo of *Wally Powers Live* appeared. Then the man himself. Sporting his trademark bow tie, he leaned across the desk. Everything about him said tonight would be special.

". . . JonBenet Ramsey and O. J. Simpson," Wally Powers said. "Tonight we have as our special guest Alice Iverson, the wife . . . the widow . . . of Philip Iverson, who was murdered last week in San Francisco. Welcome to our show, Alice."

The camera angle widened and there was Alice Iverson.

"Kinda has a Sharon Stone thing going tonight," Kenny murmured.

He was right, Jane thought. Resplendent in a cream-colored Chanel suit, Alice Iverson looked like a movie star pitching her next film.

"Alice," Wally Powers began, "your husband was on this program many times. I considered him a friend of mine."

"He was a friend of mine, too, Wally. My best friend." Alice Iverson took a sip from a water glass to her left. "Our lives were blessed with many enduring friendships. Philip and I always looked upon our friends as part of our extended family."

"How are you holding up?"

"There is so much work to be done, and that sustains me." Alice favored the camera to her left. Her better side. "I've pledged myself to two things: ensuring that Philip's Make It So Foundation will continue to thrive. And . . ." She suddenly teared up. ". . . and finding my husband's killer."

Wally Powers offered her a box of Kleenex.

Alice Iverson shook her head bravely.

"And the Oscar goes to . . ." Kenny snorted.

"C'mon, Ken," Lou Tronick said.

Jane looked around. Lou and the others were captivated by what they were watching. The late-shift guys were gathered around the TV in the lunchroom. These battle-hardened cops who had seen it all, been through it all, watched in silent fascination.

Alice Iverson, the queen of image, had them in her hands.

"What do you have to report on the search for Philip's killer?" Wally Powers asked. "Any progress at all?"

"As far as I know, there isn't any. My husband . . . his memory . . . deserves better than this."

"He certainly does," Wally Powers said dramatically, his rich voice resonating through Interrogation Room One. "If ever a man of this century were to be an American saint, then Philip Iverson surely would be that man." He found his key camera. "Back with your calls after this."

■

ELLEN SCHUBERT WATCHED the program with a renewed sense of outrage.

Her cat dozed next to her on the couch. She touched the fur on its arthritic hind legs. Pressing a little deeper, massaging, she could feel the softness of what had once been powerful muscles.

Taken by time.

Time, Ellen thought. After years of tormented but tolerable peace, the pain . . . and the secrets . . . came flooding back.

She was relieved she hadn't taken her sleeping pill yet.

She had another letter to write.

CHAPTER 37

■

JANE LAY IN the tub, bubbles crackling like burning paper, watching the bathroom ceiling take the first light of day.

The trucks would be coming soon.

She remembered them from her childhood in this house. The milk truck, the newspaper truck, the garbage truck. Predawn rumbles delivering and taking away.

"You're up early."

Jane caught Kenny's reflection in the small white television at the foot of the tub. "I never really fell asleep."

"I was afraid you were going to say that." He sat on the edge of the tub and picked up Poppy's long-handled scrub brush. Without speaking, he asked Jane a question.

Without speaking, she said yes.

Kenny lathered the bristles with lavender soap. Jane leaned forward, her breasts pressing the mountain of bubbles down and to the side. Kenny ran the brush in gentle circles along her spine. "Tell me."

Jane sighed so deeply a snowball of bubbles broke away and clung to the faucet. "I'm fighting for traction here . . . on *both* cases . . . and I feel like I keep slipping backward." She turned her head to face Kenny. "And that brings up all the old doubts. All that suppressed scary stuff that reduces down to 'can I do this'?"

"Of course you can. You're the best at—"

"I know I'm a good cop," Jane interrupted. "But is that enough anymore? Am I missing something? Some gut-level instinct that the great cops have. Because if I'm not up to this, if this job is bigger than me, then someone could die. *Die*. And if a better cop were in my job and could have prevented that death . . . well, it's . . ."

"A lot."

"Yeah."

Kenny put more pressure on the brush, working Jane's shoulders now. "Look, there are no guarantees. Someone else may die. But if we've done everything in our power with everything we know, then it's not our fault . . . It's just the game."

Jane smiled.

"What?"

"You sound like Ben Spielman."

The phone rang.

Jane started to get out of the tub as Kenny reached across to the counter for the portable. At this hour, whatever this call was about, their interlude was over.

"Hello." Kenny listened for a moment. "We're on our way."

Jane stopped in the middle of drying her legs and looked up.

"That was Cheryl." Kenny put the phone down. "Trudy Nightingale from night-shift dispatch just called her."

"Don't tell me."

"It's not that. Another letter turned up. Looks like it's from the same woman as before."

The window over the tub rattled as a truck worked its way down the street.

Jane dropped her towel. "I'm ready in two minutes."

Lieutenant,

Things are not as they seem.
The devil's grave is a place to dance.

He was not Matthew or Mark
or Luke or John.

The dead will speak.
Blood will tell.

Blood in our hearts,
blood in our souls . . .

Blood on his hands.

I know this is true.
I am dead too.

01436937471

"This time it wasn't mailed," Aaron Clark-Weber said. "The sender—the *woman,* according to Ruth Holmes—dropped it off at one of those all-night mailbox places. A clerk saw that it was addressed to the police and called us. I'll take the original back to my lab, but you can bet there'll be no prints, no saliva . . . nothing to trace us back to whoever wrote this."

"Nothing," Jane said, "except her words." She held up a copy of the letter and read out loud. " 'He was not Matthew or Mark or Luke or John.' As the resident Catholic here, this one's easy. These are saints. She's saying that Philip Iverson wasn't a saint."

"Right," Kenny said. "Last night, Wally Powers was . . . what's the word?"

"Beatifying," Jane said.

"*Beatifying* Philip Iverson. The woman who wrote this was sitting and watching that show and getting angrier and angrier and—"

Lou Tronick picked it up. "—and she got so angry that she blasted out this letter." He scooped three sugars into his coffee. "Then why isn't she just coming forward? Telling us what she knows?"

"Because she's afraid," Jane said simply. "Anyone know if that mailbox place has a security camera?"

Mike Finney wrapped a dougnut in a paper napkin. For later. "I checked and they do. But it's broken."

"Then send someone out there," Jane said. "See if there's a bank or ATM or jewelry store in the area that has surveillance cameras. If so, pull the tapes and bring them in."

"Will do," Finney said.

"The thing is, guys," Jane said, "there's a woman out there who knows, if not *who* killed Philip Iverson, then possibly *why* he was killed. And she's trying to tell us. Not only that—look at these numbers, the same as last time—she's even telling us how to get to her."

"Every law enforcement computer in the country," Lou Tronick said, "came up empty in sequencing those numbers. Basically they ruled a thousand things out—phone numbers, credit cards, and such—but they haven't been able to rule anything definitive in."

"Stay on it," Jane said. "These numbers mean something to the woman who wrote these letters. Therefore, they mean something to us."

Roz Shapiro stood in the doorway, a manila interdepartmental envelope in her hand. She waited for a pause in the conversation and stepped into Interrogation Room One. "Follow-up on that victim from yesterday."

Jane took the envelope and opened it. "Where's Linda French?"

"Not in yet," Roz said.

Jane shot a look to Kenny. All the other cops on the team were working voluntary overtime during this crisis. Linda wasn't required to put in the extra hours, but still . . .

"Give her a call please. Tell her what we've got." Jane opened the report and scanned the pages. "Mario Tonelli had no history of drug use as far as we know. No arrests. No rehab. No military service."

Finney went to the blackboard and updated the information.

"Uh, pardon me, Lieutenant." Cheryl Lomax stuck her head in. "Becka Flynn's here to see you."

"At seven-thirty in the morning?"

"Says it's important."

CHAPTER 38

■

"YOU SEE TODAY'S papers?"

Becka Flynn sat in the guest chair in Jane's office. She was dressed in black sweats, her red hair pulled back in a ponytail. This early in the morning and without makeup, Jane thought she looked little more than a teenager.

Jane sat on the couch, not wanting to have her desk and the formality it implied, between them. "Not yet. I got here before they came."

"This latest killing has them all in a frenzy," Becka said. "The *Chronicle,* to their credit, is trying to be a little subdued. Talking about a serial killer who seems to be branching out, stuff like that. But the *Trib* went totally nuts. 'Lock your doors . . . Trust no one . . .' and other exercises in journalistic integrity."

"That's all we need," Jane said. "How's your station going to handle it?"

"We've got an editorial meeting in half an hour to talk about just that." Becka took a sip from a water bottle. "But I wouldn't count on us taking the high road."

"And that's okay with you?"

"That's *not* okay with me," Becka said. "Why do you think I want out of this local-news-babe thing so badly?"

Jane regarded her friend and thought about how much they had in common. Then something occurred to her. "You didn't come here this early in the morning just to talk about newspapers, did you?"

"No, I didn't." Becka put the water bottle on the table between them and leaned forward. "Something came up."

Jane straightened on the couch. "This is me listening."

"Years ago, when I was a punk reporter at the *Chronicle,* I had to go to all these fund-raisers as a seat filler. The paper would buy a table and make the new kids go eat rubber chicken and listen to Norm Crosby."

"Ouch."

"Tell me about it. Anyway, I was watching Alice Iverson on *Wally Powers* last night and it hit me. Josh Stolberg."

"The lawyer?"

Becka nodded. "Not just *the* lawyer. Philip Iverson's lawyer on a bunch of personal stuff. I sat next to him at a couple of black-tie things. He was a handsome, flirtatious guy. One night, we got to talking and he gives me his card. Hinting very strongly that if I wanted to get anywhere in this town, he could help me."

"In exchange for?"

"In exchange for the usual."

"And did you?"

"Fuck no. The guy's a total lech." Becka pulled herself forward on the couch. "So I dig up the card—I never throw anything away—and I call him. Just trying to shake the bushes for this story I'm working on about Philip Iverson."

Jane rolled Josh Stolberg's name around in her mind. "I haven't heard of him in years. Didn't he retire?"

"Sort of. He's doing seven-to-fifteen at Shanley."

"He's in prison?" Jane grabbed a pad off her desk. "For what?"

"The bane of the white collars: tax evasion. It may all be unrelated, but who knows? It also might be the first little blemish on the robes of Saint Philip."

Jane looked up from her notes. "Or . . . maybe Saint Philip wasn't such a saint."

Becka went for it. "What do you have?"

"Nothing I can divulge right now. But when the time's right, you'll get it first."

"How about if I try to guess and you just say yes or no?"

"This isn't *All the President's Men,*" Jane said. "I can't let you pursue it, okay?"

Becka settled back into the couch. "Then at least give me something on the bums. What do you have that the press doesn't have?"

Jane thought of the holdback, the closed eyes of the victims. But she couldn't give that up, either. "I'm sorry, there's really no quid pro quo here. I've got two huge homicide cases chewing holes in me, and I can't compromise either one of them."

"I understand." Becka stood up. "I hate it, but I understand. You going out to Shanley?"

Jane reached for her bag. "You bet I am."

"Then you better hurry."

"Why?"

"Because Josh Stolberg is dying."

■

THE PAUL B. SHANLEY Federal Medium Security Correctional Facility was just north of the airport.

A series of low white buildings, it looked like an office park or a junior college. Except for the razor wire.

Jane and Kenny deposited their service pistols in the law enforcement officers' weapons locker. Kenny folded the receipts into his back pocket. Then they were issued oversized bright orange visitor's passes to be worn in a conspicuous place at all times.

Kenny pressed his over the lapel of his sport coat. "These so the guards can pick us out in case of a riot . . . or so the prisoners can?"

Their escort failed to see the humor. "We don't say 'riot' in here." He keyed the call switch for the elevator and the doors opened.

"What do you say?" Kenny asked as he and Jane got in.

"Situation." The guard reached inside, inserted the key in another slot, and gave it a twist. "The doors open, you'll be on two. Just step out and Officer Macey will take you to the infirmary."

"Thanks for all—" Jane began.

The doors closed.

"Imagine that," Kenny said. "A humorless prison guard."

The elevator rose for five seconds, then stopped. The doors parted and another corrections officer appeared. A thick black man with a shaved head, his massive biceps strained against the confines of his short-sleeve uniform shirt.

"You must be Officer Macey," Kenny said, wasting a good smile.

Macey nodded by moving only his eyes. Then he turned on his heel and strode away. "Come," he said after he'd gone about ten feet.

Jane and Kenny followed him down the light gray corridor to the prison infirmary. Macey stopped at the third door on the right. Pulling a retractable key ring from his belt, he unlocked the door and threw it open. The keys snapped back to his belt.

Jane and Kenny entered.

The walls of the room were painted yellow. Everything in the room took on its pall and was somehow diminished by it.

On the far side, beneath a high slit of a window, was a single bed.

Josh Stolberg slowly turned his head toward them. "You the cops who called?"

"Yes, sir," Jane said as they crossed the room. "I'm Lieutenant Candiotti and this is Inspector Marks. SFPD Homicide." Jane had seen photographs of Josh Stolberg from the late eighties and had always been taken by how virile and handsome he was. The man who lay before them looked startlingly old; his teeth and skin and hair withering with his dying.

Stolberg held out a trembling hand and pointed to a plastic cup on the steel table next to the bed. Kenny picked it up and passed it to him. After a long, dribbling sip through the straw, Stolberg held the cup out before him. The ice rattled against its sides as his hand continued to shake.

Kenny took the cup from him and returned it to the table. The lower door of the side table was partially open. Kenny brushed the back of his hand against Jane's hip. She followed his look.

Diapers.

Stolberg made an effort to sit higher in the bed, but actually slipped down lower. He fought to catch another breath. "You here about Philip?"

"Is there anything you can tell us," Jane asked, "that could either shed some light on why he was killed or who may have done it?"

"If there were, Lieutenant . . . and I'm not conceding anything one way or the other . . . but if there were, it would fall under attorney-client privilege."

"Mr. Stolberg," Kenny said, "your client is dead. The purview of attorney-client privilege ceases with the death of the client."

Josh Stolberg looked at the stripe of daylight that fell across the wall. "You're forgetting one thing, Inspector."

"What's that?"

"Philip Iverson was my friend."

"What about Alice Iverson?" Jane asked. "Doesn't she deserve some answers?"

Stolberg pressed his head back into his pillow and sighed. He started to say something, then shook his head.

"Sir," Jane said, "have we come all this way for nothing?"

Josh Stolberg turned his face to the wall. " 'Fraid so."

"Please help us," Jane said gently.

The bed creaked as Stolberg rolled onto his back. "Leave me alone," he rasped. "Everybody walked away happy." He closed his eyes and lay still, his breaths coming in long wheezing gulps. Then he was snoring.

Kenny tugged at Jane's elbow and they moved to the door.

CHAPTER 39

—■—

"YOU SEE HIS eyes when I mentioned Alice Iverson?" Jane asked as Kenny blasted up the northbound on-ramp of the Bayshore Freeway.

"You bet. So what was that look he gave us? Fear, anger, what?"

"I went there, too," Jane said. "But there was something else."

"What?"

"Guilt."

Kenny veered across four lanes of traffic and cut over the double yellow lines into the car-pool lane. "One thing we know about people in prison . . ." he began.

Jane finished the thought for him. "They're never guilty."

"Something happened between Josh Stolberg, Philip Iverson, and/or Alice Iverson. Something that has to do with this case."

"I agree," Jane said. "And what about when Stolberg said 'everybody walked away happy'? What the hell does *that* mean?"

Kenny was doing eighty-five. He bore down so hard on the pickup truck in front of them that the man driving it had to swerve out of the way. Kenny looked in the mirror as the pickup returned to the car-pool lane and the driver gave him the finger.

Jane tucked her hand under Kenny's right thigh. He slowed to eighty. "Something happened with those guys," he said. "Maybe before they hit the big time."

Jane looked out the window. The sun was low on the horizon. Another day, she thought, spent running down leads and innuendo. But, at last, she felt the first bit of traction on this case. "You know what else all this is telling us?"

Kenny turned to her. "What?"

"Those letters are real. Whoever wrote them knows."

"Knows what?"

"Knows the secret Josh Stolberg wants to take to his grave." Jane grabbed the radio mike. "3H58 to Dispatch."

"Go, 3H58."

"Cheryl, is Finney still there?"

"Lieutenant, he's *always* here. Hang on."

Jane lowered her window slightly, bringing a stream of cool evening air into the Explorer.

"Hello, Lieutenant."

"Mike, I need you to do a couple of things."

"Okay."

"Have someone pull *all* court records on RiverPark, Make It So, and any other companies owned wholly or in part by Philip Iverson. All the way back, and this is important, to the beginning. Back to when RiverPark was a start-up. *Before* it was a start-up. Get me everything up to and including the day he died."

"Will do. Anything else?"

Kenny smiled at Jane. "This guy's amazing."

"Yes, Mike. Pay particular attention to any court filings that include the name Josh Stolberg as the attorney of record."

"Got it."

"And, Mike, make sure that the latest letter from our secret admirer has been sent to Ruth Holmes at FBI."

"Already done, Lieutenant. She's in India. But we got it to her. Time change is screwing us up a bit, but I'll stay on it."

■

"Hungry?"

"Starving."

They were sitting in traffic behind a double-parked delivery van in Haight-Ashbury.

"Think of a place," Kenny said. "And after I kill the driver of that truck, we can do takeout."

"3H58."

"Go, Cheryl."

"Chief McDonald was just here. I told him you were still down at Shanley. Just in case."

"Thanks. What was his mood?"

"The usual. Sour. Said something about, and I quote, 'fucking Wally Powers.' I think he'd just come from the mayor's office."

Jane closed her eyes and squeezed the bridge of her nose between her thumb and forefinger.

Kenny touched her arm. "Jane, look."

Jane opened her eyes and turned to where Kenny was pointing.

A. J. Guthrie was walking purposefully along the sidewalk. Something ahead of him that Jane and Kenny couldn't see had his full attention.

Two motorcycles worked their way around the delivery van and Kenny was able to inch the Explorer forward. A.J. continued past a homeopathic pharmacy, a guitar shop, a Wells Fargo Bank. Jane lowered her window. As he neared the corner, A.J. quickened his step and caught up with someone about to cross the street. He put his hand on the shoulder of a young blond man, preventing him from stepping off the curb. The man turned toward A.J., toward Jane and Kenny.

"Motherfuck," Kenny said.

It was Jeff Levy's male hooker.

"3H58." Cheryl's voice crackled over the speaker.

The male hooker started at the sound. He whirled, spotted the Explorer, and made Jane and Kenny for cops. A.J. was just reaching out to grab him when he shoved him in the chest and tore down Stanyan Street.

Kenny jammed the car into park, grabbed his two-way, and threw open his door. "Call it in!" He raced across the street to A.J. "Was that him?"

"Yeah! He's getting away!"

"No, he's not!" Kenny flung himself down the sharp incline of Stanyan Street. "Go with Jane!" he shouted over his shoulder.

Jane jumped out of the Explorer. "Sheriff, over here!" She ran around to the driver's side and climbed in. A. J. Guthrie, limping slightly, got in the passenger side and slammed the door closed.

Jane popped the car into reverse and backed the rear wheels onto the sidewalk. Then she pulled it into low and maneuvered around the double-parked delivery van. "There's a flasher under the dash."

A.J. retrieved the dome light from beneath the glove compartment and attached its magnetic base to the roof. Jane flicked a switch near the steering wheel and the light began strobing red. Then she pressed a button with her left foot. The siren in the grille shrieked, startling the drivers in front of her. They cleared a path for the Explorer.

Jane thumbed the mike. "3H58 to Dispatch!"

"Go, Lieutenant."

"In pursuit. Haight-Ashbury. Going down Stanyan toward Golden Gate Park. Subject is no-name male hooker we've been looking for. He's on foot. Use the sketch for description." Jane caught a glimpse of Kenny running headlong down the hill two blocks ahead. A flash of worry triggered through her mind. She pushed it away. "Subject is wearing . . ." Jane looked to A. J. Guthrie.

He took the mike. "Subject is wearing a black jean jacket over a white T-shirt, black Levi's, black cowboy boots, and that white pukka-shell necklace."

"Who you with, Jane?" Cheryl asked. Making sure.

"Sheriff Guthrie." She rocketed through a stop sign. "Stay with me, Cheryl."

"I'm not going anywhere, Jane."

"3H58!" It was Kenny.

"Go, Ken."

"This fucker's fast. He just crossed Lincoln and—" The sound of screeching tires came over the radio. "Okay. He's in the park. Cutting across MLK. Suggest you set up a perimeter. Stanyan to Crossover. Lincoln to Fulton."

Jane stood on the accelerator. "Cheryl, you get that?" The Explorer's tail shimmied for traction, then shot forward.

"Got it, Jane. Patrol will seal it off. Backup's on the way."

Even as Jane approached the park, she could hear sirens keening behind her and to the left.

Kenny called in again. "Jane!"

"Go, Ken."

"He's going toward, no *past,* the Tea Garden. Heading for either the planetarium or the flower conservatory. Shit!"

"What?" Jane screamed. "Ken? Ken!" She barreled across traffic on Lincoln Way and turned up Martin Luther King Drive.

"Cheryl," Jane called into the mike. "Do you have Kenny?"

"No, Jane."

Thin static buzzed over the speaker. Jane frantically searched the dark tree line on the right.

"3H58."

It was Kenny.

Jane said a silent prayer of thanks. "Go, Ken."

"Son of a bitch took a shot at me."

"Are you hit?"

"No. But I'm more than a little irritated."

"Cheryl," Jane said into the microphone, "suspect just fired on Inspector Marks. Get me a SWAT team."

■

THE-THIRTY-MILLION-CANDLEPOWER NIGHT SUN hanging from the underside of Air Two illuminated an entire acre of Golden Gate Park.

Jane stood in the back of the SWAT van. She watched as two patrol units led a stream of park visitors out of harm's way. Lieutenant Scott Hicks and his SWAT team were going through their final gearup, getting ready to move in on the Conservatory of Flowers.

An elaborate nineteenth-century building made entirely of glass, the conservatory had just closed for the day when the suspect crashed through a ten-foot pane and hid inside. It was a bit of luck, Jane thought. People, visitors, were potential hostages. Now he was in there alone, trapped without leverage or hope of escape.

Jane jumped down and joined Kenny and A. J. Guthrie.

"I tracked down this pimp I used to know from the old days," A.J. said. "He was still working the same stretch of motels on O'Leary. Anyway, he knew a client who liked pretty boys and wasn't ashamed of it. Victimless crime and all that. So I went to talk to him and he led me to the Haight." He nodded to Jane. "Then it all hit the fan."

An SFPD light truck arrived. News vans began showing up, Becka Flynn's among them. K-9 units. Catering. Medical teams. Two fire trucks.

Settling in for a siege.

Jane signaled for a supervising sergeant to come over. "Keep the perimeter airtight. No press or civilians inside. No exceptions."

The sergeant nodded crisply and hurried away.

"Hey, Lieutenant?"

Jane turned.

Scott Hicks, his M-16 hanging loosely on his shoulder, tilted his head toward the conservatory. "We're locked and loaded. On your go, ma'am." Blond, boyish, and ruthless, he was in command of SWAT One.

Jane considered her next move. She had an armed suspect who wasn't going anywhere. It was unnecessary to risk anyone's life to bring him in early. "Have your guys take their positions. See if they can pick him up in their night scopes. I'm not ready to send in the troops just yet."

"Yes, ma'am." Hicks turned back to his men and began assigning their firing lines.

"Air Two to command."

Jane thumbed the mike on her two-way. "Go, Air Two."

"We're picking up some movement on the infrared. He's coming to the front door."

"Affirmative that!" the SWAT sniper shouted from his spotting point. There was a rush of metal on metal as the rifles were armed.

A sergeant held a bullhorn out to Jane. She took it and moved toward the conservatory. Kenny came up next to her. "Stay low," he whispered.

Jane leaned into him for a second, then held the bullhorn to her lips. "Attention, you in there! You have zero chance of getting out of this! We are prepared to wait as long as it takes. But every hour you make us wait, every minute of our time and effort you waste, we're going to make sure is held against you when we bring you in." Jane lowered the bullhorn, pausing to give the suspect a moment to assess his dilemma. Then she brought it back up again. "Throw your weapon down to the courtyard, NOW!"

Something small and dark clattered down the stone stairway. The SWAT sniper peered through his scope. "Gun."

Jane winked at Kenny.

The doors opened and the suspect, his thick blond hair whipping in the downdraft of the helicopter, stepped into the cylinder of light falling from the Night Sun. "Don't nobody shoot me!" he shrieked.

"Got him sighted, Lieutenant," the sniper called to Jane.

Jane held up a finger, indicating for the sniper to stand down. "Turn around," she commanded over the loudspeaker. "Put your hands behind your head. Now clasp your fingers together and walk backward down the steps!"

As the suspect began to do so, Jane nodded to Scott Hicks. Six members of the SWAT team swarmed the suspect, threw him to the ground, cuffed him, and searched him. Then they yanked him to his feet.

As he was dragged back to the command area, Jane was reminded of how utterly beautiful he was. Beautiful and young. She crossed to him. "How old are you, son?"

"Sixteen, ma'am."

Squinting into the light and dust, he took in the manpower and equipment around him. "You folks got some strict fucking vice laws in this town."

CHAPTER 40

■

"DANIEL JOSEPH NELSON. Folks back home call me Joe."

The male hooker sat in the hot seat in Interrogation Two.

Jane sat across from him. "Please speak into the microphone for me, Joe."

"Sorry, ma'am."

"Where are you from?"

Joe leaned his upper body forward until his lips almost touched the microphone. "Austin, ma'am. That's in Texas."

Jane looked over to Kenny. Behind him, watching through the interior window, A. J. Guthrie stood with his arms folded across his chest. Daniel Nelson was partly his collar and Jane had consented to let him observe.

She resumed her questioning. "How long have you been in San Francisco, Mr. Nelson?"

" 'Bout two months."

"Like it here?"

"Be all right if it wasn't so cold. I miss the sun shining all the time." His dark soulful eyes filled with tears. He looked down, a tear falling into his lap. "I miss my parents, too."

Jane knew he was playing her. "Why did you fire at Inspector Marks?"

"I was scared. Besides, I didn't exactly shoot *at* him. More like *toward* him." Joe looked to Kenny. "Sorry, sir."

Kenny pushed away from the wall and charged at him. "Sorry don't cut it, you little fuck!"

Forgetting that he was cuffed to his chair, Joe tried to raise his hands to protect himself.

Kenny crossed the room in three steps. "You shoot your little-dick piece-of-shit gun at me and then you say 'sorry'? What if you had hit me? You want to go and shoot a police officer? What if the bullet had hit a school bus or gone through the window of someone's home?" He thrust his face into Joe's. "You are one lucky son of a bitch, Joe, that didn't happen."

He pulled away, letting his fury subside.

Joe trembled so badly his shackles rattled against the chair.

"You ever want to see your parents again," Kenny went on, "you tell the lieutenant everything she wants to know. No games. No bullshit. No playing it cute. You hear me?"

"Y-yes, sir."

Jane gestured for Kenny to return to his place by the window. When he did, she noticed that Linda French was now standing next to A. J. Guthrie. They talked quietly as they observed the interrogation. When she turned back to Joe, she saw that he was ready to talk, the facade gone.

Jane knew she was on thin ice; interrogating a minor without an attorney or Social Services present. She had called for both and was told that because of how late it was, it would be a couple of hours. Jane didn't have a couple of hours. She couldn't afford to let Daniel Nelson stew all night, anticipating questions and rehearsing answers. She wanted what he had to say to be fresh, unadorned. If this witness had anything in his statement that differed from Jeff Levy's, then she needed to move on it immediately.

She'd deal with the system later.

Joe shifted his weight against his constraints, then leaned toward the microphone. "I was cruising the Castro and this man comes up and starts talking to me about my necklace. Then he asks am I a working man and I'm like yes. Three hundred bucks. He says fine and I get in his car."

"What kind of car?"

"Beamer. Big new one."

Jane slid a photo of Jeff Levy's BMW across the table. "This one?"

Joe studied the picture. "Looks like it."

"Go on."

"So I want to take him to this place where I . . . uh, do my work? But he said he didn't have time. That's when I saw he was wearing a wedding ring and it all kinda made sense why he didn't have no time." Joe sat forward, pushing his head past the microphone. "I gotta pee, miss," he said softly. "Real bad."

"Coupla minutes, Mr. Nelson. Then you can use the bathroom, have a meal. Maybe get some sleep."

"Thank you." He sat back. "Should I keep going?"

Jane nodded.

"So this guy takes me to this parking garage at some fancy hotel. I couldn't really see the name of it, the fog was so bad. We go up to something like the fifth or sixth floor and park. He gives me my money, three bills, and makes his seat go back. Then I undo him and start . . . getting all extracurricular with him when I hear these shots."

Jane and Kenny both spoke at the same time. *"Shots?"*

"More than one?" Kenny asked.

"Yes, sir. Two a' them."

Kenny caught Jane's eye. This was it.

"First there was one," Joe continued. "Then a little wait. Then another. When we heard the first one, my guy said for me not to stop. It was just a backfire, he says. Well, sir, I'm from Texas, I know what a gunshot sounds like. Then came the other one and the mood was kind of broken. He did himself back up and you ain't never seen nobody drive as fast as him."

Jane stood and hurried across the room. She ripped open the door. "Finney! Call Lieutenant Clark-Weber at home and tell him to meet us with his team at the parking structure of the Golden Gate Grand." She glanced at A. J. Guthrie. "We got something."

The corner of his mouth lifted into a grin. "Anything I can tell Mrs. Iverson?"

"Not yet. But that was a good piece of police work, Sheriff."

"Hey, ma'am!" Daniel Joseph Nelson called from Interrogation Two. "I gotta pee!"

■

THE EXIT SIGN glowed green above the stairwell door.

Jane and Kenny pulled the door open and stepped onto the windy deck of Parking Level Seven. "Sure wish somebody would hose down that stairway." Kenny handed Jane one of the flashlights he'd taken from the Explorer. "Nice place like this and it smells like a toilet."

A blue Dodge minivan was parked in the spot where Philip Iverson had died. The patch of concrete that had been scrubbed clean of his blood had already darkened and nearly matched the rest of the surface.

"Here's the deal." Jane held up one of the folders she was carrying, the one with the crime-scene photos from the night of the murder. "Without all the cop vehicles parked everywhere, we have a chance to look at this place with fresh eyes. Like when you put down a crossword puzzle and pick it up later."

"I don't do crosswords."

"Ken."

"Okay, crosswords." He motioned for her to go on.

"Pretty Boy Joe said there were *two* shots. If we can find either the second bullet or where it hit, then we have a chance to learn more about the geography of Philip Iverson's murder. That will hopefully lead us to more questions, which will lead us to—"

"—more answers." Kenny looked around. "Want to wait for Forensics?"

"I don't want to wait for anything." Jane put the folders on the roof of a Mustang convertible and, skirting a wide grease stain, started walking. "Look up and down."

"And all around."

The sounds of an orchestra came from the hotel. Jane stopped and looked down to the Crystal Ballroom across the way. Through the floor-to-ceiling windows, she watched couples in formal dress waltzing beneath huge crystal chandeliers.

Jane felt that tug again.

The pull on her psyche that reminded her she was an outsider. Being a cop was part of it. Not really having any friends who weren't in law enforcement was another. She thought of Becka Flynn and reminded herself to give her a call. To cultivate what she and Becka both wanted. A deeper friendship.

"C'mon, Cinderella," Kenny said gently. "We can think about the ball later. It's back to work with you now."

Jane turned to him. "*Why* were there two shots?"

"Maybe the first shot missed and it was the second shot that killed Iverson."

"All I know is that Philip Iverson had one slug in his brain. I want that other bullet." Jane touched her toe to the scrubbed patch of cement. "Let's use this as ground zero. You go back toward the stairway. And I'll go this way."

"Let's do it."

They switched on their flashlights and started walking slowly away from each other, searching beneath parked cars, scanning the low ceiling, feeling the walls for any sign of the second bullet.

Jane turned sideways to get between two cars that were parked too closely together. When she reached the low retaining wall, she crouched down and played her light over the floor, the railing, and finally the ceiling.

"Y'know," Kenny called as he trained his light along the wall leading to the stairwell door, "the missing bullet might have lodged in someone's car. It could be a hundred miles from here."

"There you go thinking again," Jane shouted back. "I'll have Finney coordinate calling the owners of all the cars and limos from the Man of the Year Banquet."

Kenny swept his light across a gray Volvo station wagon and then up to the ceiling. Then he focused his light on the stairwell door.

Walking backward, he played the beam across the fire extinguisher, across the call box. Something caught his eye. He stopped. Aiming his flashlight at the base of a concrete pillar, he came around the front of the Volvo and squatted down. There was a two-inch scar on the north side. It was circled in yellow chalk, the kind used by the forensics team. Kenny realized that this was from the ricochet that had hit A. J. Guthrie. He was about to mention it to Jane when she called out to him.

"Ken!"

He bolted up.

Jane was running toward him. "There!" she called. "Behind you!"

Kenny turned, and he saw it, too.

A pinpoint of white light was coming from a tiny hole in the green glass of the exit sign over the stairwell door.

Kenny handed his flashlight to Jane and climbed onto the steel guardrail. He pried the glass out of its frame with his pocketknife and peered inside. Reaching in with his thumb and forefinger, he pulled something out. "You are a genius." He jumped down, just missing the slippery patch of grease, and opened his hand.

A bullet, flattened and misshapen, lay in his palm.

"Twenty-two?" Jane asked.

"Looks like it."

Jane surveyed the area. "We're pretty far from where Iverson was killed. And he was shot point-blank, so the bad guy had to be over there, too."

"And the entry point on that sign is in the opposite direction. What the hell happened?"

"We've been thinking that Iverson and his killer were the only two people in the world that night. Ken, someone else was here!"

"An accomplice?"

"Or a witness." Jane held out her hands. "Bear with me on this." She pointed to where Philip Iverson had fallen. "The killer does his deed over there. Then he hears Jeff Levy's car, so he starts to flee. He turns back to the stairs and he sees someone."

"Someone watching him."

"So he shoots at him. But he misses."

"I'm with you so far," Kenny said. "But where'd the someone end up?"

"He either got away . . ."

"Or he didn't."

The stairwell door opened and a well-dressed couple came out. The man was in a tuxedo, his jacket over the shoulders of the woman with him. They were happy, glowing from dancing in the ballroom. The man said something and the woman tossed her head back and laughed.

Jane noticed her diamond necklace, her diamond earrings, her dress, her shoes. She looked down and saw the grime on her own knees from crawling around looking under cars. The woman smiled at Jane and would have stepped in a grease stain in the handicapped spot if the man hadn't deftly swept her aside, turning the movement into a little dance step. Still laughing, the man unlocked a black Jaguar with his key remote and opened the passenger door.

Jane turned back to Kenny. "Let's go call this in. I want this place secured." She started toward the stairwell door.

But Kenny didn't move.

"Jane," he said softly. "Look at this."

Jane turned and followed the beam of his flashlight to the grease stain on the floor.

There, in the center of the oily black patch, was a pair of footprints.

"Jesus," Jane said. "Who would stand in the middle of something like that?"

"Someone too scared to move," Kenny said.

"Let's think this through," Jane said. "These prints could have gotten here anytime before or after the shooting."

"If it was before, why didn't our guys see it when they were here?"

Jane snatched the crime-scene photos from the roof of the Mustang and dumped them out on its hood. "This is why." She held up a wide-angle shot of the entire scene. "Here's where we are right now. And here's . . . where that grease stain is." She pointed to the photo.

"Under Linda French's car." The man started the Jaguar and backed out of his parking place. "And the last time we were here, when Sheriff Guthrie was shot, there was an SUV parked in that spot. And what did we do? We sealed off the area so the owner couldn't move it and no one thinks to look under it."

The Jaguar rolled past them, tires squealing on the slick surface.

"It's a huge fuckup," Kenny said. "On Linda's part for parking there. On Forensics' part for not being more thorough—"

"And on my part," Jane said quietly, "for not making sure every square inch of this place was covered. Both times."

"I wouldn't go that—"

"It all floats upward, Kenny. That's the good news and the bad news about command." She knelt down next to the grease patch. "I'll beat myself up later. Gimme some light."

Kenny aimed the flashlight directly on the footprints.

Jane stared at them. They had a peculiar herringbone pattern that most likely came from some sort of tennis shoe. "Ken." She held out her hand and Kenny gave her his flashlight. Illuminating the footprints with both lights, Jane noticed something that took her breath away. "Oh, my God. Look at this!"

Kenny got down on one knee and leaned over the prints. "They're mismatched!"

"Willie Temple," Jane said, her voice little more than a whisper. "He had those mismatched tennis shoes. Do you know what this means?"

"Yeah, Philip Iverson's death is connected to the murder of Willie Temple."

"To *all* of the other murders." Jane opened the folder and riffled through the papers. Kenny held the light for her. "Here, look. Iverson's TOD is just before midnight. And check this out. Willie Temple's Time of Death is estimated at twelve o'clock midnight the same night. Willie Temple witnessed Philip Iverson's death and—"

"—and then was killed to shut him up."

"But why at Pier Twenty? And why all the other killings? And what about the snake imagery?"

"Shit, Jane." Kenny looked at the footprints again. "I don't know."

Jane had been there before on other cases. Questions led to answers, which led to more questions. The cycle didn't stop until the murderer was stopped. But she felt something for the first time since these killings began. She felt closer. Closer to the truth. Closer to finding the killer.

"Don't know what?" Aaron Clark-Weber asked as he approached.

Jane and Kenny shot to their feet.

"Aaron." Kenny held out the bullet. "This a twenty-two?"

Aaron took the bullet from him. He'd handled thousands of these over the years. "Yes, it is. Where'd you get it?"

Jane didn't answer him. "Soon as your team gets here, I want this entire place resecured as an active stage-one crime scene." She indicated the grease stain. "And make a mold of those footprints. C'mon, Ken!" She whipped open the stairwell door and plunged through it.

Kenny raced after her, letting the door thud closed behind him.

Aaron Clark-Weber looked from the footprints to the bullet in his hand. Then to the door. "Nice to see you, too."

CHAPTER 41

■

SO MANY HOMELESS had sought refuge in Santuario that even the dining hall was filled with sleeping people. On the picnic tables, the benches, the floor, everywhere.

"We're just one shelter," Reggie Mayhew said as he stepped outside to talk to Jane and Kenny. "It's like this all over the city." Once they were on the sidewalk, all semblance of civility on the reverend's part dropped away. "What the hell you want from me this time, Lieutenant? You got some old bank robbery, maybe a B and E you wanna try and pin on me?" He crossed his arms, everything about him signaling defiance and distrust.

"I'm here to ask for your help, Reverend."

This caught Mayhew off guard. "What with?"

"We want to go talk with Loretta Temple," Jane explained. "She's understandably pissed off at cops."

"And we thought," Kenny added, "that it would help if you came with."

Reggie Mayhew looked from Kenny to Jane. "What do you want with that poor woman?"

"Some evidence has turned up in her son's murder," Jane said. "We want to look in Willie's property bag. We could get a warrant and just march in there, but it doesn't have to be like that."

Reggie raised his eyebrows. "What kind of evidence?"

"All we can tell you," Kenny said, "is that it's very important."

Jane put her hand on Reggie's arm. "And we need to move fast. Will you help us?"

Reggie Mayhew patted her hand and smiled. "You know what you're doing here, don't you, Lieutenant?"

Jane nodded. "My homework."

■

"THIS IS THE *KGO Mid-Evening Report*," Becka Flynn announced into Camera One. A picture of Mario Tonelli was supered in over her left shoulder. Below it was the legend THE KILLING STREETS.

"Police have confirmed that twenty-seven-year-old Mario Tonelli was the latest victim of San Francisco's elusive serial killer. His body was found stabbed to death on the rooftop of an apartment building in Potrero Hill." Becka turned slightly to the right and addressed Camera Two. "The method of the killing and undisclosed other clues have linked Mr. Tonelli's murder to those of the three homeless men before him. But there are a number of disturbing differences. Mr. Tonelli was not homeless; he lived in the building where his body was found. Nor was he unemployed. In fact, Mr. Tonelli worked as a producer at KKSF Radio."

The station ran a tape from the day before. Becka Flynn was at the police perimeter talking with Jane. "My sources indicate," she continued in voice-over, "that the word the police are using to explain this latest tragedy is *escalation*. There's growing concern among law enforcement officials that the serial killer is no longer targeting just homeless men . . . that anyone could be next. And San Franciscans throughout the city are all asking the same question: 'Are our streets safe?' "

Becka's face once again filled the screen.

"As I mentioned before, Mario Tonelli was a media colleague; having been on staff at KKSF Radio for the past three and a half years. Our Norma Chavez was at the radio station earlier today and filed this exclusive interview with Madeline Frohman, KKSF's news director—"

Loretta Temple pressed the mute button on her remote.

She sat in her corner chair, staring blankly at the TV set. Wisps of gray hair peeked out from all around her wig. A bedroom door opened. Andrew Temple came out with his brother's property bag. He put it on the coffee table in front of Jane and Kenny and went to sit with his mother.

"Thank you," Jane said softly.

Kenny used his pocketknife to undo the police seal. It was typical, Jane thought, that the survivors of murder victims often just left their belongings, untouched, in a closet.

Reggie Mayhew watched from near the front door as Kenny opened the bag and laid it on its side. He pulled out the plastic bag containing the money Willie Temple had in his pockets the night he was killed. Then the package of Kent cigarettes, the Zippo lighter, the opera schedule.

Jane put her hand on Kenny's shoulder.

He looked up.

Loretta and Andrew Temple were staring at them, the pain in their faces made all the more haunting by the gray-white light coming off the television. They were looking, for the first time since the murder, at reminders of Willie Temple from when he was alive. From when he was their brother and their son.

"C'mon," Jane whispered to Kenny.

They gathered up the things and rose. Reggie Mayhew opened the front door for them and they went outside.

"Shit," Jane said. "That was so insensitive of me."

"I'll talk to Mrs. Temple," Mayhew offered. "Make it all right again."

Kenny sat on the top step and dumped the bag out on the narrow porch. Jane bent down and picked up the tennis shoes. Then she turned them over and held the soles up to the yellow porch light.

Black grease was caught in the ribs of the two different herring-bone patterns. What she had originally thought of as the grime of a homeless man's existence held the secret of his murder.

Kenny put everything back in the bag and pulled open the screen door.

Reggie Mayhew was kneeling next to Loretta Temple, talking to her in a low voice. Andrew sat on the arm of her chair, comforting her. The anger he had displayed at the first meeting with Jane and Kenny had long ago succumbed to the weight of his grief.

Jane crossed the room. "Mrs. Temple, may I take your son's belongings with me? There's a good chance something in here could help us find Willie's killer."

Loretta Temple looked to Reggie Mayhew. He nodded. Then she turned to Jane. "I'll say yes, miss, if you'll do something for me."

"Of course. What is it?"

"Still ain't no obituary 'bout my boy."

Jane squatted down in front of her. "I promise you, Mrs. Temple, that I will get your son's obituary in the paper."

"Not just any paper," Andrew said. "The *Chronicle*."

Jane rose. "Mrs. Temple, do you have a picture of your son I can take with me?"

"For the *Chronicle*?"

"Yes, ma'am," Jane said. "For the *Chronicle*."

■

"HI, BECKA," JANE said into the phone as Kenny sped toward the Golden Gate Grand Hotel.

"Hey, good to hear from you. What's up?"

"Saw the newscast tonight."

"And?"

"And I'm concerned," Jane said, "that you might be stirring a pot that doesn't need stirring right now."

"We went 'round and 'round in the editorial meeting today," Becka said, "on exactly how to treat this story."

"And this sort of sensationalistic stuff is the best you could come up with? I mean, what's with that slogan, 'the killing streets'? C'mon, Becka."

"You don't even want to know the ones we didn't go with. Tell you what, though, I take your point and I'll talk to my boss. Hang on, let me close my door." Becka put Jane on hold for a moment. "Okay, I'm back. I just got a call and I need to tell someone . . . CNN is circling me. There's some talk about them flying me down to Atlanta in the next couple of days. Can you believe it?"

"Of course I can. They'd be lucky to have you."

"You're a good friend. I'll keep you posted. Anything else doing?"

As they closed in on the Golden Gate Grand, Jane could see a couple of motorcycle cops directing traffic. "Stuff is happening on the murder case and—"

"Which one?"

"Actually both of them."

There was a long silence on the other end. Jane knew Becka Flynn was looking for something to write with.

"*Both* of them?" Becka finally said. "What can you tell me?"

"Becka, I haven't even told the chief yet."

"We're getting reports of police activity at the parking structure of the Golden Gate Grand," Becka said. "Anything you can tell me about that?"

"Only that it's true. For now you'll have to draw your own conclusions." Kenny pulled into a parking place and waited for Jane to finish. "Can I ask you for a favor?"

"You bet."

"Do you still have any friends from back when you worked at the *Chronicle*?"

CHAPTER 42

■

"THEY'RE A PERFECT match," Aaron Clark-Weber said. "No question." He handed Willie Temple's tennis shoes back to Jane.

Parking Level Seven looked much the same as it had the night of Philip Iverson's murder. Yellow perimeter tape encircled the area where Aaron's Forensics Team worked. A mold of the footprints from the grease stain had been made in quick-set plaster. It sat on a card table next to a small glassine baggie containing the twenty-two slug.

"I'm sorry we missed it before," Aaron said. "It's bad police work on my part."

"We all made mistakes that night," Jane said.

A patrol officer came up with the Asian security guard who had been on duty the night of Philip Iverson's shooting.

"Sir," Jane said, "thank you for coming in tonight."

"I no have no choice," he spit. "Police comes. Take me from other job."

"I apologize for that." Jane held out her hand and Kenny passed her the picture of Willie Temple that Loretta had given them. "You can be out of here in five minutes. And I'll make sure someone drives you back." She showed him the photo. "Do you recognize this man?"

The security guard only had to glance at the picture. "Yeah, I know him. He Willies."

Jane heard Kenny catch his breath. "Is this a place he frequented?"

"What means?"

"Did he come here a lot?" Kenny asked.

"Yeah, yeah. All the times. If rich peoples here, Willies here also. My job is chase him away. No bother rich peoples. He always go nice. I feel bad. He soft man. No angry or nothin'." He nodded to a group of party-goers who were waiting for access to their cars. "I see rich peoples all the times. But no more Willies."

"Thank you, sir." Jane addressed the cop who had brought him in. "Take this gentleman's statement, and then get him back to his work."

Aaron Clark-Weber approached Jane and Kenny. "I'm just catching up to you guys here. Are you telling me you think Willie Temple killed Philip Iverson?"

"Never even crossed my mind," Kenny said. "But anything's possible."

"Not likely," Jane said. "The security guard said Willie was non-violent. Plus, what happened next? He goes out and becomes the first victim of a serial killer?"

"That would be a big night for anyone," Aaron said.

"Think about it," Kenny offered. "The stairwell stinks of urine."

"Right," Jane went on. "Wanna bet the cigarette butts in there are Kents? So Willie Temple is sitting on the stairs, keeping warm, smoking—"

"Peeing," Kenny interjected.

Aaron picked it up. "Waiting for the Man of the Year Banquet to break up so he can hit on the zillionaires for spare change."

"Just like all the other nights he's done this," Kenny said. "Remember the opera schedule?"

Jane nodded. "Right. But this night isn't like all the other nights. Because this night Philip Iverson gets murdered . . ."

Kenny looked over to the grease stain where Willie Temple had been standing. "And Willie Temple sees it. The killer spots him, shoots at him, and misses. The bullet goes into the exit sign over Willie's head, and Willie gets away."

Jane watched as a forensics tech loaded the footprint mold into the van. "But not for long. Iverson's killer catches up with him later and stabs him to death. Has to be."

"Then why," Aaron asked, "does the bad guy go out and kill all those others?"

"To distract us," Jane said. "He's trying to keep us from looking any deeper into Willie's murder. Because there must be some clue there that will lead us back to the killer. He wants to bury Willie in a haystack of other bodies and dilute the significance of his death."

"I'm with you," Kenny said, ". . . up to the snake thing."

"Yeah," Aaron said. "All my resources are stumped. What the hell's that about?"

Jane looked from Kenny to Aaron. ". . . I don't know."

CHAPTER 43

■

"WE THINK WE know the why of Willie Temple's murder," Jane said to Chief McDonald. "And we believe these two letters"—she indicated the blowups of the anonymous letters—"contain the why of Philip Iverson's murder."

"If we can just unravel the secrets of the letters," Kenny said, "which we believe are authentic, or determine what was so important about Willie Temple that the killer then went on to murder three more times in order to divert the entire police department, then we'll know the *who*."

"And then, sir," Jane concluded, "we've got him."

Chief McDonald sat on a folding chair, his feet stretched across to another, in Interrogation Room One. He wore an SFPD windbreaker over a gray sweatshirt, blue jeans, and white sneakers. The chief let his feet fall to the floor and leaned forward to study the blackboards. Then the letters.

Aaron Clark-Weber sat on the table, his evidence laid out around him. Linda French and Lou Tronick stood against the back wall next to the interior window. The curtains were drawn. This was a closed briefing. Principals only.

"All of you concur," Chief McDonald asked as he stood up, "that Philip Iverson's murderer and the serial killer of four other men . . . is the same person?"

Jane and Kenny had already weighed in with their opinions.

"Far as I'm concerned, sir," Aaron Clark-Weber said, "it's sound theory. And I'd pursue it vigorously."

The chief looked across the room. "Lou?"

"I'm on board, Chief."

"Inspector?"

"Me, too, sir," Linda said.

Chief McDonald turned to Jane. "I'm on board, too, Lieutenant. Keep this under wraps. Last thing we need is for the press to start blabbing what we know." He started for the door. Linda French stepped aside, allowing him to pass. He turned the knob and leaned into the door. Then he turned back. "There's some good police work going on in this room. Thank you for all you've done. Now let's nail this son of a bitch to the wall."

After he left, Jane motioned for everyone to come closer. "Guys, I know you're all whipped, but we've got a lot more work to do."

Lou Tronick poured himself his tenth cup of coffee the day. "Whatever it takes, Jane."

"We still don't know if Willie Temple was a witness or an accomplice," Jane said. "It's going to be shitty, but we have to dig deep into his life." She looked to Linda French. "I want you to go to his mother's house and get me the names of everyone they can remember from his past. Old roommates, army buddies, anyone. His old flophouses. You know the drill."

Linda sighed, clearly unhappy with the assignment.

"Problem?" Jane asked.

"No . . . no problem."

Jane turned to Lou Tronick. "Lou, I want you to concentrate on Willie Temple's last days. Was he hanging with anyone? Did one of his buddies kill Philip Iverson and then kill him to keep him quiet?"

"I'll follow that string, Jane," Lou said. "But Reggie Mayhew said Willie was a loner. Part of the poor fellow's tragedy was that he didn't have any friends."

"That's a good point," Jane conceded. "But give it a try." She turned to Kenny. "Just to track where we stand, now that we know the killer of Willie and the others is tied in to Philip Iverson's murder, then the anonymous letters are even more important to us. Anything new with decoding those numbers?"

"We've pulled every court case Philip Iverson, RiverPark, and Make It So were ever involved in. Like any multinational corporation, there's a ton of them." Kenny shook his head. "But so far . . . nothing."

"Okay, let's stay on it." Jane rose and moved toward the door. "Linda, my office, please."

■

"NOW THAT THE murder cases are linked, I'm taking point on both of them."

Jane spoke to Linda French from across her desk. "You will still be involved in the case, but you'll now report to Inspector Marks."

Linda stood in place, her face flushing with resentment.

"Further to that," Jane went on, "I have to tell you that your parking your car so close to the Iverson murder scene was a major blunder that has cost us a lot of time and missed opportunity. I've got no choice but to enter it in your file."

"And whose file, Lieutenant," Linda French asked tightly, "will reflect the fact that a second bullet went missing all this time?"

Jane regarded her evenly. "I've already dictated my notes to the file on that matter. *My* file." She pushed back her chair and got to her feet. "I had hoped for better from you, Linda. And I'll continue to hope that you'll learn from this and become a good homicide cop." She came around her desk and offered her hand. "Let's make the best of this and move on."

Linda French glared at Jane. "*You* make the best of this."

Without shaking Jane's hand, she turned and stormed out of the office.

■

KENNY WAS LYING across Jane's couch. Aaron Clark-Weber sat on the floor, stretching out his arthritic knee. Jane sat in the guest chair, sharing a mushroom-and-garlic pizza with the two people she trusted most in the department.

She looked out to Linda French's empty desk. Linda had left the bullpen about half an hour ago, presumably for Loretta Temple's house in Daly City.

"So," Jane said, "I ask her previous supervisor over at Robbery why he'd written her such a favorable performance review. And he tells me 'to get her out of my department. She's a pain in the ass.' "

Kenny tore off another slice of pizza. "Pain in the ass is one thing. Sloppy police work and a bad attitude are a whole 'nother story."

Jane took a sip from Kenny's beer. "Then I ask the guy why he didn't just get rid or her, and you know what he says to me?" She looked to Aaron. He busied himself with eating his pizza with a knife and fork. "He says," Jane went on, " 'All due respect, Lieutenant, but *you* try firing a woman in this city.' "

Kenny opened another beer, conceding the first one to Jane. "What'd you say?"

"I told him, and I quote, 'I will.' "

"Confession?" Aaron said.

"Sure," Jane answered. "What is it?"

"Well, earlier on, when we were presenting all the evidence in the first bum killings, and you were so impressed with her work?"

"Yeah?"

"That was all me. I had been working with her for a couple of days and she just didn't have the chops. I guess it was just easier to do everything myself."

"She had no trouble," Kenny said, "taking all the credit for it."

"One other thing," Aaron said to Jane. "One time when Linda and I were driving over to meet Professor Akiyama in Berkeley, she let slip that you were her first supervisor she couldn't charm."

Jane remembered the time she and Linda were in the elevator at the morgue. Linda had said that Jane was her role model. Now, Jane realized, it was all bullshit.

"She's had too many people covering her ass for too long a time,"

Jane said. "Including me. Well, it's over. From now on, it's sink or swim for Inspector French."

Mike Finney came to the door, a smear of pizza sauce on his chin. " 'Scuse me, Lieutenant. But we were watching the news in the lunchroom? And, in the opening? Your friend, Miss Flynn, said she had something big on the Philip Iverson case." He cast his eyes down to the pizza box. Kenny handed it to him and sat up to turn on Jane's TV.

". . . stunning new developments," Becka Flynn was saying, "on tonight's eleven-o'clock broadcast."

The station went to commercial.

■

ELLEN SCHUBERT SMILED.

She had been mired in her swamp of grief for so long, she almost forgot what it felt like.

But now, as she watched that pretty red-haired girl on the news, she knew that something was about to happen.

Finally.

If the people at KGO had figured it out, she thought, then surely the police had, too.

She bent over and scooped her cat up off the floor.

"You're my good girl."

■

"IT WORKS BOTH ways, Jane," Becka Flynn said over the phone. "You've got something you can't give me; I've got something I can't give you."

"That's a load of naive First Amendment crap, Becka, and you know it!" Jane was furious with her friend.

Becka was silent for a moment. "Okay, come down to the station after the eleven-o'clock news. I'll hand over everything I have. Deep sources included."

Jane understood it was a conciliatory gesture. But it wasn't enough. "Becka, I've got bodies piling up. I've got a killer out there who might get spooked by whatever you put on the air. It might even cause him to act again. I'm not prepared to take that risk. Are you?"

"Remember I told you about CNN? They called again. With all the face time I'm getting covering these cases, they're flying me to Atlanta tomorrow. The news director said something about Washington, D.C. He also said something about flying in other reporters from Boston and New Orleans, so I'm not the only one they're considering."

"I know how important this is to you. Believe me, I know all about ambition. About being alone. About wanting to start over. But this is bigger. Becka, this is as big as it gets. Please do the right thing."

Jane could feel Becka struggling on the other end of the line. If she told Jane what she knew, and Jane convinced her, or prevented her, from broadcasting it, then Becka would lose a possible career-changing opportunity. On the other hand, Jane had to believe in her friend's innate sense of decency.

"Okay." Becka sighed. "Come by the station *before* I go on the air. I'll be down in makeup, and we can go over what I have and where I got it."

Jane closed her eyes in relief. She was grateful to learn what Becka knew about the case. But she was also gratified that her friend had come down on the right side of a very difficult choice.

"Thanks, Becka. See you tonight."

■

KENNY SPREAD THE contents of Willie Temple's property bag out on the evidence table in Interrogation Room One.

Jane checked the items against the manifest.

Linda pulled the opera schedule out from under the Zippo lighter. "If you want, I can work off of this. Try to see if someone saw Willie with anyone suspicious. I also want to keep crossing what we know and what we need to know about the other vics. Just in case."

Jane glanced at Kenny. "Just in case" meant just in case her theory about Philip Iverson's death being linked to Willie Temple's was wrong. It was a legitimate line of reasoning. "Good idea."

Linda was trying in her own way, Jane thought, to apologize for her earlier outburst. With all they had to do, she was willing to let it ride.

Mike Finney rushed into Interrogation Room One. "Lieutenant . . ." he began, so distraught he could hardly find the breath to speak.

"What is it, Mike?"

"Lieutenant, we got a call from KGO . . . Becka Flynn's been murdered."

CHAPTER 44

■

THERE WAS A snapshot on Becka Flynn's refrigerator of a red-headed six-year-old in a Sleeping Beauty costume. Another showed the same girl in a riding outfit sitting on a chestnut mare. Beneath that was a school photo. "For Aunt Becka, I will love you always, Shannon."

Jane understood.

She could feel in her soul what it felt like to be alone; to display pictures of someone else's children when you have none of your own.

Numb with sadness, Jane wove her way through the Homicide and Forensics Teams toward the bedroom.

Becka Flynn's body was on the floor next to the bed.

Blood from the stab wound in her chest had turned her white carpeting a rich and deep red. Like her hair, Jane thought as she came into the room. She bent down and studied Becka's face. There was a bruise high on her forehead near the hairline. "Blunt trauma?"

"Don't know yet," Aaron Clark-Weber said softly.

Jane nodded and peered in closer. With her sprinkling of freckles, her closed eyes, and her lips still moist, it seemed to all the world that Becka was merely asleep. That soon she would stir and make a joke about all these people in her house.

"Jane," Kenny said, "come look at this." He took her by the arm and led her to the other side of the bed. On the door of the nightstand was a crude drawing of a small snake.

In blood.

"Did you type it?"

"It's hers."

"Why so small?" Jane crouched down to examine it more closely. "And where are those dots?"

Kenny knelt beside her. "I was talking with the guys about that. They're thinking that it could mean a couple of things. Either the killer didn't have time to get more elaborate. Or . . ."

"Or what?"

"Or he's starting over."

Kenny stood up and helped Jane to her feet. There was a carry-on suitcase next to the dresser. A faxed confirmation for Delta Flight #1949 to Atlanta at seven-thirty the next morning was tucked under the handle.

"Any sign of forced entry?" Jane asked. "Neighbors hear anything?"

"No and no," Kenny said. "She either let him in, which of course means she knew the killer or had nothing to fear from him when he presented himself."

Jane looked across the bed as the Forensics Team continued to work on Becka's body. "Or he followed her home and made his move when she opened the door."

Two coroner's deputies squeezed into the small bedroom with a black body bag. Jane and Kenny passed into the living room.

"She came home to pack for her CNN meeting tomorrow." Kenny stepped aside as two cops lifted Becka's computer off her desk and carried it outside. "She had a reservation at the Airport Sheraton for tonight, presumably so she wouldn't have to get up before dawn to make such an early flight."

"She didn't want to look tired for her big interview." Jane sniffed a little laugh. It was so typical of Becka to think ahead like that. "Who found her?"

"When she didn't show for her makeup call, the station sent a newsroom intern over. Gretchen Brodie." Kenny pointed to where a twenty-year-old black woman sat in the bay window seat. She had her arms wrapped around her chest and, staring at the floor, she rocked gently back and forth.

Her life from this moment on, Jane knew, would be changed forever.

"After pounding on the door for a couple of minutes," Kenny continued, "she went and got the condo supervisor. He unlocked the door, but it was the kid who found Becka's body."

Jane motioned for Aaron Clark-Weber to join them.

"I'm sorry about this, Jane," Aaron said. "I know she was a friend of yours."

"Thanks. What are you turning up?"

"You saw the snake thing in there. We got some good latex traces."

"How about the red cotton fiber?" Jane asked.

"Not yet," Aaron said. "But as we learned at the parking structure, that doesn't mean it's not here." He nodded and made his way back into the bedroom.

Jane watched as the coroner's deputies lifted the body bag onto the gurney. It landed heavily, without grace; made awkward by its own awful weight. Jane closed her eyes and tilted her head back, holding in the tears.

Kenny leaned into her. Jane pressed against him, drawing on his strength as Becka's body rolled past. A uniform opened the front door and the coroner's deputies hefted the gurney down the three steps to the street. Jane noticed Becka's BMW 325i being secured onto an SFPD flatbed. Becka was lifted into the coroner's wagon. The flatbed and the wagon pulled away from the curb at the same time.

"Lieutenant?" A young patrol officer was standing at a respectful distance. "Can I show you something?"

"Sure."

She and Kenny followed him to the bookcase behind Becka's desk. An answering machine sat on the middle shelf next to a tall KGO Post-it stack. Using the tip of his pen, the cop pressed "play." The tape whirred into rewind, clicked once, then went forward.

"Hi, Miss Flynn. It's Danny from Mr. Christopher's office at CNN. Please check your fax machine. I've sent you confirmation of your Delta flight to Atlanta. Looking forward to meeting you."

Then the next message.

"Becka? Becka, are you there? This is Gretchen. We're wondering where you are. I'll try the car again."

And the last.

"Hello, Miss Flynn." A woman's voice. "I'm returning your call. Yes, I'll watch your broadcast tonight. I'm most anxious to hear what you have to say. Perhaps we can talk after."

Alice Iverson.

And then it struck Jane, like two pieces of a jigsaw puzzle clicking together to reveal a larger picture.

"Ken, c'mere." Jane led him to the small dinette. They sat down and she pulled her chair closer to him. "This all makes sense now," she began. "In fact, it proves our theory. Becka went on the air tonight saying she was going to release some big information on Philip Iverson's murder. Iverson's killer naturally wants to prevent that, so he stabs her to death, making it look like the homeless killings, then that radio producer's killing. Just another murder in the whole escalation."

"To make it seem," Kenny said, "like this *wasn't* about Philip Iverson."

"Exactly." Jane watched as Stacey Moran from Forensics emptied the kitchen trash bin into an evidence bag. "He doesn't know we already suspect the other murders are a cover-up." Stacey then went to the desk where Becka's computer had been and dumped the contents of the wastebasket into a second evidence bag.

Jane leaped to her feet. "Stacey! Hang on a minute." She hurried over and grabbed the bag. Then she turned it upside down. Papers and other discards floated down to the floor. Jane shook the bag.

A bright orange visitor's pass landed on the pile.

Becka Flynn had been to Shanley Prison.

"Josh Stolberg," Jane said. "Becka got him to talk."

■

"THE CANCER'S TAKING over and he's slipping into an advanced stage of dementia," the prison infirmary's chief of staff explained. "His organs are failing. First his liver, then his kidneys." He looked through the observation window. "And soon . . . his heart."

"Is there any possibility," Jane asked, "that he could ever be lucid again?"

"Even briefly?" Kenny added.

They stood in the darkened corridor in a circle of light from an overhead lamp. Other than their voices, there was virtually no sound in the prison hospital. These were not ordinary patients and this was no ordinary hospital facility. All of the doors were thick, closed . . . and locked.

"Lieutenant, I know how important it is that you speak to Mr. Stolberg." The doctor shook his head. "But it just isn't going to happen. He has no mental capacity, as we know it, remaining. There's a very good chance he won't live another twenty-four hours. Mrs. Stolberg is in with him now . . . to say good-bye." He turned to go. "I'll be in my office if you need me."

"Thank you, Doctor," Kenny said.

Josh Stolberg lay with his head drooping forward, a string of slobber falling across his chin. His wife passed in front of the observation window and went to the bed. She cleaned her husband's face, and then lowered the bedsheet. His thin, gray body heaved with every breath.

Mrs. Stolberg pulled on the Velcro tabs of her husband's diaper and removed it. After wiping his crotch and genitals, she put on a fresh one and pulled the sheet back over his chest. Then she touched his face with her hand and bent over to kiss him on the lips.

"This time tomorrow, she'll be a widow," Kenny said softly.

"We've got a widow of our own to deal with," Jane said.

CHAPTER 45

———■———

ALICE IVERSON WORE her grief as if it were part of her wardrobe.

Jane imagined Alice getting up in the morning, showering and dressing. And then, before she faced the day, she would don the widow's mantle. It was what people saw first, the presentation of pain, rather than the pain itself.

The mahogany shutters in the library of the Iversons' apartment sliced the morning sun into horizontal ribbons. Jane sat on the couch across from Alice, her gut jumping with suspicion.

"There's little to tell really," Alice Iverson said. She was wearing a starched white blouse, beige slacks, and Belgian loafers. "Miss Flynn called me yesterday and left a message with my service. She said she wanted me to watch her on the late news last night, and asked if she could call me afterward to follow up."

Kenny shifted his shoulders, scratching his back against the edge of the bookcase. "Did you respond?"

Alice didn't even bother to look at him. "You know I did, Inspector. That's why you're here. You heard my voice on Miss Flynn's answering machine."

"And what would you have said to Becka Flynn," Kenny asked, "had you had the chance?"

"That's all too hypothetical for me this early in the morning." She turned slightly, still not facing Kenny directly. "*Really*, Inspector."

"Mrs. Iverson," Jane said, "did Becka Flynn give you any indication about what she was going to say on the air last night?"

"No, nothing. She just wanted me to watch the broadcast." Alice Iverson turned to Jane. "Let's make this a two-way street, Lieutenant. My husband was murdered over a week ago. You and the rather considerable resources of your department have been, as you've said to the press, devoted to finding his killer. Just what have you learned so far?"

"We believe," Jane said, "that Becka Flynn was killed because she knew something about your husband's murder."

For the first time in this encounter, Alice Iverson seemed to be completely engaged. "Do you have any idea what that may have been?"

Jane nodded. "We have our suspicions."

"For God's sake, Lieutenant, stop being so obtuse. What exactly are your suspicions?"

"You know something, Mrs. Iverson?" Jane leaned forward on the couch. "You're wrong. This is not a two-way street. I am under no obligation to tell you anything. I would appreciate it if you would take words like *obtuse* and its implication off the table and just co-operate in this interview."

But Alice Iverson wasn't backing down. "Lieutenant Candiotti, my husband is *dead*! I am really quite tired of your evasions."

Jane felt her own anger welling in her chest. "There is no evasion on my part, only prudence. Your confrontational attitude is not going to get me to disclose anything more than I deem appropriate."

Alice Iverson glared at Jane.

Jane now recognized something in Alice she'd not been able to identify before.

Hatred.

"This interview is terminated, Lieutenant." Alice Iverson rose from the leather club chair. "I think it best that all requests for further communication between us be handled by my attorney."

Jane used the arm of the couch to pull herself up. Kenny crossed the room and opened the door.

"Speaking of attorneys, Mrs. Iverson," Jane said. She now stood face-to-face with her. "What can you tell us about your husband's history, and your own, with Josh Stolberg?"

A flicker of uncertainty betrayed Alice Iverson's careful facade.

Jane remembered where she had seen that same look before.

On Josh Stolberg's face when she had asked him about Alice Iverson.

These two people, Jane thought, were sitting on a secret. She pressed the point. "You know something you're not divulging. When you decide that you really want to solve your husband's murder, you'll tell me the truth. Until then, you stay the hell out of my way." She brushed past Alice, their shoulders bumping.

"Lieutenant," Alice Iverson said, hissing.

Jane turned.

"And if I don't?"

Jane came back at Alice and thrust her jaw into her face. "Believe me, Mrs. Iverson, you do not want to fuck with me anymore."

■

JANE WAS STARING at Becka Flynn's name atop a new column on the second blackboard. It was unbelievable to her, but there it was.

Kenny stood next to the blackboard, briefing the Homicide Team. "Nothing in Becka's home computer or her computer at KGO had anything of interest to us."

Jane leaned against the back wall. She was hurting over Becka's death and still seething over her confrontation with Alice Iverson.

"M.E.'s report," Kenny went on, "tells us what we already know. The bruise on her head was most likely not fatal. No defense wounds, nothing under the nails." He glanced over to Jane. "And so on."

Ordinarily, Jane realized, the inspector-in-charge would have gone into far greater detail in reading from a medical examiner's report. Details about the nature of the fatal wounds, the organs involved. But ordinarily, the victim wouldn't have been a friend of the homicide lieutenant. Jane lowered her chin in a tiny nod of gratitude.

"We still haven't found the red fiber," Aaron reported. "But if it's there, we will."

"It's not entirely outside the realm of possibility," Lou Tronick offered, "that the killer might want to change his shirt every, I don't know, four or five murders or so."

"Good point," Kenny acknowledged. "But it's still an anomaly, and we should treat it as such. We're also pursuing the fact that Mario Tonelli worked in radio and Becka Flynn worked in TV. Might be some kind of media thing there. Might not."

Linda French sat to the side of the room going over her notes, removed both from the center of activity and from the conversation. She had had little to offer in the two hours they'd been sifting through the accumulation of evidence. In that time, her mood had deteriorated from detachment to petulance.

Jane was even more resolute that Linda would have to go.

"On the subject of anomalies," Aaron added, "Professor Akiyama agrees with the possibility that the diminution of the snake symbol may mean some sort of retreat on the part of the killer. The question is: Is the bad guy going away like Zodiac . . . or is he starting over?"

"Either option is unacceptable to us," Jane said. "If he crawls into some hole like Zodiac did, then we have to find him and dig him out. I am *not* going to have this asshole walking the streets of our city knowing he murdered all these people. Mocking us. And, guys, we just have to prevent him from the other option."

The door opened. Mike Finney carried in a deli tray. "Dinner."

"Mike," Jane said as Lou Tronick took the tray from him, "what's happening with the numbers on those letters?"

Finney crossed to the easels where the blowups stood. "I attacked these every which way from here to Sunday. They're simply not court cases."

"What about other states besides California?"

"Sorry, Lieutenant."

Linda French lifted her head from her notes. "Swiss bank account?"

"Been there, too," Finney said. He watched possessively as Lou Tronick made himself a corned-beef sandwich. "Switzerland and most other countries use a combination of numerals and letters."

"Insurance," Lou Tronick offered. "Maybe it's the number of an insurance policy. Lord knows Philip Iverson had to be insured up the wazoo."

Finney shuffled his feet. "I hadn't thought of that, Inspector." He seemed almost embarrassed at the omission.

"It's a good impulse," Jane said. "Mike, why don't you and Lou jump on that right away?"

"Check foreign carriers, too," Kenny added.

Roz Shapiro came in with a cardboard box of Starbucks and soft drinks. She put it next to the deli tray. As she crossed to leave the room, she handed Jane the afternoon edition of the *Chronicle*.

Becka Flynn's murder was the lead story.

■

JANE SAT AT her desk and read of the murder of one of San Francisco's rising stars in journalism. Cameron Sanders, a senior correspondent for the *Chronicle* and an old friend of Becka's, had written the story himself.

"Check this out." Kenny sat in the guest chair. He held up the metro section. Below an article about that evening's Chinese New Year celebration was a small black-and-white picture of Willie Temple. Becka Flynn had done Jane one last favor on the day she died and gotten his obituary printed in the city's leading newspaper.

Seeing it now, Jane understood why Loretta Temple had been so insistent that her son's obituary should run in the *Chronicle*.

It lent him an aura of legitimacy in death that had been denied him in life.

Kenny lowered the paper. "Some fucking day, huh?"

Jane dropped the front page onto her blotter. "Some fucking day."

"Look under your desk."

"What?"

"Just look."

Jane pushed her chair back and bent down. Her overnight bag was wedged behind the wastebasket.

"It's packed," Kenny said, "with half your birthday present." He stood and came around the desk. "The other half"—he massaged her shoulders—"is a night of passion and fireworks—sexual and otherwise—on the fortieth floor of the Shanghai Dragon Palace."

Jane purred and let her head fall forward. "And sleep?"

"We are so married."

CHAPTER 46

■

KENNY SLIPPED THE strap of Jane's camisole down over her shoulder. "Ever make love under a mirrored ceiling before?"

"Not in my forties." Jane straddled Kenny and fell forward. Placing her hands on either side of his head, she brushed her right breast across his mouth.

"Speaking of forty," Kenny said, "we're forty floors up and I can still hear all those people on the streets down there."

"That's because every one of them has firecrackers." Jane reached down and took him in her hand. "Now shut up and fuck me." She lowered her hips onto him. A shiver of release coursed through her body as he entered her. "Slowly," Jane whispered. "Slowly . . . husband."

She sat back on his thighs and moved up and down, flexing her legs, absorbing him. Closing her eyes, she arched her shoulders and increased the tempo. When she opened them again, Kenny was smiling at her.

"What?"

"Two things. One, I love my wife." He reached up and touched her lips. "And B, you gotta see this."

Jane looked up.

For just an instant, she thought the couple in the mirror over their bed was someone else.

They looked so young and happy.

In that moment when Jane realized she was that woman who was looking back at her, she suddenly filled with emotion. She took Kenny's hand and put his first two fingers into her mouth. Sucking on them, she intensified her pumping. Rising on her knees until Kenny was almost out of her, then dropping back down onto him. Again and again.

Jane moaned and dug her nails into Kenny's chest, their skin slapping together in a rhythmic frenzy. At last, Jane tossed her head back and watched the woman in the mirror above have a long, delicious, shivering orgasm.

Exhausted, she fell across the pillows. "Wow."

"No shit, wow." Kenny pulled her to him. "Wait a minute. Aren't firecrackers illegal?"

■

THE LIGHT WOKE them.

Then the noise.

Brilliant flashes of bursting colored light filled the sky outside their room. Then a concussive booming followed as sound caught up to light.

Jane and Kenny sat up in bed. Their room filled with the ricocheting beams of starburst fireworks. "Happy birthday." Kenny kissed her on the forehead. "And Happy New Years, Chinatown-style."

A flurry of fireworks roared across the floor-to-ceiling windows in rapid succession. Flaming and smoking fragments fell back to earth.

"Like it?" Kenny asked.

"Better than sex."

"Ouch."

Jane laughed and threw her arms around Kenny's neck. "Thank you so much for this."

"Thank *you*," Kenny said, "for making everything in my life better."

"You're welcome." Jane touched her forehead to his. "I'm gonna call room service. Want anything?"

"Everything."

Jane sat on the side of the bed and retrieved a pair of sweats from her overnight bag. She pulled the sweatshirt over her head and wriggled into the pants. "Ahh, cozy."

"Sexy." Kenny got on his knees behind her and nuzzled her hair.

Jane picked up the telephone receiver, switched on the bedside lamp, and dialed room service. As she did, she thought she saw, out of the corner of her eye, a small dark dot appear on the window where the fireworks were lighting up the sky. A heartbeat later, the mirror over the bed shattered, raining shards of glass down onto her and Kenny. Then the bedside lamp was thrown back against the wall.

Jane felt Kenny's body fall on top of her. He pushed her to the floor. Just then, the huge window filled with a thousand tiny cracks. It crumbled inward, bringing with it the cold night air and the roar of the fireworks.

"Someone's shooting at us!" Kenny yelled. He crawled to the small desk. His sport coat and shoulder holster were draped over the back of the desk chair. Jane groped under the bed for her purse. She found it and pulled out her service weapon. Bullets thudded into the wall just above her head.

Kenny toppled the desk and pushed it into the gaping hole where the window had been. Jane scooted across the glass-strewn carpet. "Do you see him?"

The television exploded.

"There!" Kenny shouted. "Where the building els. Third window in."

Two bullets pierced the side of the desk, splinters of wood erupting into the air. Jane spotted the muzzle flashes. "I see him!"

Together, they rose to their knees and fired. Round after round tore into the window across the way.

Jane reloaded her pistol. "Think we got him?"

"You're the marksman." Kenny slammed another clip into his Glock. "What do you think?"

The impact of a bullet screaming toward them sent a piece of window frame flying into the room.

Jane caught a glimpse of movement. A door was yanked open, a body raced through a sliver of light from the hotel corridor, then the door was slammed closed. She pulled on her tennis shoes and tugged at the action of her pistol.

"C'mon!" She whipped open the door and hurtled into the hallway.

■

THE LOBBY OF the Shanghai Dragon Palace was teeming with people.

Families, college kids, businessmen, and tourists; all had come to Chinatown for the fireworks and parade.

Just to the right of the bell captain's podium, a dozen elevators stood six and six across from each other. The last one on the left opened, and Jane and Kenny, their weapons under their shirts, raced out.

Jane searched the crowd as she hurried to the reception clerk.

In his haste, Kenny bumped into a man on a pay phone. "Sorry," he called back as he ran to join Jane at the front desk.

Jane turned and gasped. "God, Ken, are you hit?"

Kenny looked at his T-shirt. There was a wide streak of blood across his sleeve. "It's not mine!" He remembered the man he had jostled. He spun around. The pay-phone receiver was dangling off the hook. Beyond it, the man was shoving his way through the revolving door. A dark trail of blood seeped from a wound in his shoulder.

"There!" Kenny took off after him.

Jane grabbed the desk clerk by the arm and screamed into his face. "I'm a cop! Call 911 and tell them we have shots fired. Officer needs help. Got it?"

The clerk nodded briskly. "Got it."

But Jane was already gone, racing across the lobby and out the bellhop door.

She entered another world. Hundreds of exploding firecrackers danced on the pavement in front of her. Music from half a dozen marching bands collided with one another in the canyon of China-town's buildings.

Jane quickly surveyed the area as the parade watchers thronged around her. Elementary-school children in flowered masks waved from the centerline of the street. An enormous Chinese dragon bobbed and floated from curbside to curbside to the cheers of the thousands of people overflowing the sidewalks.

In an odd bit of juxtaposition, Jane saw Mayor Lucien Biggs, a dy-namic black man in his late fifties, waving his trademark fedora from the back of a mock cable car.

Across the broad avenue, through a float commemorating Chinese-American cooperation in the arts, Jane spotted Kenny fight-ing his way through the mass of people. She looked to the right. The gunman was twenty feet ahead of him.

As the fireworks continued to burst overhead, Jane flew around the float and made it to the other side. But Kenny was racing head-long away from her. She saw the gunman career around a corner, into an alley just past an acupuncture studio; Kenny in close pursuit.

Jane grabbed the arm of a young uniformed cop working crowd control. He reflexively pulled away and reached for his weapon. "I'm Lieutenant Candiotti," Jane said. "SFPD Homicide. Call code 3H58." The cop's partner, an Asian woman, came over. Jane addressed both of them. "I'm in foot pursuit. Suspect is male Caucasian, six feet, sandy-blond hair. GSW to left shoulder. Armed and dangerous. I need you to seal off the far end of that alley."

The female officer snapped her pistol from its holster. "You call it in yet?"

"Yes. Now go!"

The cops raced into a Chinese grocery. They tore down the center aisle and burst through the back door.

Seconds later, Jane reached the mouth of the alley and, horrified, skidded to a stop.

Kenny was on his knees beneath a fire escape.

The gunman stood over him, about to fire into his head. His pock-marked face was pulled into a grimace.

Jane whipped her pistol out from under her sweatshirt. "NO!" she shouted. But her voice was absorbed by the din of the parade. There were a dozen people milling about the alley entrance. They were blocking her way, their attention riveted on the celebration in the street. Jane couldn't get a shot. "Get down! I'm a cop! Get DOWN!"

The few revelers who could see or hear her fell to the ground. But there were still too many bodies between her and the gunman. Frantic, she threw herself forward, shoving people out of her way. Even as she did, she saw the gunman pull back on the hammer, his finger curling on the trigger, and she knew she'd never get there in time.

There was a commotion to her right.

A. J. Guthrie stiff-armed a young couple aside. He took three long strides and in one fluid motion tore his .357 Magnum from beneath his coat.

The gunman sensed how close he was and started to turn. But before he could come around, A.J. fired twice into his chest, sending him flying backward into a row of steel fifty-five-gallon drums.

Kenny jumped to his feet and scrambled to get his pistol.

The gunman still clutched his weapon. When Sheriff Guthrie stepped forward to retrieve it, the gunman began to raise it toward him. A.J. fired one round into his forehead, blowing out the back of his skull.

And it was over.

The wailing of sirens cut through the music and the shouting and the firecrackers. The two crowd-control officers came running up from the back of the alley.

A.J. watched numbly, his gun hanging in his hand, as Kenny began tearing the clothes off the gunman's body.

Jane hurried over to him. "Are you okay?"

"Yes!" Kenny turned the gunman over. "Shit, it isn't him!"

A.J. moved in closer. "What are you doing?"

"Looking for a bite wound," Kenny explained. "Willie Temple's killer had a chunk of flesh bitten out of him."

A.J. slipped his pistol into his shoulder holster. "How in the world do you know that?"

"Because," Jane said, "we found it in Willie Temple's mouth."

"Jane, look at this." Kenny squatted down and pulled something out of the gunman's back pocket. A pair of latex gloves.

"I want to know who this guy is and where he lives," Jane said. "And then I want a team tossing his place as soon as possible."

Kenny nodded. "I'll call it in."

A.J. took a cigar from his shirt pocket and tried to light it with a match. But his hands were trembling. He looked to Jane, embarrassed. "All these years," he said, "I ain't never had to pull my weapon." He glanced down to the gunman. "Let alone do something like this."

Jane reached out and steadied his hands until the cigar was lit. "Thank you, Sheriff," she whispered. "Thank you." She let go of his hands. "Why are you here?"

A.J. let a stream of smoke curl over his upper lip. "Mrs. Iverson called me and instructed me to personally contact you. So I called the precinct. Your Miss Lomax said you were both out. I guess I kind of badgered her into telling me where you were. I apologize if that was overreaching, but it was important."

"Well," Kenny said, "under the circumstances . . ."

Two more patrol officers, their guns drawn, ran into the alley. Kenny flashed his shield and directed them to the gunman. A half-dozen other cops were hustling toward them from the other end of the alley. An ambulance, its siren whooping intermittently, nudged its way through the crowd.

Jane touched A.J.'s arm. "What was so important, Sheriff?"

"I kinda hate to tell you this, but"—he drew deeply on his cigar and politely turned his head to blow out a thin stream of smoke— "Mrs. Iverson, through her attorney, is going to Chief McDonald about you."

Jane shook her head. "Won't be the first time."

"This one's different," A.J. said. "She's claiming that you lost your temper and shoved her. And then you threatened her. She wants you removed from the case."

Jane shook her head in disgust. "Y'know, Sheriff, after what we've all been through tonight, nothing Mrs. Iverson does either surprises me or worries me. Let her do what she has to; and let the chief do what he has to. They can spin their wheels with all their bullshit . . . I've got a job to do."

The ambulance arrived at the alley entrance. A police van pulled up behind it and ten officers in riot gear poured out to secure the area. A.J. watched blankly as the man he shot was surrounded by the black-clad cops.

Then he suddenly found himself on the other side of an adrenaline rush. Spent, he leaned against the cool brick wall and wiped his forehead with his sleeve. He let the cigar fall from his fingers. It landed in a puddle and went out. "Damn, but if I ain't beat to shit."

CHAPTER 47

———■———

THE HOMICIDE TEAM was gathered in Interrogation Room One.

"ID on the shooter from last night is Kimball Wayne Ashe." Kenny held up a sheet of paper. "Forty-four. Escaped con. Drugs, assault, manslaughter. Quite the résumé." He dropped the page on the table. "Aaron had a team work Ashe's apartment in the Tenderloin all night long."

Jane turned to Aaron. "What'd you find?"

"A lot," Aaron Clark-Weber said. "Blood traces on the front door-knob and the bathroom faucet that are consistent with two of the homeless victims. A knife that may be the murder weapon . . . we'll know tonight. A box of latex gloves. And then one of my guys found a red flannel shirt in a trash bag at the bottom of a Dumpster behind his building."

"So all this means," Kenny said, "that this guy's involved in the serial killings. Which *also* means he's involved in Philip Iverson's murder."

Something about the gunman was eating at Jane. "Ken, how big was Kimball Ashe?"

Kenny read from the report. "Five-eight, one-fifty."

Jane shook her head. "All of our science has been telling us the se-rial victims were killed by a large man."

"Don't have to be a big guy," Kenny said, "to shoot Philip Iverson in the head."

"Point taken," Jane acknowledged. "Maybe he was there, maybe not. We know because of the flesh thing that we're looking for more than one man. Here's what we need to do: find out Kimball Wayne Ashe's relationship to Philip Iverson. However obscure, however many degrees of separation . . . we do that and we're there."

Mike Finney came to the door. Behind him Jane saw A. J. Guthrie come out of the elevator and head down the hall to his shooting-team debriefing. He seemed, Jane thought, as lost as a bird at night.

"Chief McDonald called from his car," Mike Finney said. "Wants to see you in his office at noon."

"Tell him I'm busy," Jane said, unable to conceal her irritation with the chief.

". . . Okay."

Through the window, Jane could see Roz Shapiro and a couple of uniforms gathered around the television in the lunchroom. She crossed to the open doorway.

The announcer spoke in a low voice she couldn't quite hear from across the bullpen. But Jane was able to make out the exterior of a Southwestern-style church on the screen. The sun was brilliant, completely unlike the winter light of San Francisco. People streamed up the steps of the church. Jane noticed the KGO logo floating in the bottom right corner. And she remembered.

Becka Flynn was being buried today.

■

SITTING IN HER darkened living room, the drapes drawn tight, Ellen Schubert watched the funeral of Becka Flynn.

It had been Becka's promise of a break in the Philip Iverson murder case that had filled Ellen with hope. Now that hope was gone and Ellen knew she had to come forward. If not for herself, then for the others.

The coverage of the funeral came to an end and the station went to a break.

Ellen's cat didn't stir when she got up from the couch and went to her desk. She had reread the files last night. Blocking out the sounds of fireworks from Chinatown, she had relived their secrets.

She found herself in the mirror over the desk. The time, the shame, the loss had all taken their toll. Her hand trembled as she reached for the telephone.

■

CHIEF MCDONALD LOOMED in the doorway.

Then he stepped into Jane's office and, leaning forward, put his hands on the back of the guest chair. " 'Busy' when your chief calls you is *not* an option. Do you understand me, Lieutenant?"

Jane stood up to meet him head-on. " 'Busy,' sir, is what happens to a homicide lieutenant when there's a murder case of the highest profile *on top of* a serial killer running loose in the city. 'Busy' is what happens when that lieutenant's chief tells her to solve those murders at all costs."

"Even at the cost of threatening a murder victim's widow?"

"It never happened. We had some strong words, and that was it."

"Not according to her." Chief McDonald straightened up. "I want you to apologize to her. Strike that. I'm *ordering* you to apologize to her."

"That, sir," Jane said evenly, "is not going to happen."

"What is it about you, Lieutenant, that has to be so goddamned confrontational in every situation?"

"And what is it about you, Chief, that reflexively believes the word of someone like Alice Iverson instead of an officer in your own command?"

A blur of movement in the squad room caught Jane's eye.

Devon Haskell seemed to be running backward. Then Jane saw that Kenny was grasping him by the lapels and was propelling him across the bullpen. They crashed into the large window of Interrogation Room One, the upper half of Haskell's body shattering the glass.

Jane bolted past the chief and ran out of her office. Just as the other cops were converging on him, Kenny's fists shot out. The first blow caught Devon Haskell in the temple, the second just under the right ear.

Haskell was stunned for an instant. Then he lunged at Kenny. But Mike Finney caught him in a powerful bear hug, and Devon, his feet still churning, struggled to free himself.

"Gentlemen," the chief bellowed, "stand DOWN!"

Kenny lowered his fists. Finney let go of Haskell.

The chief strode up to Jane. "Lieutenant, you're losing control. My office at noon. No excuses, no nothing. You will be there." He grabbed Haskell by the arm and tugged him toward the waiting elevator.

A. J. Guthrie emerged from his debriefing. He saw what was happening and stood back at a respectful distance.

Everyone in the bullpen waited for the elevator doors to close before moving again. Everyone except Cheryl Lomax. She was speaking into her headset at the dispatch console.

Just as Jane was turning to confront Kenny, Cheryl was rising from her chair. "Lieutenant," she called out, "I got a woman on the phone. Says she wrote those letters!"

"Send it to my office." Jane tore across the squad room, ran into her office, and snatched up the phone. "This is Lieutenant Candiotti."

"I wrote those letters."

"How many letters?"

"Two."

Jane grabbed a pencil. "What's your name?"

"I'd rather not say."

"I understand. Just your first name, then, so I have something to call you by."

There was a long pause. ". . . Ellen."

"Okay, Ellen. Good." Jane made a note. "Can you tell me what those numbers mean?"

"Yes."

Jane's heart leaped. "What? What do they mean?"

The woman hesitated. "Not on the phone."

"Then meet me somewhere."

"I . . . I can't."

"Are you afraid?"

"Yes."

"If you meet me, I can help you," Jane insisted. "If you don't, then I can't." Jane thought she heard the woman weeping. "Let me help you," she said gently.

". . . Okay," the woman finally said. "Ruby's Deli in half an hour. I'll be wearing a yellow scarf . . . with flowers."

"And I'll be wearing—" Jane began.

"I've seen you on television."

The line went dead.

Jane dropped the phone and ran back out. "It was definitely her."

"Did you get a name?" Kenny asked.

"Ellen somebody. I'm meeting her at Ruby's Deli in half an hour."

A. J. Guthrie came up behind Kenny. "Which Ruby's? There's two of them."

"Yeah," said Finney. "One in the Financial District. Another in Russian Hill."

"Get your stuff," Jane said to Kenny. "We'll split up and cover both of them." She raced for the stairwell door.

CHAPTER 48

JANE SAT IN an unmarked police sedan across the street from Ruby's Deli in Russian Hill.

She watched the foot traffic work its way along Kearney Street.

Her pager vibrated. Jane glanced at the readout. *Anything? Call me. 3H61.* She dialed Kenny's cell phone.

He answered on the first ring. "Any action over there?"

"Nothing yet." Jane's eyes flicked back and forth, taking in every woman in every car, in every doorway. A taxi pulled up next to Jane's car. "Hang on." A middle-aged woman got out. She paid the driver, then lugged a cello out from the backseat. The cab drove away and the woman wheeled the cello down the street. "False alarm."

"Had a couple myself."

"Ken," Jane said solemnly.

"You're pissed at me, huh?"

"That . . . and disappointed. It's hard enough with us being married and working together like we do. But we're the ones who have to set the higher standard."

"I know that, but Haskell's been riding me pretty hard for weeks. Truth is, I'm a little impressed with myself for maintaining as long as I did."

"Then get over yourself. You simply don't get to explode in your usual Y-chromosome way just because someone's giving you shit. Plus, now I've got the chief on my ass way worse than before."

"Tell me something, Jane," Kenny said quietly. "Did Chief McDonald stop by the precinct to compliment you on your restraint with Alice Iverson?"

"Ken, it's true I can't stand that woman. But my little nonincident with her had everything to do with solving a murder case . . . and nothing to do with my ego. You *have* to see the difference."

Kenny took a moment to absorb all this. "Okay . . . I get it. You're right and I'm sorry."

"Thank you, honey." Jane felt a rush of emotion. "Ken . . . last night, in the alley . . ."

". . . I know."

"I almost lost you. What kind of life is this? What kind of jobs do we have where you almost get shot in the head by some loser junkie ex-con? What are we gonna do?"

"If you want out, then you should resign. I'll support us until you find something else . . . or we have a baby. Whatever you want." Kenny paused, a hum of static connecting them. "But if you left, then I would be . . ."

"Sad?"

"In charge of the department," Kenny said. "I've been thinking a lot about what you said before. And you were right. I've got some definite issues working under you."

"How serious are these issues?"

"They're serious, Jane. They color everything I do. How I live, how I work."

"Then we *have* to keep talking about them, Ken. Otherwise we're living in two different worlds and that's no way to be married." Jane waited for Kenny to respond. When he finally did, he changed the subject.

"It's five past twelve. Looks like we've got a no-show."

Jane sighed, doubly frustrated by their conversation and the fact that Ellen never came. "Dammit, Ken."

"Lou should be there any minute to relieve you," Kenny said. "If our mystery woman turns up, I'll get you out of your meeting with the chief. Talk to you later." And he rang off.

Jane squeezed the phone in her fist, angry at the world.

Lou Tronick parked his car in a yellow loading zone and crossed to her. "I got a newspaper and a passion for deli food. I'll cover this one for you. Long as it takes." He could see that Jane was reluctant to leave. A bus pushed its way up Kearney Street, and Lou had to press into her car. He put his hand on her arm.

"Go, Jane."

Jane started the car, pulled it into drive, and sped away.

■

IT WAS KILLING her.

Jane was in the Hall of Justice, taking the elevator to Chief McDonald's office. The woman who wrote those letters was the key to unlocking everything. Philip Iverson's murder, the serial killings, Becka Flynn's. Everything.

And she didn't show.

The elevator came to a stop on the twelfth floor. As soon as Jane stepped out, a captain on the chief's staff came up to her. "You're late, Lieutenant."

"I had a rendezvous with someone material to the murders."

"And?"

"She didn't show."

The captain was already moving down the corridor. "Tell it to the mayor."

"The mayor?" Surprised, Jane hurried after him.

They turned right at the end of the hallway and there, before them, was Chief McDonald's windowed conference room. Mayor Lucien Biggs sat at the far side of the gleaming mahogany table, with his briefcase and fedora beside him. An aide brought him a plate of fruit salad from the lunch setup.

The chief was at the head of the table, chatting with another captain. The mayor said something to them and they all laughed.

The mayor, the chief, a deputy chief, two captains, and two lieutenants were marking time. Waiting for Jane.

The thought crossed her mind that here was the top brass in San Francisco, and they were all men.

Her pager pulsed on her hip. *911! 3H61.*

Jane turned to the captain. "I have to make a quick phone call."

"Not a good idea, Lieutenant." He was just about to open the door to the conference room. "Can't it wait?"

Jane speed-dialed Kenny's cell phone. "No."

He answered on the first ring. "Jane?" He was breathless, agitated.

"What is it?"

"A woman was just found stabbed to death in a Russian Hill apartment. The notepad on her desk had your name and phone number on it."

"Jesus. Is it her?"

"She had a yellow scarf tied to the strap of her bag. A yellow scarf with flowers."

Jane kicked her heel back into the wall. "God *damn* it!"

Everyone in the conference room looked up. The chief spotted Jane and started to rise.

"What do you want to do?" Kenny asked.

The chief was at the door, motioning toward Jane.

"I'm there in fifteen minutes!" Jane said into the phone. She turned and tore down the hall.

"*Lieutenant!*" Chief McDonald called after her.

But she was gone.

■

THERE WERE BLOODY paw prints all over the apartment.

The cat growled from under the bed as the living room filled with more and more police personnel.

Jane crouched down to get a better look at the body. It lay on the parquet floor of the entryway. The wound in her chest had bled out until she was an island in a broad pond of her own blood.

The bloody smudges near her eyes indicated that they had been closed by her killer.

"What's her name?" Jane asked.

Kenny flipped open his notebook. "Ellen . . . Schubert. Been living here something like twenty-five years. Neighbor saw the cat in the hall. Its feet were covered in blood."

"Forced entry?"

"Nope."

A photographer snapped a picture of Ellen Schubert's purse. It was upside down under a side table, the yellow scarf saturated with blood.

The cat's low moan sounded like a child crying.

Jane crossed to the tall mirror over the desk. Scrawled along the length of the glass was a refined depiction of a snake. There was one teardrop to the right of its head. The blood from the snake dripped in long thin rivulets until it caught on the mirror's lower frame. It welled at the bottom and overflowed, splattering onto the computer monitor. A screen saver of a cat playing with a ball of yarn danced across the screen.

Jane saw herself in the mirror, the bloody snake a separate dimension between her and her reflection. She followed the tiny streams of falling blood to where they landed on the monitor. Then she noticed her own name and phone number on the scratch pad next to the telephone. A pencil lay across the pad.

The blood from the snake drawing was now traveling down the screen of the monitor. Jane stared at the screen, watching the image of the playful cat still dancing behind thin red rivulets. Ellen Schubert had a secret, she thought, and she had written two telling letters to her . . . on this computer.

Jane took the pencil from the pad and used the eraser end to touch the space bar on the keyboard. The screen saver dissolved away. The monitor bloomed white and a file appeared.

"Ken," Jane called in a hushed whisper.

Kenny hurried over.

Jane nodded to the screen.

SCHUBERT, BIEDERMAN, ET AL.

V.

RIVERPARK ENTERPRISES & PHILIP IVERSON

01436937471

CHAPTER 49

■

*** PERSONAL & CONFIDENTIAL ***

P—

Per your request, I am presenting our conversation of last night for your review.

Going in, I must reemphasize that I am uncomfortable committing this information to paper. But I understand that you need it in order to make what I agree is a very difficult decision.

As we have learned, Engineering has discovered that the water table formed by the Halaby River has effectively been compromised by RiverPark's manufacturing site. At present we do not know the full extent of the pollution, but the numbers suggest it could grow to be substantial. There are indications that there may be—in fact, probably will be—adverse affects to some portion of the downriver population that uses the Halaby as its principal source of water.

The questions you put forth to me regarding the potential for litigious action by that population against RiverPark should be considered very carefully.

As we discussed, RiverPark is on the verge of the kind of unparalleled success most companies dare not even dream of.

Would litigation of the sort alluded to above be damaging or even preventative to that success?

Most likely.

Is there a way to address the situation, perhaps compensate the potential litigants, and still have RiverPark maintain its momentum?

Yes.

I propose:

RiverPark continue its manufacturing business as usual. Then, at a time in the not-too-distant future, we will "discover" that the plant is a polluter. At such time, we will immediately stop the pollution, make plans for relocation (perhaps to a country in Central or South America where the environmental concerns are minimal compared to those in the U.S.). Then, and only then, should we alert the U.S. government and the public.

We would then present the potential victims and their families a generous offer of compensation. If we can defer this offer—and its attendant negative exposure—for a period of as much as twenty-four months, my conservative estimate is that RiverPark will gross in the area of $5.5 to $6.5 billion.

If the company can establish that sort of foothold, there is no upper boundary in sight for how high we can go. Compared to that astronomical sum, compensation to potential litigants at 100 or even 200 percent of their asked-for damages seems to be an acceptable risk—not to mention something of a PR coup on your part.

I trust that the information contained herein will remain solely between the two of us.

Please do not hesitate to call with any further questions.

J.

"That son of a bitch!" Jane dropped the memorandum onto a stack of papers recovered from Ellen Schubert's apartment.

Kenny quickly scanned the contents of another file. "You know what we have here, don't you?"

"Yes," Jane said, "we have answers."

"Ellen Schubert was right about one thing: Philip Iverson was no saint. No wonder he had what his wife so delicately called a midlife crisis."

Jane pushed the papers away. "Let's talk this through. Make sure we've got it right." Mike Finney came in with a cappuccino for Jane and an iced coffee for Kenny. "Mike, you want to hang?" Jane sipped her coffee. "Maybe help us reason this out?"

"If you think I'd be useful."

"We think," Kenny said. "Have a seat."

"Best I can tell," Jane began, "we've got two things going on in these files. RiverPark, back when the manufacturing site was still up in Dos Rios, had some problems safely disposing certain chemicals it used to clean its storage tanks."

Kenny pulled a sheaf of pages from the top file. "Right. And the Halaby River ended up getting polluted."

"So Mr. Iverson," Finney said, "was responsible for fouling the Halaby. Why would anyone kill him for that?"

"We're still unraveling here," Kenny said. "This goes way deeper."

"The water table in Dos Rios was affected," Jane explained. "People got sick. Some were permanently disabled. Children were especially vulnerable . . . and Mike, three kids died." She referred to another report. "The families got together to sue RiverPark."

"But before they filed in court," Kenny went on, "Philip Iverson, by then a wealthy man—"

"And knowing he was going to get a lot richer if he could avoid both a prosecution and the accompanying bad press," Jane interjected.

"—settled *before* it ever reached the court system."

"Which is why," Finney realized, "we could never cross those numbers with a court case."

"Exactly. It was a brilliant preemptive strike. There *was* no court case." Kenny stood up and paced while he talked. "Philip Iverson was about to be sued for something like fifty million dollars. And what did he do? He settled for *one hundred* million dollars."

"On top of that," Jane continued, "he promised to donate a substantial percentage of his corporate profits to charities dedicated to helping children. Hence, Make It So, the RiverPark Scholarship Program, the hospitals, et cetera. The bereaved families were faced with an impossible choice: go to court and destroy Iverson, or let the legacy of their dead children be the foundation for all the money Iverson would donate to help generations of children to come."

"So Philip Iverson, with the grudging consent of the parents of the children whose deaths he was responsible for, becomes a modern-day Alfred Nobel," Kenny added. "He goes on to give away part of his fortune every year to compensate for the misery he caused in amassing it."

Jane held up a thin sheaf of papers. "Iverson had certain stipulations about the settlement. Stuff that I think anyone would have agreed to, given the situation."

"And given the aforementioned shitload of money." Kenny stopped pacing long enough for a quick sip of iced coffee.

"One," Jane went on, "there could be absolutely no mention of all this in the press." Jane indicated a memo. "None whatsoever, or the deal was off."

"And B," Kenny said, "the money was given out in the form of strictly supervised trust funds with binding confidentiality clauses. So if anyone said anything, they would be out of the money, with no legal recourse."

"Was the lady who wrote the letters," Finney asked, "one of the mothers who lost a child?"

"Good question, Moby," Kenny said. "Yes, she was."

Finney was pleased to be holding his own. "Could she or her husband be involved in the killings?"

"We went there, too," Jane said. "Her husband was so distraught over the death of their daughter, he committed suicide on the first anniversary of her funeral."

Mike Finney was getting more confident. "Then how about—"

Kenny held up his hand. "Whoa, Moby. We haven't gotten to the best part. The lawsuit—Schubert, Biederman, et al.—was drawn up in 1979. The date on this memo, our little smoking gun, is early 1976."

"The son of a bitch *knew* that he was compromising the drinking water of an entire town," Jane said, picking up the memo and shaking it angrily, "and he deemed that pollution"—she picked up the memo and shook it angrily—'to be an 'acceptable risk'."

"Those kids died," Kenny said, "from fucking friendly fire. And why? So that Saint Philip could one day be richer than God."

"What about the numbers in the two letters?" Finney asked.

Jane gathered up the pages. "They were just the internal filing system used by Iverson's lawyer. Nothing exotic. Ellen Schubert probably thought they were a court-case designation like we did. But they weren't . . . because there never was a court case."

Kenny stood over Finney. "And Iverson's attorney at the time, the only other person who knew the truth about Iverson and RiverPark and Make It So? The man who wrote this memo?"

Finney thought for a second. Then it hit home. "Josh Stolberg!"

"Right. This is the dirty little secret he took to his grave." Jane came around her desk.

"But," Finney asked, "how did Ellen Schubert get this memo?"

Kenny stopped pacing. ". . . We don't know."

"But we do know," Jane said, "that Philip Iverson's greed killed those children . . . and that same arrogant, insatiable greed is responsible for the deaths of all those homeless men, Mario Tonelli, Ellen Schubert, her husband . . . Becka Flynn." She pulled open her door. "And, in the end, it's what killed him." She dropped the files on Finney's lap. "Schubert, Biederman, et al. Somewhere on that 'et al' list is the break we need." She started into the bullpen. "Guys, we're an inch away. Let's close this case."

CHAPTER 50

■

"I KNOW YOU'VE suffered, Mrs. Biederman," Linda French said into the phone, "but if we could just speak in person. I only need a few minutes of your time, and a little information . . . Hello? Mrs. Biederman, hello?"

Linda put the phone down and crossed an X next to "Ava Biederman."

Interrogation Room One had been converted from war room to boiler room. Kenny, Lou Tronick, Linda French, and Mike Finney had shoved four folding evidence tables into a square and were calling the names on the *Schubert, Biederman, et al* list.

"Anything pops," Jane said as she came in, "I don't care how small, let me or Kenny know about it. We just need one person willing to talk to us to get another step closer. Couple more steps and we're there."

Lou Tronick crossed another name off his column. "That's the problem."

"What is?"

"The 'willing to talk to us' part." He dipped a piece of leftover doughnut into his coffee. "These folks are scared shitless, Jane."

"They're all quiet, simple people," Kenny said, "who made a deal with—to use Ellen Schubert's word—the devil. It happened so long ago, it's become their way of life, and they don't want to risk losing their trust funds. They're all older now, a lot of them are still sick, and that money is all they and their families have in the world."

"I'm hitting stone walls," Linda said, "on every call."

Jane looked to Kenny.

He held up his list. "Half my calls hang up on me as soon as I tell them who I am."

"Then call again."

"I do. Same thing."

"Me, too," Lou Tronick said. "Maybe it's my voice. I kinda have this nasal thing going." He tossed off a half smile.

But Jane was in no mood.

"Sorry," Lou said. "Just trying to cut the tension."

"I don't want the tension cut." Jane saw Roz Shapiro crossing the bullpen, coming toward her. "I want you all to *feel* the tension and push harder. Someone on this list has to talk." She started toward the squad room. "If you hit another stone wall"—she glanced at Linda French—"knock it down!"

"Lieutenant," Roz Shapiro said. "I've got Chief McDonald on line two."

Jane looked to the ceiling and shook her head. Then she pushed past Roz Shapiro and pulled the door to Interrogation Room One closed. She wanted the pressure to build in there; to mix with the tension and create an emotional fuel that needed only the slightest spark to ignite it. It's what, she thought as she strode toward Ben Spielman's old office, her former boss would have done.

▪

"THIS IS CANDIOTTI."

"Lieutenant," the chief said into the phone, his voice measured and calm, "I saw the IR on that Schubert woman. What do you have?"

Jane was surprised at how calm he sounded. "The incident report doesn't tell the half of it, sir. We think we got some good evidence from her apartment."

"How good?"

"Names," Jane said. "My team is going through them as we speak."

"The mayor will be pleased." The chief's implication was inescapable.

"Sir," Jane began, "I had been in contact with Ellen Schubert only hours before. Just when I got to your office, I got a call that she'd been killed. I *had* to leave."

"Lieutenant, there were any number of ways you could have handled it. Not the least of which was to call me yourself from the car to tell me what was going on."

Jane sat heavily in her desk chair. "You're right, Chief. I apologize."

"Accepted." There was a short pause. "As long as we're communicating with each other, I think we need to talk about what happened with your husband and Inspector Haskell."

Jane noticed the door to Interrogation Room One open. Kenny came out, pulling on his jacket. "Sir, I've spoken to my . . . Inspector Marks . . . and told him that his behavior was unacceptable. When I get a chance, I'll write up a full report and discuss what further action is warranted with the disciplinary review committee."

"You send that report to me. I'll read it . . . and tear it up."

"Sir?"

"Lieutenant, your husband is an excellent cop. I don't want his file trashed because of some stupid incident with an ambitious kiss-ass like Devon Haskell. I know all about their history at the Academy. The thing with that woman, the whole bit."

"All due respect, Chief, but how . . . ?"

"You know how people in this department are always talking about friends in high places?"

"Yes."

"Well, *I'm* that friend in this high place. And we would both be well served—and our already difficult jobs would be a lot less difficult—if you would just help me ease this constant sense of conflict between you and me."

"I'll do my best, sir."

"That's all I ask. Now get off the damn phone and find me that killer. Good-bye, Lieutenant." He rang off.

Kenny stuck his head into Jane's office. "You still have a job?"

"Apparently."

"Do I?"

"Yeah." Jane shook her head. "I think the chief must be taking some kind of anger management course or something. He hates Haskell and he's gonna let you off without a reprimand in your file."

"Amazing."

"Where you going?"

"Taking your advice." Kenny held up a sheet of paper. "Gonna go knock down a few stone walls."

"Ben always said all the science in the world can't beat legwork. You get anything, I want to know about it right away."

Kenny slipped the page into his coat pocket and started to go. "Almost forgot."

"What?"

Kenny's lips creased into the beginnings of a smile. "Love you."

Jane felt her jaw unclench, her face relax. "Thank God." She watched him go, grateful to be sharing her life with this man. The phone rang. She picked it up. "Hello."

"Jane, A. J. Guthrie here." His voice was tight, hurried. "Can you meet me at Dighby's in an hour?"

"Things are a little intense right now, A.J. What's up?"

"I have something for you."

Jane sat up. "Tell me more."

"When I see you."

CHAPTER 51

■

"LET'S DO THIS quick." Ava Biederman snuffed out her cigarette in an overflowing ashtray.

"I'll try, ma'am," Kenny said. "Thank you for agreeing to see me."

"I didn't."

"Well then"—Kenny shrugged—"thanks for not slamming the door in my face."

He stood across from Ava Biederman in the oak-paneled den of her large ranch-style home. The walls of the room were lined with narrow shelves that were filled with thousands of miniature liquor bottles. Thin lengths of fishing line were strung along the front of each shelf to hold the bottles in place in case of earthquake. The room was dark, shadowed.

Ava Biederman sat in a love seat, away from the windows, away from the lamps. She was, Kenny figured, around sixty. Her yellow-gray hair was just a little too long for someone her age. At first Kenny thought it was the hairstyle of a woman who was trying too hard, but then he realized she had just given up.

"You're sure it was Ellen?" Ava Biederman took a pack of Merit Menthols from the coffee table. She tapped a cigarette sharply against her watch and lit it, pulling the smoke in with what was almost a gulp.

"Yes, ma'am. We're positive."

"Shame." Ava Biederman let the blue-white smoke drift out her nostrils. Her way of smoking, Kenny noticed, had a masculinity about it. "After all her suffering." She tugged on the cigarette again. "How'd you find me?"

Kenny stepped forward and showed her the top sheet of *Schubert, Biederman, et al v. Philip Iverson.* Her head falling in tiny nods, she looked at it for a long time.

"Of course," she said at last. "Hers was the first, Ellen's. But in a way she was lucky. Her little girl died quick." The dry white ash of her cigarette fell in her lap. She didn't bother to wipe it away.

Kenny knew that one of the best interview techniques was silence. He leaned back against the corner of the bookcase and waited.

"Mine . . ." Ava Biederman shook her head, her jaw quivering. "Mine died slow . . . the leukemia took him away from me in pieces." She stabbed out her cigarette and pulled a new one out of the pack. "I didn't know Ellen Schubert before. She found me . . . and the others . . . got us all together so's we could maybe try to do something about . . . what happened. At least stop him from hurting anyone else."

"Stop who?"

"You know who." Ava Biederman glanced up. "Philip Iverson."

Kenny gestured for her to continue.

"Most of us were too shocked, too stunned, to do anything. But Ellen Schubert was angry. You never saw no one so pissed off. She made phone calls, got us an attorney, and organized us all like she was some kind of Erin Brockovich." She lit the new cigarette and let her head fall back against the love seat. "Mr. Iverson was so torn up over this, over the fact that he might be responsible, he settled all our claims without us having to go through a trial. It was more than generous, we thought at the time. All's we had to do was agree to stay quiet on it." The smoke rose from her cigarette, curling toward the ceiling. "That and bury our babies."

Kenny waited, silent and respectful.

"And everything was quiet for years. Most of us moved away. We weren't supposed to talk to each other or nothin'. The checks always came, regular as a phone bill." She tapped the cigarette on the edge of the ashtray. "Then about a year ago, the first letter showed up."

Kenny fought the impulse to intervene. He let her go on.

"It was from a lawyer." Ava Biederman's eyes filled with tears. She pushed back in the love seat, deeper into the shadows. "And it said that Philip Iverson . . . knew." She straightened up, her body responding to this fresh rush of pain. "The bastard *knew* what he was doing to our water the whole time. For years before. He could have done something about it. And he didn't." She raised her eyebrows, almost in a plea. "And our children died."

"What was the lawyer's name?"

"Josh Stolberg."

Kenny nodded. A deathbed confession.

"Coupla months later, another letter comes. With even more stuff about how much Mr. Iverson knew and when he knew it. This time Ellen Schubert calls me up. She wanted to do something about it. Maybe sue Mr. Iverson. But I was afraid, scared I'd lose my money. I asked her if she talked with any of the others. And she said yes, all of them."

"Had they gotten these letters?"

"Yes."

"In all of those other families," Kenny asked, "was there anyone who was so angry, so torn up, who might have killed Philip Iverson?"

"Yes."

Kenny pushed away from the bookcase. The miniature bottles rattled against themselves. "Who?"

Ava Biederman looked up to him, holding his eyes with hers. "Me." She brought the cigarette to her lips. "But I didn't. Better answer to your question woulda been 'all of us.' You lose a child, 'specially like that, your mind goes to some ugly places. It's acting on it makes the difference."

She reached over to a nearby shelf and pulled a small framed picture from among the bottles. "Albie was my life. Mr. Iverson took him away from me. Times are I wished I had the courage to kill that prick myself." She turned the picture toward Kenny. "I buried him in that same Little League uniform."

Kenny took the photograph from her and tilted it into a smoky shaft of light coming from the window. He looked at the face of the young boy smiling back at him. "Mrs. Biederman," he said, his heart hammering, "can I borrow this?"

"Only if I get it back."

"I promise." He started for the door.

"Inspector," Ava Biederman called.

Kenny stopped.

"You catch whoever killed Mr. Iverson, you tell him something from me."

"What's that, ma'am?"

"You tell him . . . thank you."

CHAPTER 52

—————■—————

Dighby's was a cop bar.

Rather, it was an old cops' bar. Dark and dank with the smell of thousands of beers and thousands of cigarettes, it was a safe haven where retired cops went to drink away their days and nights. No questions asked.

A. J. Guthrie sat at the bar, a whiskey with ice sweating through a flimsy paper napkin. "Thanks for comin'," he said without turning around.

Jane took a seat. "Eyes in the back of your head?"

A.J. smiled. "Mirror over the bar."

The bartender exchanged A.J.'s drink for a fresh one and looked to Jane.

"Coffee," she said. "Black."

"Gonna be a long night?"

"You never know." The bartender set a cup of coffee in front of her. She took two Equals from her purse and stirred them in. "What do you have for me, Sheriff?"

A.J. turned his drink in his hand, the napkin turning with it. "Something happened I thought you should know about."

Jane held her hand over her coffee, letting the steam billow against her palm. "Tell me."

"I went to tell Mrs. Iverson what I knew about the case." He caught her eye in the mirror. "Just briefing my boss the way you have to brief yours. Anyway, I told her about Ellen Schubert dying. And about the files, the names and all . . . and—"

"Wait a minute. How'd you know about what was in those files?"

A.J. dropped his gaze, studying the bar top. "Someone on your team told me."

"Who?"

"I don't want to get no one in trouble."

"Sheriff, that is not the issue here."

A.J. nodded. "It was Linda French. But it's not her fault. It's mine. She's new and I guess I sweet-talked the information out of her before she realized what she was saying."

"I'll deal with her later," Jane said evenly. "What happened when you told Alice Iverson what you had?"

"She fired me on the spot. Wrote me a check for more than what she owed me and told me she wouldn't be requiring my services any longer." He took a long pull on his whiskey.

"Any idea why?"

"No, ma'am. But the funny thing is, she seemed different all of a sudden."

"How so?"

"She seemed nervous." He swiveled on his stool until he faced Jane. "I've known Mrs. Iverson for a long time, twenty years maybe, and that's the first time I've ever seen her not in control . . ." A.J. patted his shirt pocket. "Her hand was trembling when she wrote me that check. I been a cop forever. I know scared . . . and I know guilty . . . when I see it." He took a cigar from his pocket and rolled it in his fingers. "Used t' be, a man could smoke in a place like this."

"Did Mrs. Iverson say anything when she let you go? Give you any indication one way or the other?"

"Hardly nothing at all. Just thanks and good-bye. Makes it three jobs I been fired from." A.J. rose from the stool. He dropped some bills on the bar and looked around. A couple of old-timers looked his way; most didn't. "When I was a rookie, I promised myself I wasn't gonna end up like these guys." He turned to his reflection in the mirror. "But now I can see . . . I already have."

Jane swiveled on her stool. "You sure you're okay to drive?"

"I'll be fine, thanks." Sheriff Guthrie headed for the entrance. "I ain't goin' far." He pulled the door open and stepped into the blue light of Dighby's neon sign, his body in silhouette. Then he turned back to Jane. "Lieutenant," he said, his eyes boring into hers, "you watch out for Alice Iverson. There's badness in that woman." He let the door creak closed and was gone.

Jane took a last sip of her coffee, trying to figure out the best way to go back to Alice Iverson. Her pager vibrated. She pulled it out of its plastic holder and pushed the backlight button as the message scrolled in the darkened barroom.

I know who the killer is! I'm just outside Dos Rios. Meet me at RiverPark ASAP! 3H61.

3H61 . . . Kenny.

Jane spun away and ran toward the front door. A few weary heads turned to follow her.

When she burst into the bracing night air, she plucked her two-way from her bag. "3H58 to Nineteen."

"Go, Lieutenant."

"Cheryl, patch me through to Inspector Marks."

"Will do." There was a beat of silence, then Cheryl came back on the line. "All's I'm getting is heavy static, Lieutenant."

Jane remembered the interference caused by the mountains around Dos Rios. "Keep trying. When you get through, tell Kenny I got his message and I'll meet him at RiverPark."

"Got it."

"Also, I need a twenty on Alice Iverson. Have Lou track her down."

"Lou's in the field. Inspector French is here. Want me to put her on it?"

Jane crossed the sidewalk and ripped open the door of her sedan. "No." She started the car. "Have Finney do it. 3H58 out." Cranking the wheel hard to the left, she peeled away from the curb.

CHAPTER 53

∎

THE HALABY RIVER pushed itself along the grounds of RiverPark.

Jane skidded to a sideways stop across from Philip Iverson's parking place. As she scrambled out of the car, she noticed the lot was empty. Where was Kenny's Explorer?

Pulling her two-way from her bag, she ran to the front door of the main building. The hot white plate of the moon was reflected a dozen times in the slanted windows.

"3H61," she called into the radio.

Nothing.

She tried the Precinct. "3H58 to Dispatch."

Static.

The signal still couldn't connect in these mountains.

Jane tested the lobby door. Unlocked. She dropped her two-way into her bag and pulled out her weapon. Then she leaned into the door with her shoulder.

Faces of children watched Jane cross the broad lobby.

The huge black-and-white photographs caught the moonlight from the tall windows. Eerie images of a smiling Philip Iverson surrounded her as she arrived at the security desk. Leaning over, she peered into the surveillance monitors. Other than a live shot of herself in the center monitor, there was no movement anywhere in the building. She hissed a whisper, trying to raise the security guard. "Anyone here?"

Nothing.

Jane crossed to the elevators.

She tried the button beneath the photograph of Philip Iverson and the sick young girl. The elevators were shut down for the evening. She was about to turn away when she noticed the small bronze sign. MR. IVERSON →.

Jane looked to the right. A staircase led to the mezzanine level. Her pistol ready at her hip, she slowly climbed the stairs.

■

"3H61 TO DISPATCH."

"Go, Ken."

"Cheryl, I'm up working my way down Route 12, closing in on the 101 South. I need Jane."

"Then we have a problem."

"What?"

"Jane checked in a little while ago. Wanted me to tell you she got your message and she'll meet you at RiverPark."

"Are you sure?" Kenny asked, a sense of dread rising. "She said *I* called?"

"And that it was important."

"Call for backup. CHP, local, whatever you can find, and get them to RiverPark. 3H61 out!"

Kenny threw the Explorer into an abrupt left U-turn. He jammed the accelerator to the floor and the car sideslipped on the gravel shoulder, straining for traction. Its rear wheels finally grabbed the roadway and the Explorer rocketed back up Route 12.

■

JANE MOVED IN a crouch up the last few steps. The reception area to Philip Iverson's office was lit only by moonlight.

Her heart racing, she started to cross toward the office door. When she reached the secretary's desk, she paused. Something wasn't right.

A presence, a smell, a feeling.

She wasn't alone.

Her training told her to fall back and summon backup. But Kenny had called for her. What if he was in trouble? He could be anywhere in this vast complex.

Jane turned to go back to the vantage point at the top of the stairs. But something caught her eye. The phone on the secretary's desk.

A red light suddenly came on.

Philip Iverson's line.

Someone was in the office . . . and wanted her to know it.

Jane thumbed the safety off her pistol and pressed her back against the wall. She reached out with her left hand and tried the knob. It turned. Standing to the side, she pushed on the door. It fell open.

Jane swung low into the doorway, her gun in a two-handed grip. Ready for anything.

CHAPTER 54

◼

SHERIFF A. J. GUTHRIE sat at Philip Iverson's desk.

He had his .357 Magnum trained on Jane's forehead. "I kinda have you outgunned, Lieutenant." Without taking his eyes off of her, he returned the telephone to its cradle. "Maybe you oughta drop your weapon so's I don't have to blow your head off."

Jane quickly assessed the situation.

She was standing in a backlit doorway. A.J. was sitting in vague shadows. Her gun was aimed in his general direction. His was pointed at her face.

Her shoulders sagged as she brought her pistol down to her side. She relaxed her fingers and it fell to the floor. "But," she asked, ". . . how?"

A. J. Guthrie sipped at his thermos cup and smiled. "Back roads." He motioned for her to sit in the guest chair.

Jane sat down, her eyes level, her jaw set. "Where'd you get my beeper code?"

"Inspector Linda French is a little too easily convinced of things she shouldn't be." A. J. Guthrie lay his .357 Magnum on Philip Iverson's desk, its muzzle less than three feet from Jane's chest. He took a cigar from his shirt pocket. Roughly scraping a wooden match across the desk, he lit it, blue folds of smoke rising. "I know it's not polite," he said as he dropped the match on the desk, "but given the circumstances . . ." The snapshot of him and his son on a fishing trip was leaning against the telephone.

"Tell me what's going on, A.J."

A. J. Guthrie looked around the office. The framed photographs, the citations, the trophies. "What's going on, Lieutenant, is the inevitable." He shrugged. "I thought I was better. I thought I was smarter. But I wasn't." He drew on the cigar, its tip glowing then quickly fading. "And this office, the seat of Philip Iverson's empire, is where it all ends."

"All what ends?"

"The killing." He tapped a thick ash onto the blotter. Leaning forward, he blew it toward Jane. "Except for one more."

Jane watched as the ash disintegrated and fell to the carpet in tiny gray flakes. She brought her eyes back up to A.J. and saw that the sadness that haunted him had returned.

And she understood.

"Your son didn't die in a car accident."

"No, ma'am."

"He got sick, didn't he?" Jane asked. "Like the others."

"And he died like the others." A.J. rocked back in Philip Iverson's desk chair. "I couldn't save him. His last moment in this life was spent looking into my eyes. And he just . . . passed. I would have given my life for him to draw just one more breath. To have had him for just that one more second." He put the cigar onto the desk and watched as it burned a black scar into the wood. "But he was gone. Looking right at me. But gone. I held his head to my chest for half an hour. Not believing that such a terrible thing could ever happen to anyone. The nurse came. She touched me on the shoulder. Gentle. And I put him back on the pillow. And I kissed him on the lips . . . his blue lips." A.J. swatted at a tear as if he were chasing a fly. "Then I . . ."

"Then you closed his eyes."

"That's right, ma'am; yes, I did." A.J. glanced at her, pulled out of his reverie. "But you've been right about a lot of things, haven't you, Lieutenant?"

"You killed Philip Iverson; that I understand. But why Willie Temple? Why all the others?"

"Your theory on the other murders was also right." A.J. rolled the cigar one turn closer to his gun. "Willie Temple saw me shoot Mr. Iverson and, sadly, I had to kill him, too. The others had to die to make you think you had a serial killer loose in your city."

Jane shifted in her seat. Her gun was where she had dropped it. Near the door. Too far. "So, to distract the Homicide Department from finding Philip Iverson's murderer, you kept sacrificing innocent men."

"After Willie Temple, it just made sense to keep taking homeless men. Lonely men who were adrift . . . like me."

"Then why did you kill Mario Tonelli?"

"That was a mistake." A.J. chewed on the inside of his bottom lip and sighed. "The way he was dressed, plus him smoking dope and all . . . I thought he was just another bum. Then, when I checked his wallet, I knew I'd fucked up. So I had to turn that mistake to my advantage and make you all think I was upping the ante." He touched his finger to the cigar, rotating it another turn closer to his pistol.

"All those men . . . all those lives." Jane turned it over in her mind, playing back everything she knew about the case. The victims, the survivors, the suspects, the evidence. Smoke from the charred desk mingled with the smoke from the cigar. Jane watched as it curled sideways, drifting over the discarded match. And then she knew. "It's the cigarette lighter, isn't it?"

A. J. Guthrie nodded. "You're a good one, Lieutenant."

"Not so good," Jane said. "I should have spotted it before. Willie Temple had a Zippo with a Marine Corps insignia among his personal effects. But he was in the army, and you—"

"And I was in the marines." A.J. looked at the cigar. Then back to Jane. "I dropped my lighter when I was chasing Mr. Iverson. Willie Temple picked it up, but I didn't realize it until after I left his body at the pier." His head fell forward for an instant. Then he brought it back up and took a long sip from his cup.

Now Jane recognized the odor she had smelled earlier . . . liquor.

A. J. Guthrie had had at least two whiskeys at Dighby's that she knew of. And he was still drinking. Her only chance of getting out of this presented itself. She had to keep him talking . . . and drinking. "Then what about the snake imagery at the crime scenes?"

A thin smile cracked across A.J.'s face. "There's a beauty to that." He pushed the cigar two turns nearer the .357. "When I was on Zodiac, I had this theory. You know how it usually goes: Someone kills someone else, then tries to take away any evidence he was ever there. Wiping away fingerprints, shoe and tire prints, picking up stuff, whatever." He took another drink. "But what if Zodiac was doing the opposite? *Adding* stuff. Polluting the crime scenes with all his symbols and gibberish, setting the machinery of San Francisco's police department off on a wild-goose chase. You know as well as I do, once that machine starts turning, it's impossible to stop."

Jane twisted in her seat, stretching her back. Cataloging the terrain for when she was forced to make her move.

"But," A.J. continued, "my superiors were too invested in the drama of their huge high-profile case, and cops being cops, they just flat-out ignored me."

"So you corrupted the crime scenes of the men you killed with those snake figures and red fibers and latex traces, and we ran around in circles chasing our tails."

" 'Fraid so."

"And you worked your way into our . . . into *my* good graces by conniving Alice Iverson into hiring you as her private investigator."

"Keep your enemies close." A.J. rolled the cigar again. This time he left his hand on the desk, inches away from the pistol.

"But someone shot you at the parking structure."

"We were there looking for my lighter when your Linda French pulled a gun on me."

"We?"

"Me and Kimball Ashe. He opened fire, trying to scare off Linda. There was a ricochet—no way to foresee that—and I got hit. Kinda lucky when you look back on it. I get a flesh wound and—"

"And a world of sympathy from me."

"You're a good cop, Jane. But you ain't perfect." He gripped his gun and raised it. "Nobody is."

▪

THE EXPLORER WAS airborne.

It bounded over the driveway at the entrance to RiverPark and thudded heavily onto the gravel of the parking lot. Kenny brought it to a shuddering stop next to Jane's police sedan. He was out and running in seconds; the Explorer's engine still turning, the driver's door still open.

Ripping his Glock out of its shoulder holster, Kenny entered the lobby of the main building. The dull gray glow from the surveillance monitors drew him to the security desk. Kenny swept the console with his gun. Movement on one of the monitors caught his eye. The security guard passed from one screen to another. From the monitor marked MAINTENANCE to the one marked GROUNDKEEPING.

Kenny started back outside. Then he remembered how immense RiverPark was. If Jane was in danger, he didn't have time to waste running to the far reaches of the complex.

He pulled out his cell phone and pressed the speed dial.

▪

"WHAT HAPPENED THAT night in Chinatown?"

A. J. Guthrie looked at her along the length of his gun. "I can see where you might think I was setting you up," he said. "But I was really setting Kimball Ashe up."

"Why would he even get involved?"

"Ashe was an escaped con I knew from my old days on the force. He was lookin' at life without parole and didn't really have any leverage. Way I saw it, he was the ideal pigeon to pin the serial murders on. It was the perfect plan, all the way down to planting evidence in his apartment." A.J. smiled. "But like all perfect plans . . . it was flawed. I was going to play local hero and take him out, while saving your husband's life." He pushed the thermos cup away. "But I hadn't counted on one crucial thing."

"The piece of flesh."

"Exactly." He raised his shirt with his left hand to reveal a blood-stained bandage. "Who woulda thought that a chunk of me would still be in Willie Temple's mouth? I took something for granted I shouldn't have. I'm a better cop than that."

"Don't give me that bullshit." Jane knew she was provoking him, but she had to change the course this was taking. "You're a disgrace to your badge. Sure, you've had a devastating loss, but you know what, Sheriff? You're hiding behind it. Hiding behind the sweet face of your dead son in some sort of sick compensation for a lifetime of inadequacy."

A.J. laid the picture of his son flat on the desk. He put his hand on top of it and pressed down, as if gathering strength from it. "You can't begin to know how it feels to go through what I've gone through."

"You're right," Jane said, hissing. "Or the thousands of other parents who've lost children. You cloak yourself in some sort of collective grief, but you're not the same as them." She leaned forward, hurling her words at him. "When you die, Sheriff, you *will* leave that ripple you were so concerned about. A ripple of shame. On yourself . . . and on your son."

The fury in A. J. Guthrie's eyes came up so suddenly that Jane shrank back in her seat. He jumped to his feet, threw the desk chair aside, and started toward her.

Then her cell phone rang.

She and A.J. stared at her bag. Glancing up, Jane spotted Kenny just cresting the stairs. His gun in one hand, his phone in the other. He had called her number and was using its ring as a beacon.

"It's all about sacrifice." A.J. now stood in the middle of the room. "Some make it willingly . . . some have it thrust upon them. My son did. Ellen Schubert did. Killing her turned it for me. I hated doing it. That's when I knew it had to stop."

Jane caught a flash of movement through the drawn blinds. She looked to A.J. He had seen it, too.

The phone continued to ring.

Jane tensed. She knew that Kenny would come through the door. He had to. It's what she would have done.

"My son was sacrificed," A.J. went on, "for the fortune that provides the money that saves all those others. There's irony in that. But no satisfaction. And for that, Philip Iverson was also sacrificed."

Jane saw the doorknob turn.

Her phone was still ringing.

A.J. backed up next to the desk. He brought his .357 up.

Jane flexed her entire body, ready to leap for her weapon.

Kenny pushed at the door. It started to open.

A.J. pulled back on the hammer.

The phone rang once more. Then it stopped, its echo hanging on the edges of silence.

Suddenly Jane kicked out of her chair and thrust herself across the room.

A.J. raised his massive pistol.

As he did, Jane's body fell against the door, slamming it closed with Kenny still outside. In the same motion, she groped for her gun. Her fingers brushed the barrel and she was just about to flip it into her hand when a booming gunshot erupted, filling the office with a thunderous explosion.

"NO!" Kenny shrieked as he flung himself through the door.

Jane rose from the floor, her pistol at eye level. She followed Kenny's gaze to the desk.

A. J. Guthrie was sprawled across the toppled chair. The back of his head and part of his brain were flattened against a portrait of a beaming Philip Iverson and a group of college-bound Make It So kids.

The .357 Magnum lay clutched in his right hand, blue cordite smoke snaking from the muzzle.

His eyes were open.

Kenny strode across to Jane and pulled her into an urgent embrace. "Thank God I found you."

She took his hand and pressed it to her cheek. "Why were you even looking for me?"

Kenny took the photograph he had gotten from Ava Biederman from his shirt pocket and placed it on the desk next to the picture of A.J.'s son.

It was the same child.

CHAPTER 55

———■———

"CLEAN OUT YOUR desk."

Linda French stiffened in her chair. "What?"

Jane watched through her office window as Kenny and the others broke down the war room. She shifted her attention back to Linda. "I'm relieving you of all duties in my department pending a formal inquiry into your competence. Regardless of the outcome of that inquiry, you are through in Homicide."

"You can't do this. I've worked my way up the ranks. I've earned everything I ever—"

Jane cut her off. "Inspector French, you've had a greased path ever since you joined the SFPD." She pulled a manila folder from her bottom drawer. "Your career has been built on exaggerated performance reviews from male superiors who were either eager to have you move on so they could get rid of you, or . . ."

"Or what?" Linda French demanded.

"Or who were afraid to say anything unfavorable about a female colleague. Playing the politically correct card while you advanced through the department."

Linda shot to her feet. "This is discrimination, Lieutenant. My attorneys will—"

"Will what? Sue?" Jane came around from behind her desk.

"Please, Inspector, I beg you to file on me." She pressed forward. "Because when you do, I'll have the opportunity to make public what I'm now required to keep confidential. I'd love the chance to talk about your continued poor judgment, your habitually deficient skills, your reliance on others to do your work, and your eagerness to accept the credit."

Linda French retreated until her back was against the door.

Jane moved in. "You gave Sheriff Guthrie vitally important information about an ongoing investigation without my knowledge or approval." She was shouting now, her face burning red. "You gave him my pager code, goddammit! Inspector, this is Homicide. Life and death. And you don't have what it takes."

Jane thrust her arm out. Linda French flinched. But Jane was reaching for the door. She pulled it open. "We desperately need women on the force. But only the best." She motioned for her to leave. "If you even *think* of filing on me, I will drag your ass through so much mud, you won't be able to get a job as a meter maid. You have five minutes to get out of here."

Linda started to speak.

Jane jabbed a finger toward her face. "Don't," she said through clenched teeth. "You don't need the last word." She stepped aside. "Give your shield to Inspector Marks and . . . just go."

Salvaging what little dignity she could, Linda French brushed past Jane and stormed into the bullpen.

■

"IT WAS MY fault," Alice Iverson said. "I never should have let A.J. talk me into hiring him." She sat on Jane's couch, sipping water from a paper cup.

She even did that, Jane thought, with a certain elegance.

Jane sat in the same chair Linda French had used half an hour ago. She glanced into the squad room. Linda's desk was empty. Her badge was in an envelope next to Kenny's keyboard. "You and I got off on the wrong foot, and I'm sure that influenced your decision to bring

Sheriff Guthrie in on the case. I apologize, Mrs. Iverson. I'll try to do better next time."

"There always is a next time for you, isn't there?"

"Unfortunately."

Alice Iverson put the paper cup on the coffee table and rose. "Those poor men who were killed by A.J. It's such a pity for them and their families."

"He lived his life in so much pain," Jane offered, "his only solution was to hurt other people."

"And Mrs. Schubert . . ." Alice shook her head. "And that lovely news lady . . . Is there any way I can convince you to accept the reward?"

Jane stood as well. "I appreciate it, but no. I was just doing my job."

"I could give you enough money to change your life."

"My life's changed enough, thank you."

Alice smoothed her skirt. "Like you said, we got off on the wrong foot . . . and sort of stayed there. I apologize for my part in that." She held out her hand. Jane took it and was surprised at the strength of her grip. "Thank you, Lieutenant. For all you've done."

"You're welcome. Thank you for coming by."

Alice Iverson reached down to the couch for her purse.

"Mrs. Iverson?"

She turned back, her blond hair falling across her face. "Yes?"

"About the money . . ."

Alice tucked her hair behind her ear. "Are you reconsidering?"

"No. But if it needs to go somewhere . . ." Jane wrote something on her notepad and handed it to her. "There's a homeless shelter I know that could use some help."

■

"Something's wrong."

Kenny was at the evidence table in Interrogation Room One. Jane stood with her back to the blackboards, eating a yogurt. "Moby went over to the Hilton where A.J. was staying. Aaron's guys gave him this box of stuff." He reached into a cardboard box and pulled out two sheets of paper.

"These are the same letters Ellen Schubert, Ava Biederman, and the others received along with that secret memo from Stolberg to Iverson. The one about RiverPark polluting the Halaby River years before they went public about it." He handed the letters to Jane.

They were written on Stolberg, Kerner & Gest stationery and signed by Josh Stolberg.

"Philip Iverson's late, great personal attorney makes a deathbed confession." She passed the letters back to Kenny.

"Exactly what I thought . . . at first." Kenny pointed to the date on the second one. "I called Shanley Correctional. They checked their records. Josh Stolberg was non compos the entire week surrounding this date. His chart is quite specific. He was suffering from advanced dementia."

"But," Jane said, "the first time we saw him he was lucid. Obnoxious and uncooperative, but lucid."

"That can happen," Kenny countered. "Good days and bad days. But, Jane, there's no way he wrote this letter."

Jane dropped her yogurt into the trash can. "Then who did?"

■

LEILAH STOLBERG STOOD among the packing boxes in the living room of her Pacific Heights home. She wrapped another framed photograph of her and her husband in happier times and slipped it into a carton.

"Mrs. Stolberg," Jane said gently, "will you please look at these?"
Kenny handed her the letters.

Leilah Stolberg slid her reading glasses down from the top of her head and examined the pages. "My husband didn't have much at the end." She looked to Jane and Kenny, her eyes wet and distant. "But he had his pride. He wanted to die as well as he could, given the . . . indignities . . . of his situation." She pushed her glasses back up and passed the letters over to Kenny. "Josh wrote that memo, but he didn't write these letters. It's not his language . . . or his signature."

A pair of moving men in dark brown overalls came in. They stacked a load of boxes onto a two-wheel dolly and left. "She asked him to, but he refused," Leilah Stolberg said. She watched the men wheel the boxes through the spacious entry hall. The walls were bare. The chandelier was gone and the furniture was shrouded in padded blankets.

"Who?" Jane touched her arm, bringing her back. "Who asked him to?"

Leilah Stolberg looked from Jane to Kenny, then back to Jane. It was as if she had forgotten they were there. "Sorry?"

"Who asked your husband to write these letters?" Jane said again.

"Why . . . Alice Iverson, of course."

CHAPTER 56

∎

ALICE IVERSON MOVED through the water as gracefully as a bird in flight.

Completely in her element, she powered through her laps in the Olympic-size swimming pool on the enclosed roof of her San Francisco apartment.

She was making Jane and Kenny wait.

"Coming on two miles, miss," Mr. Kim announced.

Alice executed a perfect flip-turn, stretching her body for more glide. She came to the surface and sliced through the water, each stroke thrusting her forward until, with one final reach, she touched the side. With an agile downward push, she lifted herself out of the pool.

Peeling off her bathing cap, she allowed Mr. Kim to drape a white terrycloth robe around her shoulders.

"Hello again, Lieutenant." Alice Iverson sat on a beige chaise lounge and wiped her legs dry. She looked to Kenny and nodded. "Inspector."

Mr. Kim poured her a frosted glass of ice water. He turned to Jane and Kenny. They declined.

"I called Bob Lewis, Lieutenant," Alice said. "He's cutting a check for Santuario today."

Jane stepped over a shallow puddle and sat on a deck chair. "You move fast."

"I try to."

Kenny handed her copies of the two letters that Ava Biederman, Ellen Schubert, and the others had received. "These look familiar?"

Alice Iverson dried her hands on her robe and picked them up. "Interesting." She offered them back to Kenny.

He let them hang between them. "We have copies."

"The question is, Mrs. Iverson," Jane said, "have you seen these letters before?"

Alice Iverson turned to Jane. "Hypothetically?"

"If you have to."

"Hypothetically . . . maybe." She let it rest there, apparently finished with the conversation.

"We know you asked Josh Stolberg to write these," Jane said.

"And we know," Kenny went on, "that he refused; and that he was incapable of writing the second one on the day it was dated . . ."

"And we know," Jane continued, "that isn't his signature."

Alice Iverson glanced at the pages. "Then who wrote them?"

"You did," Jane said.

"You wrote the first letter," Kenny said, "exposing your husband's complicity in the deaths of those children. When nothing came of that, you wrote the next one."

"You would have kept on writing them," Jane continued, "until someone in his grief and outrage stepped forward to do something about it. Which is exactly what happened."

"You're crazy." Alice Iverson swung her legs to the floor. As she did, her robe fell away, revealing her thighs.

"FBI," Kenny said, his eyes level with Alice's, "has already confirmed that Josh Stolberg's forged signature on both of the letters matches your handwriting."

"So what are you saying?" Alice sniffed derisively. "Should I get a lawyer?"

Jane rose and stood next to Kenny. "You seem to do a pretty good job of impersonating one yourself."

Mr. Kim moved toward the exit door.

"Sir!" Kenny called. "Why don't you have a seat?"

Mr. Kim looked from Kenny to Alice Iverson. She nodded. He sat on a deck chair by the wall. Uneasy with being seated in Mrs. Iverson's presence, he rested on the edge of the chair, ready to rise at any moment.

"Let's say . . . hypothetically," Alice Iverson began, "that I *did* write those letters. There's no crime in that. In fact, the content of these letters is merely the truth. They say that Philip knew about the pollution for two and a half years before the cleanup." She crumpled the pages in her hand, her eyes tossing a challenge at Jane. "It could be argued that I did those families a service by shining a light on what really happened. It could be argued that they *deserved* to know." She directed her gaze at Jane. "But Sheriff Guthrie, in his grief and outrage, as you say, committed the murders. Not I. The simple fact is, I haven't committed any crime, Lieutenant."

"That's where you're wrong!" Jane snapped. "Now that we've tied your handwriting to the signature, you've committed two crimes: forgery and impersonating an officer of the court."

Alice Iverson waved her hand at Jane as if shooing away a nuisance. "Please, this is all so bothersome."

"Those may only be misdemeanors," Jane pressed on, "but we always have the civil courts to pursue. You can still be held liable for your husband's death and, by extension, all the others. Even if we fail, your precious image, your perfect golden persona, is going to be obliterated by all the shit that'll be thrown your way." Jane stepped forward. "And you know what? A lot of it's going to stick; and all those doors that are always thrown open for you everywhere you go? They're all gonna slam in your face."

"Mr. Kim!" Alice Iverson shouted, her voice bouncing in the cavernous space.

Mr. Kim stood up quickly. "Yes, miss."

"My guests were just leaving."

"Yes, miss." Mr. Kim strode toward Jane and Kenny. He reached out to guide them to the exit.

Kenny raised his hand, allowing his coat to fall open. "Don't," he warned.

Mr. Kim glanced at Kenny's Glock and backed off.

Jane wasn't done with Alice Iverson. "There is no such thing as the perfect crime. Even in your world. You made the mistake of forging those letters. If you fucked up there, then you fucked up somewhere else." She started to go, then wheeled around. "I am going to find some minuscule, seemingly insignificant, missing detail in this little scheme of yours . . . and I will take it and I will ram it down your throat. Count the days, *Alice,* because I'm coming back for you!"

She pushed her way past Mr. Kim and pounded toward the door.

Kenny leaned over Alice Iverson and gestured to her legs. "Cover up now. You'll catch your death." He shouldered Mr. Kim aside and caught up to Jane.

"Did you really run those signatures?"

Kenny held the door for her. "Not yet. Ruth Holmes gets back tonight. Little trick I learned from you."

They passed through the door and headed for the private elevator. "Then you were what?" Jane asked. "Bluffing, lying?"

"I prefer to think of it as . . . testing the veracity of the suspect. And this time the suspect—"

"Failed." Jane stopped. "Alice Iverson had everything anyone could possibly ask for from life, and she wanted more." She looked back as the door was closing. Alice Iverson was on the phone, laughing. "I'm gonna bust that bitch, Ken. Someday, somehow, I'm gonna bust her."

The door clicked shut.

CHAPTER 57

◾

FOR THE FIRST time since Philip Iverson's murder, Interrogation Room One was dark.

Applications for Linda French's spot on the team were already being faxed in. Word traveled fast when there was an opening in Homicide.

Jane sat at her desk, riffling through the faxes. Catching up on paperwork. The aftertaste of the previous day's confrontation with Alice Iverson lay at the back of her throat like something she needed to be rid of.

"You wanted to see me?" Mike Finney stood in the doorway.

"Come on in." Jane got up and joined him on the couch. "I want you to apply for Linda's place on my team."

Finney's mouth fell open. "Really, Lieutenant? I—"

"Really." She put her hand on his arm. "Mike, you're a smart, resourceful, imaginative police officer." Finney blushed and Jane realized that this was probably one of the few times in his professional life that anyone had ever complimented him. "I talked this over with Ken, and as your immediate superior, he agrees. What do you say?"

"I . . . I say yes." A rush of tears filled his eyes. "And I say thank you."

"Good. Now go call Vicki and tell her the news."

Mike Finney stood quickly. "I'm on a diet, Lieutenant. I'm gonna be around a long time to enjoy my son." Beaming, he crossed the bullpen to his cubicle.

Kenny looked up from his computer and smiled at Jane.

Her pager pulsed. *What'd he say? 3H61.*

Jane caught Kenny's eye and mouthed the word *yes.* Then she noticed people in the squad room turning toward the elevators. Kenny felt it and turned as well.

Chief Walker McDonald emerged from the left elevator, handed his briefcase to his new bodyguard, and made for Jane's office.

Lou Tronick raised his hand in a half wave from the coffee setup. Chief McDonald passed by without looking over.

Jane's beeper vibrated again. *Uh-oh. 3H61.*

"Jane," the chief said as he entered her office, "Linda French has filed on you."

Jane shook her head. "What are the charges?"

"Dismissal without cause and . . . gender discrimination."

"Fuck her, Chief," Jane said coolly. "She's a shitty cop. There's no room for shitty cops anywhere on the force. Especially in Homicide."

"I agree completely."

This caught Jane off guard. "You do?"

"I read your performance review and talked to her previous supervisors. You will have the full weight of the department's resources behind you."

Jane started to thank him. Then it dawned on her. "Chief, I've been walking a tightrope since this case began. I've had Reggie Mayhew and Alice Iverson on my butt; my husband in trouble and Linda French filing on me. And each time, you've cleared the way. With all due respect, sir, what the hell's going on?"

Chief McDonald gestured for her to sit down.

Jane took the guest chair. The chief sat on the arm of the couch.

"Lieutenant . . . Jane . . . I know you've been contemplating leaving the department. I'd hate to see that happen. You're one of my best commanders, and once you learn the political ropes of the upper echelons, there could well be a captaincy waiting for you."

"That's . . . well, that's flattering, Chief." Jane sat back in the chair.

"But let's be totally honest here. The only political rope you're concerned about is the one you're hanging on to so you can make a run for Mayor Biggs's office."

Chief McDonald raised an eyebrow. "I am not without my ambitions, Jane. Neither of us is."

"That's right, sir. But we're not here to talk about my ambitions. We're here to talk about yours." Jane felt a smile play at the corner of her mouth. "If I, the first female homicide lieutenant in the department's history, resign—especially under the cloud of Linda French's bogus filing—that's not exactly the best atmosphere for you to start climbing that rope."

Chief McDonald's face lifted in a tight grin. "Granted."

"On the other hand," Jane went on, "if you get the chance to promote a female to a captaincy—something almost unheard of in big-city police departments—well, let's just say it could have its advantages for someone as adept at the politics of the upper echelons as yourself."

The chief regarded her. "Advantages, Lieutenant, for everyone." He rose and offered his hand. "What would you say if I came back to you with captain's bars?"

Jane stood and took his hand in hers. "I'd say no, Chief."

"What?"

"Accepting a captaincy on this police force is a huge responsibility . . . and a major distraction. As you've seen in my report, I've got some unfinished business with Alice Iverson, and I can't allow anything to get in the way of that."

"I understand, Lieutenant. But I would be remiss if I didn't point out what a spectacular, and rare, opportunity this represents to the other women in the department."

"I fully appreciate that. But if you need an answer now . . . it's got to be no." She let go of his hand and opened the door. "Maybe I'm not as ambitious as you thought, sir."

Chief McDonald straightened his coat. "Ambition isn't a crime, Lieutenant. Squandering a chance like this one . . . is."

He nodded curtly and left.

CHAPTER 58

━━■━━

THE FACES OF the dead were everywhere.

Jogging on these misty February mornings, Jane pushed herself even harder, taking a longer route each time. In the week since her last confrontation with Alice Iverson, she had moved up to five miles a day.

Chasing demons, she thought, or running away from them.

The faces of the dead were everywhere.

Willie Temple's face was the sullen panhandler who sat huddled outside the Starbucks shaking a Styrofoam cup at all who passed. Philip Iverson's face, pale as a candle as he lay in the morgue, was the man at the bus stop. It wasn't until the third time Jane jogged by that she noticed he wore the same suit every day. Ellen Schubert's face was Mrs. Tasca, Davey's mother, who worked at the Italian deli. They were about the same age, and since her husband Vito had died, she had the same weary weight about her.

And Becka Flynn.

Becka Flynn's face was everywhere. She was the college girl laughing on the cell phone in her SUV at the stoplight. She was the young nun herding the kids to class at Jane's old school. She was the new mother pushing her pink infant in the canvas jogging stroller.

Jane turned onto Oak Street and amped her jog into a final sprint.

Her breathing quickened to match her pace, sending smoky puffs of air to mingle with the light haze.

And there was A.J.'s face in the mist. Weathered and lined and lost. He was the face of the men not yet old who had surrendered to the gravitational pull of their pasts. He was Mr. Polucci, the mechanic who had never married. He was Jacob Turner, a friend of Poppy's and Aunt Lucy's who had survived the Holocaust.

He was Ben Spielman.

Jane saw Kenny up ahead and she slowed, savoring the sight of her husband working in the garage. He was bent under the open hood of the Explorer, a spark-plug wrench in his hand. Guitar music leaked out from his yellow Discman earphones as he worked. Jane recognized Steve Earle's new album, the blues as always, and she smiled at how wonderfully predictable Kenny was.

"Hey!" she called as she climbed the gentle slope of the front yard. But Kenny couldn't hear her. His back to the street, he continued working.

Jane held out her hand and brushed Kenny across the shoulders. He turned and pulled his headphones down to his neck. "Good run?"

"Five miles plus."

"Then that's a good run."

Jane reached over and took a stray eyelash from his cheek. "Feeling any better about working with me?"

"Working *with* you was never the problem. Working *for* you is."

"I understand how complicated it is for you and I'll try to be more sensitive to it."

"Fair enough." Kenny kissed her on the forehead.

"And you'll . . . ?" Jane prodded, urging him to keep talking about it.

"I'll try not to beat people up when I get frustrated with you."

"Glad to see you're finally getting in touch with your feminine side."

Kenny smiled. "It's your feminine side I want to get in touch with."

"Okay then, Inspector." Jane peeled off her nylon jacket. "I'm gonna take a bath." She rose on her toes and kissed him. "You could use one yourself."

"Ten minutes."

She kissed him again, her tongue finding his. "I'll make it worth your while."

"Five minutes."

Jane tied her jacket around her waist and, waving back to Kenny, headed for the house.

She didn't notice the car parked down the street.

Nor did she see the driver open the glove compartment and remove the pistol. Chambering a round, the driver got out of the car and started toward Kenny.

■

JANE SLIPPED INTO the bath.

The water's heat captured her, folding itself around her. Moaning slightly against the ache in her legs, she lay back. The water rose over her shoulders. She dipped a washcloth in the tub and put it over her face. Stretching her legs, she touched Poppy's long-handled brush with her toes.

Jane closed her eyes, breathing through the washcloth, and felt herself relax. And with that calm came Becka Flynn's face. A life in afterimage. Her freckles, her brick-red hair, her green eyes.

Eyes closed in death.

A sob erupted from Jane before she even knew she was crying.

She pressed the washcloth into her eyes and listened to the ratcheting sound of Kenny's spark-plug wrench. He would be up soon. In the water with her. And all would be right again.

Jane pulled the washcloth away. Reaching back to the counter for the remote, she turned on the television. She flicked past *Sesame Street* and some vaguely familiar soap-opera stars selling cosmetics until she found the KGO News.

Norma Chavez, a pretty young Hispanic woman, was sitting in Becka Flynn's old seat at the anchor desk. A photograph of Chief

Walker McDonald floated on the screen behind her as she finished a news story. ". . . his hat into the ring for the June primary. Mayor Lucien Biggs said he welcomed the challenge and looked forward to taking the Democratic nomination into the November election."

The chief's picture faded away as Norma Chavez found the lens of another camera. "Speaking of Chief McDonald's day job . . ." A photo of Philip Iverson came up. "As KGO first reported last hour, the chief's office has released, just this morning, what in police jargon is called a holdback. Often in major cases, especially those involving multiple homicides, the police will retain—hold back—a crucial piece of evidence. This helps ensure that when they capture a suspect or someone confesses, they have the right person. In the Philip Iverson serial murders"—an old photograph of A. J. Guthrie appeared—"the killer, Albert James Guthrie of Dos Rios, California, had the unusual habit of closing his victim's eyes. SFPD public information officer Rene Alvarez had no comment as to why Mr. Guthrie did this. But theories range from the religious to the psychological to the macabre. More on this in our noon broadcast."

A live helicopter shot of the Golden Gate Bridge replaced A.J.'s photo. "A tanker truck carrying thirty thousand gallons of milk jackknifed on the Golden Gate . . ."

Jane pressed the mute button and fell back in the tub. She knew that if she allowed herself to relax again, the image of Becka Flynn's face would come back to her.

This time she welcomed it.

Something, some inexplicable anomaly, had been gnawing at her for days. Jane could feel it finally emerging, struggling its way through her subconscious. Closing her eyes, she willed herself to receive the memory of her friend's face.

Becka Flynn came to her.

Her smile, her impossibly white teeth. The sprinkling of freckles, dense on her forehead, light on her cheeks and neck. Her hair, that luxurious red hair that turned the head of every man in the room whenever they were out together. Her green eyes—shamrock green, Becka had once called them.

Jane sat up so quickly water sloshed over the edge of the tub.

Becka's eyes.

When Jane had knelt over Becka Flynn's body that night in her condo, she had noticed that her eyes were closed.

Like all the others.

Now the anomaly presented itself. Unlike all the others, Becka's eyes had no blood on them.

She either died with her eyes closed . . . or someone other than the killer had closed them for her.

Jane forced herself to remember A.J.'s last words to her at River-Park. He had confessed to killing Philip Iverson, Willie Temple, the serial victims. Even Ellen Schubert. But he had never mentioned Becka Flynn.

She lifted herself half out of the tub and called out the window.

"Kenny!"

■

THE FIRST BLOW caught Kenny at the base of the skull. He staggered forward, fell to one knee, and tried to get up.

The second one thudded against his right temple, sending him sprawling under the Explorer.

Blood trickled from his ear, running down the yellow wire of his headphones.

CHAPTER 59

———■———

"KEN!" JANE CALLED. "Hey, Ken!"

That damn Discman, she thought. She snatched up the portable phone and dialed KGO. It was a number she knew by heart from her time with Becka.

"Newsroom."

"Yes, is your intern working this morning?"

"We got two, ma'am. Sunil Ray and Gretchen Brodie."

"Gretchen. Is Gretchen there?"

"Somewheres."

"Could you find her for me? It's important."

"Hang on a sec . . . Yo, Gretch-en! Call for ya!"

There was a brief moment in which Jane could hear over the phone the same newscast she was watching on the bathroom TV with the sound off. Then the handset clattered against something hard.

"Oop, sorry. This is Gretchen."

"Gretchen, this is Lieutenant Candiotti from SFPD Homicide." She heard Gretchen take a quick breath. "I need to ask you something and it's crucial that you think hard and tell me the truth. Will you do that for me?"

"I . . . I'll try."

"Good. When you found Becka's body that night . . . did you touch her?"

"Well . . . yes, ma'am. I did."

Her heart racing, Jane stepped out of the tub. "What did you do?"

"I closed her eyes, ma'am. I mean they were all open and everything. I remembered my dad doing it to my grandpa when he died. I thought that's what you're supposed to do with a dead person." There was a long pause. "Am I in trouble?"

"No, Gretchen, you're not. Thank you very much for your help."

Jane hung up and was just pulling on her robe when she heard the downstairs door. Then footsteps creaking on the stairs. As they reached the second-floor landing, she reached for the doorknob. "Ken, we've got to—"

The door was flung inward with such force that Jane was knocked sideways against the sink.

"Your husband is indisposed," Alice Iverson said. Jabbing her pistol at Jane, she forced her deeper into the bathroom.

Jane stared at the gun. The muzzle's perfect black circle was pointed at her chest. She moved to her right, forcing Alice to follow her with the pistol. "You killed Becka Flynn."

"She called me and said she had something big on my husband's murder. The implication was she had information that would link me to the letters."

"Josh Stolberg's confession."

"He always was a sucker for a pretty face."

"But what was the big deal?" Jane asked. Her mind raced through an inventory of the bathroom, searching for something to use as a weapon. "You've as much as admitted to me that those letters were written by you."

"The big deal *was*—" Alice Iverson waggled the gun at Jane, signaling for her to stop moving. Jane took another sidestep and came to rest near the foot of the tub. "Philip's murderer was still at large."

"Did it ever occur to you," Jane pressed, "that if the killer had found out those letters had come from you, he might have actually been grateful?"

"Unfortunately, I didn't have that guarantee. Most of the people I sent letters to were so bereft, they weren't rational anymore; which is what I was counting on. But I sure as hell didn't want to put *my* name in front of them." She kicked the door closed with her left foot. "Had I known at that point it was A.J., I could have dealt with him. But I didn't . . . so I went to see your friend."

"And recognizing you, she let you in. Which explains the lack of forced entry."

"She practically *pulled* me into her place. The warm trail of her big story got a whole lot hotter when I showed up. But I didn't go there to kill her. I went there to—"

"—bribe her."

Alice Iverson nodded.

"Just because you sold your soul for money," Jane said, "you assume everyone else will, too."

"Everyone else does."

Jane shook her head in disgust. "But not Becka. You were up against the one person you couldn't manipulate. So you killed her."

"It never would have happened if she hadn't insisted on—"

"On what?" Jane spat. "On running with the story?"

"On calling you."

Jane caught her breath.

"I tried to stop her. There was a struggle. I was stronger." Alice let that thought linger, knowing Jane understood she was now in a similar situation. "Your friend fell and hit her head pretty hard on the corner of the nightstand."

Jane remembered the bruise on Becka's forehead. "And then you finished her off; covering your ass by making it look like the serial killings."

"I was in too deep," Alice said.

"And for once your money couldn't buy you out of trouble." Jane took a half step back. "You left a very convincing crime scene."

"A.J. had briefed me well: what kind of knife, the latex gloves, the snake symbols. I found a knife in her kitchen that was close to what he'd described."

"And the gloves?"

"In the bathroom. What woman doesn't use them to touch up her hair?"

Alice was right, Jane thought. She had a pair of her own in the cupboard under the sink. She leaned back until she could feel the tub with her legs. Getting her bearings in a room she'd been in thousands of times. "Then, when the news came on this morning's early broadcast about the police holdback . . ."

"I knew it would be that one minuscule detail you'd come after me with."

"So you preempted that by coming after me first. Just like you did with Becka." Jane arched her back, ready to lunge. Just then she heard the downstairs door creak as it opened.

Kenny, she thought. At last.

"Jane, honey!" Aunt Lucy called from the entry hall. "It's me. I brought a sauce!" The refrigerator opened and closed and Jane knew Aunt Lucy had gone into the kitchen.

"Say a word," Alice hissed, "and she's dead." She advanced until the tip of the gun was inches from Jane's face. Then she snatched a towel from the rack over the tub and wrapped it around the barrel. "Wouldn't want anyone in this nice little neighborhood to hear anything, would we?"

"What did you do to my husband?"

"Let's just say . . . he's at rest."

"Oh, my God." Jane cringed. "Please." She screwed up her face and turned away.

It was a ruse.

By averting her eyes, she was able to find what she had been looking for. A weapon. She looked back. "How do you plan to get away with this?"

Alice's finger pressed against the trigger. "Not everyone is as honorable as your friend. You'd be surprised what money, big money, can do."

"You pompous bitch," Jane seethed. "You and your husband just go through life buying your way out of trouble. Checks to the families of the children he killed. Checks to the Make It So kids. Checks to Eddie Lukic and all your other boyfriends."

"The difference is," Alice said, "this will be the end for me. For Philip, it was a lifestyle."

And then it hit Jane. The last piece finally falling into place. *"He was giving it all away,"* she said in a rush of understanding. "I kept trying to figure out why anyone who had as much as you would want your husband dead. And now it makes sense. He was consumed with remorse, drowning in it; and the more he gave away, the more he needed to keep doing it."

Alice's mouth twisted into a grin. "He gave till it hurt."

"Because he felt so dirty," Jane pressed on. "His blood money was the only way he could feel worthy again."

"That's enough," Alice warned.

But Jane pushed on. "And there was only one way to stop him before it was all gone . . ." She glared at Alice, challenging her to make her move. "But you were too imperial, too chickenshit, to do it yourself!" Jane sneered at her. "Just like now!"

Alice Iverson narrowed her eyes. "That's where you're wrong!" She thrust forward, closing the distance between them, and jammed the gun against Jane's head. "You can't talk to me like that!" she shouted. "No one can talk to me like that!"

"Why not, *Alice?*" Jane taunted. "Because I'm not good enough? Because no one is good enough?"

"Shut up!" Alice scraped the muzzle of the gun into Jane's hair.

Jane saw the sinews in Alice's forearm tense . . . and she was ready.

At the precise instant Alice squeezed the trigger, Jane dropped to one knee and grabbed Poppy's long-handled brush from the top of the faucet.

The gun went off.

The towel shredded as the bullet tore through it, shattering the window over the tub.

Jane lashed out with the brush, again and again. Catching Alice first behind the knee. Then in the shoulder. Then in the neck. Alice, in her frenzy to ward off the blows, kept pulling back on the trigger. The towel around the muzzle caught fire, each shot becoming louder as it burned.

Out of the corner of her eye, Jane saw Aunt Lucy running across the lawn toward the Tascas' house.

The mirror over the sink exploded and fell in on itself. The shower door crystallized and burst into countless shards of glass.

Jane threw herself onto the bed of broken glass and slammed her shoulder into Alice's legs. Her left knee buckled with a sickening pop. Alice, howling in pain, swung the pistol wildly and continued to fire.

The ceiling light blew out. A slug hit the toilet tank and ricocheted into the doorjamb.

Scrambling across the glass pieces, shredding her hands and legs, Jane tried desperately to regain her footing. But Alice stepped away and, wincing against her ruined knee, brought the gun to bear on Jane's back. She shook the burning towel from the gun and prepared to fire again.

Thrusting upward with all the power in her legs and upper body, Jane rammed the top of her skull into Alice's chin. Alice staggered backward, her jaw broken. As she did, Jane grabbed the hair dryer from the countertop and smashed it into Alice's face.

Alice stood there for a second, stunned. Then Jane pounded the hair dryer into her forehead, splitting her flesh. Before Alice could recover, Jane walloped her again, hitting her just below the left eye and obliterating her cheekbone.

Even though Jane knew Alice was unconscious on her feet, she swung the hair dryer again. It caught her on the left ear, whipping her head around. Alice fell backward against the counter, her broken jaw hanging open. But still Jane came on. Driven by adrenaline and hatred, she brought her arm back, ready to put the full force of her weight into one final blow.

Someone grabbed her from behind.

Jane whirled, trying to strike out.

It was Kenny.

He grabbed her wrists and pulled her toward him. Then he wrapped his arms around her. "It's over, honey," he whispered hoarsely. ". . . it's over."

Jane, her chest heaving, her breath coming in gasps, let the bloody hair dryer slip from her fingers.

Alice Iverson moaned and slumped heavily, gracelessly, to the floor; her body coming to rest in front of the TV. As she did, Jane noticed something strange.

On the television, with the sound off, KGO News was airing a segment on Alice Iverson, California's tragic queen, presenting a blowup of a Make It So check to Reggie Mayhew in front of Santuario. She was beaming, beautiful, her honey-blond hair catching the sun.

She looked, Jane thought, perfect.

CHAPTER 60

∎

JANE GINGERLY CARRIED the tray in her bandaged hands. In the three days since her fight with Alice Iverson, the glass cuts in her palms and fingers were healing nicely.

"Sausage and peppers," she said as she came into the living room. "Aunt Lucy strikes again."

Kenny shifted to a sitting position on the couch. His head was still wrapped from the blows from Alice's pistol butt. But the doctor had said he was out of danger and the effects of the concussion would soon pass.

Jane set the tray on the coffee table and looked at the television. "Is that Jimmy Connors?"

"And John McEnroe."

"Don't tell me, it's that old sports channel."

"ESPN strikes again."

The phone rang. Jane picked up the portable. "Hello."

"Sorry to bother you at home, Lieutenant," Mike Finney said. "But are you watching TV?"

"Mike, we're *always* watching TV."

"I mean the news. Check out KGO."

Jane rang off and, using the remote, changed the station.

A helicopter shot of a white van pulling into a parking lot came into view. "This is Norma Chavez," a voice announced, "in the air over the Christine Murphy Women's Correctional Facility, where Alice Iverson, widow of billionaire Philip Iverson, is arriving from Alameda County Jail."

The doors of the van slid open and a woman stepped out, her blond hair swirling in the wind. "As many of you know," Norma Chavez continued, "Mrs. Iverson has recently been arraigned for the murder of Becka Flynn, a reporter at this station."

The camera zoomed in and Alice Iverson's face came into focus. There was a line of butterfly bandages across her forehead. Her left eye was swollen and bruised. Her broken jaw had been wired shut in a perpetual grimace.

"Jesus," Kenny said. "Her face looks like a disaster area."

Jane studied the image on the screen. "Too good for her."

Alice Iverson, her hands shackled to a thick leather waist belt, her ankles chained together, limped and shuffled toward a low beige building. She was wearing a shapeless orange jumpsuit with a brace over her damaged left knee.

"What if," Kenny began, "what if I hadn't stopped you?"

"I don't know," Jane said, still looking at the television. "I've never lost it like that before. I let my emotions get the better of me and I—"

"Acted like most people would have, given the same circumstances."

"That's just it, Ken. We work in a world where we have to be better than most people."

Kenny pulled her to him and kissed her hair. "Nobody's perfect, honey."

Jane rested her head on his chest and watched as Alice Iverson was escorted through the heavy door of the women's prison. "No," she said. "Nobody's perfect."

CHAPTER 61

—————■—————

THE OLD WOMAN was there again.

Sitting on a bench on a rise in the land, she fed the pigeons and the sparrows and the squirrels. She was well preserved and well dressed; maybe even, Jane thought, wealthy.

A breeze caught a corner of the blanket Jane was resting on. She reached over and smoothed it down before continuing.

"Kenny's a lot better. I'd like to think it was his loving wife who got him through the postconcussion thing. But I'm afraid it was equal doses of ESPN and the History Channel." She smiled at the memory of Kenny lying on the couch for two weeks; the remote in one hand, some wondrous plate of Aunt Lucy's cooking in the other.

"He's been back at Nineteen about ten days now," Jane went on. "You know how it is. When you're working Homicide, you never run out of customers."

The sun bounced off the bay like gleaming stones skipped along the water's surface. A flight of brown pelicans swooped low, hungry and searching.

Jane shielded her eyes with her hand and watched as the birds veered to the south and dipped from view.

"I'm still on my leave of absence," she said. "I'm not sure if I want to go back. But the promotion is awfully seductive. I asked the chief

for an extension, and he said to take all the time I need. It's not that he's such a great guy—or such a bad guy, for that matter. I just think he's distracted with the campaign."

Jane rose to her knees and gathered the blanket in her arms. "I've got to get going. Kenny's meeting me at Buddy's Hardware to pick out paint for the baby's room . . . my old room." She put her palm flat against her belly, then reached out and touched it to her parents' headstone.

Then she leaned over and kissed it—first her mother's name, then her father's—taking its coolness as she left behind her warmth.

"I love you so," she whispered as she stood up.

Jane walked slowly, thoughtfully, beneath the broad umbrella of the giant oak. The sun dappled the ground as it filtered through new leaves. When she got to her car, she turned for one last glimpse of her parents' grave.

And beyond it, under a tree of her own, the old woman was still there.